FIN

James Delingpole was born in Worcester and lives in London with his wife and two boys. As well as writing novels, he writes about music, TV, the Internet and lots of other stuff for newspapers and magazines. His first novel, *Fish Show*, was published by Penguin.

Also by James Delingpole

Fish Show

JAMES DELINGPOLE

FIN

PICADOR

First published 2000 by Picador

This edition published 2001 by Picador
an imprint of Macmillan Publishers Ltd
25 Eccleston Place, London SW1W 9NF
Basingstoke and Oxford
Associated companies throughout the world
www.macmillan.com

ISBN 0 330 48045 6

Grateful acknowledgement is made for permission granted
by A. P. Watt Ltd to reprint the excerpt from
'The Three Beggars' by W. B. Yeats.
Copyright © Michael B. Yeats.

1 3 5 7 9 8 6 4 2

A CIP catalogue record for this book is available from
the British Library.

Typeset by SetSystems Ltd, Saffron Walden, Essex
Printed and bound in Great Britain by
Mackays of Chatham plc, Chatham, Kent

FOR THE ANIMALS

CHAPTER ONE

'Save Our Sharks' says the new, kiddie-friendly cartoon propaganda poster in the atrium of my local swimming pool. And I'm thinking, 'Fuck. Is nothing sacred?' I mean, whatever next? Save Our Cancerous Cells? Save Our Plague Bacilli? Is the dork who devised this campaign living on the same planet as the rest of us? Did he not read the awful, awful story about the couple from Louisiana who ended up being abandoned on a reef forty miles from the coast of Australia? Or the one about the surfers who were snapped up in South Africa? Does he not know about the Matawan Creek incident? About the *USS Indianapolis*? Has he never seen *Jaws I, II* or *III*? *Mission of the Shark*? *Blue Water, White Death*? Has he never watched *Shark Week* on the Discovery Channel? Well I do, did and have. More often, perhaps, than is healthy for someone who's convinced that somewhere out there is a fin with his name on it.

But what can you do?

I'll tell you what you can do. You can be afraid. Be very afraid. For given half the chance those finny bastards will have the lot of us.

All of which, naturally, I'm bursting to get off my chest by the time I reach the hatch where you pay for your swim ticket. I suppose I could save it all for Sam, for when I get home. But I doubt she'll be in the mood for another of my shark-related rants. Especially not after last night. And anyway, you don't want to let these thoughts fester in your head – not for a whole hour. I'll just have to tell whoever's on duty.

With any luck it'll be Moroccan Babe. Moroccan Babe has olive-coloured skin, braided hair, dark, glistening eyes and an incredibly wide mouth which has enjoyed a starring role in many a wank fantasy. Normally I try not to converse with her at any length, lest her real personality impose itself on my mental image of her as a sultry, North African temptress. But I think I'll make an exception with my shark problem. She'll probably find it strangely endearing.

Or maybe it will be Mr Freebie. Mr Freebie is so-called because, if the supervisor's not around, he lets me in free. He once glimpsed me talking about something or other for five seconds on a daytime news bulletin and is consequently convinced that I'm a major celebrity.

But no. Today's cashier is Kenneth, a middle-aged black man with a round, very solemn face. He wears starchy white shirts with bad embroidery on the front, and unlike his colleagues – who prefer the *Sun* or the *Mirror* – he's always reading a classic work of English literature.

This, it must be said, is far more information than you need about Kenneth. I only see him for – what? – maybe a total of one minute every weekday, so he's hardly what you'd call a major character in my life. The thing is, though, he intrigues me. Like, what's a man of his age and intelligence doing in such a crap job? What's with the strange shirts? And why does he always look so troubled – so doomed, almost?

It's the troubled bit that decides me against launching into my shark tirade. It really isn't what Mark needs to hear

at 7.30 in the morning. Instead, I just say something gratui-
tously weird.

'Has Hackney Council gone mad?' I say. 'Do they really
mean to stock our pool with maneating sharks?'

Kenneth blinks owlishly. I gesture towards the poster.

'I believe,' explains Kenneth in his studiously correct,
West African accented English, 'that it is designed to make
our children more aware of environmental issues.'

'Ah, that'll be it,' I say. And I give him a big grin to
show that I was just being silly.

'You are a very funny man,' he replies. And he breaks
into a rare smile, which almost makes my day bearable.

But not quite. The problem is I'm still haunted by last
night's row with Sam. It's her total lack of empathy that
bothers me. I mean, how could she possibly have failed to
share my horror at the awful, awful tale of that hapless
couple from Louisiana.

I'll try it out on you and you can decide for yourself.

OK. So there's this couple from Louisiana – Thomas and
Eileen Lonergan – and they're really into scuba-diving. And
they pay to go out on this dive boat from Port Douglas in
Northern Australia with a party of twenty-three other divers
to explore the Great Barrier Reef, forty miles offshore.

Two days later, by his own account, the skipper of the
dive boat *Outer Edge* first notices that the Lonergans are
missing. He finds a bag of belongings onboard and thinks,
'Jesus Christ, it's got a wallet and papers in it.' There's an
extensive search by the police and the Royal Australian
Navy. But there's still no trace of the Lonergans. Not, at
least, until the following month when their scuba vests are
found washed up on a beach a hundred miles north of Port
Douglas. And the rumours start to fly. Maybe the Lonergans

have done a Lord Lucan and staged their own deaths; maybe Mr Lonergan had a death wish and killed his wife before committing suicide. Maybe. But then – and this is the bit that spooks me – another four months later, a diving slate is found in a mangrove swamp with a message apparently scrawled on it by one of the Lonergans. The message reads, 'We have been abandoned by . . . *Outer Edge*. Help!'

At which point the verifiable facts end and the specu- lation begins. For example: quite how big a cunt did that skipper have to be to return home without noticing that two of his passengers were missing? And how exactly did the Lonergans die? By drowning or by . . .

Well, you know how I think they died. And an Australian diver who spoke at the trial of the *Outer Edge*'s skipper – who was subsequently acquitted of unlawful killing – was of much the same opinion. He said they had probably been eaten by tiger sharks soon after the boat left. 'Tigers are very cautious sharks,' he said. 'They just circle and watch. They may do this for an hour before moving closer and may follow you for another hour before they take that first bite. And then you don't have a hope.'

God, can't you just imagine it? There are the Lonergans, finning amid the coral, basking in their good fortune at having got to try one of the world's truly great dive sites. They've been underwater for quite some time now. They really should think about surfacing. But not yet. Not quite yet. They're having too much fun. They've still got fifty bars of air left in their tanks, more than enough to get themselves back safely to the boat. And besides, the Great Barrier Reef is a long way from Baton Rouge. They won't be coming back here in a hurry. Why don't they just give it ten bars more? Surely there's no harm in that?

It's a decision that's going to cost them their lives, though they don't know that yet. They don't even know it when they surface and see – Jesus Christ! – the *Outer Edge* receding into the distance. The skipper's incompetence is so crass it's almost funny. Won't this be a fine story to tell the folks back home. Abandoned on the Great Barrier Reef.

Well, *almost* abandoned. Because obviously, any second now the skipper – and Jesus, he's going to be given a piece of their mind – is going to notice his error, turn the boat round and scoop them out of the water. There's no way, there is just *no way* that the skipper of a professional dive boat would ever leave port with twenty-five passengers and return home with only twenty-three. Is there?

That's what the Lonergans keep telling one another. They're getting a bit edgy now. They need reassurance. Because, let's face it, the situation they're in is not what you'd call happy. In fact it's very, very unhappy. They're forty miles from shore, too far to swim, even if they knew what direction to head in. And they're floating around in waters chock full of some of the world's deadliest predators: stonefish, sea snakes, box jellyfish, sharks. All of which, they're naturally very, very keen to avoid right at the moment.

Which is ironic, because only an hour ago, these were precisely the sort of critters they most wanted to see. Especially the sharks. Every diver wants to see sharks. They're cool, they're mean, they're surprisingly beautiful. And they're not particularly dangerous, provided you know what you're doing. You dive with a big group of buddies (sharks are scaredy-cats, as a rule – more frightened of us than we are of them); you don't stray too far from your boat (if something does go wrong, you want to be out of the water fast);

and you don't spend too long on the surface (underwater you're generally fine – the shark thinks you're just another big fish and steers well clear; on the surface you're not – the shark thinks you're wounded, he thinks you're food); and above all you don't panic.

So why are experienced divers like the Lonergans panicking? Because they aren't in a big group of buddies; because they're miles from their boat; because they're floating on the surface, that's why. Wouldn't you panic? Of course you would. We all would. We'd all be absolutely shitting ourselves.

Still, human nature being what it is, the Lonergans never quite give up hope. Hope, after all, was the one thing remaining in Pandora's box when all else had fled (which has always struck me as a pretty false consolation: I mean if things like 'sudden dramatic rescue' and 'lucky escape' have gone, what use is hope?). So all the time they're telling themselves: the boat's going to come back, the boat's going to come back. Even after they've seen the first distant fin; even after that distant fin – and perhaps there's more than one – has started circling closer and ever closer; even after the shark has made its first dummy run; even after it has closed in to 'bump' its prey. And 'bumping', as every diver knows, is the shark's way of telling you that you're finished. Next time round, he's going to bite you for real.

And by this time, of course, you – the Lonergans – are telling yourself, 'This is not happening. It can't be happening. No way was I meant to die in such a horrible way as this.' Yet another part of your brain – the implacably logical part – is telling you, 'Oh yes, it is happening. So you'd better make the best of it.'

Time, you realize, for a prayer; time for your life to flash before you; time for you to think about all the things you wished you'd done but now never will; time to say goodbye to your loved one, to tell them how much they mean to you and how you wished it could have ended some other way – any way but this. Time, at some point, to scrawl that last hopeless message on your diver's slate.

Time to die.

So that's what I'm thinking about now as I make my way into the changing room, too preoccupied to grunt the usual cursory 'morning' to the early swim regulars: Mr Bicycle, who's always leaving just as I arrive, in his all-weather bicycle gear; Mr Insufferably Jaunty, who sings in the shower, used to work on an aid project in India and now spends his life being very, very happy; Mr Fat Blubbery Bastard and his skinny sidekick, Mr Grinny Beard, who gabble away to one another incessantly, telling unfunny jokes and giggling like schoolgirls, from the moment they arrive until the time they leave. I don't know their names and I don't want to know their names. It isn't natural being so happy at this time of day.

The only regulars I have much time for are the trio of pensioners I know as Bob, Not Bob and Not Not Bob. Bob is a little boy trapped in an old man's body who spends his pool sessions – yes – bobbing around in his favourite lane (the middle one) waiting for someone he recognizes to emerge from the changing room. When they do he bellows 'Morning,' at them. And they reply, 'Morning, Bob.' Which is how I know his name. His daily dip is, I suspect, the pinnacle of his social life.

Not Not Bob is a bald gent with a friendly face who

always makes a point of smiling at me the first time we swim past one another each morning. We have never actually spoken.

Not Bob is the one person I have conversed with at any length. I really ought to know his name by now, but we've reached that stage in our relationship where it would be embarrassing – rude almost – to ask. He uses my name frequently. And every time he does, I wince. I have to pretend that I'm one of those people who never uses anyone's Christian name. Obviously, if I took the trouble to find out his name now, my ruse would be exposed.

One of the things I like about Not Bob is that, though he must be in his mid-seventies, he looks so healthy and cheerful. This gives me hope. Or at least it would if I believed there was the slightest chance of my reaching such a fine old age. He has a full head of very white hair and a lean muscular body, the result no doubt of his days heaving carcasses around Smithfield Market.

We have, needless to say, enjoyed many long rants about the government's handling of the BSE crisis. But the subject I most like to get him on to – not too often, lest he think I'm a ghoul and clam up – is his experiences during and just after the last war.

Listening to men like Not Bob makes me feel very 'end of *King Lear*'. 'We that are young . . .' and so on. I wonder how I would have coped in the heat of battle. Would I have cowered in my foxhole? Or would I have charged headlong into the raking machine-gun fire? Would I have had 'a good war'? Like most of my generation, I'll probably never know. And though part of me is grateful for having been denied the opportunity of being blown to smithereens for my country, another part is perversely resentful. Can a man ever feel truly complete without having undergone the ultimate test?

Instead, I must fight my battles vicariously, devouring military history books – especially those with detailed accounts of the experiences of men on the ground – like John Keegan's *Six Armies in Normandy*. From Keegan's book, I learned something rather upsetting. It was America, not Britain, that really won the war. By the time of the D-Day landings, our military manpower had come close to exhaustion. Only by allowing America to bear the brunt of the fighting could we be sure of having an army powerful enough to lay claim to its fair share of the spoils when the allies finally conquered Germany.

I mention this fact because it relates to something Not Bob told me one morning. For most of the war, he worked as a stoker in the Navy. But in 1944, much against his will, he was drafted into the Army as D-Day cannon fodder. By the time he knew what was happening it was too late. Along with many of his shipmates, he disembarked at Liverpool and was put on a sealed, heavily guarded train which took him directly to his new army barracks. The idea was to stop the resentful ex-sailors deserting. But many did, all the same, some of them dying as they jumped train.

My other favourite Not Bob anecdote concerns his days patrolling Palestine in 1946. One day, by then a sergeant, Not Bob was helping to man a roadblock. 'We had these two armoured cars parked at intervals halfway across the road. You couldn't get straight through. You had to drive between them, in an S shape. So one morning, we're standing round, checking papers, getting sunburnt, when suddenly this covered Bedford truck comes tearing up the road towards us. And we know straightaway, he's not planning to stop.

There's just time to take cover as he smashes straight into the first armoured car, knocking it sideways. The truck's driver goes right through the windscreen. Dead instantly. But out of the back, firing sten guns, comes this bunch of terrorists, none of them more than twenty. And one of them is a pregnant girl. Now you don't want to shoot at a pregnant girl, do you? It just ain't natural. But what can you do? There was one of us killed and two wounded. And the one that was killed was my best mate. So we returned fire. It was stupid, really. They never stood a chance. All of them killed or badly wounded. When we got to the girl she was still alive. Our medics did what they could, which wasn't much. Once they knew they'd lost her, they tried for the baby. No good. They called us "baby killers" after that.'

Tales such as this I reserve for my post-swim treat. Before my swim, I am in no mood for talking or listening. My head is a fug of sleepiness, stale marijuana, alcohol, confused thoughts, dark imaginings, anxiety and self-hatred. Sometimes it gets so bad that I cry out to myself 'Die! Die! Die!' Or 'Noooo!' Today, preoccupied as I am by the terrible fate of the Lonergans, I groan so volubly that Not Bob calls back from the neighbouring cubicle, 'You all right there, my friend?'

'Yeah, yeah,' I reply. 'Just thoughts.'

Just thoughts. If only.

Not all my morning thoughts are horrible. Sometimes, if I'm in the middle of an interesting project, my mind might slide towards a constructive idea. Or if I've had an erotic dream and still haven't woken up properly, I can sometimes continue the scenario from the point where it was cruelly ruptured by the alarm. Or I might just catch sight of a loose panel in the ceiling and drift into a fantasy where a group of silent assassins have come to wipe us all out, like at the beginning of *Three Days of the Condor*. And I'll wonder whether I would have time to haul myself up into the rafters and replace the loose ceiling panel before the killers could find me. And then I'll probably conclude that, no, I wouldn't.

As I say, not all my morning thoughts are horrible. Just most of them.

And this, I think, is probably the main reason why I pursue this ridiculous daily health regimen. Not so much to cancel out the effects of all the cigarettes I smoke, nor to keep my body in good enough shape to ensure Sam doesn't chuck me for a younger, healthier man, but as a ruse to purge myself of my inner demons. For exercise read exorcize.

This is why, when I wet my hair before pulling on my swim cap, I don't wait for the shower to warm up. I just plunge my head and body straight under, enjoying the frozen agony.

And it's why, instead of mimsying into the pool down the ladder, I dive straight in, relishing both the ecstasy of that split second of mid-air anticipation and that liberating shock of cold as I hit the water.

Today, it's even colder than usual – the heaters must have broken down or something – which is good because it means I have to swim extra fast to stop myself dying of hypothermia. And the faster I swim, the harder it is for me to think all those thoughts I'd rather not think.

That's the theory, anyway.

But I've only done a few lengths when the evil death thoughts start trickling back. I'm not sure what it is that has triggered them. Maybe it was a Rorschach shape glimpsed, on one of my backstroke lengths, in the peeling paint of the pool's arched ceiling. Or perhaps the torpedo surge, glimpsed from the corner of my eye, of a passing swimmer. Or, perhaps, it's just the effect of being immersed in water.

Whatever, I'm back there, with the Lonergans, hoping against hope that the boat returns before the tigers close in for their final run. I'm with the survivors of the *USS Indianapolis*, floating for three days in the shark-infested Pacific, shuddering as my shipmates are snatched into the depths, one by one. I'm on a sinking ferry in the Philippines, wondering whether to go down with the boat or leap into the sea and risk a fate far worse than drowning. I'm diving in the Red Sea when I feel some large evil presence behind me. I'm – God knows why, because this is something I'd never ever do – I'm in a shark cage. A great white shark cage. And something must have gone badly wrong because instead of floating on the surface, the cage is sinking, deeper and ever deeper, towards the black ocean floor a million miles below. And I know I've got to get out because the pressure's building and in a few minutes more I'll implode. But I can't get out because those steel bars surrounding me, imprisoning me, are all that stand between me and the savage jaws of the monstrous white shark circling, unseen, in the murk beyond. So do I die or do I die? And why am I thinking these thoughts? Why can't I just get on with it – do my lengths, get out, have a shower, go home, die in fifty or so years' time of natural causes – like any normal person?

I'll tell you why. Because all the things I've been telling you about – that shark poster, the story of the Lonergans – they're all signs. Omens. Omens like the ones in *The Omen*.

You know the bit I mean? Well, there's this photographer character in *The Omen*, played by David Warner. And this David Warner photographer has noticed something rather horrible about the pictures he has been taking. Whenever he has snapped someone who's about to be killed in a hideous fashion by the powers of the Antichrist child Damien, he notices, when he develops the photograph, that a strange blemish has appeared across that person's body. And when he photographs the person again, he sees that the blemish has grown more distinct. And the more distinct that blemish grows, he realizes, the closer that person is to the time of their vile death.

Then, one day, the photographer notices something particularly grim. He has taken a self-portrait. And this too is now disfigured by one of those ominous blemishes. He now knows he is going to die soon. He also has a pretty good idea of how he is going to die because the blemish takes the form of the instrument of his death. Yet when he tries telling anyone about the ghastliness of his predicament, no one will believe him. They think he has gone mad.

I know just how he feels. There are blemishes on my photographs too. Not real ones, obviously. This is real life not fiction. But as far as I'm concerned it amounts to the same thing. The imaginary blemishes on my imaginary photographs are growing more distinct with each passing day. And they take the form of a black triangular fin.

But will Sam listen when I explain my theory? Will she bollocks. She thinks it's just a form of hypochondria. Despite the fact that I have presented her with the most compelling evidence to the contrary.

Like yesterday morning, for example. Before I picked up the newspaper, I said to myself, 'If there's a story in today's paper about sharks, then it's a sign from God that I'm totally fucked.' It's a game I play quite a lot. When I'm going up an escalator, say, I'll tell myself that if I get to the top before someone steps on to the down escalator then I definitely won't get eaten by a great white shark. And what invariably happens is that someone does get on to the down escalator, so I have to tell myself, 'OK. That one didn't count.' Which is fair enough, I reckon, because as a rule in life it's bloody difficult getting to the top of an up escalator without anyone stepping on to the down escalator first.

The thing with the newspaper, though, that really bothered me. I mean, what are the chances of opening your paper and finding that the first story you've turned to concerns one of the most horrific shark stories ever? Pretty slim, I'd say. Is it any wonder I got so agitated?

'Oh fuck!' I said. 'I'm fucking fucked this time.'

Sam, as usual, ignored me. She doesn't do mornings.

So I left it till the evening before I elaborated. There was a shark programme playing in the background on the Discovery Channel at the time. Which I might have interpreted as yet another ominous sign if I didn't know that there's *always* a shark programme playing on the Discovery Channel.

I waited until Sam was skinning up, so that she couldn't run away, and then told her what had happened.

'And suppose there hadn't been a shark story?' she said, wearily.

'I would have been bloody relieved,' I said.

'No you wouldn't. You would have kept making the same pact day after day until, eventually, you did find the shark story you wanted. It's just wishful thinking.'

'Oh right,' I said. 'Like, deep down I actually want to be eaten by a shark.'

'You said it.'

This gave me the perfect opportunity to remind her of

the many occasions in the past when I have most definitely not wanted to be eaten by a shark.

Seychelles, 1978. 'Shark! Shark!' screams my mother, dragging my brother and me ashore. Actually, the fin she's seen belongs to a dolphin. But from that day forth, I can never again associate the sea with uninhibited fun.

Porto Ercole, 1983. 'There are no sharks in the Mediter- ranean,' insists my father, before betting me fifty thousand lire that I can't swim as far as a frighteningly distant-looking buoy. I win but it's a pyrrhic victory. I've never swum in water that deep before and by the time I've finished, I never want to do so again. I've just reached the buoy when I become convinced, absolutely convinced, that something is stalking me. Years later, I discover that I might have been right. I have been swimming only a few miles from the spot where, the previous year, an Italian diver was 'taken' – what an awful euphemism that is – by a great white shark.

Key West, 1988. A tuna-fishing expedition. I'm reeling in a huge fish, the base of my rod tucked into a sort of codpiece device strapped around my crotch, when suddenly, with a terrible yank, I find myself being dragged over the stern. The skipper grabs me just in time. We pull in the tuna – what remains of it. The skipper examines the ragged crescent where half the tuna's body should be. 'Big,' he says. 'Very big.'

Lamu, Kenya. 1993. I'm windsurfing in the mouth of a muddy-brown estuary. God knows why since murky, tropical river mouths are prime shark-attack territory. Still, at least I'm on the water rather than in it. No, I'm not. Oh Jesus, I'm in, I'm in, I've fallen in. I may not be good at windsurf- ing but if ever there was an international haul-yourself-out- of-the-water-so-quickly-that-the-sharks-don't-have-time-to-get-you competition, I reckon I'd be world champion. I daren't risk tacking my way back to the shore. I'm too exhausted. I might fall in again. So I sit, trembling, waiting for someone to rescue me. I let the sail drag in the water, to slow my progress. I put my hands round my knees and keep my feet planted firmly in the middle the board. And I scan the surface of the muddy, turbulent water for any sign of disturbance.

What was that? A fin?

Oh please, God, not a fin, please.

Two hours of hell later, I'm finally rescued. I'll never go windsurfing again.

'And there's something else I've just realized,' I said to Sam. 'The dates. The dates! Oi! are you going to give me some of that or what?'

Sam passes me the joint.

'Don't you see? '78, '83, '88, '93. These shark experiences. They come in five-year intervals.'

'How mathematical of them.'

'But don't you see what this means? Now it's 1998. And in a few weeks—'

'No!' snaps Sam. 'No bloody way.'

'You don't know what I'm going to say.'

'If it's got anything to do with cancelling our holiday the answer's no.'

'Of course I'm not going to cancel the holiday. I was just thinking we might want to go somewhere a bit less hot. Like Iceland maybe. It's meant to be really cool. Damon Albarn's got a bar there and everyone takes loads and loads of drugs.'

'We're going to the Red Sea and that's final.'

'If we go next year . . .'

'If we go next year you and I won't be an item.'

'OK. Have it your way. Just don't blame me if I die.'

'Joe, sweetheart. You are not going to get eaten by a shark, I promise. Not this year. Not next year. Not ever.'

'So you say. But there's something about me you don't know, something so horrible that I've never dared tell anyone before.'

'Shit!' says Sam.

'What?'

'Oh, nothing. Just remembered a phone call I was meant to make at work,' she says.

'Sam, this is important. It's probably the most important thing I'll ever tell you.'

'Just give me five minutes, OK? I might still catch him on his mobile.'

'Oh, never mind.'

'Go on then. But make it quick.'

'Forget it, I said.'

'Huh,' says Sam, making for the phone. 'It can't have been that important.'

Bitch.

So I don't tell Sam the horrible thing that I've never dared mention to anyone before. And I'm never going to either. She wouldn't listen. She doesn't care. She'd only put it down to paranoia.

But just because you're paranoid doesn't mean they're not out to get you. They are out to get me, they definitely are, my finny Eumenides. They're pursuing me even now, as I swim up and down the lanes of my local pool, those evil, evil shark thoughts that I came here to avoid.

'Stop!' I tell my brain. But my brain won't listen. Not even when I try distracting it with the usual pointless mental and physical challenges. I try swimming a length in under twenty seconds; I try swimming two lengths in the time it takes Not Bob to do one; I try keeping pace with the really fast Olympic swimmer in his private cordoned-off lane. None of them works. I try revising my list of desert-island films: *Withnail and I*, *Au Revoir Les Enfants*, *Badlands*, *Brazil* ... And my list of desert-island Nam movies: *Apocalypse Now*, *Platoon*, *The Odd Angry Shot*, *Go Tell the Spartans*, but definitely not crappy old *Full Metal Jacket*, which scarcely counts as a Nam movie at all. It was filmed in London Docklands, for fuck's sake. I try playing the four-minute warning game, which entails deciding which of the people in the pool I would most like to shag in the final moments before the Apocalypse. Or rather, given the limited options, which person in the pool I would find least unbearable to shag. Then, to give myself a really hard time, I list every single swimmer in order of shag preference. You can imagine how nauseous I feel by the time I get to Fat Blubbery Bastard.

But nauseous is good. Nauseous is much better than the alternative, which thinking those horrible thoughts about ... Oh God. Here we go again.

Squeezing together my fingers and cupping my hands tight, I claw my way through the water, stretching my arms to their furthest reach, working my thigh and stomach muscles, pumping my legs and thrashing my feet.

Behind me, I can feel it drawing closer.

I surge forward, mouth gasping, eyes stinging, lungs bursting. Faster and ever faster.

Now I can hear screams.

Just two more strokes. But they'd better be big and they'd better be quick.

It's snapping at my heels.

One more. Quick now, heave yourself out of the pool. And get those fucking legs out now.

As I slip clear, the water turns into a boiling crimson soup of swirling fins and severed limbs.

This time I made it. How much longer will my luck hold?

BASKING SHARK

I like basking sharks. A lot. So much so, in fact, that I get awfully upset by the scene in Ring of Bright Water *when the Gavin Maxwell character rows out to butcher a hapless basker, just so as he can feed his wretched otter Midge.*

Why do I like the basking shark? Because despite being the second largest fish in the sea (after my other favourite shark, the whale shark) and having a huge and terrifying mouth, he is in fact a total wuss. He eats plankton, not humans.

CHAPTER TWO

Of course I'm not really so warped or stupid as to imagine that I'm in any serious danger of being eaten by a killer shark in my local swimming pool. I've given it a lot of thought and the chances are ludicrously small.

I mean, how on earth would you get it into the pool? First you'd have to go to all the trouble of shipping it safely from its hunting grounds in Australia or America all the way to Hackney. Then you'd have to make an enormous hole in the swimming pool's roof and winch it slowly into the water from a helicopter. And if the shark wasn't killed by the trauma of being out of its natural environment for so long, it would surely die within minutes of being exposed to fresh chlorinated water. And even if it wasn't, you'd be highly unlikely not to notice the presence of a twelve-foot maneater in the pool, before you dived in.

So no. I have never actually been pursued by a ravening shark on the final length of my morning swim. Nor has the water ever really been transformed into a boiling soup of spurting arterial blood and severed limbs. It was just a dramatic device, designed to illustrate the sort of shark-related shit that goes through my head every single day.

But just because this shark action all takes place in my head doesn't make it any the less real or frightening. In fact one of the strange things I've noticed in a lifetime of shark phobia is that I'm often more scared of the bastards when I'm sitting at my desk or swimming in a pool or lying in bed than when I'm floundering about in genuinely shark-infested seas. I don't quite understand the reason for this phenomenon – Joe Davenport's Great Big Shark Paradox – but I suppose it has something to do with the fact that phobias are, by nature, irrational.

Irrational, at least, to those who don't share them. I cannot understand, for example, why anyone should be afraid of spiders. Especially not in Britain, where only the tiniest minority of our vast arachnid population has fangs powerful enough to penetrate human flesh. And even those that can bite you almost certainly won't because spiders are intelligent and unaggressive. And even if they did bite you, it would probably hurt less than a wasp or a hornet sting. And even if it did hurt a bit, you'd be in no physical danger because the few species that can do you harm – the black widow, say, or the Sydney funnel web – all live abroad.

But if you explained all this to an arachnophobe, they'd look at you as if you were mad. 'But you don't understand,' they'd say. 'Spiders are horrible. They're big and black and hairy, with hundreds of eyes, and thousands of legs, and ginormous biting jaws. They lurk and they scuttle and they pounce on you when you're least expecting it. They ensnare you in their horrid sticky webs and plunge their fangs into your soft, vulnerable flesh. They're evil!' Yeah, you reply. But you're not a fly.

Fear of dentists, on the other hand, I can understand. When they say it won't hurt, it always does. And when they say 'You may experience some slight discomfort', you know they're going to take you through purgatory.

Wasps too. They're very scary. And hornets. Partly, I'm sure, it's atavistic: the warning signal we instinctively infer from those stripey, black and yellow jackets. But mainly it's common sense. Never mind all that bollocks about 'If you leave them alone, they won't hurt you'. It's simply not true. Wasps and hornets do sting, they do attack for no reason, and they really do hurt. QED.

And scorpions. What total bastards they are with their flat, elongated carapaces, segmented like a squashed Michelin man; their sharp, probing pincers; their flicky, curvy whip-lash tails topped with bulging poison sacs and that stabbing scimitar sting. I don't like them at all.

And I'm positively terrified of stonefish, grizzly bears, polar bears and alligators. And my fear of crocodiles is exceeded only by my terror of sharks. But I've said quite enough on this subject for the time being. I'm not some sad monomaniac, you know. I do have a life beyond shark fear. Though not much of one, right now, as you'll soon see when I tell you about Marc and Jennifer's party.

Marc and Jennifer Stone live in the sort of enormous Kensington home that I'd own myself if there was any justice in the world. It's on one of those broad, tree-lined, stucco avenues where all the cars are either Volvos, Mercs, or top-of-the-range BMWs, except for the odd Peugeot Junior or Golf GTI, reserved for the spoilt elder child and the impossibly overpaid nanny. Confronted with such smug exclusivity, you're sorely tempted to do something naughty like scrape a key along the nearest Beemer's paintwork, or bend down in the middle of the road with your trousers round your ankles, yelling, 'Kiss this, you filthy rich fuckers!' But you don't because, apart from the fact that you're almost certainly being watched by a resident convinced you're a burglar, you actually feel rather clever and special to have been invited to such a smart address.

In fact, that's the main reason I'm here in the first place. I hardly ever go to parties these days, for reasons which will become apparent. But an invitation from Marc and Jennifer Stone is not something you turn down lightly, especially when you scarcely know them and don't want to jeopardize your prospects of being invited again.

At the top of the stone steps, the front door is opened by a man wearing a white shirt and a red sash. Another one takes my coat, and yet another one takes my bottle of cheap undrinkable red that some tight-fisted bastard brought to one of my dinner parties, conceals it quickly, and offers me a choice of Krug, Bellini, buffalo grass vodka or a Margarita. I realize then that this is in an altogether different league from your average PBAB affair. All the guests look infinitely richer and more successful than me. They're also mostly older, but that's no consolation. I feel like a piece of dog turd which has been scooped from the pavement on a Lobbs brogue and deposited on the carpet of Buckingham Palace.

'Why me?' I wonder.

'Joe! Glad you could make it,' says Marc. Then he answers my question. 'Is Sam not with you?'

I tell him that she should be here any minute now.

'Nice shirt,' says Marc.

And it is a nice shirt. It's a red, deep green and saffron plaid number which I picked up in the sale at Gap. I was a bit worried about it at first. It reminded me of the sort of thing middle-class thirtysomething dads wear – invariably with fawn jeans and Timberland boots – when they're pushing their toddlers round the park on Sunday afternoons. It made me think I'd suddenly grown staid and bourgeois.

But then I realized 'What the hell? It suits me. It's comfortable. I like it.'

But I still have a nasty suspicion that Marc's compliment is loaded. As I can tell by the plethora of Ozwald Boateng suits, Paul Smith jackets and Voyage dresses, this is very much a fashion party. And I'm wearing anti-fashion. Now there's nothing wrong with anti-fashion per se. In fact there are few better ways to make your mark at a party than by looking scruffy while everyone else is dressed to the nines. But I'm not looking scruffy enough. What I should have worn is my standard, workaday, don't-give-a-damn kit of ragged black levis and holey black wool M&S polo neck. Then people could have been absolutely sure of my intentions. 'Look at him! He's so cool. He really doesn't care!' As it is, it just looks as if I've tried a bit and missed by a mile.

My instinct is to get one of the waiters to retrieve my beautiful, double-breasted buckskin Gigli coat – so smart, fashionable and expensive (£1,000, if I hadn't got it in the sale) that it would surely eclipse all the other garments in the room. 'See,' I could say. 'I do understand fashion really!' But I sense that this might make me look a bit sad, mad or desperate.

Instead I reply, 'Nice jacket.'

As soon as I've said it, I realize that this isn't enough. It sounds insincere, as if I'm only saying it because he's just complimented me. So I tell him, in extravagant detail, precisely why I think his jacket's so wonderful. I like the deep pile of its dove-grey velvet. I like the Chinese-style fastenings, the Nehru collar, and the silk lining, a glorious shade of – now what colour is it exactly? – kingfisher blue.

When I ask if I can give it a stroke, Marc says, 'I meant what I said about your shirt, you know.'

'And I meant what I said about your jacket!'

Marc smiles enigmatically. This is the problem with Irony Culture. No one thinks you mean anything for real any more.

To our mutual relief, some of Marc's real friends arrive, enabling me to escape into the garden for that essential, party-arrival fag. Outside I roll up, down half my Margarita and take stock. On the plus side I can see that the party has great potential. There's lashings of free, top-quality booze, which makes me really glad I didn't bring the car. The canapés look pretty excellent – pizzas, hamburgers and hot dogs but all in miniature, bite-sized form, like something from a Lilliputian fast-food emporium. And unless I'm very much mistaken, this is exactly the sort of house where half the guests arrive laden with top-quality cocaine.

Now the downside. I'm wearing a stupid shirt. I've offended the host. You can't smoke inside and it's too cold to stay outdoors for very long. The canapés aren't as brilliant as I thought: I've just tried a hamburger and it tastes like one of those evil, one hundred per cent fat-gristle-hoof-and-testicle, BSE-flavoured jobs you find in greasy caffs. The booze is far too tempting and strong, which means I'll get pissed too quickly and make a fool of myself. I don't know anyone and I don't want to because they all look too old/boring/snooty/famous/ugly/gorgeous to talk to. I don't want to see any of my friends, if they ever arrive, because I'm feeling low and miserable and full of self-hatred and they'll only gloat, or try to tell me life's really not so bad, or gossip about my condition to all my other friends, or express sympathy in a cloying, sick-making way. No one's ever going to offer me any coke. And even if they do, it won't be enough. And even if it is enough, it'll only make me feel more miserable when I come down tomorrow. And in any case, there's no coke in the world strong enough to conquer my condition because right now I hate myself and I want to die. Or, failing that, go home.

'Joe?'

It's the girl with the fabulous cleavage and huge, long-lashed cow eyes whom I keep bumping into at parties like this and whose name I can never remember.

'Hi!' If I sound pleased enough to see her, maybe she won't notice that I haven't used her name.

'You don't know who I am, do you?'

''Course I do. How could I ever forget a girl with such stupendous breasts? But are they safe out here? Won't they shrivel up in the cold or something?'

'Our girlie equipment isn't like yours,' says fab cleavage, nodding towards my crotch in a way that would be extremely erection-inducing if I weren't (a) attached, (b) terrified that Sam might appear at any minute, (c) distracted by the fear that despite my descent-into-jokey-crudery ruse, she's still going to test me on her name. 'Anyway,' she continues, 'apart from being crude and disgusting, how are you?'

'Oh, you know. Pretty shit.'

'But you're doing so well! I read you everywhere.'

'Yeah, that's what everyone says. But it doesn't seem like that to me.'

'Well, take it from me, you're doing all right.'

'Then why aren't I more rich and famous?'

'It'll come.'

'Will it, bollocks. There's no future in journalism. I mean it's great to start off with. Loads of money. Name in print. Massively steep career curve. Then, all of a sudden, it flattens out and that's it. You're fucked. Unless you're editor material, which I certainly ain't, the only way of making more money is to work even harder. 'Cos you don't get a better rate just because you're old. That's what's so unfair. You know, when I started out I was earning more than any of my friends. Even the ones in the City. Ten years on, I'm the poorest of the bunch. And the differential's going to get even greater, the older we get. Now if I'd gone into something like law—'

'You still could.'

'Go back to school for three years? And live on baked beans and water? Forget it. No. The thing I need to do, I reckon, is to get into screenplays. Even if your film's never made, you still get paid a fortune. Or TV. Know anyone who works in TV?'

'Apart from me, you mean?'

'Oh, right, yeah. Maybe you can give me some advice, because I've got this brilliant idea for a show. It would be absolutely perfect for late night on Fridays, maybe on Channel 4. What I'd do—'

'So you're the presenter?'

'Well, yeah. I know I haven't got a massive amount of TV experience but I think I'd do this one really well. What I'd do, basically, is travel round the world doing incredibly cool things. Test driving superbikes and jet skis and sports cars; staying in luxury hotels, checking out the local delicacies and drinking fine wine; hanging out with film stars and supermodels. That sort of thing.'

'It's an interesting idea, but—'

'No, wait. I know what you're going to say. Me and a thousand other wannabe TV stars, right? But the clever thing about this show and the reason I'd be so good at doing it is that it'll mix the highbrow and the lowbrow. Sort of *Beavis and Butthead* meet Bernard Levin. Or something. Anyway, to give you an example, I might spend one section checking out some hot new club in Ibiza, before cutting to a French chateau where I'm tasting some grand-cru claret. Because that's what I'm like. I can read without moving my lips. I'm into art and literature and fine wine and culture but, at the same time, I'm pretty groovy and into stuff like music and bikes and drugs. Not that we'd be allowed to road test those, I suppose. But you get the idea.'

'I do, Joe, but the problem is, as I said the last time you suggested it to me—'

'No? We've already had this conversation? Oh fuck fuck fuck fuck fuck fuck fuck. Don't go on. It'll be too painful. Look, I'm really sorry, I – Oh fuck. Oh fuck! You must think I'm a total twat.'

'Of course I don't. I already said I think you're very good at what you do. And listen. People are pitching me ideas all the time. A lot of them much sillier than yours. So keep your chin up. Take care.'

'You're going?'

'Yes, Joe. I'm going indoors. My stupendous breasts need warmth, remember?'

'Oh. Right. Yeah. Your breasts.'

Now I really hate myself. Now I really want to extra, extra double-die with cyanide on top. I'm boring, I'm repetitive, I'm a failure, I regularly make a fool of myself in front of pretty girls whose names I can't remember. I'm going to have to commit mini-suicide with another cigarette. And another Margarita.

No! Not a Margarita. You'll never cope with the morning-after paranoia. Stick to fizzy mineral water and fags.

So I do. Which makes the party even less fun than it was

already. In the next hour, not daring to go into the warm lest I bump into the girl with the cow eyes and the enormous cleavage, I endure a series of terrifyingly pointless conversations with people I've never met and never want to meet again.

There was a time when I might have enjoyed this: giving strangers the privilege of discovering just how wonderful I am, telling them about all the thrilling assignments I've had of late, all the film stars I've interviewed, all the gigs I've reviewed, all the countries I've visited. But at the moment I'm just not up to it. It's time for me to take a back seat and listen to people telling me about their lives for a change. The problem is, other people's lives seem to be very, very boring.

I meet a dealer in classic twentieth-century furniture. 'Biedermeier?' I hazard, revealing the full extent of my knowledge. 'Not exactly,' he says. And I'd be quite happy for the conversation to end right there. But it doesn't because in a fit of masochism, I keep urging him on with interested 'mms' and the occasional intelligent question. Being as I'm probably the one non-classic-twentieth-century furniture collector in the universe ever to have expressed any interest in this man's tedious profession, he's more than happy to oblige.

Eons later, I'm offered a lifeline by three Americans who sidle up and exchange warm greetings with Mr Not Biedermeier. It emerges that they'd like to reminisce about a recent business trip to Austria. For some unaccountable reason, however, I refuse to take the hint. One of the Americans gives me a mock-polite smile which means 'Who the fuck are you?' Mr Not Biedermeier obliges with a limp introduction.

'Which paper?' an American asks.

'Oh, just freelance,' I say.

The conversation returns to Austria and still I linger.

'Do you know Austria?' another American asks, eventually.

I do actually. Can't stand the place. I travelled to Vienna when I was interrailing at university and found it chock-full of unrepentant Nazis. When I tried changing some traveller's cheques at the station, a stentorian crone complained that my current signature bore no resemblance to the one on my passport. 'That's because the passport's five years old. My handwriting was more childish then,' I explained patiently. 'Zen you must change your passport,' barked the woman. 'I don't think that's really necessary. No one pays much attention to that sort of detail.' 'But if your signature has changed, zen your passport must change also.' 'Excuse me, madam. I came here to change some traveller's cheques. Not to receive a lecture on the state of my passport.' 'In Austria—' 'I'm not Austrian, damn it. I'm British. Now are you going to change these cheques or shall I take my custom elsewhere?'

'No, I don't, I'm afraid,' I reply. 'But I've heard it's *lovely*.' And with that, I make my escape.

Only to end up talking to a lawyer about legal reform; a banker about offshore banking; and an advertising executive about the dark secrets of Ronald McDonald, which is just starting to get interesting when I get a blast of alcoholic breath and a warm peck on the cheek.

'There you are! God, you're freezing. Come inside, why don't you? Everyone's here.'

Sam drags me up the wrought-iron staircase which leads to the drawing room.

'Where've you been?' I ask. 'I've been getting bored shitless.'

'Sorry, hon. Got a bit carried away,' says Sam wiping her nose.

'Oh God. You haven't?'

'I'm sure you can score some too. There's loads here.'

'I was actually rather hoping to leave quite soon.'

'*What?* Get some powder up your nose. That'll sort you. Look, I'll go and ask Marc.'

'Hang on—'

But Sam's already gone, shimmying across the stripped-wood floor in a baby-blue, skinny-fit T-shirt, which reveals far, far too much midriff, attracting lecherous glances from every man she passes, and basilisk stares from every woman. Even after five years, I still find myself looking at her and thinking, 'Jesus! What a babe! However did I manage to pull that?'

'Way out of your league that one. Jailbait, almost,' says a voice I'd sincerely hoped not to hear this evening. It belongs to Tom Bland, a tall, preternaturally balding thirty-year-old who isn't nearly as good-looking as he thinks he is, and who, depending on circumstances, is either my best friend or my worst enemy.

'Speak for yourself, tosser.' Tonight, as he has been ever since the publication of his first novel, he's my worst enemy. Naturally, I do not want him to know this, which is why I must strive to remain bullish and combative.

'Good party,' he says.

'Yeah,' I reply. 'I didn't know you knew Marc and Jennifer.'

'I don't, really,' he says.

This is precisely the answer I had expected. It's one of the things that annoys me most about Tom, this unerring knack for being in the right place at the right time. He's the one who appears at the bathroom door, just seconds before you lock it for your clandestine line of coke; the one who always finds himself sitting next to the prettiest girl at dinner; who gets invited on month-long Caribbean cruises by a very rich friend of a friend of a friend; who gets asked to be best man at the weddings of total strangers. Perhaps I wouldn't mind so much if he ever showed the slightest sign of gratitude for his outrageous good fortune. But he doesn't. He thinks it's his due.

'Sorry I couldn't make your launch, by the way,' I say.

'Oh. No worries. I'd probably have missed you anyway. You know what it's like – well, actually, I don't suppose you would – but they're a total nightmare. A fun nightmare, obviously, because you're the star. Everyone has come just to worship at your shrine. But people can be so insensitive. They keep wanting to talk to you about this and that but what they don't understand is that you haven't got time. You've got too many books to sign. Then there are all the diarists, trying to milk you for gossip. You give them a really good anecdote but it still isn't enough. They hover on the edge of your conversation. Hoping you're going to say something even better, I suppose. Well, you'd know. You used to do that sort of thing.'

'Mm.'

'But how are things with you? I don't get much time to read the papers these days, I'm afraid. Still getting stuff printed?'

'Loads.'

'Now, come to think of it, I did see one of yours the other day. An interview with someone quite extraordinary. Bearded chap. Used to be on children's TV in the seventies.'

'Rolf Harris.'

'That's the one. What on earth was that all about?'

'Well, he's a sort of a cult figure. You know, *Animal Hospital*. Glastonbury. Ironic, so-bad-they're-good records.'

'Ironic is he? You'd know all about that, I suppose.' Tom, you may have gathered, doesn't. He is quite the most-out-of-touch thirtysomething I know. He wears clothes by Mr Byrite; he buys his cassettes from racks at petrol stations; he thinks clubbing's what you do to seals; he has never watched *Frasier*, *The Fast Show* or *King of the Hill*, and even if he did, he wouldn't find them funny. Girls, apparently, find this naivety charming. I think girls can be extraordinarily foolish.

Tom pulls out an unbranded, low-tar supermarket cigarette and lights it from the stub of the one he's just finished smoking.

'But anyway,' he continues, 'you're happy with the way things are going?'

'Very.' I search my brain for some forthcoming assignment that will make Tom jealous. Finding none, I have to add rather lamely, 'I'm having to turn quite a lot of work down.'

'That good?'

'Mm, well, casting modesty aside for a moment, I think I've got about as far up the ladder as it's possible to get.'

Tom studies his footwear for a second and I know the remark has hit home. He was a journalist too. Still is theoretically. And an overabundance of work has never been one of his problems.

He looks up. 'All downhill from now on then?'

'No. No. I didn't mean that. It's just that I'm thinking of branching out a bit. You know. Bit more radio and TV, maybe.'

'Right. So Marina was saying.'

'Eh?' I feel a sudden lurch in my stomach and at first I can't work out why. Then I realize who Marina is and what a terrible error I've made. 'Girlies will gossip.'

'Oh, I think she was just a bit concerned. She'd somehow got the impression you were quite down.'

'Silly thing. I was only trying to play the sympathy card. They love it when they think you're vulnerable, don't they, girls? Gives them a chance to mother you. Which gives you the chance to get inside their knickers.'

My attempt to speak to Tom in the sort of language he understands backfires horribly.

'Are things not going well between you and Sam?'

'Oh, for goodness' sake, I'm not seriously intending to get into bed with Marina.'

'Why not? I can highly recommend it. For further details turn to the end of chapter two of *Founder's Day*.'

'Wow! Does she mind?'

'I rather hope she never has the chance.'

'That'll depend on how well you've disguised her.'

'Hmm. Well, I gave her slightly bigger tits and a job at the BBC instead of Channel 4.'

'That's not fiction. That's autobiography.'

'I believe the term is roman-à-clef.'

'Well, if that's all you need to do to get a novel published – bang on about your ex-shags – I think I'll have a go myself.'

'I hope you're not serious.'

'Why not?' Only with a considerable effort of will do I bite back an 'if you can do it, anyone can'.

'It's just . . . It's just not that simple. If you had any idea how hard it was to write that book—'

'The research sounds fun.'

'No, seriously though. As Proust said. Or was it Gide? Oh, I forget the story but the point is that writing a novel is not something you choose to do. It's a compulsion. A disease. It's the most horrible thing imaginable.'

'You seem to be coping rather well. The ghastliness of being worshipped at your launch party. The horrors of being mobbed by lowly hacks all dying to give your tome a plug—'

'There are compensations, certainly. But if anyone were to come up to me and say, "I'm thinking of writing a novel. What do you advise—?"'

'Which of course everyone does now that you're so well established.'

'I'd say never. Not at all. Don't even think of it. Because when you write a novel, you move on to a completely different emotional plain. I know it may sound pompous but I'm only saying this because you're a friend. You're doing well as a journalist. Really well. And—'

'Tell him like it is, Tom. He might actually listen to you,' butts in Sam, with the tact and sensitivity of the true cokehead. She plants a slobbering kiss on Tom's cheeks and ruffles my hair. 'Moan. Moan. Moan. I'm so depressed. Why aren't I more famous? He's been driving me up the wall. Now be a sweetheart, hon, and get me another voddie. You've been hogging Tom for far too long.'

'Um, actually I was hoping we might head off fairly soon. I'm feeling a bit queasy.'

'But I've only been here ten minutes. Just get some powder up your nose, that'll sort you.'

'You were going to ask Marc.'

'Oh that's right. I meant to ask you. What did you *say* to him?'

'Nothing.'

'He seemed very put out.'

'I promise you. All I said was I really liked his jacket.'

'But it's a lovely jacket.'

'I know. That's why I said I liked it.'

'Maybe he thought you were being ironic.'

'I wasn't!'

'Yes, but you do have a funny way of putting things.'

'Excuse me. You're supposed to take my side.'

'She does have a point, though,' chips in Tom. 'You can sound pretty sneery. Like the other day, when I was wearing that suit—'

'That was different.'

'What was wrong with it?'

'Nothing, Tom. It was absolutely divine.'

'See. See!' Tom and Sam chorus.

I leave Sam to relay a few more details about what a miserable bastard I am and scan the room for a suitable sulking ground. I settle on one side of a large, marble fireplace, the other side of which is occupied by an equally bored-looking girl. I rest my bottled beer (Budvar – our host has taste) on the mantelpiece, lean against the wall, one leg crooked over the other, and gaze listlessly into the throng. Everyone is drunk now, the indoor smoking ban has been relaxed, and the cumulative noise of the shouted chit-chat is deafening: fortunate really, since it drowns out the Mark Morrison album playing in the background.

I pull out my dwindling pack of Golden Virginia. Then, after a lengthy quest through remote pockets in search of the elusive blue Rizlas, I roll a cigarette with slow, therapeutic relish. It's at times like this that I thank the Lord I'm a smoker. I pinch the strands of stray tobacco from one end of the cigarette. I raise the fag gently to my lips. Light up. And am instantly transformed into Humphrey Bogart, Alain Delon, Cary Grant, James Dean and anyone else who has ever looked cool with a fag.

'Mind if I have one?' says the bored-looking girl. She's at least as tall as me, with broad shoulders and a boyish face which should appeal to my latent homosexuality but somehow doesn't.

'Sure.' I shove the packet towards her.

She uproots a tangled plug of tobacco and spreads it unevenly on the paper. Realizing that she's used far too much, she subtracts a bit of tobacco. Then she adds a bit. Then she takes some away again. Finally satisfied, she runs her wide tongue along the adhesive strip, drenching it in spit. She looks up for a moment, perhaps asking for help. Unfortunately, I don't fancy her enough to oblige. And anyway, I'm rather enjoying her incompetence. Instead of rolling the cigarette into shape, she folds the sticky strip into place, first one side then the other. She pops the thinner end of the bedraggled cone into her mouth and waits.

Belatedly, it occurs to me that she needs a light. This is unusually remiss of me, since I consider lighting girls' cigarettes one of life's great pleasures. Especially when the girl looks down the length of the cigarette, directly into your eyes. This doesn't happen.

'Thanks,' says the girl, handing me the tobacco. She turns quickly towards her side of the mantelpiece.

I hadn't been planning to talk to her but now I feel I should.

'Apparently they give you cancer.'

'So I heard,' she says, with the trace of a smile. The paper on her cigarette is burning faster than the tobacco, causing the end to droop.

'Is that smoking OK? I can roll you another if you like,' I say.

'No. Thanks. This is fine. Much better than a realie,' she says.

'You call them realies? I thought I was the only one.'

'Really?'

We both laugh.

'I'll tell you what really annoys me,' I say.

'What really annoys you?'

'When you're rolling up and someone says "Do you want a real one?" like they're doing you some massive favour. And you're like "Fuck off! I don't smoke these things because I'm poor, you know. I smoke them because I prefer the taste."'

'Healthier too.'

'I don't know about that. They probably haven't got so many chemicals and preservatives in them. It's why they keep going out. But not having a filter must do some serious damage to your throat.'

'Gives you a better hit though!'

'Yeah!' Our eyes meet properly for the first time. Hers are deep brown. Much prettier and more animated than the ones I'd mentally ascribed her. I feel a twinge of unease. 'That's just what my girlfriend would say,' I add, looking towards Sam.

'In the T-shirt? She's very pretty.' She says this without a hint of bitchiness.

'Mm.' Now I wish I hadn't said anything. The poor girl's just trying to make normal, friendly conversation and here am I implying that she's trying to leap into bed with me.

There's a silence which, if I don't say something soon, is going to end in a 'Well. Nice meeting you . . .'

So I say, 'Have you ever played that game where you talk to somebody at a party without asking them what they do for living?'

'Like we are now?'

'Uh. Yeah. I suppose. It's just that, I don't know whether you feel the same, but I'm a bit sick of going through that "So you're a barrister? How amazing! Had any interesting trials recently?" routine. You know, by the fifth time you've done it it gets a bit tedious. Not that I am a barrister, by the way.'

'I'd already guessed,' she says.

'Oh fuck. Am I so inarticulate?'

'No. But you've already told me you weren't going to tell me what you do.'

'I didn't say I wasn't. I was just wondering "Do you reckon it could ever work?" Or is it one of those obligatory hurdles you have to jump before you can move on to the interesting stuff.'

'Oh, I think we should move straight into the interesting stuff,' she says.

'Only the thing is, I'm actually quite keen to know what you do.'

'Stop cheating.'

'Yes, but now we have to move straight into the interesting stuff, I feel slightly pressured. What if what I have to say isn't interesting enough?'

'Try me,' she says.

'Can't you go first?'

'It was your idea.'

'Oh, all right. I've got this theory – and you're bound to be the person who proves it wrong – but I've got this theory that everyone in the world has a good shark story.'

'A good shark story?'

'Damn! I knew you'd be the exception.'

'No. No. I do as a matter of fact. A really good one. Well, really horrible anyway. It happened to a friend of mine. In Hong Kong.'

'The bastards. They love harbours, you know. They follow the big ships.'

'I know. But this wasn't in the harbour. It was in one of the bays outside. Would you mind rolling me that cigarette. This story makes me a bit squirmy.'

'Thick or thin?'

'Medium.'

'So,' I say, nursing the tobacco into shape, 'you have a thing about sharks?'

'Doesn't everyone?'

'Not my girlfriend. She thinks being afraid of sharks is deeply abnormal. If you ask me, it's deeply abnormal not to be.'

'Right.'

'In fact, I've never told anyone this before. But I think it's probably one of the reasons I smoke.'

'What? So the cancer gets you before the sharks do?'

'Hey. You know that one?'

'Sure.'

This time, when I light the cigarette, she looks me directly in the eye.

'So your friend's swimming in this bay in Hong Kong . . .'

'No. She's not swimming. She's gone for a walk on the cliffs overlooking the bay. It's an isolated spot, several miles from the main beaches. And it's taken a very long time to get there. It's scorching hot and she's dying for a swim. The water below looks crystal clear and inviting. But she can't work out how to reach it, because the drop's so sheer. She knows there must be some way down because she can see someone there already. A lone swimmer—'

'Oh God. Here we go.'

'So she stands there watching this swimmer enviously. He's really not far away, so eventually she calls out to him and asks the way down. He stops and waves in the direction she's supposed to go. And she's just heading off when something catches her eye. A dark shape in the water. But for some reason, she doesn't think anything of it. And this, my friend says, is one of the things that most upset her about it afterwards. She'd never seen a real shark before and this thing, this shape, looked nothing like the ones you see in films. There wasn't a huge triangular fin cutting through the water. Or not that she could see. There was no scary music to tell her that she should be frightened. It was a beautiful, sunny day. And things like that just don't happen on beautiful sunny days.

'So for a short time, and it really can't have been more than a few seconds, she looked away and carried on walking. The next time she looks, this shape has got much bigger. And she can now see that it's moving directly towards the man—'

'We going then, or what?' says Sam. Loosely translated this means, 'I have been unable to procure any more coke.'

'Hang on. We're just in the middle of a story.'

Sam glances at the girl, susses that she's no threat, and rewards her with her best smile.

'Sorry,' she says. 'A few minutes ago he was dying to leave.'

I send Sam off to fetch the coats. 'Right,' I say to the girl. 'The shark's closing in.'

'The shark's closing in, but still it doesn't really hit her. She can see it's a fish. A big, big fish. But it just doesn't look very menacing. It's gliding towards the man slowly, almost casually, as if it doesn't mean him any harm. Then suddenly she hears a dry, rasping scream. "Shark!" it goes. "*Shark.*" And she realizes then that it's her voice that's doing the screaming.

'And she sees the man look up at her, just for a second, before the shark's upon him. And she can see the shark's head thrashing from side to side, like a cat, that's what she said, like a cat with a bone stuck in its throat. And the water turns a horrible red. And then, just as suddenly, it's over. The man's still there floundering in the water. But the shark's gone.

'Or so she thinks. But as she watches the man struggling towards the shore, willing him on at every stroke, she sees the shark coming back. "Swim!" she screams. "Swim!" And the shark's getting closer. "Swim!" And thank God, just in time, the man manages to pull himself on to this strand of beach. She can see he's bleeding heavily and that she needs to get help fast.

'She tells the man that she'll be back very soon. And she runs and she runs and she runs and at last she finds someone to tell what's happened. And it's so awful. She's hysterical and the person doesn't understand English. So she has to follow him back to find someone who can, and this person's old and moves really slowly, and she's going out of her mind with frustration. Finally, she finds someone who does understand her and once she's made absolutely sure they're going to fetch help, she runs and runs all the way back to the clifftop.

'The man's still there, legs half in the sea. The water, full of blood. He's not moving and she's sure he must be dead. But when she calls out to him he answers back, very feebly. And she feels so helpless watching this man lying there. And she wants to be down there with him to comfort him but she knows that even if she could find the way down, he'll probably be gone before she makes it. So she stands there, shouting encouragement. Telling him help's on its way and that he's not alone. He mustn't feel lonely. And she wonders whether the man would lose less blood if he pulled himself out of the water. Or whether the effort involved would kill him. And she feels more useless and helpless than ever before. All she can do is shout. Keep shouting. Until help arrives.

'By the time it does she has shouted herself hoarse. But she thinks that maybe, just maybe, it has all been worthwhile because the doctor who has been winched down from the helicopter gives a thumbs-up when he's examined the swimmer and dressed his wounds. She watches the man being winched up into the helicopter. And that's the last she sees of him.

'Only after reading the next day's paper does she discover whether he survived.'

'And did he?'

'No. Bled to death before he reached hospital.'

'Jesus. That is terrible. That is one of the most awesome shark stories I've ever heard. Beautifully told too. Thanks!'

'That's OK. It's nice to meet a kindred spirit.'

'Hey. You never told me you name.'

'And you never told me your shark story.'

'Is that the deal?'

'It is now.'

WHALE SHARK

Apart from the basking shark, this is the only shark to which I am prepared to give the time of day. He has attractive white spots all over his enormous body (up to forty-six feet long) and it is perfectly safe to dive alongside him while he goes about his innocent business, hoovering up plankton and small fish.

That said, it wouldn't half be a bugger if you ended up accidentally being hoovered up too.

CHAPTER THREE

There's an incredibly important question which I'm dying to ask my cousin. But I daren't just yet because it's only 11 a.m. and he'll be working and I know I should be too.

Under normal circumstances, I would be. I would have made my first cup of coffee; I would have rolled my first couple of cigarettes and completed my statutory half-hour's paper-riffling and vacant screen-gazing. I would have made my second well-the-first-one-was-so-nice-and-it-kills-time-and-anyway-I-haven't-got-quite-enough-caffeine-in-the-system-yet second cup of coffee. And having accompanied panied it with another brace of cigarettes, I would have concluded by now that enough time had been wasted and that there were enough stimulants coursing through my veins for me to get off my slack arse, stop making any more excuses and start earning some money.

Not today, though. And if you ask me it's all the fault of that wretched Tom Bland. If he hadn't made out that novel writing is only marginally less difficult than climbing Everest blindfolded with both hands behind your back and ten-ton weights round your legs while pterodactyls peck and claw your skull, I would never have risen to the challenge. But I have and what makes it so much worse is that the bastard was right. Novel writing is living death.

I say novel 'writing' though actually I haven't quite reached that stage. For the last hour, well maybe half-hour if you take into account the two-coffee, four-cigarette preliminaries described above, I have been sitting in an armchair, pen poised above a notepad, waiting for inspiration to strike.

But it hasn't struck. Instead my head has filled with thoughts which have absolutely no relevance to the book I am planning to write. The book I am planning to write will explore grand themes like the passage of time, the experience of growing old, the evanescence of friendship, jealousy, rivalry, and thwarted ambition. The thoughts that have been filling my head, however, consist mainly of things like 'What am I going to have for lunch?' 'Do I have any spots that need squeezing?' 'Aren't my fingernails a bit long?' and 'Would it unblock my channels if I had a quick wank?'

Only with a considerable effort of will do I manage to find space between these vexed and potentially lethal questions for the odd vaguely useful idea. The fruits of this struggle can be seen on my notepad. It says, 'Oxford?' 'Evil hate figure (Tom?) frustrates hero. Dies horribly. Poss. Shark,' and 'JOB!!!???' The final jotting concerns a problem I am finding exceedingly difficult to resolve: what sort of job to give to my hero.

Obviously, this good-looking, intelligent, incredibly sympathetic character is based on me. But I don't want to make this too obvious. Otherwise, I'm just going to end up with a piece of cheap, autobiographical trash like – to pluck an example from the air – *Founder's Day*.

This means I'm going to have to change my physical features slightly and give my character a different name. It also means that I'll have to make him do something other than journalism for a living. But not something so radically different that I'll have to spend loads of time doing research. So banking's out. And law. And advertising. And anything to do with science. Or business. Or most of the arts.

PR's a possibility. I can get all the insider knowledge I need from Sam. But if I give my hero a job in PR, the readers are going to have trouble finding him sympathetic. Damn! What other jobs are there that are exactly like journalism, but aren't journalism? My thoughts begin to drift once more until they settle on the vitally important question that I'd like to ask my cousin Bill but daren't because it's only 11 a.m. and I know he'll be working and that I should be too.

I manage to hold out till 11.03, largely thanks to the intervention of a leaflet advertising a local pizza-delivery company which I hear being posted through the letterbox and rush to intercept, thinking it might be something exciting or life-changing, like a £1,000,000 premium-bond prize. Having read it through carefully and decided that, on balance, I'm still better off collecting my pizzas from the place in Stoke Newington which does them with authentically crisp, thin bases, I discard the leaflet and pick up the phone.

'Bill,' I say.

'Cousin,' he replies.

'I have an incredibly important question to which only you can provide the correct answer.'

'Tell me this important question.'

'Do you think I should get a Sony Playstation or a Nintendo 64?'

'Playstation. I already told you that.'

'Yes, I know. Only I've read some reviews that say the Nintendo's better.'

'Look. Who's cooler – Crash Bandicoot or SuperMario?'

'Not Mario, obviously. He's a total twat.'

'OK. And which has the cooler soundtrack: *Goldeneye* or *Wipeout*?'

'Yes, all right. But what about the technical stuff?'

'Technically, the N64's better. Clearer graphics and twice the memory.'

'So—'

'So nothing. N64's never going to be any use for our generation. It's meant for kids. That's why they have all these babyish cartoon characters. And we have Lara Croft. Now who would you rather shag: the fox in *Lylat Wars* or Lara Croft?'

'Well, now you put it like that . . .'

'Good. Any other vital questions you need answering? Because I haven't got an incredibly tricky job which I should have finished by yesterday or anything.'

'Oh. Sorry. There was one other thing.'

'Yes?'

'I heard you had a bit of an orc infestation round at your place. Any chance I could pop round and help you finish off a few? I'll be really, really quiet. Promise.'

As I fear, Bill says no. He's far too busy but if I want to come round later, half-two say, he might just be able to slip me in for an appointment.

I should be relieved by this. After all, playing video games on a weekday mid-morning is a pretty obscene waste of life. But actually I feel somewhat resentful. Perhaps he is busy, but I've a nasty suspicion that the main reason he's putting me off is that he's scared of his wife. I can just imagine her lecturing him. 'Yes, I know he's family, Bill, but what you gotta remember is that me and Apollo' – Yes. Horrible isn't it? She really did insist on christening my one-year-old godson Apollo. Perhaps I'd mind less if she'd meant to name him after the god of music and poetry. But no. Carrie comes from the Valley. She named him after a space rocket – 'that me and Apollo, we're family too. And you know, maybe your cousin should be a little more understanding of that. Because you know, Bill, time is money. And the more time you spend playing games with your cousin, the less you'll have to supply the needs of me and li'l Apollo.'

Still, it has given me a good idea for another character. I jot down a few notes, before I forget. 'Laurie. Californian ex-model. Bitch from Hell. Dies horribly.' Then it occurs to me that despite the cunning change of name, Carrie might recognize herself. She is, after all, Californian, an ex-model and a bitch from hell. So I scrub out Californian and write New Yorker. And I change ex-model to failed actress. Then I remember that besides being Californian and an ex-model Carrie is also a failed actress who used to live in New York, which worries me for a moment, until it strikes me that, being incapable of dealing with any form of literature which isn't accompanied by glossy photographs, she's not going to read anything I write anyway.

Now I am free to move on to more fertile territory. What sort of horrible death, other than shark attack, can I mete out to this Laurie character? No sooner have I started than I realize that this is a grave mistake.

I think of death by grizzly bear, which entails first having your face ripped off by razor-sharp claws designed for scaling fish; death by being eaten alive by soldier ants; death by falling from an incredibly high cable car; death by being sliced in half by a sheet of glass which has fallen off a glazier's van, like in *The Omen*, which naturally leads to death by being sliced by sizzling lift wire, death by being spiked by a bit of falling church spire, and death by drowning underneath the ice, while your family looks helplessly on and urgent, sub-Carl-Orff horror music plays in the background.

What bothers me about all these grisly scenarios, and the many others now competing with one another for space and multiplying like mutant pupae in my morbid brain, is that the person suffering them doesn't look at all like Laurie. He looks like me. Which, if you subscribe to my theory that the very act of envisioning a horrible death makes it that much more likely that it's going to happen to you, is not a very healthy way of spending your time.

The sensible response here seems to be to switch off and move on to something more pleasant. When I try this, however, another part of my brain says, 'You useless, lazy, worthless bastard! Don't you realize that if you keep running away from your innermost thoughts, you will never write a decent book. You will be doomed to remain a journalist till the end of your days. You will never become rich or famous!'

Assailed on two fronts by the forces of guilt and fear, I suddenly remember why it was that I wanted to go round to my cousin's house to play video games. Because it's the one pastime one hundred per cent guaranteed to stop you thinking about things you don't want to think about. And just a few feet from where I'm sitting lies the answer to all my problems. It's in a box whose cover I can scarcely bear to look at, partly because the illustration is so painfully tacky (it's done by Boris Vallejo in the style of his seventies sci-fi/barbarian paintings), and partly because it features a particularly evil-looking shark. I prefer the other side. 'You are Ecco,' it says, 'a powerful young dolphin . . .'

Unless you're French, in which case you're 'Un dauphin

jeune et vigoureux'; or Danish: 'En ung och start delfin'; or
Italian: 'Un energico e giovane delfino'; or Finnish: 'Nuori,
vahva delfini'.

I was all of these things, once, though I haven't been for
a good three years. I got about as far as level eighteen and
then had to give up because, infuriatingly, I lost all the entry
codes and couldn't be arsed to start all over again.

Looking at the illustrations on the back, though, I'm
sorely tempted. They show four of my favourite levels: the
challenging Atlantis section, where you swim between submerged, Graeco-Roman-looking ruins; the exciting prehistoric one, where you call out with your sonar to the
pterodactyl, who carries you with his talons over a seemingly
impassable rock into the next pool; the early one where you
encounter a friendly killer whale, and he says something
gnomic like 'I know not of your pod. Seek out the Big Blue';
and the one where you have to swim slowly past the octopus
known as Eight Arms.

If you don't swim slowly past Eight Arms, of course, he'll
kill you with his poisonous tentacles. But this is the sort of
knowledge which only comes with long experience. In the
same way, it takes hours of hard play before you work out
how to penetrate the barrier of boulders by smashing them
with a conical shell which you push with your snout; and
how to replenish your life energy by gobbling up tiny,
colourful reef fish; and how to distinguish between an evil,
killer clam (they release brown bubbles) and a friendly
replenishing one (blue bubbles).

How gloriously, life-enhancingly useless this knowledge
is! What a spectacularly decadent and pointless way of
spending one's time! To think that in all those wasted hours,
I might have translated Proust or discovered the meaning of

life or learned how to turn base metal into gold or – let's get really stupid – written a chapter of a novel! And instead, I've been perfecting the art of manipulating an electronic mammal through a labyrinth of subaquatic tunnels. Great.

But the terrible thing is, it is great. Right now I can think of nothing that would give me greater satisfaction than to propel Ecco the dolphin forth on his next big adventure; to hear that familiar ambient soundtrack, soothing yet urgent; to thrill to the 'wraaggh! wraggh!' horror noises of attacking sharks and jellyfish or the pleasing 'thock' which comes when Ecco has swallowed another fish; to meet once more all my old friends – the pterodactyl, the killer whale and the gargantuan Big Blue.

Only by exerting an almost superhuman degree of self-control do I manage to prevent myself from thrusting the Ecco cartridge into the Megadrive. The novel beckons, I remind myself. The critics are salivating. My public are holding their breath ... A bit like Ecco has to when he's deep in the undercaves and you can't find any pockets of air to replenish his dwindling oxygen supply but you know you've got to keep pressing on to find the next glyph and—

Stop it, Joe! Stop this at once! Think of the reviews.

'Joe Davenport is a young writer of great promise.'

Oh, come on. You can do better than that.

'Joe Davenport is a genius.'

Yeah. Yeah. And?

'Joe Davenport is funnier than Stephen Fry, cleverer than Will Self, cooler than Irvine Welsh and has a better prose style than Martin Amis.'

Getting there.

'Joe Davenport is funnier than the distilled essence of the funniest episodes of *The Simpsons*, *King of the Hill*, *Frasier* and *Father Ted*; he is cooler than the collected works of Quentin Tarantino and William Burroughs, in an ice storm; his prose style makes Martin Amis look like Jeffrey Archer.'

Almost.

'Joe Davenport is God.'

Excellent. Now all we have to do is think up a plot, a structure and half a dozen well-rounded characters; bash out 100,000 words; find an agent; send out a half-dozen manuscripts; start a bidding war; get paid an unfeasibly large advance; sell the film rights for even more; get rich; get famous; and live happily ever after.

Simple.

But let's not get ahead of ourselves. Before we get on with the trivial business of writing this novel, there are a few pressing details that need attending to. Starting with that irksome carbuncle I can feel swelling and throbbing on the hairline by my left temple.

No. This isn't just an excuse I've made up to put off the tedious task of thinking up my plot and developing my characters. It's serious. If Martin Amis doesn't write when he has an irksome carbuncle swelling and throbbing on the hairline by his left temple – and I'm sure he doesn't – then I see no reason why I should.

What Martin Amis would do, I'm sure, is allow himself to go off and squeeze the spot – but only on the strict condition that having done so, he should not attempt to explore any other parts of his face for further squeezing material. No sir. The moment he had squished that carbuncle down to the last drop of clear juice, he would be back at his desk, devising another clever sentence.

So that's exactly what I'm going to do myself.

When I get to the bathroom, unfortunately, things don't

quite work out as planned. It's the carbuncle's fault, not mine. Instead of exploding between my forefingers in a volcano of red and yellow pus, it just swells into a more pronounced mound. I try again, squeezing from another angle. Still it won't budge, though it has now been pressed into a slightly different shape which probably means it's going to turn cancerous and kill me. The pain's so great I daren't risk another assault.

It's only fair, I decide, that I should have some reward for all this frustration and suffering. So I head straight for the fertile squeezing ground beneath my right nostril and, with only the mildest pressure, ease forth a wriggling mass of eager blackheads. I smear them on the bog roll and pause to admire their loathsome off-white greasiness and their putrescent stench. I find a clean section of paper and repeat the process, working my way first up the right-hand side of the nose, where the blackheads are sparser, thicker and more deeply entrenched, then up the (oddly less productive) left-hand side.

Though I am now in serious breach of my Martin-Amis-style no-extra-spot-squeezing contract, I'm enjoying myself far too much to stop. There is still my chin to explore; and my forehead; and my cheeks; and the mouth region which, though superficially unpromising, sometimes yields those wonderful little surprise blackheads which you can only find by inspecting yourself very closely in the mirror and pulling the edge of your lip taut. By the end, my face is a mass of livid blotches, red lumps and nail scars, which is good because I deserve to look hideously ugly as a punishment for having wasted so much valuable writing time. And I mean to go straight back to my thinking chair and make amends, I do, I do, but as I examine my battle-ravaged features one more time, it suddenly strikes me that I really ought to do something about those lethal fingernails.

This is not as irresponsible an idea as it seems. Yes, I am perfectly well aware that cutting one's nails is almost as dodgy a displacement activity as squeezing one's spots. But the point is that if I get it done now, I won't be able to use it as an excuse next time I'm looking for a reason to avoid doing real work.

During my quest for the nail clippers, which leads me from the bathroom cabinet through all the drawers in the bedroom to the kitchen shelves and back to the bathroom cabinet where they were hiding all along, I am reminded that nail clipping is a far more complex and challenging pursuit than is commonly credited.

Like gloves, scarves, car keys, spectacles, video instruction manuals, TV remotes and the bits of paper on which you have jotted down the entry codes for your video games, nail clippers are always there when you don't want them but never when you do. The logical solution to this, I suppose, would be to keep them permanently in a dedicated nail-clipper drawer. But it never works in practice, partly because you can rarely be arsed to replace them once you've finished, and partly because you secretly want to guarantee yourself more time-wasting the next time round.

Now the act of fingernail clipping itself is not, per se, a terribly demanding activity. Apart from the risk of cutting down too low and penetrating the raw, pink skin beneath your nails, it can be achieved safely and efficiently in under a minute. Where it gets complicated is when you decide that while you're at it, you might as well deal with your toenails as well. And your toenail, as we know, is an altogether trickier customer. He's tough, volatile, smelly and inaccessible. Which is why you have to think far more carefully about where you're going to deal with him.

The loo is an obvious candidate: rest your foot on the seat, point your toes into the bowl and all the stray clippings should end up safely, flushably in the bottom of the bog. Doing it on the edge of a wastepaper bin is similarly effective, with the added virtue that the clippings make a satisfying tick as they hit the metal sides. The downside is that the bin's thin lip can be hard on the sole. Also, as with the loo option, you have to do it standing up and doubled over – which buggers your back.

That's why, as a rule, I go for the sitting-on-the-edge-of-the-bed option. If convenience and hygiene are your priorities, you can incorporate the bin into this method. Personally, though, I prefer to live dangerously and let the clippings fly where they will, all over the carpet. Or, if in playful mood, to turn it into a game of tiddlywinks, using my skill and judgement to control both the angle of exit and the distance the clippings travel. Then comes the matchless satisfaction of locating the clippings. First, the big juicy crescents. Then the tiny, filigree ones which sometimes lodge awkwardly between the filaments of the carpet. And finally, the best part of all – digging with that special prodder (the one shaped like a scorpion's sting) down the sides of your big toes to extract that rank paté of sock-fur and yellowish gunk; raising it cautiously towards your nostrils, having a good sniff, and reassuring yourself that, yes, it really is as revoltingly cheesy as you remembered.

Once I've done all this, I feel almost as drained and disgusted with myself as I would if I'd had a wank. Which I'm definitely not going to do despite the fact that I'm in the bedroom and the bed's unmade and the sheets haven't been changed for a while, all of which is somehow conducive to lewd thoughts.

But that's no excuse. I AM DEFINITELY, DEFINITELY, DEFINITELY NOT GOING TO HAVE A WANK!

Definitely not.

Not at all.

Never.

Well not never, obviously, but not right now. It would be wrong. Irresponsible. Desirable, perhaps. But very irresponsible. And I know I'd only end up feeling even worse afterwards than I already do having wasted so much time on my spots and my nails. And yes, all right, maybe the pleasure of the moment would be enough to outweigh the post-masturbatory tristesse. But that's still no excuse.

Instead, I must steel my resolve by having a quick lie down. Just a very, very quick one – no more than thirty seconds. Or a minute. Or perhaps slightly longer if I find I'm having useful, novel-related thoughts. Then I'll leap up, hurry back downstairs to my thinking chair, and work flat-out till lunchtime.

But suppose I were to have a wank, all the same. Mightn't that clear my head, get all those distracting sexual thoughts out of my system, so that by the time I get back into my thinking chair, I'll be overflowing with brilliant ideas?

Not if we are to believe Flaubert, no. Every time he had sex he said, 'There goes another chapter.' Clearly he believed that creative energy and sexual energy were one and the same.

Yeah. But he was talking about proper sex. Wanking's

different. And anyway, let's face it, the sooner I have a wank the sooner I can stop wasting time by debating whether I should have one or not.

If there is a good answer to that, I cannot think of it.

I unbutton my flies, somewhat grudgingly since I am already aware that this is going to be a relatively pointless exercise. This is not a pleasure wank. This is a boredom wank. A nice distinction, perhaps, but a very important one. With pleasure wanks, you hit the ground running. You start off with a full erection or, at the very least, a trouter. You have a very clear idea in your head as to what you're going to wank about: that girl who flashed you a lascivious look on the tube, say; or the naughty little chambermaid who's just tidied your hotel room and who was clearly dying to rip off her uniform and take you right there on the bed if only you'd had the courage to ask. Just a few fevered strokes on your pulsing manhood and you're there.

No chance of that today, I can see. The little fellow – he certainly hasn't earned the right to wear a macho porn-mag tag, like cock, dick, prick, pork sword, love missile or tadger – has shrivelled so deep beneath the matted pubic hair that he might just as well be a vagina. I pull him free and tease him with a few tentative strokes. No response. I try again, this time more forcefully. Still nothing.

What I need, obviously, is a bit of inspiration. But what form will it take?

How about the killer one-night stand I picked up at university when I was feeling like shit with flu, who gave me the mother of all blow jobs and later came at such noisy length that the Canadian mathematician across the corridor lodged a protest with the dean?

Or Jenny, the outdoors-in-wellies-suspenders-and-rain-coat girl?

Or Sarah, in a tent at Glastonbury?

Or Kim on E?

Or Sophie, in her father's Volvo?

On and on I trawl through my mental wank bank, fast-forwarding through my 'best all time' fucks, stopping when I've found one that might do the trick, rewinding and pressing play. Just like *The Chart Show* really. Except that this is like *The Chart Show* on a particularly bad day when it's wall-to-wall swingbeat, teen fodder and boy bands. Because today those videos just aren't doing anything for me. And this is a matter of some concern. Normally, you see, if there's one method one hundred per cent guaranteed to bring a man from limp to hard in under ten seconds, it's the remembrance of shags past. Provided that they're not shags with current girlfriends, who don't count because they're far too familiar and available. Former girlfriends, on the other hand, are a wanker's dream. They come in a number of shapes and sizes – 'Hmm, today, I think I rather fancy a short-haired blonde with medium breasts and long legs. Karen from Ibiza '93. Come on down!'; they are far easier to visualize than, say, an anonymous babe you spotted fleetingly on a bus; they offer an entertaining range of sexual proclivities (those that swallow, those that scream, those that like it from behind, etc.) and scenarios (behind the bushes, a thin wall's breadth away from her parents' bedroom, on a beach).

And most important of all, there was an actual, genuine moment in your life when you really did have sex with them. You're not making it up. It really, really did happen. Only now those moments are even more exciting than they were at the time, partly because you're recalling it through a haze of tumescent nostalgia, and partly because she's now an ex and consequently an exotic, tantalizingly unavailable stranger.

The failure of my trusty 'these you have fucked' technique leaves me no option but resort to the 'these you haven't fucked but would quite like to' method.

Right. So who's to be the lucky girl?

One of Sam's girlie friends maybe. That chick, whatsername, who popped round the other day straight from the gym. Black vest revealing the sweat glistening above her firm breasts, a feral smell, gobblers lips and—

No. Hang on. It's not gym girl who has the gobblers lips. It's Ailsa. With the razor-cropped hair and intense blue eyes. Yes. Yes. Something stirs below. Go on. Go on!

Right, so I'm at home. There's a knock on the door. 'Is Sam in?' says Ailsa, who for some reason is hardly wearing any clothes. 'I'm afraid not,' I reply, 'but you're welcome to come in for a coffee.' Ailsa pouts with her pouty gobblers lips and stares at me intensely with her intense blue eyes. 'Actually it wasn't really Sam I wanted to see. It's you. You see, ever since I first laid eyes on you I've been dying to fuck you and—'

Oh, come on. A bit more realism please.

Right, so there's a knock on the door and Ailsa's there and for some reason her tits have doubled in size and she's now wearing a blonde bob. Probably because she's turned into another of Sam's fanciable friends. Camille, I think it is. And this time she's soaking wet, which means, of course, that she needs to take all her clothes off. 'Would you mind just helping me with my knickers,' she asks in her sweet Mancunian voice. 'Only I'm so, so wet that—'

Yes? Yes??

Sorry. Before we go on, I need to remember exactly what this girl looks like. Generic blonde with Mancunian accent just isn't good enough. We need detail, here. Detail.

I can't remember any more details. I've only met the girl a couple of times and the last was six months ago.

Ailsa then.

She's a bit fuzzy too.

All right. What girls can you remember? When did you last see something vaguely attractive and female and probably begging for it which wasn't Sam?

Er. That party in Kensington. The one where I embarrassed myself hideously in front of – yes! Yes! *Yes!* The girl with enormous breasts whose name I can't remember!

OK. Now slowly this time. And keep it subtle.

Right so, she's just going indoors because her breasts need warming. 'Anything I can do to help?' I say.

I said 'subtle'.

'Cheeky!' she says with a lascivious smile and beckons me to join her. We head inside, shivering. Not just from the cold but because we can read each other's minds. 'It's a lovely house, this,' she muses. 'I wonder what it's like upstairs. Shall we go and explore?' 'Why not?' I say, a lump forming in my throat. And in my trousers.

Now we've found a bathroom and locked the door and, oh God, let's skip the explanation as to how we got into this position, we're just doing it. Kissing passionately as we tear each other's clothes off in a frenzy of yearning and naked lust.

'Oh God, you're so wet and soft!' I say slipping my fingers deep between her legs.

'Oh God, you're so big!' she replies.

But when I look at her face I realize that I'm with someone completely different. She's turned into the girl who told me that brilliant story about sharks. Which is odd because Shark Girl isn't nearly as attractive as the girl with enormous breasts. Not that we care right now because she's doing it for me just as well. If not better. It won't be long now.

And I take her breasts in my mouth and plunge my tongue into her cunt and now it's soixante-neuf and now she's begging me to fuck her hard and harder and harder and she's coming and I'm coming, I'm definitely coming and—

There.

I wipe myself clean. Button up my flies. Leap out of bed. And return to my thinking chair.

I was quite right of course. I feel like shit.

But at least now that I've squeezed my spots, cut my nails, had a wank and resisted the temptation to play *Ecco the Dolphin*, I can give the novel my fullest attention. There's still a good hour and a half's thinking time to go before lunch. Well, a good hour anyway, because I'll have to leave by 12.30 in order to get to the Italian shop for my special sandwich bread and charcoal roast ham before the lunchtime queue builds up.

Another coffee to gee me up. Another fag. And then—

Good Lord. It can't be half twelve already, can it? Where did the time go? Oh well. I'll just have to make it up with some extra-hard thinking this afternoon. Except that that's when I'm supposed to playing orcs at my cousin's. Damn!

Damn! Damn! Damn! Damn! DAMN!

BRILLIANT.

I have just had the most brilliant idea. Like all the most brilliant ideas, it has come when I was least expecting it, from deep within my subconscious. Which, strangely enough, effectively proves the thesis of my brilliant idea: that brilliant ideas come when you are least expecting them, from deep within your subconscious.

This means that I haven't wasted my morning at all. Or only those parts of it which I spent in my thinking chair, searching in vain for inspiration. Because when you're trying to think, you're shutting yourself off from your creative unconscious. Whereas when you're not trying to think — spot squeezing, say, or wanking, or toenail cutting — you're allowing the mind all the space it needs to come up with a succession of ever more brilliant ideas.

My cousin is not so easily persuaded.

'Sounds like a waster's charter to me,' he says, once I've explained why I'm feeling so uncharacteristically chipper.

'Well, it has a very sound intellectual precedent. Think Zen. Or that poem by Yeats. You know, where the crane is trying to catch a fish.'

'No.'

'Oh. Well, this crane is trying to catch a fish. And just like me it suddenly dawns on him that the reason he's failed is because he has been trying too hard. So he says to himself, "Maybe I shall take a trout / If but I do not seem to care."'

'And you're saying, "Maybe I shall write a novel, if but I spend my time wasting orcs."'

'Er, yeah. Sort of.'

Bill sets me up on his Apple. He's now so rich that he

can afford two, one for games and Internet use, one for his graphic-design business.

'Let me know when I've been playing for too long,' I say.

'Oh? Is that a problem now that orcs count as work?'

'The mind is a fickle thing, Bill. Imagine how awful it would be if I played for four hours and then suddenly decided my theory was total crap.'

While Bill works on his latest project – the dinosaur design which will appear on a fizzy drinks special-offer multipack – I busy myself with mine – the eradication of the orcish navy, oil platforms and coastal defences.

It is tense, demanding work. Twice, I am forced to quit and reset the scenario, having had my oil rigs, dockyards and foundries utterly destroyed by strange missiles which seem to come from nowhere.

'That'll be the orcish submarines,' explains my cousin.

'What? How am I supposed to deal with them if I can't see them?'

'You fly over them in your gnomish flying machine.'

'You might have told me earlier.'

'You never asked.'

'Only because I was scared you'd get all snappy with me.'

'And was I snappy?'

'A bit.'

'What? When was I snappy?'

'You said "of course". As if I was being really stupid.'

'Maybe you were. I never had to ask for anyone's help when I was on that level.'

'All right. I won't ask next time.'

'Don't then.'

Not for the first time, I find myself thinking what an utterly selfish bastard my cousin has become since he got hitched to Carrie, had a brat and became richer and more successful than me. But there's no point in escalating the row. Not while he holds the trump cards of Lara Croft, *Tekken II*, *Doom*, *Warcraft II*, *Civilization*, *Sim City*, *Command and Conquer* to my measly *Ecco the Dolphin* and *Sonic the Hedgehog*.

Anyway, the thrill of battle with the orcish hordes soon distracts me from my sulk. Things are going much better now that I've learned how to spot the orcish submarines. They are shaped like turtles and are gratifyingly easy to destroy. My campaign progresses swiftly. Soon, I have trounced the forces of darkness, been promoted to general and established a commanding position on the next level.

'Um, Bill?'

'Ye-es.'

'Which do you think is more essential: a mage tower or a gryphon aviary?'

'The gryphons are very useful against dragons.'

'Are they a problem?'

'Total bastardville.'

'I thought things had been going a bit too easy. When do they start attacking?'

'Could be any time.'

'Ah! Aaagh! Speak of the devil! He's burning my port. What do I do? What do I do?'

'Send in some gryphons.'

'I haven't got any.'

'Elvin archers?'

'They've just been frazzled by the dragon! Help! *Help!*'

'Keep your voice down.'

'I can't. I can't! I'm under attack.'

'*Shut up!*'

I stab 'pause' and turn round to tell Bill what a moody little shit he is. Then I see the expression of unbridled terror on his face and I realize what's wrong.

'Carrie,' he mouths, unnecessarily.

'Aagggghh!' I mouth back, equally unnecessarily.

'Hon,' calls the dread voice from down below. 'You OK?'

'Fine, honeybun.'

'Is someone with you?'

'No.' Bill gestures for me to hide behind the door.

'It sounds like someone's with you.'

'Really? Oh. That! No. I was talking to a difficult client. On the phone.'

'Hey, can you take Apollo? He's being really difficult.'

'Just give me a second. I'll be right there.'

'Now, hon! He needs his daddy.'

From the stairway comes the sound of weary footfalls. There's a rap on the door.

'Can I come in?'

'Sure.'

The door swings open. I hold my breath.

'Come to Daddy, darling!'

Apollo totters forward towards his father's open arms. Pauses halfway across the room. And looks back for reassurance from his mother. Then he spies me. I try to pretend that I'm not there, which makes him more interested in me than he has ever been before. He walks towards me, gurgling.

Bill scoops him up.

'I've got him,' he says.

Apollo thrashes in protest. He wants to join in with his godfather's hiding game.

'You're hurting him!' says Carrie.

This gives Apollo just the excuse he needs to thrash and kick some more.

'Let go of him!' yells Carrie.

'If you'll just leave him with me, he'll be fine.'

'I'm not leaving while my child is in pain.'

'He's not in pain. He's only doing it because you're encouraging him.'

'I'm his mother and I'm telling you that that child is in pain.'

Apollo, evil, manipulative rat that he is, knows that this is his cue to let out a long scream.

'I'm his father and I'm telling you—' protests Bill.

But now Carrie has seized her poor darling from his father's brutal clutches. 'You call yourself a father? Do you have any idea what I have been through this afternoon? I ask you to take care of your son just for a few minutes. And you can't even manage that. Come on, Apollo! We're leaving your father to his stupid computers and his difficult clients.'

'It's my stupid computers which keep you and Apollo in Nicole Farhi.'

'Asshole,' says Carrie, stomping almost directly towards where I'm standing. There's no way she can avoid seeing me. Absolutely no way. Unless her rage is so blind that – yes, she's almost past. And—

She stops. Does a double take. And fixes me with a glare which could slay dragons.

'Hi, Carrie!'

'Hi, Joe,' she says breaking into a smile and offering me her cheek. God, what an operator! As I kiss her, a thousand and one excuses rush through my head, all of them lame. Perhaps Bill will be able to come up with something.

'Well, that's blown our plan, hasn't it, Bill?' I prompt.

'Uh, yeah,' he replies with a blank look.

'We were hoping to keep it a surprise,' I say.

'A surprise? For me? How nice,' says Carrie.

'Er, yes. Sam and I were wondering whether you'd both like to come round to dinner next Friday.'

'Oh,' says Carrie, somewhat underwhelmed, 'that would be nice.'

On my way back home across the park, all the evil thoughts that I'd put on hold by playing orcs come surging through my brain like burst-dam water. Old favourites like 'I'll never be rich and famous', 'I'm a failure' and 'I'm going to die a horrible death' meld with nagging newcomers like 'I'll never be allowed to play video games at my cousin's ever again', 'Oh my God! Carrie's coming to dinner!' and 'Fuck! I've just gone and wasted a whole fucking day!'

With luck, a mugger will leap out from behind one of the scabby trunks that line my route to punish me for my ineffable uselessness. Or, failing that, maybe I'll step on a dog turd and spend a distracting minute or two smearing it off my shoe. You can't see them in this fading light. It's like walking through a minefield, never knowing whether your next step will be the fatal one. Which reminds me of a really harrowing Nam movie I saw. Not that there are many Nam movies that aren't harrowing, but anyway. There's this scene where a platoon is moving line abreast across a paddyfield. Nerves straining. An ominous silence. Charlie could be waiting in ambush. The camera pans from soldier to soldier. We know something awful is going to happen.

It does. There's a gentle crunch. The sergeant yells for everyone to stop right where they are. One of the men has stepped on a mine. A particularly grisly mine designed to scare you and all your buddies shitless before you die. Because it isn't triggered by pressure. That would be far too quick and pleasant. It only goes off once the pressure has been released. All the soldiers dive for cover, save the unfortunate soul who's stepped on the mine. He's sweating and shaking and screaming with fear. Can you imagine what it would be like to be in his boots? I can.

I'd be thinking, 'Why me? Why not one of the other guys? Why didn't I just step off this mine straightaway and take a few of the bastards with me? They deserve this just as much as me.'

I'd be thinking, 'So this is it! This is how my life is going to end. Not under a bus, or in an office, or in bed attended by my grandchildren, or any one of the other possibilities which used to be infinite until the second I stepped on this mine and narrowed them down to just one. I'm going to die here. In a paddyfield. In Vietnam. And the things I can see from the spot where I'm standing – the rainforest, the water buffaloes, the rice plants, the water, the mud, and my buddies – are the last things I'll ever see.'

I'd be thinking, 'When shall I step off this mine and get it over with. Now? Now? Now? Now? Or Now?'

I'd be thinking, 'Maybe the mine's a dud. Maybe the sergeant can find me a weight and slip it on top of the mine at the same time as I ease myself off. Maybe it'll explode but only take off my foot. My leg. Both my legs. My whole lower body. I don't care. I just want to live!'

I'd be thinking, 'I want my mommy.'

I'd be thinking, 'I'm surrounded by my buddies. I can talk to them. They can talk to me. They're so close I can hear them breathing. And yet the gulf between us is so vast, I might as well be all alone. I'm lonely. So lonely. God, I'm lonely. I'm going to die alone.'

I'd be thinking all these things and more. I know I would because I'm thinking them all right now, waiting for death inside the body of an imaginary soldier somewhere in the Plain of Reeds.

REEF SHARKS

There are lots of different reef sharks: blacktips, greys, Carib-beans, etc. They are mainly of interest for two reasons. First, because they are the sort of shark divers are most likely to encounter on scuba holidays. Second, because they are not at all averse to biting anyone who annoys them, be they swimmers who have inadvertently waded into their territory or divers trying to hand feed them. Still, if you've seen a reef shark on your diving holiday and you're trying to impress me, don't bother. As dangerous sharks go, they're pretty pathetic.

CHAPTER FOUR

Here's a piece of information I really didn't need. The snowy-haired biddy from number 48 is a virgin.

She didn't tell me this herself, of course. The most we've ever said to one another is '*Mor*-ning,' in that sing-song voice you reserve for people you see every day but don't care to get to know.

Ever since our paths first crossed, I've always made sure to give her a really big smile. This was because I'd persuaded myself that she was a sweet, lovely old dear. She looks like a granny from a Fairy Liquid ad: very clear, pale-blue eyes, rosy cheeks and amazingly wrinkle-free skin, which, if it weren't for the cotton-wool hair, would make you think she was closer to sixty than the seventy she probably is.

Her specialities are looking radiant and doing good works. She is a stalwart of the rather hideous modern church up the road whose bells wake me up on Sunday mornings. She does the 'heavy shopping' for my next door neighbour Mabel, who's too old and too busy caring for her bedridden husband Arnold. And she even helped me once, by taking in a huge pile of parcels that was delivered when both Mabel — who normally performs this service — and I were out.

She is so good and kind and generous, in fact, that I can't look at her without feeling bad. That's another reason why I always smile so hard at her. I want her to know that just because the majority of the younger generation are workshy, slovenly, foul-mouthed, disrespectful and often criminally inclined, I'm a jolly nice young man whom she can trust not to beat her up and steal her handbag. But I often wonder whether those clear blue eyes haven't seen straight through me. 'You, young man, are a drug abuser!' they seem to say. 'A thinker of unclean thoughts, a practitioner of pre-marital sexual intercourse!'

Yes, I suppose deep down I've always loathed the sanctimonious old bat. I hate her too-friendly greetings; I hate the way she gossips noisily at 7.45 every morning on Mabel's doorstep; I hate the fact that – via Mabel, to whom I confide rather more than I should over the garden fence – she knows far more about me than I know about her. But what I hate most of all is that the one, nauseating fact I do know about her is that she's a virgin.

I discover this from the decorator, Ed, who has spent the morning repairing the paintwork on our front window.

'Your neighbour,' he says, over a lunchtime sandwich, 'she isn't half racist.'

'Mm. Yeah. It's a generational thing. Rivers of blood.'

'And her friend's even worse. "The blacks this. The blacks that." And she doesn't mind who's listening, I can tell you.'

'Ah,' I say, through a mouthful of prawn sandwich. I'm actually trying to read the newspaper.

'Some things, I'm telling you, I wish I hadn't heard. Like her *internal examination*.'

'Do I really want to hear this?'

'I didn't have the choice. I was stuck up the ladder. She was lying there in hospital when this doctor came round with a group of medical students. And he says to her,

"Madam. I hope you don't find this embarrassing. I mean this as a compliment." Then he says to his students, "Come and look at this. Here is something you won't see very often these days. A genuine case of *virgo intacta*!"'

I stare into my sandwich's squidgy mayonnaise interior and think of that unbroken septuagenarian hymen.

'Thanks, Ed,' I say at last. 'Thanks for sharing that one with me.'

'And thanks for sharing that one with me,' says Sam later. She's poaching the smoked haddock for the fish pie. I did all the potatoes so I'm at the table taking a fag break.

'You haven't heard the epilogue,' I say.

'More geriatric gynaecology?'

'Dustbins. You know those new tall wheelie bins we had delivered last week?'

'No.'

'Well, we did. They're meant to be easier for the bin men to deal with or something. Anyway, the point is the bin men didn't empty them this morning. Just the old bins.'

'Fascinating,' she says.

'You wouldn't say that if it had been you who had to shift all the rubbish bags out of the old bins into the new one. One of the bags was crawling with maggots. I almost threw up. So you can imagine how mighty fucked off I was when the "operatives" – have you seen that? On the back of the dustbin lorry? It's Hackney PC-speak for bin men.'

'Are you going to fix me a vodka or what?'

'Excuse me! *I* listened to all *your* office gossip.'

Sam sighs. 'The bin men didn't empty the new bin.'

'Right. So there's this pullulating mass of maggots and rotten meat which is going to sit outside our house for another frigging week. Not my idea of fun – as I happen to mention to the Virgin. Just by way of something to say, you understand. She's knocking on Mabel's door. I'm fiddling with the lock on ours. I give her a shit-eating smile and say, "Really! You'd have thought the bin men could have emptied all the bins." And you know, I expect her to nod, and say, "Ooh, yes. Terrible, isn't it." As Any Normal Person would. Instead, she looks daggers at me and says, "They're not coming till next week." And I say, still smiling but more strained now, "Well, they might have told me. Jolly annoying, isn't it? I mean, if they can do the old ones, why not the new ones?" And she gives me a look as if I've just called her an old cunt – and I bloody well should have done after what she says – she says, "Don't be *stupid*! They're not coming till next week!"'

'Is that it?'

'Jesus. Do I have to spell it out? I'm trying to make pleasant conversation with this repellent old witch. And for *no reason whatsoever* she calls me stupid!'

'And what am I supposed to do?' says Sam, brandishing a coppery strip of haddock skin.

'Nothing. Just be sympathetic. Like I was when you were boring on about your afternoon with that stupid rapper.'

'Excuse me, but I think there's a slight difference between trying to get a coked-up musician out of bed with two underage prostitutes for the exclusive magazine interview he should have given three hours ago. And being called stupid by some silly old woman. Sorry you can't see it. But I'm sure if we conducted a straw poll in the street as to which story was more exciting—'

'Oh, I see. All my problems are invalid unless they involve someone famous.'

'I'm just talking about the degree of pressure.'

'Which, of course, is something I know absolutely nothing about.'

I tense as Sam plants a big kiss on my cheek. 'There, poppet. I'm sure you've had a horrid day too. Now, don't you think we should do something about dinner?'

'Yeah. Like call it off now.'

I only say this to punish Sam for her callous indifference to the traumas I have suffered on yet another scarily unproductive working day. But as the words come out, I realize that I mean them. Tonight's dinner is going to be no fun at all.

'They're your friends,' says Sam.

'Nadia is not my friend.'

'It's Nadine,' corrects Sam. 'And how do you know she's not your friend when you've never met her?'

'Oh, so she's not the sour-voiced Scottish hag who dissed me when I rang you at work last week?'

Sam shrugs. 'You've got your cousin,' she says.

'He's no fun when Carrie's around,' I say.

'Tom,' she says.

'He's only coming so he can flirt with you.'

'Tom Bland flirt with me? That'll be the day,' she says.

'Will it?' I say.

'You really think he fancies me?' she says.

'You needn't sound so pleased,' I say.

'Well, you have my full permission to flirt with Nadine, Carrie and whoever Repton's bringing along.'

'Fag hag loser bitch?' I say.

'God, you're so judgemental,' she says. 'She could be really nice.'

'Which is better: The Cross or Top Shop?'

'I don't see—'

'Quick, quick. Or your credit cards will all be snipped,' I say.

'The Cross,' she says.

'And when did you last go to Top Shop?'

'Um—'

'God, you're so judgemental. Their new collection could be really nice.'

'It's not the same.'

''Course it is. I don't need to see Repton's fag hag loser bitch to know that she's a fag hag loser bitch. One, Repton's gay – ergo, fag hag. Two, Repton says she's been having a miserable time recently and needs cheering up – ergo, loser. And the bitch part? Pure, blind, misogynist prejudice.'

Yes, yes. I know I'm being horrible. If I were in Sam's Emma Hopes, I too would choose this moment to retreat upstairs and have a long, hot soak in a bath rich in Jo Malone lavender oil, leaving me to get on with the tedious business of shelling the prawns and mashing the mash for the fish pie. But if I were me – and I am me – I'd carry on behaving exactly as I am now because I bloody well have a right to be evil and cross and horrible when I'm about to have one whole precious evening of my valuable and fast-dwindling life hanging out with people I mostly don't know or can't stand, listening to drivel like:

'What do you do? Oh, really?'

And: 'Delicious fish pie!'

And: 'Would you mind passing me a drop more red?'

And: 'Lovely colour that top you're wearing – who's it by?'

And all the other pointless things people always say at dinner parties when they don't know each other well and probably never will because they're completely incompatible.

Then, when the alcohol starts kicking in, they'll move on to politics, current affairs, art, the theatre, music. Passions will be aroused; voices raised; points contested; sides taken and bullshit shat in ever-increasing quantities until the moment comes when, tearful with boredom, kippered with fags and far, far drunker than I'd planned, I leap on to the table and scream, 'For fuck's sake, we're not at university any more. This is real life! So will you stop all this serious bollocks and move on to something a little more trivial!'

My only chance, I suppose, is to find some subtle way of steering the conversation towards something more interesting.

Maybe I could suddenly break out with the theme tune of the *Flashing Blade* and see if anyone joins in. It's a small step from there to *Robinson Crusoe, Belle And Sebastian, The Aeronauts* and other Classic Black and White Morning Childrens' TV Series We Have Loved from the early seventies.

Or I could impersonate the Soup Dragon; or speculate on the precise nature of the bizarre ménage à trois in Hector's House; or ask whether anyone else's favourite episode of *Roobarb and Custard* is 'When Thursday was Thor's Day'; or lament the awful moment when the makers of *He-Man and the Masters of the Universe* stopped Skeletor being the embodiment of hooded, cackling evil because he was scaring the kids and turned him into a wuss.

Then, if things were going well, I could move on to the most important subject of all. It would only take an innocent remark like, 'Anyone see *Mission of the Shark* last night? God, wasn't it scary?' Or, 'Which reminds me. Did you read that terrible story about the South African diver . . .' Or, if all else failed, 'Don't know about you lot. But personally I'm shit-scared of being eaten by a shark . . .'

I'm sure Repton would back me up. So to speak.

Yes. Repton. Perhaps I should tell you a bit more about him before he arrives since he is probably the most important person in my life after Sam. Repton and I have been sort-of friends since school. I say sort-of because even though we used to hang out together quite a bit – same house, same year, same interests – I think we secretly hated one another. At least, I secretly hated him. He was much taller than me (he's even bigger now – well over six foot), he never got spots and he always beat me in the subjects that mattered like English, French and History. He was also weirder than me – weird in an indefinable way, which only became definable later – which was especially galling since, obviously, I wanted to be the school eccentric even though, and this was what buggered up my plan, I could never decide what form my eccentricity would take. I just wanted to be different. And Repton, damn his eyes, was more different.

Things got worse at Oxford when Repton got a scholarship and I didn't; pulled all the most attractive girls, which I didn't; and got invited to join all the screamingly pretentious and/or screamingly homosexual dining societies like the Lily and the Piers Gaveston, which again I bloody didn't.

Under the circumstances I'm surprised we carried on being friends. But we did, somehow, until the truly miraculous evening in our mid-twenties when Repton took me for a bibulous dinner at the Caprice – he could afford it, by then he was making a mint in post-production, whatever that is – and told me there was something I ought to know, he realized that he'd been living a lie and that, um, he was gay.

Actually, I'm sure he didn't really say the 'something I

ought to know' or the 'living a lie' or the 'um' bits because Repton's too original for that. But he definitely said that he was gay in a slightly apologetic tone which implied, quite deliciously I thought, that our friendship might never survive such a heinous admission.

Well obviously, I wasn't going to let slip an opportunity like that. I looked at him balefully, my lower lip quivering and said, 'Repton. I feel utterly, utterly betrayed. To think that, until this evening, I might seriously have considered making you my best man. I might even have chosen you to be godfather to my firstborn child. No chance of that now, you filthy, filthy pederast.'

Pity I'm such a crap actor. Especially when I'm drunk.

'Cunt!' said Repton, merrily. He reached under the table and gave my knee a hard squeeze.

'Off! Off! You filthy—' I said.

'Don't worry,' he said. 'You were never my type.'

'Why not?' I said.

'Too low rent,' he said.

I ordered up another bottle of fizz. He was paying, after all.

'So you're quite pleased for me?' he said.

'Well, yes. Obviously. But more importantly I'm pleased for myself.'

'Less competition?'

'I was thinking more of the unrivalled opportunities for taking the piss. Plus, whenever some lefty toerag picks me up on some homophobic remark I've made, I can honestly reply, "I'll have you know that my best friend is gay. And if he doesn't mind when I use terms like 'fudge packer', 'uphill gardener' and—" er. You don't, do you? Mind, I mean.'

'I'd be worried if you didn't,' says Repton.

'Good. Because obviously, I don't really mean it when I—'

'Now I'm getting worried,' he says.

'Sorry. Arse bandit,' I say.

'Better,' he says.

'God, though. I don't half envy you. I mean, suddenly, you're an oppressed minority. What I wouldn't give to be an oppressed minority!'

'There are disadvantages,' Repton says. 'Being oppressed, for example.'

'Sure, sure,' I say. 'But think of the upside. You're halfway to being black. If anyone annoys you you can claim to be a victim of prejudice. You'll have the whole of Hampstead riding to your aid. You can be angry and proud and chippy and hysterical. You can go on protest marches.'

'Hunting permitting, I presume?'

'But that's just it, don't you see? Once you were just a soulless, heartless, cute-red-furry-animal murderer from the ruling Tory-fascist junta. Suddenly you're the voice of enlightenment. Your opinions will get taken seriously!'

'And you imagine that little aperçu hadn't already entered my chromosome-defective brain?' he says.

'Blimey! So that's the real reason for all this?' I say.

'Of course it isn't, you fool.'

'Bloody good one, though. Do you think maybe I should consider converting too?'

'Joe. You would make a truly crap homosexual.'

'That's not what all my gay showbiz chums tell me.'

'Right, because they all know you so well.'

'Well, I do fancy girls who look like boys. That's got to mean something.'

'Yes. It means you fancy girls who look like boys. So did Ernest Hemingway. I never did, particularly, so I shouldn't leap to any dramatic conclusions.'

'Oh. Pity. Because I was going to ask you, if you did have any old flames with a suitably ephebic demeanour, perhaps you could pass them on now that my need is greater than thine.'

'I do know one actually.'

'Oh?'

'Problem is, she's got a boyfriend.'

'That's no good.'

'Mm. Shame, really. She might have been right up your street.'

I'm reminded of this conversation when Repton turns up at my door, uncharacteristically early, with Fag Hag Loser Bitch in tow. Perhaps this is the girl he meant. She certainly looks quite a bit like a boy. A worryingly familiar boy. So worryingly familiar indeed that I'm really grateful that Sam is still in the bath. Like all girls you've been going out with for any length of time, she has this uncanny ability of knowing exactly what's going through your mind no matter how carefully you try to arrange your features into a Lee Van Cleef mask of manly inscrutability.

Not that my features qualify for Lee Van Cleef mask of manly inscrutability status right this second. Far from it. They've come over all wobbly and Jim Carrey. First they register 'Whaaat? How on earth? Is this weird or what?' shock. Then they move on to suspicion: 'Is this some sort of sinister plot?' and delight: 'Hurrah! A kindred spirit!' which quickly gives way to embarrassment: 'Didn't she feature in one of my wank fantasies the other day?' and confusion:

'*Why* did she feature in one of my wank fantasies the other day? She's not that much of a looker.'

For Fag Hag Loser Bitch is Shark Girl.

'Joe,' says Repton. 'This is my good friend Martha. You will adore her!'

'I'm glad about that,' I say, not meeting her eye.

'Me too,' says Martha, with a guilelessness that makes me feel rude not to have looked up.

And she does have nice eyes, I'm reminded. Brown ones that draw you in like a magnet.

'Are you going to let us in or what?' says Repton.

'Oh. Yes. Sorry.'

I lead them into the kitchen. Repton has brought champagne as he always does because it's the only form of alcohol he'll allow to pass his lips other than grand cru claret and burgundy. Martha has brought one of those well-aged Riojas that taste magnificently of blood, sweaty sex and ordure, which I know you can't get for less than £12.99 a bottle. Normally I'd make a big deal of such generosity. But instinct tells me to avoid any more interaction with Martha than is strictly necessary.

'So, um, you got here OK and everything?' I say to Repton.

'Flash floods in Marylebone. Riots in King's Cross. Sarin attacks at the Angel. But apart from that – Are you feeling all right, Joe? Would drugs be of any assistance?'

'Yes. I imagine.'

'Phew!' Repton reaches into his pocket. 'For a nasty moment there I thought you'd turned into a Rotarian. *How was your journey? Don't mind if I do. Drop of the old red infuriator, squire? Thanking you.* Something bothering you?'

'Oh, just tonight's nightmare guest list,' I say.

'Flattered, I'm sure. Aren't we, Martha?'

'I didn't—'

'Damn,' says Repton. 'I'm all out of skins.'

'Bugger. I think we are too. SAA-AAAM!'

Sam confirms from upstairs that we too are out of skins.

'Where's your nearest?' asks Repton, making to leave.

(NO. NO! Don't leave me alone with this dangerous, predatory female!)

'It's all right,' I say quickly. 'I'll go.'

'What about your other guests?'

'Oh yes. Them.'

'Anyway, Martha's gagging for it. And only you can give her what she wants.'

Suddenly my cheeks feel very warm. So, by the looks of it, do Martha's.

'Red. White. Whatever you've got open,' she says. 'Friend of yours?' she adds, once Repton's gone.

'Absolutely not. You?'

'Never seen him before in my life.'

I pour us a glass each of her Rioja.

'So that makes two nightmare creatures we both have in common,' I say.

'You remembered,' says Martha.

'Never forget a good shark story,' I say.

'Then you'll also remember our deal.'

'Too late. I already know your name, *Martha*.'

'You needn't say it like that, *Joe*.'

'Like what?'

'Like you've uncovered some dark and terrible secret.'

'Well, Martha is quite an – um – unusual name.'

'You mean a crap name.'

'No.'

91

'Repton always says so.'

'Repton's a very rude young fellow.'

Martha smiles. 'He's right though. I think if I'd had any choice in the matter, I would have gone for something a bit less biblical.'

'Yeah. I guess you are much more of a Fifi Trixibelle Tigerlily Heavenly Hiraani.'

Martha laughs. I really wish she wouldn't laugh at my jokes. They're not *that* funny.

She looks at the stereo and nods experimentally to the music. 'This is nice,' she decides.

Oh God, oh God. She even has the same taste as me.

'Yeah, it's all right,' I say. 'Bentley Rhythm Ace.'

'Should I have heard of them?'

'Probably not. They've got quite a dodgy reputation. Crap live, I reckon. But this album – well – you just can't argue with it, can you?'

She shakes her head dreamily in time to the beats. Lost in the music. Sam never does that when we listen to Bentley Rhythm Ace. She thinks they're boring.

'So tell me about this nightmare guest list,' says Martha.

'God, you just don't want to know. We've got this poison-tongued homosexual. Some chick whose parents were, like, these mad fundamentalist Christians and who's got this stupid hang-up about sharks.'

'My kind of people,' says Martha. 'Anyone else?'

'My cousin Bill, who's fine when his wife's not around. But she is, her name's Carrie. A nightmare bitch called Nadia. A total lech called Tom Bland. And my beauteous girlfriend Sam.'

'Sam. I remember. Have you been together long?'

'Five years.'

'Almost married.'

I laugh nervously. 'And you?'

'The less said the better.'

'Oh come on. A nice girl like you—'

'Thanks for the vote of confidence. But if I were to tell you it had been fifteen months since I last had sex—'

'Oh dear.'

'Sorry. That was probably a bit more information than you needed.'

'No. No. Not at all. I—'

'What's this about sex?' says Sam, making for the fridge.

'Hey, babe, this is Repton's friend Martha,' I say in a 'hey, she's just another guest, we were only chatting innocently and we haven't been getting on really, really well or anything' kind of voice. And just in case Sam fails to get the message, I add, 'We've met her before. *Apparently.*'

The *'apparently'*, I realize as soon as I've said it, is an unnecessarily cruel flourish. Especially since Sam, rummaging in the freezer for the ice tray, is completely oblivious to any emotional undercurrents which may or may not exist between me and Fag Hag Loser Bitch. If she has thought about it at all – and I'm sure she hasn't – she probably just imagines I'm doing my best to be nice to the poor girl I was maligning not half an hour ago. Martha, on the other hand, has definitely noticed. I can tell by the way she takes a huge gulp of her Rioja.

'Oh, I remember,' says Sam vaguely. Which of course she doesn't. By now she has glanced at Martha and sussed that she poses no sexual threat whatsoever, so she can afford to be polite. 'Zoe's and Caspar's, wasn't it?'

I suppose the decent thing to do here would be to undo the effects of that thoughtless 'apparently' by reminding Sam that it was at Marc and Jennifer's. The problem about doing the decent thing is that (a) it might draw Sam's attention to the fact that my 'apparently' was a ruse to disguise the fact that I remember exactly where we met Martha before and (b) it would signal to Martha that I'm feeling bad about having betrayed her, thus implying that our relationship has already reached a state where I should care about such nuances.

So I say, 'Yes, that's right. I think.'

And Martha looks evilly at me and says, 'Yes. They don't half give a good party, Zoe and Caspar.'

'God, don't they, though!' agrees Sam. 'Have you known them long?'

'Not terribly—' says Martha. And as I flee gratefully to answer the doorbell, I can feel her eyes boring into my back.

It's Sam's friend from work.

'Hello there. I'm Nadine. And you must be Joe,' she says.

'Not Nadia. Nadine!' I repeat to myself in my head. 'Nadine. Nadine. Nadine.' Because she's clearly the sort of girl who'd have your balls smeared on toast if you got it wrong.

'I've heard a lot about you,' she says, squeezing past me through the entrance to the kitchen.

'Oh. Er, good,' I say.

Now I'm really nervous. She's an ultra-petite Scots girl, with cropped red hair, very pale, freckled skin, and a sassy 'come, fuck me' manner. I'd happily oblige too. Breasts way out of proportion to her tiny frame; terrifyingly brief, A-line skirt; suspenders and, at a lewd guess, no knickers. I can just imagine it now – hoiking her up into the air, her legs splayed and ready, and then just . . . *spearing* her with my –

' – Bobby Brown,' says Nadine to Sam.

Did I hear aright? Did Nadine mention the name of He Whose Music I Hate More Than Anything In The World. With the possible exception of Steely Dan, Luther Vandross, Boys II Men, Michael Bolton and – well, actually, there are quite a lot of people whose music I hate at least as much as Bobby Brown's. But the point is that their names weren't mentioned by Nadine, whereas Bobby Brown's was. Worse still, she's holding what looks very much like his latest album above the portable stereo. *My* portable stereo. The one that's currently playing my cherished Bentley Rhythm Ace CD.

'Um—' I'm about to protest when Sam gives me a look. Nadine's finger is poised above the machine.

'How do I . . .?'

'Let me.' I dart forward.

Too late. She's missed 'stop' and hit the eject button. The exposed CD makes a stricken whirr as it spins to a premature halt.

'Oops.' Now the evil Nadine whom I most definitely would not like to shag, not ever, is taking out the CD. Not by the edge, but holding the middle.

'I'll do it.' I snatch the Bentley Rhythm Ace CD from her, pointedly inspect the greasy thumbprint on the shiny underside, and snap the disc back into its case.

'He's very protective,' explains Sam to Nadine and Martha, in that voice women reserve for silly boyfriends and naughty pets.

'Don't tell me,' says Nadine. 'He keeps them all in alphabetical order?'

'And by category. Dance. Rock. Drum 'n' bass . . .'

'But no swingbeat, funnily enough,' I say.

'Och, Bobby Brown isn't swingbeat,' says Nadine. 'He's R&B.'

'Rubbish and Bollocks?' I put it slowly in my portable stereo, giving Nadine plenty of time to take the hint.

'Joe thinks all black music's crap,' explains Sam.

'That's right. I'm always listening to white-boy music. Lee Perry. Augustus Pablo. Tricky. LTJ Bukem . . .'

'If you'd rather play something else,' says Nadine, at last.

'Thanks.' I reach for the pile of CDs I set aside earlier. It includes Underworld – *Second Toughest in the Infants*; Death In Vegas – *Dead Elvis*; Julian Cope – *World Shut Your Mouth*; and, for the unlikely event that things turn mellow later on, Neil Young – *After the Goldrush*; OP8; and Belle and Sebastian.

'Joe!' says Sam. 'Nadine's our guest.'

'So's Martha,' I say. 'And she likes this one. Don't you, Martha?'

'Oh. I'm easy,' she says, treacherously.

'Well, I'm the host . . .' I say.

Plus, I'm about to add, being as I write about music for a living, my ears are more sensitive and easily offended than most people's; plus I've already devoted a considerable amount of time and thought to choosing precisely the right sort of music for the occasion; plus I hate Bobby Brown so much that I might just go into a huge sulk which won't be fun for anyone, will it?; plus . . .

But the doorbell interrupts. And by the time I've answered it and returned to the kitchen with Bill and Carrie the battle is lost.

Carrie puts her hands in the air and waggles her hips. 'Hey! Bobby Brown!' she says boogieing towards Sam, Martha and Nadine. 'Party on down!'

Bill, who shares my abhorrence of swingbeat and related musical atrocities, gives me a pained look. I grab us both a consolatory beer and, not without a guilty glance at Martha, I lead Bill into the garden. That's what the letting agent called it, anyway. It consists of a few square feet of raised patio, bordered on three sides by elongated cat toilets in which no plant can bear to grow, save weeds, some rather creepy-looking ivy with thick, twisted stems and centipede legs and a terrifying, indestructible Russian vine which, like cockroaches and scorpions, will inherit the earth when the Apocalypse comes.

In the middle sits its one redeeming feature – a fish pond which I built with my very own hands. Bill and I stand at the edge, peering through the weed and green murk in search of its inhabitants, Percy, Jimmy, John Paul and Bonzo.

'I can only see three,' says Bill.

'You're right. Bonzo's missing.'

'Maybe he drowned,' quips Bill, 'in his own vomit.'

I light a cigarette to mask the pervasive whiff of feline piss.

'It's that fucking cat!' I decide. 'It's that evil, evil fucking cat.'

'Then the cat must die,' says Bill.

See? See how much more fun he is when Carrie's not around?

'He must. But how?'

We speculate pleasurably on ways to kill the evil cat. Not that we are cat haters, you understand. We both have pussies of our own, born in the same litter. Bill's is called Lara. Mine is called Black Cat. But, unfortunately, like their owners, Lara and Black Cat are pampered, sophisticated types who wouldn't have a clue how to take care of themselves in a fight with the neighbourhood lowlife.

Black Cat's worst enemy and mine is the aforementioned

evil, evil fucking cat. He is almost twice Black Cat's size with scurfy black and white fur and a droopy, pink lower jaw which, when he's close enough – which isn't very often because he's devilishly cunning when humans are around – you can see dripping with foul, evil cat saliva. He craps and pisses in my flower bed; he terrorizes Black Cat; he has even been known to creep through our cat flap, eat Black Cat's food and spray on our furniture. I hate him and he must die!

Bill and I have just gone through the punji-stakes-under-the-patio, poisoned-fish, airgun, and large-weight-from-my-office-window options when Repton reappears. Martha trails behind him.

'Hey, Repton! We were just discussing the best way to kill the cat that's been murdering my goldfish. Any suggestions?'

'Um. You'll have covered firework-up-the-bottom, presumably?'

'Too pleasurable, I think,' I say.

'And how would you know, sweetheart?' says Repton, sitting on the edge of the fish pond, the better to roll our urgent spliff. 'And excuse me,' he says, suddenly looking up at me. 'I thought you were supposed to be taking care of Martha.'

'Oh, sorry,' I say to Martha. 'I thought you were busy with girlie talk.'

'Martha doesn't do girlie talk,' says Repton.

'Except with you,' she says to Repton.

'Except with me,' confirms Repton.

'And she doesn't like being trapped in a room with Bobby Brown, either,' says Martha.

'You're cool,' says Bill. He introduces himself to Martha. 'Don't you think she's cool, Joe?'

'Oh, definitely,' I say. Non-committally.

'She's not the one you told me about?'

'Er. Don't think so,' I lie. Because of course she is. Bill shares my enthusiasm for girls who look like boys. He doesn't share my gift for discretion.

'Who's this?' says Martha.

'Oh, just some girl I met,' I say.

'A girl who looked like a boy,' says Bill. 'Like you. We like those, don't we, Joe?'

'Uh, yeah, because we're both latent homosexuals,' I say blushing furiously.

Martha is not to be sidetracked. 'Well, being a girl who looks like a boy I'm always keen to meet other girls who look like boys. Can you remember her name?'

'No.'

'She never said,' chips in Bill. 'They had this deal where – Ow!' Bill rubs his knee, looking up at me angrily.

'You're embarrassing our guests,' I tell him

'Oh, very much so,' says Martha, pleased as punch.

Repton passes me the joint. 'Only toke on a little. Never more than a spot. Or something may happen. You never know what.'

'After you, then,' I say.

'You have turned into a Rotarian,' says Repton, retrieving the joint.

He lights up.

'Skunk?' I ask.

'Superskunk.'

'Bugger. Sam hates it when I get monged before dinner.'

'I doubt she'll notice.'

'Oh?'

Repton makes a girls-getting-drunk-very-quickly gesture. 'Tequila slammers,' he explains.

'Carrie too?' asks Bill anxiously. 'I'd better—'

'No, Bill,' I command. 'This is war. We need all the good men we can get.' I glance guiltily at Martha. 'And women.'

She smiles, still looking disgustingly triumphant.

When my turn comes the joint has little effect. I take a few extra-hard sucks just to make sure. Still nothing.

'Oh sorry. Very rude of me.' I pass the joint to Martha.

She shakes her head.

'It's really not that strong,' I insist.

Then it strikes.

'Wow!' says Bill. 'It's like a jungle out here!'

'Mm,' agrees Repton. 'Prehistoric.'

We gaze towards the tangled mass of ivy and Russian vine. If you stare very hard at it, as I am right now, you can almost make out the herds of brontosauri grazing underneath. And the predatory tyrannosaurs thrashing through the dark foliage. And the pterodactyls soaring overhead with their menacing beaks spiking forward like the V1 rocket which Mabel next door once told me flew right above our house, so low that it blacked out the sun – like a huge black cross, it was – and everyone was in their garden at the time because it was a blazing Sunday afternoon in August. Which is a story I have a really, really strong urge to tell everyone this instant, because let's face it, it's incredibly interesting. But the small part of my brain charged with keeping things together is advising me otherwise. 'That way paranoia lies,' it says, pointing out that my mind has been drifting somewhat from the subject currently under discussion. There has been slippage. And if I suddenly start talking about V1s everyone will start giving me anxiety-inducing 'what the hell's he on about?' looks. Which is, in itself, a very paranoid-making thought. But let's not dwell on that. Let's make a real effort here and claw our way back through those vanished seconds and try to recall what was going on just before we got sidetracked by Mabel's V1 blackening the sky above the house like a circling – Victory!

'Prehistoric or what?' I say. 'And it's impossible to kill.'

'Piranhas. That's what you need,' says Repton.

'Piranhas?' I fail to see how even the most vicious piranhas could help me destroy my Russian vine.

'That's an old wives' tale. They only attack when there's a severe shortage of food,' says Bill.

'So starve them,' says Repton.

'An estuarine crocodile would be better,' says Martha.

Bill looks at Martha, then at me in a way I'm supposed to find deeply significant but which only serves to confuse me even more than I already am. Which is very confused indeed. It's like being trapped in a coma where your friends and family are chatting by your bedside. You can hear every word they're saying and you're aching to join in but you can't. You're paralysed in a semi-conscious dream world, where you speak exactly the same language as they use in the one outside, only with a completely different syntax, grammar and vocabulary. And whenever you think you've got a fix on what's going on, the rules keep changing. The conversation is just a string of non-sequiturs.

'Does it have to be estuarine?' asks Repton.

'Oh, for sure,' says Martha. 'They're the great whites of the crocodile world. They're the ones who got all those Japanese soldiers in the – um – in the . . .'

'Mm,' says Bill. 'I know where you mean. In the – Joe'll know. Joe. Joe? *Joe?* "Earth calling Joe. Earth calling Joe."'

'Yes?'

'Where did the estuarine crocodiles eat all the Japanese soldiers?'

'Um . . . Fuck, this stuff's strong!'

'I did warn you,' says Repton.

'. . . Never more than a spot . . .' says Bill. 'Where do I know that line from? Joe?'

'Yes, Joe,' teases Repton. 'Where does that line come from?'

'Oh, leave him alone, boys,' says Martha. 'It's Doctor Seuss. "A Fish Out Of Water". Joe knew that. Didn't you, Joe?'

'Yeah,' I say, uncomprehendingly. '"A Fish Out Of Water".'

Let's fast-forward. We have to. There's no point even trying to make sense of the ensuing hour. Or hour and a half. Or however long it is before the effects of Repton's noxious weed have worn off sufficiently for me to make sense of my surroundings.

But before we go on, I want to make it clear that I wasn't that far gone. I can hold my weed, you know. I'm not a total lightweight. I do remember at least some of the things that went on between. Like:

The satanic death-look Sam gave me on realizing that I was in no fit state to help her serve up the fish pie.

Becoming obsessed with my teeth and the process of chewing and the lumpy progress of the fish pie down my gullet. Discovering that my throat had grown parched and disconcertingly sensitive; that the water I drank to lubricate it had mutated into liquid diamonds.

Someone saying, 'Could you pass that red?' Someone else saying, 'Lovely fish pie.'

Experiencing a nagging, ill-defined sense of unease.

Having a long internal debate as to where I should seat Martha. If I put her anywhere near Tom Bland, there's a serious risk that his tentacular arms will stray all over my beloved Shark Girl's body. He'll seduce her, dump her and ruin her life. But if I put her anywhere near me, Repton might get suspicious and Sam might think I'm flirting with her in order to pay Sam back for flirting with Tom Bland, which Sam will then take as her cue to flirt with Tom even more, forcing me to be yet more flirtatious with Martha so that Sam feels compelled to trump me by having a clandestine affair with Tom, or perhaps even a not-clandestine one, perhaps she might even snog him at dinner, or make love to him here and now on the table in front of us, or am I being paranoid? Well, yes. Probably. But on balance it does seem to make more sense to go for the let-Tom-Bland-ruin-Martha's-life option.

Tom Bland arriving late with a bottle of wine so disgusting that, in a burst of temporary togetherness, I opened it, poured him a huge measure and kept it on the dresser behind me so that I could recharge his glass, and his alone, whenever he asked for more.

Portishead's *Dummy* replaced Bobby Brown. An improvement, no doubt, but by no means ideal. For a time, during that six-month period after its release when only cool people knew about it, it was definitely my favourite stoner album. Then everyone started raving about it, including Carrie, who completely ruined it for me by drawing my attention to the lyrics which, she insisted, were about 'a woman's hurting'.

Nadine cross-examining me in a voice that combined sweet reasonableness and insidious menace as to my musical preferences: 'Is there really no black music you like?' My political persuasion: 'You never did? Really? Do you know I think you're the first person of my age I ever met who voted Tory.' And my background: 'Och, well, public school. Is that where you met your friend Repton by any chance?'

It's about this point that I become aware that I am having every bit as miserable a time as I had predicted. This owes much, I am sure, to the seating arrangements. I have been exiled to the boring end of the table, between Carrie and Nadine, where the conversation has been confined to child-care, the unreasonableness of men, therapy, the Celestine Prophecy, the Bible Code, the mystery of the Nazca Lines. On all of which subjects, I have nothing positive to contribute.

At the other, fun, end, everyone's laughing, flirting (Tom, the odious lech with both Sam *and* Martha), bitching about mutual friends, and talking about the sort of things that I'd like to be talking about: the 'My Lovely Horse' sequence from last night's repeat of *Father Ted*; the grisliness of the recent chairlift disaster in Andorra; a bus accident that Martha once witnessed in India; nasty diseases that everyone has caught on their travels.

Normally, this would be my cue to butt in and trump the lot of them with my tropical double whammy: acute amoebic dysentery and bilharzia. But I can't because Nadine's just asked me that loaded question about Repton. And since by now I've grown heartily sick of her mock-polite attempts to have me admit that I'm the fascist racist wanker she'd so dearly love me to be, I reply, 'You mean, am I a closet shirtlifter?'

For the first time all evening, Nadine looks coy. 'That's not what I meant at all.'

'It's what you implied. Hey, Repton. Nadine wants to know if you ever slipped me one in the school showers.'

'All I asked was—'

'Oh well, you know what they used to say,' says Repton. '"What's the difference between Joe Davenport and the Eiffel Tower?" Not everyone's been up the Eiffel Tower.'

'He's teasing, doll,' says Sam to Nadine. 'Joe's far too squeamish.'

'That's what you think.'

'It's what I know.'

'He does like girls who look like boys though,' offers Bill.

'Yeah. So do you.'

'Of course. That's why we both like Martha so much.'

Bill tends to get like this, unfortunately, after a few glasses.

'Oh, that's so unfair,' says Sam. 'Martha doesn't look at all like a boy. She's—'

'Gamine,' says Tom.

'So useful having a top author around,' says Sam.

'Gamine *means* boyish,' I say wearily. It's meant to put down Tom, but then I panic that Martha might think I'm getting at her. I give her a solicitous look, which Sam catches. And I think, 'Fuck! *Fuck!* However did we get here?'

Salvation comes in the unlikely shape of Carrie. 'It's such an English thing, don't you find?' she says to Nadine earnestly. 'This flirtation with homosexuality.'

'Aye. That and public school. You'll not be sending Apollo, I imagine.'

'Oh. I couldn't. It's so cruel.'

Not half as cruel as entrusting him to the cares of Hackney's 'education' system, I'm tempted to say. But what's the point? It will only develop into one of those predictable arguments where neither side gives any ground. Nadine and Carrie will contend that it's unnatural to tear a boy from his parents' bosoms at the tender age of eight, that he'll always have trouble relating to women, that the whole system is elitist and outmoded. I'll counter that there's nothing wrong with elitism, that eight-year-olds are infinitely adaptable, that the system never did me or Bill any harm, and that, anyway, at least you end up learning something which is more than you can say for the state system. And Nadine and Carrie will both splutter, 'What's wrong with the state system?' And I'll deliver an impassioned speech on the perils of 'child-centred' education, on the disastrous legacies of sixties liberalism, the idiocy of the 'real books' system, and – oh God, it's just too dreary. I've got to get out before I flip.

'Uh, here's an idea,' I announce. 'Why don't all the men move round two places?'

'Are we boring you?' says Nadine.

'Not at all. I think I'm the one who's been boring you.'

'Great,' says Sam, 'so now you're offering to come and bore me and Martha.'

'I'm happy where I am,' says Tom, beaming at Martha and Sam.

'Or we could always chill out next door,' I suggest.

'We haven't had pudding yet,' says Sam.

'Oh. Right. How about a pre-pudding joint then?'

'*Mister* Control Freak!' says Sam.

'I'm only trying to jolly things along a bit.'

'So we *are* boring you!' says Nadine.

'Oh, forget I said anything.' I sigh, adding sotto voce, 'Skin up, would you, Repton?'

I put on Belle and Sebastian. Nadine and Carrie are embroiled in another of my favourite dinner-party topics, animal rights. Nadine, I discover to no surprise whatsoever, is quite the activist. She once single-handedly rescued hundreds of baby veals at Brightlingsea and liberated thousands of chain-smoking beagles. And only last weekend, she helped save an innocent fox from being torn to pieces by savage hounds.

'Really? Which hunt?' I say, toking on the joint which Carrie has just rejected.

Nadine eyes me suspiciously. 'The Belvoir.'

'I think you'll find it's pronounced "Beever". As in split.'

Oh God, did I really say that? Better not have any more. I pass the joint on to Nadine, who shakes her head. She is not a happy bunny.

'I only ask,' I say airily, 'because you might have bumped into Repton. You were out last weekend, weren't you, Repton?'

'Have been for six years now, sweetheart.'

'*Hunting*, you old queen!'

'Mm. With the South Dorset. Why?'

'Nadine here rides with the Belvoir.'

'Does she really? How wonder ... ah—' Repton looks anxiously at Nadine. 'He's joking?'

'You could call it that,' she snaps, rising suddenly to her feet.

Exit Nadine pursued by Sam. When they return, Nadine is sniffing slightly.

'I'm sorry. I didn't mean to—'

107

'That's OK,' says Nadine with a smile. 'I'm sure it's not your fault you're a fascist.'

'Strangely enough, hunting and fascism aren't necessarily compatible,' I say. 'You do know that Hitler was fiercely anti-field sports.'

'And he was a vegetarian,' adds Repton.

'That's what I love about you carnivores,' says Nadine, 'your arguments are so original.'

'That'll be because of all the extra protein feeding our brains,' I say.

'I was – oh, why bother?'

'Quite.'

'Are you patronizing me?'

'No. I just think that rather than spending the rest of the evening trotting out the same weary old arguments, it might be nice to find something we all agree on.'

'And what would be the point of that?'

'I dunno. Guess I'm just a peace and love kind of guy.'

Nadine snorts. 'Except where foxes are concerned.'

'All right. Have it your way. It's my firm belief that all foxes must die. The more cruelly, the better.'

'And cats,' says Bill.

'And sharks,' says Repton.

'Yeah. Sharks especially.'

'What have you got against sharks?' asks Nadine.

'Don't start him off,' says Sam.

'They're bastards and I hate them and they must all die,' I say.

'I'm sure they'd say the same about you,' says Nadine.

'Aha, but that's exactly it!'

'Joe's convinced he's going to get eaten by a great white

shark,' explains Sam in a God-isn't-my-boyfriend-pathetic voice.

'Not necessarily,' I say. 'It could be a tiger. Or a bull. Or an oceanic white tip. That's one of the things that's so horrible about the bastards. There's a shark for every occasion. Some of them like cold water. Some like it hot. Some get you in the shallows. And some get you in mid-ocean. After your plane crashes, say. Or your boat sinks.'

'So stay at home,' says Nadine.

'What? Then they'll have won,' I say.

'Maybe you secretly want to be eaten by a shark,' says Nadine.

'Fuck off! It's the most horrible death imaginable.'

'Aye. But it's not exactly likely, is it?'

'Nadine, seriously,' pleads Sam, 'it's not worth it.'

'Oh, I find it quite interesting actually. The way men are always scared of such improbable things, whereas women tend to be so much more pragmatic.'

'Huh. Well, Martha's scared of sharks.'

'Is that so, Martha?' asks Nadine.

Martha shrugs. 'Not especially.'

'*What?* The other night you were saying – your story! your friend in Hong Kong!'

'You must be confusing me with someone else,' says Martha.

'I know damn well it was you!' I say. 'Repton. Support me here. Isn't Martha terrified of sharks?'

'Problem with this stuff is it plays havoc with the short-term memory,' says Repton inhaling.

I look angrily round the table. All eyes are on me, sceptical, mocking. I have become the victim of a terrible conspiracy. Everyone hates me and wants to make my life even more miserable than it is already.

'But you're all scared of sharks,' I insist. 'Of course you are. You just won't fucking admit it!'

'Maybe,' suggests Carrie in a deceptively meek voice, 'maybe, when you have a strong, irrational fixation, maybe sometimes you need to justify it to yourself by imposing your perspective on other people.'

'Must say, sharks have never much bothered me,' says Tom.

'Well, aren't you the brave, braw laddie!' says Nadine. Not so much sarcastic, I suspect. More, 'In case you haven't noticed, I've been eyeing you all evening and I'm up for a shag.'

'Oh good,' says Repton. 'That must make me one too. Because I think sharks are pathetic!'

'And me,' says Bill.

'You're all lying bastards, that's all I can say. Lying bastards!'

I'm not quite sure how cross I am but I might as well make the most of being the centre of attention.

I snatch the joint from Repton and put on Underworld because it's dark and menacing. If I'm not allowed to be mellow, then neither will anyone else.

After pudding – defrosted raspberries, ice cream and M&S bubbly Swiss milk chocolate – Bill and Carrie head off to relieve the babysitter, while the rest of us retire to the sitting room. I'm all ready for some Neil Young but Nadine is adamant that it has to be drum 'n' bass. I soon discover why.

It happens when Tom, who has weaselled his way on to

the sofa between her and Sam, grumbles about the 'awful racket'.

'There are ways of getting into it,' says Nadine, exchanging a conspiratorial smile with Sam.

'I think you're overestimating Tom's musical sophistication,' I say. 'You'd prefer a bit of Dire Straits, wouldn't you, Tom?'

'Proper music, mm.'

The girls, Martha included, beam at Tom. 'Oh, he's so cute,' seems to be the verdict. 'So nice to see a man who knows his own mind; who's not swayed by fickle fashion; unlike ghastly, neurotic, trivial, shark-obsessed Joe . . .'

And Tom clearly thinks this is his due because when Nadine's hand drifts across to his lap, he doesn't even flinch. It's so embarrassingly brazen I'm tempted to look away. Martha must have noticed too because she turns sharply to face Repton and asks whether it's time to call a minicab. The hand doesn't linger long though. It seems to rummage briefly in his pocket and then pulls away.

Repton proposes one more spliff for the road; I call a minicab; and Tom asks, 'Loo upstairs, is it?'

No sooner has he returned, scratching his nose, than Nadine makes the same round trip. Then Sam. They cosy up to one another on the sofa, snug as tiger snakes under a log.

'God, I love this music,' says Nadine, rapidly patting her knees.

'Fucking brilliant,' agrees Sam, hands aquiver at 160bpm.

Nadine squeezes Tom's arm. 'Hey, what do you think?'

'OK!' he says with a huge grin.

'Better than OK,' says Sam. 'This is the business!'

'Yeah!' says Tom.

'Yeah!' says Nadine.

'Cunts!' I think, sucking extra hard on the joint Repton's just passed me. I don't think it'll do much good though. I think I've smoked myself straight.

'So, Repton,' I say, coughing. 'We hardly got to speak.'

'There's always Bill's stag weekend.'

'Oh there won't be time then. I'll be far too busy shagging and snorting,' I announce, mainly for Sam's benefit.

Annoyingly she doesn't hear. But at least I get an enthusiastic leer from Repton.

'By the way, I meant to ask you,' he says. 'Is this some new trend I don't know about? I thought these things were supposed to take place *before* one's wedding.'

'You know Carrie,' I say. 'I guess she needed the insurance of a ring, a sprog and guaranteed alimony before she'd take the risk.'

'Bitch,' says Repton.

'And you're not? Betraying me like that over the sharks.'

'Oh but, darling. You're so wonderful when you're angry.'

I roll my eyes. 'As for you, Martha—'

'Call it quits.'

'Mm. Suppose I—' I glance over to the sofa. As far as its occupants are concerned, we might as well not exist. 'Oh, whatever. See you again sometime. I hope.'

'That depends,' says Martha.

'Oh yeah?' I say.

'Well, now I know how bad your memory is, there's a chance you might not recognize me.'

'I'll work on it,' I say. 'I promise. I'll never smoke any of these evil, brain-destroying drugs ever again. Just for you, Martha. Just for you.'

A horn sounds outside. Martha and Repton collect their things.

'Hey, you're not going?' says Tom, snapping to his feet. 'Let me take your address. Then I can send you my book.'

Martha obliges.

'It was good meeting you,' says Tom. 'Really good. Maybe we can meet for coffee or something. You don't live so far from me. Here. I'll give you my number—'

Which, by my understanding of female psychology, should have scuppered his chances with Nadine. But no. She's looking at him so longingly her tongue is combing the carpet.

'I think if you guys don't mind, I'm heading off to bed,' I tell the three cokeheads.

'What?' squawks Sam. 'We've only just started.'

'Oh, come on, Joe. Don't be a killjoy!' says Tom.

Even Nadine joins in with a half-hearted, 'What are we going to do for a DJ?'

'I'm sure you'll manage,' I say. 'Night night.'

When I awake, a sliver of pale, unhealthy light has stolen in through the gap in the curtains and something is pawing desperately at my groin. I roll over to face the bedside clock. It's half past four.

'Are you awake?' says Sam.

'No.'

'I want you.'

'Tough.'

'But I can't sleep.'

'Why's that I wonder?'

'Look, it was Nadine's stuff. I couldn't very well—'

''Course you could. She's your – What was that?'

'What?'

'Like an animal in pain.'

'Cats fighting?'

'There it is again. It's coming from downstairs. The fucking cats are inside the fucking house!'

'Oh. *That* noise, you mean. That'll be the fucking Tom and Nadine.'

'What? On our sofa? Jesus! I hope you gave them some sheets.'

'Don't be such a prude.'

'Listen to them. Disgusting!'

'I find it quite a turn-on.'

'You would with half of Colombia up your nose.'

'Please. Then I'll leave you alone.'

'I'm not in the mood.'

'I'll get you in the mood.'

'You can try but it won't work.'

'Don't you find me attractive any more?'

'Oh please. We're not going into this one.'

'Well, do you?'

'Sam, you're the most gorgeous, shaggable chick in the whole universe now will you let me go to sleep.'

'Say it as if you mean it.'

'Sam, you're the most gorgeous, shaggable chick in the whole universe. Now will you please, please let me sleep.'

'You don't mean it.'

'I do.'

'No you don't.'

'All right, I don't.'

'So I was right.'

'No. I'm just telling you what you want to hear. So I can get some fucking sleep.'

HAMMERHEADS

I have quite a soft spot for hammerheads because they look so crap. I mean, even if they were the most dangerous sharks in the world, which they're not, you could hardly stop yourself laughing at those stupid protrusions either side of their head. Apparently, they use them a bit like a metal detector, swinging their heads from side to side over the sea bottom so as to discover buried fish.

In shark books, hammerheads are listed as 'potentially dangerous' but I have yet to find a recorded instance of a hammerhead ever attacking a human. Still, the biggest ones can grow up to twenty feet, so you wouldn't want to get too blasé about them.

CHAPTER FIVE

I'm lying prone on the moist, brambly soil behind a fallen tree, heart pounding, gun cocked, eyes straining to catch the slightest movement in the bosky shadows ahead. My scalp is itching with nits and I think I can feel something nasty crawling across the exposed skin between the top of my left boot and the base of my combat trousers. But I'm not going to scratch or squirm because elite special forces troops just don't do that sort of thing while lying await in ambush. Not even when they're several thousand miles from the Mekong Delta, in a scrubby wood outside Nottingham, playing paintball.

Just like in Nam, I've developed a severe case of thousand-yard stare. The longer I gaze through the trees, the more imaginary enemies I see. And the more imaginary enemies I see, the less I trust my ability to spot the real enemy when he comes. It's like that scene at the beginning of *Platoon* where Charlie Sheen is on night-guard duty, struggling to keep awake, plagued by mosquitoes, tormented by the shadows, when the Viet Cong materialize like greeny-yellow ghosts. No, worse. It's like *Predator*.

I wonder if Bill's thinking the same thing. He's only a few yards away, covering my left flank from behind a silver birch. Over to my right, Repton is manning a foxhole.

Behind him, Tom Bland and a couple of other stags whose names I can't remember are guarding our team flag. Beyond Bill, two more of his friends are completing our defensive semicircle behind a giant stump. According to Tom, who studied this sort of thing in the infantry section of his school corps, our position is impregnable.

Which is just as well since up to this point, we have been doing very badly indeed. Half our unit – Bill's stag group – consists of wimpy Londoners, the other, of amiable but feckless crusties from Bristol, who seem keen to get shot by the enemy as early as possible in each ten-minute game so that they can retire for a spliff break.

While I admire this heroic indolence, it does tend to stack the odds even more heavily in favour of our large and merciless opposition: a group of big lads with squaddie accents, military haircuts and very small brains, who appear to have no lives whatsoever beyond the world of paintballing. They have brought their own camouflage jackets, protective masks, and rapid-fire, ultra-long-distance paint guns. And whereas my team is decidedly frugal when it comes to buying extra magazines of ammunition at a fiver a throw, the opposition purchase theirs in bulk and are happy to expend more in one game than we would in a whole morning.

Suddenly there's a muffled 'phut' from a distant paintball gun. Then comes the 'phut-phut-phut' of several guns in rapid-fire mode, the hiss of balls through foliage and the splat of gelatine on bark. There are shouts of aggression, outrage and pain. I am glad that I chose to stay with the defenders rather than join the Bristol crusties on the attacking party. With luck, I won't even see any action during this particular game. The enemy seem to have concentrated all their efforts on defence, which means it's probably safe to remove my protective goggles and give them a quick wipe.

As I'm doing so, Bill calls my name.

'Shhh!'

'*Joe!*' he repeats, more urgently this time.

I look round, glasses in one hand, protective mask pressed awkwardly against my face with the other. For some stupid reason, Bill has decided to stand up. Not only that, he's got his gun jokily pointed straight at my backside and . . .

'*Ow!*' There's a stabbing pain on my right buttock. 'You fucking . . .!'

More blasts of pain now. On my legs, on my back and – Jesus, that hurt – on the back of my head.

'Stop! I'm dead! I'm dead!'

The two shots that follow are the most agonizing of all. One catches me on the temple, close to my right eye. The other slaps into the back of my left hand which I've raised to protect my face.

I'm curled up in a foetal ball, wondering if it will ever end, when I recognize the voice of one of the marshals.

'No more. He's dead,' he tells my assailant.

My finger joints are throbbing and swollen; I can feel an egg-sized lump developing on my temple. When I retrieve my paint-splattered glasses, I discover that one of the arms has snapped off.

'Marshal!' I call out.

'Put-your-mask-on-now!' he screams.

'Marshal, did you see that?'

'Next time I catch you doing that you're out of the game for good. Understand?'

'Yes, marshal.'

'Do you know how fast these paintballs move? Sixty feet per second. Do you have any idea what an object moving at that speed can do to your eye?'

'Well, I've a pretty good idea. Look!'

'Put-that-mask-on-now!'

'I was only trying to show you what that fucker did to my face at point-blank range.'

'If you'd been wearing your mask it wouldn't have happened.'

'Look, I'm sorry but that's beside the point. He shot me loads more times when he knew I was already dead. He should be disqualified.'

'Are you trying to tell me my job?'

'Forget it, Joe,' says Bill. He has been almost as badly spattered as me.

We return to the 'sterile zone'. This is the area to which you retire when you've been killed. It is protected from stray paintballs by camouflage netting, making it safe to remove your mask, smoke consolatory cigarettes and drink filthy cups of tea or coffee. The majority of our team are already there, chuntering about the injustice of it all.

According to the rules of the game, you're dead as soon as a paintball explodes anywhere on your body. This means that in any one game, the enemy has no need to shoot you more than once. Yet many of our team are covered from head to foot in yellow stains, notably the hapless defenders like me, who were shot at point-blank range in the back.

The attacking element in our team has suffered too. One of the two girls from the Bristol crew, an achingly beautiful thing with matted, dyed-red dreadlocks, has sustained a direct hit on her left nipple.

'I've just the cure for that,' leers one of the few 'dead' members of the opposition.

'Swivel!' she calls back, showing him her middle finger.

Tom has noticed several instances of cheating by the opposition. Not only have they been wiping off paint after being hit and pretending they're still alive, but they have been manoeuvring through the forbidden area beyond the playing zone's official perimeter. This, he reckons, is how they managed to outflank our defences and take us by surprise.

'And when I told the marshal, he said there was nothing he could do unless he saw it for himself.'

'But they won't look, that's the problem,' I say. 'They're in league with the enemy.'

I tell everyone the story of my own fracas with the cuntish marshal.

'Cunt,' says Bill.

'Yeah,' I say. 'But not so big a cunt as the bloke who got me in the face. Anyone see him?'

The consensus has it that it was almost certainly the loudest and most obstreperous member of the opposing team, a razor-cropped moron called Shortie. Besides being short, Shortie is recognizable by his Nam-style, cam-net bandanna, and his fondness for making tough, faux-military remarks like, '2K payload from a GR2. That would sort 'em.' He considers himself a wit and a natural-born leader. His friends think so too, which gives you a good idea of just how breathtakingly stupid they all are.

The consensus also has it that a terrible revenge must be exacted upon our enemies, though there are differing views as to what form it should take.

Tom thinks it will teach them all a jolly good lesson if

we carry on playing exactly as we were before: by the rules. Yes, they might keep on beating us, but we shall win a mighty moral victory.

Happily, this suggestion goes down with the rest of the team like a cup of cold sick. Some propose that we should all just give up and head home early; others that we should start cheating even more outrageously than the opposition; while one of the Bristol crew suggests that we forget all our troubles by breaking into Jem's Special Stock Sensi.

The crusties all chuckle knowingly.

'Jem's Special Stock Sensi,' I say. 'Sounds interesting.'

'It is that,' agrees one of the crusties. 'Very interesting.'

More laughter.

'How much do you have?' says Repton.

'Plenty.'

'Uh. We've still got to drive to Nottingham,' I caution Repton.

'See, the thing is,' explains one of the crusties, 'you only needs one puff. Unless you're Jem. He sometimes has a couple.'

'Had three once,' says the crustie with the wildest eyes and the most matted dreads.

'But no one's ever had four,' chips in the beautiful girl with the wounded bosom.

'Not as has lived to tell the tale,' agrees a mate.

'Here's an idea,' says Repton. 'Why don't we just spike the opposition?'

'Mm,' I say. 'Or we could build a huge wooden horse, leave it outside their camp and—'

'All right, Mr Clever Bastard.'

'Well, what are you going to do? Roll some sort of

whopping great Camberwell Carrot, call them over – all twenty of them – and say "Here, lads. Suck on this."'

'So come up with a better solution.'

'I already have.'

My plan will require a joint's worth of Jem's Special Stock, a crack section of snipers, and, most importantly, the services of the girl with the wounded nipple. I approach her somewhat nervously, partly because she's drop-dead gorgeous and she might think I'm trying to pick her up, partly because the mission I am proposing that she should undertake is so deeply unpleasant. But the girl with the wounded nipple – Bel, her name is – turns out to be game for anything. In fact, I find her enthusiasm for the task ahead almost frightening in its intensity. It emerges that the target of our operation is the man responsible for giving her that grievous wound.

Though she has not forgiven him, she makes a very good job of pretending otherwise when he approaches her in the lunchtime burger queue.

'Er, my mates said I got you in the tit,' Shortie mumbles in a tone which veers awkwardly between new man and new lad. 'Sorry about that, yeah.'

'That's all roit,' she replies, really laying on the creamy West Country accent, like the rabbit in the Caramel advert. 'If you're good I might ask you to rub it better.'

Shortie's bulldog features have turned crimson. He clearly cannot believe his luck: this is how girls talk in porn mags, never in real life. But he's far too embarrassed to do anything about it, even if he knew how, because he's being watched by a tableful of mates. There are muted cheers when Shortie rejoins them. Louder ones and cries of 'Phwoaah,' when Shortie has given his no doubt heavily embroidered account of what the girl said.

Bel, meanwhile, has found an empty wooden table set slightly apart from the main food area. She allows herself a brief, 'if only my gallant hero would join me', glance at Shortie's table, and then sets about her veggie burger. After much ribbing from his mates, Shortie finally plucks up the courage to join her. He stays there until the next game begins, when Bel leads him by a roundabout route to our prearranged killing zone.

It lies beyond the perimeter tape which marks the official gaming area. In the middle is an oak tree, surrounded by dense undergrowth in which we rapidly conceal ourselves. And not a moment too soon. Barely have we recovered our breath when we hear the scrunch of wet leaves underfoot and then a murmuring male voice.

'Course I'm more of a lager drinker meself. So I don't think I'll need much.'

'Oh, don't worry. It's not too strong,' replies Bel. 'How about here?'

Shortie looks round apprehensively. He's thick but that doesn't preclude a certain animal cunning.

'Sure this is all right? Only if any of the lads were to find out—'

'They'd be very jealous.'

'Er, yeah. Suppose they would. Ta.'

Shortie takes the proffered joint. He's about to light it when a thought strikes him.

'Forgot me manners there. Ladies first.'

'No. No,' says Bel, brushing a finger across his flies. 'I've got other things to be doing.'

What? This was never in the plan.

'Funny,' muses Shortie, huskily. 'I thought you hated us lot.'

'Is that right?' says Bel. She's on her knees now, facing his crotch which she's caressing through the material with her palm in slow, circular motions.

Shortie's eyes are fixed straight ahead, his expression a mixture of terror and elation. He steels his nerves with a hefty drag on the joint.

'Good?' asks Bel, rubbing more insistently.

Shortie's answer is submerged in a bout of fierce coughing. 'Yeah,' he eventually manages to rasp. 'Yeah!'

Bel releases Shortie's belt and unbuttons his trousers. Slowly.

She gives the waist band of his underpants a sharp tug. And out it flops. Stubby. Engorged.

Oh God, this is horrible. I can see it so clearly, in profile and directly in my gun's sight line. My hand is trembling. I can't go through with this. I can't.

Now Bel has eased down his pants so that they hang round his trousers.

'Fucking hell!' says Shortie. 'Fucking hell!'

And as I look down at my hands, I see the lump on my finger joints, livid, throbbing and cracked with dried blood. And I think of the swollen bruise on my temple. And the way Shortie ignored my cries for mercy as I lay curled up on the ground.

Suddenly, Bel draws herself clear of Shortie.

'Now!' she yells.

I squeeze the trigger.

The terrible tale of Shortie's exploding knob is predictably high on the conversational agenda, after the stag party has showered, snorted and reconvened in an Indian restaurant not far from our budget hotel on the outskirts of Nottingham.

'And it just exploded?' asks Repton, completely unnecessarily since he's heard the story a thousand times already.

'Yup. One second it was throbbing purple. The next, electric yellow. And the sound it made as the ball hit. A sort of dull, moist thwack, like a piece of sirloin hurled against a marble slab.'

'Ouch!'

'Or what!' agrees Bill. 'And you could see it twanging under the impact. Doiiing! Like an arrow.'

'I'm telling you, it felt bad enough from where I was lying. God knows what it must have been like for Shortie. It was all I could do to keep on firing.'

'Yeah, but you managed,' says Bill.

'Well, he shouldn't have doubled over like that. Big mistake. His buttocks presented such a beautiful target.'

'All white and hairy.'

'Not for long. You should have seen the bruises! And all that yellow slime. Like spotted dick and custard.'

'I think it was jolly irresponsible,' says Tom Bland gravely. 'You almost put the poor chap in hospital.'

'We're on a stag weekend. We're meant to be irresponsible.'

'Yeah. More beer!' comes a cry from the far end of the table.

'More drugs.'

'More chicks.'

'Talking of which,' I say. 'What about that girl Bel, eh? Was she totally shaggable or what?'

'The hippie with bright red hair?' says Tom. 'Hardly.'

'Says the man who only a month ago was porking a redhead in my sitting room.'

'What's all this?' someone shouts.

'Oh, we had this ball-breaking piece of ginger minge round for dinner and Tom here . . .'

'Her name's Nadine and if you don't mind—'

'Steady, Tom. We all make mistakes.'

'She wasn't a mistake, actually. She's a very nice girl.'

'What? You're still seeing her?'

'Yes.'

'Does she know what you're up to this weekend?'

'Yes.'

'And she doesn't mind?'

'Why should she?'

'Oh per-lease. We're on a stag weekend. In Nottingham. Where the women outnumber the men by, what is it, Bill?'

'Five to one, I think.'

'There. You see. For every one of us, there are five women out there absolutely begging for it. Plus the five extra who can't have Repton. Do you honestly think that you, of all people, are going to resist that sort of temptation?'

'Are you?'

'I should bloody well hope none of us are. Anyone here apart from Tom not planning on getting laid this evening?'

'*Nooooo!*'

'Looks like you're on your own, matey. You and your strong right hand.'

'Do you think Sam will mind?' asks Tom.

'Oh, the breathtaking hypocrisy! You questioning me about fidelity! No, I'm sure she won't mind because she won't get to hear. Unless someone tells her.'

'Don't look at me,' says Tom.

'Anyway, we're allowed to be unfaithful. We've both got our own shag lists. Sam's allowed Ralph Fiennes, Johnny Depp, Richard Ashcroft, Thom Yorke and that Berlin techno DJ, what's his name, stupid haircut, huge penis, apparently – well, it's no good asking you, is it? Bill, who's that techno DJ that Sam and Carrie want to shag?'

'Marius Schenk.'

'That's the one. And I'm sure there's a few others I've missed out. She keeps updating it every ten minutes.'

'And it wouldn't bother you if she slept with anyone on her list?' asks Tom.

'Dunno. It's hardly likely though, is it? I mean that's the nature of shag lists. Everyone on them is unattainable.'

'I wouldn't know,' says Tom.

'You don't have your own personal shag list? What kind of sicko are you? Every man has his own shag list. Haven't you, guys?'

Fuelled by another round of beer – not Cobra or King-fisher, unfortunately, because they haven't yet discovered Indian lager in the provinces – we take turns to name the women we definitely wouldn't kick out of bed if they farted. Most of the obvious names come up in the first round: Uma Thurman, Meg Ryan, Michelle Pfeiffer, Claire Danes, Keanu Reeves (Repton's suggestion), Gwyneth Paltrow, Juliette Lewis, Ulrika-ka-ka-ka-ka. Then it starts to get a bit more contentious.

'Kylie Minogue.'

'What?' says Tom. 'The skinny pop star from *Neighbours*?'

'Don't you know *anything*? Kylie's cool, these days. She's the thinking man's sex kitten. She hangs out with Nick Cave.'

'Anna Friel.'

'Naah. She lost it after *Brookside*.'

'Never!'

'Christine Villeneuve,' I suggest.

'Who?'

'Only the most babesome chick in the whole of French cinema. The whole world, probably,' I say.

'What? More shaggable than Emmanuelle Beárt?'

'Or Beatrice Dalle?'

'I'm telling you. She makes both of them look like septic whores.'

'We'll have to take your word for it, Joe. We don't watch poncy films with subtitles. We like proper films.'

'Yeah. Like *Spice World*.'

'Oh per-lease. Have you seen them close up? Total hounds, the lot of them.'

'Except Posh.'

'Especially Posh.'

'You don't mean that. If they were all lying there in your bed, legs open, saying "Oh please, please take us right now—"'

'I'd say fuck off out of it and let me get some sleep.'

'You filthy liar.'

'But which order would we shag them in? That's the real question—'

Ah, the company of men! So joyously crude! So uncomplicated! If it didn't involve revolting things like sperm and erections and bottom holes, I think I'd seriously consider turning homosexual. It's so much more fun when women aren't around to censor your behaviour and weird you out with their hormonal mood swings and make you all compete against one another for their favours.

No need this evening to pull out our metaphorical penises and flop them on the table for comparison: who's the best looking? Who's got the best-paid job, the fastest car, the smartest address? Who's got the biggest non-metaphorical penis? Who's going to end up with the most toys? It's only the presence of women which encourages that sort of macho bullshit. Tonight we're all equals.

Almost. I mean, obviously, I find it a comfort to know that I'm more famous than anyone at the table save, possibly, Tom; that I earn more money than everyone apart from Tom, Repton, Bill, and maybe the computer programmer with the mad beard, and the chap who's in advertising. Oh, and Bill's painter chum from art college, who's just had a successful show open on Cork Street. Which could mean that he's not only richer but also more famous than me.

Not that any of that matters because, as I say, it's not that kind of an evening. It's about group solidarity; male bonding; who can hold the most drink; who can pull the tastiest bird; who can tell the filthiest anecdote; who's quickest with the one liners; who's loudest; who knows the most obscure stats about film, music. All right. So maybe there is a hint of competitiveness lurking beneath our laddish bonhomie, but you can bet your life that Carrie's hens, wherever they are right now, will be a whole lot worse: 'My boyfriend's got a bigger dick than yours,' 'Mine's got a bigger spending limit on his gold card,' 'Well, mine's given me an expense account at Voyage.'

Wait. I've suddenly remembered. Girls aren't like that. They never boast about their men's achievements. Quite the opposite. 'Six inches, he says. If it was that in centimetres, I'd be grateful,' 'To see his face, you'd have thought the blood was his,' 'Oh sure. He's happy enough for me to

swallow. But when it comes to returning the favour...'
'"My hand's tired," he says. One minute later,' 'How many times *haven't* I faked it, more to the point...'

God, I can just imagine them all now, cackling over my shortcomings. Carrie saying something like, 'Oh, but you've such a wicked sense of humour, Sam.' And Sam replying, 'Who said I was joking?' More witchy laughter. More drink. And heaps and heaps more drugs, if I know Sam. And their eyes trawling the room for available mates. 'Why not? If the boys are going to play away, why shouldn't we?'

'I don't suppose Carrie told you where they were all going tonight?' I ask Bill.

'There!' says Bill.

'Where?'

'Don't make it so obvious. To my right.'

I strain to look over the sea of heads bobbing around the bar. Most of them belong to tall, loutish blokes. The only representative of Nottingham's allegedly vast and wanton female population I can see is a stubby little thing with a denim jacket and short, dirty blonde hair. As our eyes meet, she gives me a faint smile. I look away quickly.

'She must have gone,' I say.

Bill glances over his shoulder. 'No. Still there. Blonde. Denim jacket—'

'The dwarf? She looks nothing like Christine Villeneuve.'

'She might after a couple more pints. Hey. She's coming this way.'

'Run away! Run away!'

Too late. There's a tug at my arm.

'You going to buy me a drink or what?' says the dwarf.

'Um.' I look to Bill for support, but he has muscled his

way to the front of the bar and begun ordering. I turn back
to the dwarf. 'Bit forward.'

'Don't you like girls who are forward?' she says.

'What are you having?'

'Lager and black,' she says.

I relay her order to Bill.

' – with a vodka top,' the dwarf adds.

'I think not,' I say in a schoolmasterly tone somewhere
between ironic and sincere. 'It will make you far too drunk.'

'Don't you like it when girls get drunk?' she says.

'And a vodka top in the lager and black,' I tell Bill.

'So. What's your name?' asks the dwarf.

'Joe. And yours?'

'Cath. Haven't seen you here before?'

'I'm not from here. I'm from London. It's my cousin's
stag weekend.'

'Come here for a laff, have you?' she asks.

'Uh. Yeah.'

''Aving a laff'. It's not a phrase I use myself, but I know
what it means. It means getting drunk and having casual sex
with the first slapper to come up to you and ask whether
you're going to buy her a drink or what. A terrifying
prospect.

Yet not totally unappealing. I mean, she's short, but she's
not really a dwarf. Nor is she beyond the acceptable bounds
of ugliness. A little on the plump side, perhaps. And definitely not what you'd call a 'trophy shag'. But she's young,
blonde and enthusiastic. Anyway, it's quite a compliment to
be chatted up by someone ten years younger than you. Even
if they are loose, desperate and pissed out of their brain.

It would be so easy. Really it would. All I'd have to say

is, 'You coming outside then?' And off we'd slope, into the night, side by side. Maybe holding hands. Maybe me slipping an arm round her waist. Perhaps even under the back of her jacket. Or her blouse. We'd weave through the throngs in the glare of the city centre – gangs of drunken lads, mobbing and leering and pissing in alleyways, groups of pissed-up girlies, screeching and laughing and chucking up on the pavement, moony-eyed couples and sullen singles – in search of somewhere quiet, secluded. We wouldn't say much. There'd be no need.

Maybe she'd have a flat nearby. More likely, we'd end up in some dark alley, or clambering over the walls and into the gardens beneath the sheriff of Nottingham's castle.

Then we'd do it. Quite what I'm not sure. Everything, I imagine. A snog. A fevered grapple with those breasts. Slip my hand inside her knickers. A hand job in return. Perhaps a blow job. Perhaps even a hard, torrid fuck in the flower-beds. And I'll bet she'd be good. I'll bet she'd be really good. She's obviously done this sort of thing before. Plenty of times. Too many times, you might almost say, if you were feeling a bit squeamish.

Which I am, I realize, despite the three lines of ego-boosting coke currently numbing my nostrils and the three pints of lager swelling my belly. Because while the lecherous part of my brain has been ripping apart the girl's blouse, burying itself in her blubbery breasts and giving her a good humping in the bushes, the boring, responsible part has been holding down a stilted conversation about where she comes from (Nottingham), what she does for a living (she's in the army), whether she comes here often (yes), and whether she'd like to come and meet my mates.

'If you want,' she says, in a tone which implies, 'It's not too late. We can still go outside and do what you know you really want to do.'

And the lecherous part of my brain is screaming, 'You plonker! You stupid, pathetic wuss!'

And the boring, responsible part is intoning, 'Don't listen. It's only your dick talking.'

'Everybody, this is Cath.'

'Hi, Cath.'

There's barely room for both of us in the snug my party has commandeered. Tom gallantly offers Cath a corner of his chair, while I squeeze on to one end of the alcove bench. Ah, the relief! Safe once more in the rank, hot, beery company of men. Cath doesn't seem unduly bothered by my failure to deliver. Not now that she's surrounded by a dozen flirtatious males, all eager to ask her lewd questions about her sex life, which she answers with shocking frankness. She is soon adopted as an honorary stag.

Later, someone suggests that it's time we moved on. There's a distinct shortage of totty and besides, there are no decent snorting surfaces in the pub's toilets.

'Where's Tom?'

'Went off to get a drink, I think.'

'He might have got in another round. Tightarse.'

A search party is dispatched to the bar. Still no sign of him.

'Hang on,' says someone – and if this were a cartoon huge, flashing lightbulbs would appear simultaneously in the thought bubbles over everyone's heads – 'Wasn't he with that girl?'

*

And it's no good trying to tell myself that she wasn't good enough; that the others would have laughed; that I've stayed true to Sam; that it wouldn't have been fun anyway. I now know that the boring, responsible part of my brain was completely wrong. Tonight I am going to score with the next woman that comes along, no matter how raddled, dwarfish, or ugly.

But the girls in the vast, noisy dive to which we repair after closing time have proved strangely unwilling to oblige. In the half hour since we arrived, not one of them has approached me. Not even to ask me the time, let alone whether I'd mind if they closed their lips around my enormous member. This I find totally extraordinary since I know for a fact that I'm quite the sexiest, hunkiest, wittiest, most desirable male ever to stalk God's earth.

From what I have gathered from our gabbled conversations, the others seem to hold themselves in similarly high esteem. Of course, this has absolutely no connection with the two fat lines of coke we all snorted on our arrival.

Wreathed in clouds of charisma, pheromones and ineffable loveliness, we have taken turns to waft around the dance floor and along the balconies which overlook it. 'Yes, girls,' our expressions say, 'your luck's in tonight. We are available.'

Bill returns from a scouting mission to report a babe sighting. I accompany him to investigate. And indeed he has a point. She has long auburn hair, a cute button nose, smooth freckly skin flushed from her exertions on the dance floor, and a fabulous lithe body.

'Top Junior Minge,' I gasp.

'Yeah. Isn't she wonderful?'

'Awesome.'

'What shall we do?'

'Um. Have another beer?'

'Good idea.'

After another beer, we check out the awesome babe again. She is playing with her hair and giving us nervous, sideways glances.

'Another line?'

'Good idea.'

Our confidence boosted, we return for a third time.

The girl is gone.

'Dance?'

'Good idea.'

We dance uninhibitedly. The Chemical Brothers is about as close as it gets to proper dance music. Mostly it's out-of-date indie – Faith No More, Jesus Jones, Ministry, Nirvana: stuff from the plaid-shirt era. But Bill and I are too wrapped up in the beauty of our frugging to care. Until Oasis comes on.

'Let's find the others.'

'Good idea.'

The others aren't doing much. Bill decides that this is what he wants to do too. I decide I'm going to do something about that babe.

Something consists of leaning against a pillar and staring at her back for as long as it takes to smoke two cigarettes. I'm about to roll a third when I think, 'This is stupid!' and I lurch forward.

'Hello.'

'Hello.'

'Can I buy you a drink?'

'No thanks.'

'Oh. Why not?'

'I'm not thirsty.'

'Oh. Er . . . Nice place. Nottingham.'

'Yeah. See you.'

I rejoin the others. They have grown slightly more animated in my absence. Someone thinks they might have spotted one of the paintballing crusties. Perhaps we'll be able to score some of Jem's Special Sensi, head back to the hotel and chill out.

'Already?' I say. 'What about the girls?'

'What girls?'

It is, I must concede, a good point well made. From the pulling point of view, the evening has been a total disaster. And from an ambience point of view. And from a musical point of view. In fact, if it hadn't been for the drugs, the last few hours would have been a total write off. Some might go so far as to suggest that it's because of the drugs that the last few hours have been a total write off. But not me. Drugs are good. Drugs are fun. Drugs make everything better. Pro-vided, of course, you know which drug to take for which sort of mood. And right now, I'm in a cancelling-out-the-effects-of-one-drug-and-taking-another sort of mood. At least I think I am. And if nothing else, the quest for a different sort of drug has given us all a sense of purpose. A mission. We must find Jem's Special Stock Sensi at once.

During our search for the Bristol crusties, however, my plans are radically altered by the occurrence of a small miracle.

'Bel!'

'Hey! Joe. How's it going?'

'Great. Cool – Pretty shit, actually. We were thinking of going.'

'No!'

'Well, I might stay a bit longer now you're here.'

'That would be nice.'

'Would it?'

'Yeah.'

I have soon established everything I need to know. Yes, she's every bit as shaggable as I remembered. No, she doesn't have a boyfriend. Well, not a serious one. Anyway, he's ill in bed. And no she wouldn't mind at all joining me in a line or two of coke.

'After you,' I say, slipping her the wrap.

'You'll be here, won't you?' she says.

'Definitely.'

As she heads for the Ladies, she throws back a smile which says, 'You won't regret it.'

And my what a wonderful sensation it is when you know, beyond all reasonable doubt, that within the next couple of hours you are going to be humping senseless a stranger you really fancy. I feel a powerful surge of warmth towards everyone in the club. Including the awesome babe who refused a drink. Poor thing, doesn't know what she's missing. Nor do the rest of my party. Heh heh heh. Look at them all. So frantic. So miserable.

'Joe!' says Bill urgently. 'We've got to go.'

'You can, matey. I'm staying here.'

'Joe, the others are waiting. We're getting out now!'

'Not a prayer,' I say. 'Do you know who I've just pulled?'

Suddenly Bill drapes an arm round my neck and yanks me bodily forward.

'Shut up! Shut up!' he hisses, keeping his head low and close to mine. After a moment he looks anxiously over his shoulder. 'They're here!' he mutters. 'All of them.'

'I know. I've just met Bel.'

'Not them, you fool. Shortie and his squaddie friends.'

'No!'

'Yes!'

'But she's got my coke!'

'Sod your coke.'

'I'll meet you outside,' I say, dashing towards the Ladies loo before he can stop me.

There's a long queue. I scan the faces from the tail end to the door. There she is. With her back turned to me. I tap her arm. The girl who turns to face me, peeved, isn't her. 'Sorry.' I move further along the queue. And this time it's definitely her. Standing by the toilet entrance. 'Bel!' I call out. 'Bel!' She smiles, gives me a little wave and goes into the loo.

I'm so intent on pursuing her that I very nearly miss the three very big, very angry lads coming towards me. It's only when one of them bellows, 'You!' that I finally concede that there are times when not even half an ounce of cocaine and passionate sex with a beautiful stranger are worth dying for.

I duck behind the queue, a protective wall of tight-bladdered girls between me and my pursuers.

You don't want to mess with tight-bladdered girls. Shortie and his mates discover this when they try to elbow through.

'Oi, fucking watchit, will you?' screeches a girl, pulling Shortie's sleeve.

He pushes her away and at once two of the girls' indignant mates are tearing at the back of his shirt. Shortie's chums attempt to rescue him. Only to be besieged by yet more angry females, like songbirds mobbing owls.

I start to run.

But where to? They're bound to have the exit covered. They do in movies, anyway, and maybe it's the coke or maybe it's just the fact that this is all far, far too horrible to be real life, but this is how it feels. Like a really bad movie.

So I don't want to go for the main exit. I want to go for one of those secret exits that the baddies don't know about. The sort, maybe, where a friendly hand suddenly pulls you into the shadows and you watch, silently, as your nemesis and his evil henchmen pass within inches of your face. Then they all split in different directions and you turn to the friendly stranger who's just rescued you and you say . . .

Can we please stop this fantasy bollocks and start finding a way out of here. Fast.

I'm on the dance floor: 'Smells Like Teen Spirit' – so the kids are moshing really wildly. I'm moshing wildly with them because I know that if you want to cross a dance floor of moshing kids, the only way to do it is to go with the flow. Shortie and his mates don't know this. They're trying to lumber through like tanks and are getting caught by dragons' teeth and flailing elbows and knees and DM boots and thrashing heads and I'm thinking 'Ha! Ha! You wankers! You're never going to catch me.'

Because ahead of me, I can see it. A door with a green exit light above it. And now I'm almost through it. Just push the bar and—

Can't move.

'Excuse me, sir,' says the bouncer holding my arm. 'This door is for emergency use only.'

'But it is an emergency,' I plead.

'It's not an emergency until I decide it's an emergency,' he says.

'But they're trying to kill me,' I say, glancing desperately over my shoulder.

'Who's trying to kill you?' says the bouncer, unimpressed.

'Drug dealers!' I improvise.

The bouncer scans the crowd. 'What drug dealers?'

I turn to point them out. 'Er – er – ' Where the fuck are they? 'They were there a few seconds ago.'

'Be a good chap, sir,' says the bouncer, patting my shoulder heavily. 'Piss off and stop wasting my time. All right?'

'But—'

There's a sudden pressure in the small of my back and I'm hurtling forward.

'Main exit's that way. *Sir*,' the bouncer calls after me.

I'm about to tell him what a cunt he is when sense prevails. For one thing, he might give me a beating even worse than the one I'm expecting from Shortie. For another, he could be my only salvation. If only I can linger in his vicinity until the club closes. They'll never dare come near me while –

'I said, *sir*, the main exit is *that way*!'

'All right, I'm going! I'm going!'

Bugger.

I mingle with the punters on the edge of the dance floor, trying to stay as close as I can to the bouncer without him actually seeing me. It's a fine balance and I can't afford to get it wrong. Somewhere nearby, Shortie and his mates are watching and waiting.

But where?

I scan the balconies, the dance floor, the bar area, the

people milling next to me. Round and round again I turn, eyes darting from face to face to face. I feel dizzy and sick. I want to be back at the hotel with the others. I can't put up with much more of this. My nerves are fizzing, my eyeballs are on stalks. What the fuck am I going to—

Ohmygod.

My back.

Something hard thudded into my back. Wetness trickling down my spine. And I know what they say about stab wounds: sometimes they feel like a punch; sometimes you don't even notice until you see your own blood.

'Sorry, mate,' says the bloke readjusting his three tottering pints.

That's it. I'm going. I don't care any more what they do to me. I just want to get it over with. I'm going to walk straight towards the main exit. If I make it, I make it. If I don't, I don't.

The most direct route, unfortunately, will take me underneath one of the balconies where the lighting's much dimmer and it's easier to run into an ambush. And though I try to move quickly, my path is impeded by the trailing limbs of zombified clubbers, surreptitious joint smokers and snogging couples. It means I keep having to look down instead of around me.

Which is why I don't even notice them until they've grabbed me tight by both wrists.

Shortie hobbles forward from the shadows. And I don't think the hobble's play-acting. He definitely looks as if he's still in enormous pain.

'Wait!' I say. Because he's bunching his fist.

'Wait?' he says. 'I've been waiting all fucking day for this.'

'I can pay you,' I say, crossing my legs and wriggling so that if he lands that punch where I think he's planning to land it, it might just stand a chance of missing its very soft, very vulnerable target. 'In drugs.'

'It's your fucking drugs that are the fucking problem.'

'Not those kind of drugs. Nice drugs. Drugs to make you feel better.' And I can't help it. I'm grinning so hard my jaw hurts.

'I don't fucking believe it. You're fucking laughing at me.'

'No. No. No. I'm laughing 'cos I'm scared. I always laugh when I'm scared.'

''E's fucking laughing at me. Do you see that, lads? He's fucking laughing at me. How are you going to show 'im it isn't nice to laugh at people?'

'Hit him,' suggests the creature to my left.

Shortie's about to oblige when the creature to my right has a better idea. 'Take his drugs and then 'it him.'

'Go on then, cunt. Show us what you got.'

'You'll have to let go of me first.'

'Do you think we're fucking stupid or something?'

There's an answer to that but this really isn't the moment.

'I won't run. I promise I won't run. You have my word.'

Shortie and his mates find the concept of 'my word' so ludicrously poncy and amusing that they do indeed let go of my wrists. That's the thing about oiks. They love it when you treat them posh. Of course, I would run if I thought I'd get away with it. But I'm still banking on the possibility that I might yet be able to smooth-talk and bribe my way out of this mess.

143

As I rummage in my pockets for my wrap of coke, however, a very nasty thought occurs. Bel has got it.

'He's taking the piss,' says one of Shortie's mates.

'I have got it. I have,' I plead.

'Then where the fuck is it?'

Just on the off-chance, I stick my fingers in that tiny, mini-pocket on the right-hand side of my jeans, where I sometimes keep my emergency stash. And quite miraculously, I manage to find four pills. Hayfever pills, actually, which I kept in reserve in case the pollen count got too high during the paintballing. But Shortie isn't to know that.

'There,' I say, triumphantly opening my palm.

'Oh yeah. And what are they supposed to be?'

'Es,' I say.

'Smallest Es I've ever seen.'

'Yeah, well,' I say, synapses on coke-fuelled overdrive. 'They're LBWs aren't they?'

'LBWs?'

'Little Bastard Whites,' I say. 'One hundred per cent pure MDMA.'

I hand them to Shortie. He examines them suspiciously.

'These aren't Es,' he says.

'That's what I said to the bloke who sold them to me. Eight hours later I was still gurning like a bastard. Straight up. Best pills I've ever done. And I've been doing Es since '87.'

God, I'm a good liar. I'm the biggest cleverest liar since Baron Munchausen. They're going to buy my story. I can see they are. Shortie's convinced. The one with acne scars is convinced. The dark-haired one is . . .

Uh. Not quite convinced. He's got the pills in his palms

now. He's holding them up to the light. Reading the print on the pills.

'I know what these are — ' he's saying.

'And I'll give you some money,' I'm gabbling. 'How about that? I'll give you some money so that even if they don't work and they do they do I promise they do, you can go and score some other ones. Look here. Twenty — forty — sixty quid. Here, here. Just take it and leave me alone.'

' — I take these things for my hayfever.'

'Right,' says Shortie, 'you have fucking had it!'

'No, please,' I say, as I try to stuff my notes into his clenching hands. '*Please.*'

As I tense, waiting for the blow, I hear a voice somewhere ahead of me say, 'Just a minute, gents.'

Shortie calls back over his shoulder, 'Fuck off out of it, mate, will you? We're busy.'

'No, sir,' says the bouncer. 'I'm afraid I won't "Fuck off out of it."'

He turns to the dark-haired one. 'You. Give me those pills.' Then to Shortie: 'You. Give him back his money.' Then to me: 'These the dealers?'

I nod vigorously.

'Good,' he says. 'So now you can do what you promised me you were going to do half an hour ago. And piss off out of here, all right?'

'I think I can manage that,' I say, scurrying for the exit.

'No, not you,' I hear the bouncer saying behind me. 'You lot are coming with me.'

The chill-out session back at our hotel is the best part of the whole weekend. For me, anyway. Not only do I get to tell at great length (and retell, for the benefit of later arrivals, at even greater length) the thrilling story of my heroic escape from Shortie and his crew. But I also get to broach almost all of those life-enhancing conversational topics – Nam, chicks, music and drugs – that make the hours fly by when you're getting totally wankered in a spartan hotel bedroom with half a dozen or so like-minded males on a stag weekend in Nottingham.

Over the next few hours we progress from the ineluctable Namness of paintballing via Great Joints We Have Smoked through the meaning of life (and, more pertinently, of that baffling 'Just' video where the man's lying down on the pavement and no one can work out why until he tells them something so dark and terrible that they all feel compelled to follow suit) and thence, inevitably, on to one of my all-time favourites: are Radiohead brilliant or what?

I have often wondered what would happen if you recorded a late-night stoner conversation and then played it back in the sober light of morning. (In fact, I did actually try it once but everyone got freaked out and refused to go on talking until I turned the machine off.) And I've a nasty suspicion that if you did you'd find it incredibly depressing. All those sudden flashbulb aperçus you'd mistaken for profound insights; all those moments where you'd thought you sounded so fluent and articulate; all those bits where you'd felt part of some privileged community of dope-smoking uber-beings, more happy, more alive than mere mortals could ever dream; all this would be revealed the next day for what it really was: the dreary, delusional ramblings of a group of head-fucked morons.

Still, you don't know that at the time, do you? If you

did, no doubt, you'd never have conversations that go something like this:

Me: 'So what do we reckon guys: *The Bends* or *OK Computer*?'

Someone: 'Oh, man. *The Bends*. *The Bends*. It's got to be *The Bends*.'

Me: 'Well, yeah. I see where you're coming from. But *The Bends* doesn't have "Karma Police" on it. Or "Lucky".'

Someone else: 'Fuck, no. You can't argue with "Lucky".'

Someone: 'Yeah, but you can't argue with "My Iron Lung", either.'

Another person: 'Or "Creep".'

Me: '"Creep"'s not on either.'

Another person: 'I know. I'm just saying you can't argue with it.'

Me: 'That's just it. You can't argue with anything they do, can you? They are total fucking gods.'

Someone else: 'Fucking right they are. Did you see them at Glastonbury?'

Everyone else: 'Or what!'

Me: 'Best Glasto set ever. Best Radiohead set ever. Except maybe that one at Brixton Academy, when Oasis were playing Earl's Court the same night.'

Everyone (jealously): 'Good?'

Me: 'Well, it was a pretty special moment. Sorted out the sheep from the goats, I can tell you. Mind you, Radiohead are never bad. I've never seen them play a bad gig. Ever!'

Everyone: 'They rule!'

Etc., etc.

Once we've exhausted our supply of superlatives, I

manage to steer the conversation towards another perennial favourite: The Terrors Of The Animal Kingdom.

My version of Martha's shark anecdote goes down very well, though it's rather spoiled when Bill starts badgering me as to whether I've heard anything from her since that dinner. (No. Nor am I expecting to.) Then Rob, the painter, gets us all back on course with a tale of how he was once chased for four miles by an angry hippo while canoeing down the Okavango River.

'But they look so cute and friendly,' someone says.

'Total bastards,' I pronounce authoritatively. 'They kill far more people than lions, you know. In fact, the only African mammal responsible for more human fatalities is the Cape buffalo.'

'Ah, but crocodiles. They're the worst,' says the bearded computer programmer, whom I have long since dismissed as a terminal bore. Now, he rehabilitates himself with quite the most brilliantly scary crocodile tale I have ever heard. It happened, inevitably, to a friend of a friend.

'So, this bloke, right, he's out with his girlfriend in Northern Australia. And they take this trip up a river in the Outback. Just them and a guide. So they're miles up the river in the middle of the bush. It's boiling hot. And the girlfriend fancies a dip so they can cool off.'

'Madness,' I say, with a hideous shudder. 'Total fucking madness!'

'Ah, but this is the thing,' continues the beardie. 'See, they'd heard there were crocs in that part of the country. So they asked the guide who, let's face it, should have known these things, whether it was safe to swim. And I don't know what he was thinking, whether he had it in for Pommie tourists or whether he was a total moron, but the guide said it was.'

'Wanker!'

'Well, you've guessed what happened next. Soon as they've dived in, this massive, great crocodile grabs the boyfriend and starts pulling him under. Girlfriend makes it back to the boat. Nothing she can do except watch her bloke get eaten.'

'They don't eat you straightaway, though. Do they?'

'That's just it. They don't like fresh meat. They prefer it rotten. So what they do is drown you and then leave your body to hang around for a few days in their underwater larder. Now the park rangers know all about this, so they go back with the girl and her guide to recover the body. They find it, tucked underneath a ledge and rope it on to the back of their boat. But here's the really nasty bit. Before they've gone far, the crocodile goes back to his larder, finds his food's been stolen and starts chasing after the boat. He grabs the body, pulls it back in the water and that's the last they see of it ever again.'

Truly, we all agree, that was the most awesomely horrible crocodile story there ever was. The only way I can think of capping it is with the terrible, terrible story about the abalone diver off the coast of New Zealand.

Before I can begin, however, Repton comes in, followed by Tom.

'I suppose you scored,' I ask Repton, sullenly.

'Perhaps you should rephrase the question: how *many* times did I score?'

'Oh, Tom!' I tease. 'You didn't let him?'

'We bumped into each other on the way back,' says

Tom, infuriatingly, endearingly literal, as ever. He sits on the end of my bed.

'Well?' I ask.

'Well what?'

'Did she howl, the Hound of the Baskervilles?'

'I say. Is that a joint?' says Tom.

'You're not getting off that easily. Tell him the stag rules, Bill.'

'Oh. Right. The stag rules are that anyone who gets laid must give a full account of their activities in every disgusting detail.'

'Splendid,' says Repton. 'Let me tell you about boy number one, Julian, with the big brown eyes of a startled deer and the tongue—'

'We don't want to know, Repton. We want to hear about Tom and the Dwarf of Death. Come on, Tom, stag rules.'

'I thought the stag rules were that *everyone* had to get laid.'

'Some of us chose to save ourselves for our beloved girlfriends.'

'What rot!'

'Ah well. I wouldn't expect you to understand lofty concepts like fidelity. Poor Nadine. I can just imagine her now, lying on her tartan sheets, gazing tearfully at the ceiling. "Och the noo! I hope ma wee Tommy has nae been unfaithful to me with some wee strumpet."'

'I doubt it somehow.'

'Shame on you, Tom. Surely you're not suggesting that that sweet Scottish maiden is as big a tart as you?'

'No. But to judge by what the girls had been planning for this evening—'

'You know? Why didn't you say?'

'Tact, maybe?'

'So go on. Tell us.'

'Private dining room with a male stripper. Then on to see that German friend of yours disc jockeying.'

'Marius Schenk?'

'That's the one.'

'Oh dear. Now I feel really threatened. Because it's really so likely that when a girl goes clubbing she ends up shagging the DJ.'

'Did I say she was?'

'It's what you were implying. And you're not getting off the hook that easily: tell us what you got up to with Dwarf Hound right this second.'

'Tell you what. If I tell you my wanking story will you let me off?'

'Is it a good wanking story?'

'The very finest.'

'Let us be the judge of that, my friend. Proceed with your wanking story.'

'OK. I was about fourteen at the time. It was a hot summer's afternoon and as you do at that age, I retired to my bedroom for a quick Joddrell—'

'Hang on, hang on. We've all experienced this one. You forget to lock the door and your mum comes in. Right?'

'Oh, no. That was another time. I never forgot to lock the door after that. So I'm lying there with my favourite porn mag – and I'll always remember her, my first true love, sporty young Bekki from Crewe – and I'm beating really frantically now because I'm just on the verge of coming, when suddenly I become aware of this presence in the window. And God knows how long he's been there, I mean it's just too painful to think about. But it's my dad and he's cleaning the window.'

'Nooo! *Noooo!*' I'm writhing in agony. 'What did you do?'

'What could I do? You know what it's like when you're in the throes of passion. And my dad, well, you know what he's like—'

'Fuck, yes. Straight as they come.'

'So he gave me this sort of jolly wave and then disappeared. For two whole days.'

'He disappeared for two whole days!'

'As I said, you know my dad.'

'Jesus, Tom. No wonder you're the way you are.'

'So. Was it good enough?'

'Tom. You have trumped us all. That was the finest wank story ever told.'

'Why, thank you.'

'And a fitting climax to the evening's entertainment. Don't know about you guys but I'm getting some kip.'

Before going to the outside bathroom to clean my teeth, I tiptoe downstairs to the payphone in the hotel lobby and dial my home number. It rings out until the answer machine clicks on. I put the phone down without leaving a message and try a few more times, hanging up before the answer machine engages. If Sam was asleep, she would definitely have woken up by now. Which either means she's awake and not bothering to answer. Or not there. I can't decide which possibility is more threatening. Not, of course, that I'm remotely worried by what Tom said to me earlier. But – Oh, fuck it. Let's try one more time.

The answer message is even more annoyingly long than

I remember. If people were forced to listen to their own messages more often, I'm sure they wouldn't make them nearly so self-indulgent. Sam's are among the worst. She will insist on prefacing them with long musical extracts or samples from *Beavis and Butthead, Ren and Stimpy* or cult movies like *Withnail and I*. Her latest one features Samuel L. Jackson's 'when you absolutely, positively got to kill every muthafucker in the room' speech from Tarantino's *Jackie Brown*. Royally entertaining in the film, no doubt, but extremely irksome at 4.30 a.m. when you're tired and slightly paranoid.

At last it ends.

'Hi, it's me,' I say. 'Hope you're being good. I am.'

When I've put the phone down, it occurs to me that this strikes slightly the wrong note. I redial.

'AK47 . . .' It's much, much more annoying second time round.

'By the way, love you!' I say. And there's really not much I can do about the fact that, having been so incensed by that fucking answer message, my tone sounds decidedly grudging and insincere.

BLUE

If you ask me, the luckiest man in the history of the world was a Russian sailor called Valery Kosyak. In 1975, he was swept overboard from his cargo ship during a storm in the Indian Ocean and was surrounded by a shoal of sharks.

He first noticed them when he felt something brush against his leg and looked down to see a pig-like snout sticking out of the sea in front of him. For the next four hours he was circled by sharks between nine and fifteen feet long. He tried floating flat on the water so that his feet wouldn't dangle and even tried talking to the sharks and swearing at them.

The first thing that amazes me about this story is that when, two hours after his disappearance, his shipmates discovered he was missing, they actually bothered to turn round to look for him. I'd always imagined that merchant seaman from the Black Sea Fleet would be much harder than that. The second thing that amazes me is that they actually found him. And the third amazing thing is that the sharks didn't kill him first.

Jacques Cousteau was pretty impressed too. 'I have heard of people surviving an hour or two among sharks,' he said afterwards, 'but four hours – never.'

My own theory on this is that either they weren't sharks but porpoises or dolphins. Or that they were blue sharks, which strike me as being marginally less evil than most. But perhaps that's because I've been taken in by their graceful good looks: long and slender with indigo blue upper bodies, bright blue sides and white bellies.

The time to worry about blue sharks is when they're in a feeding frenzy. Hunting in packs, they're capable of taking on whole whale carcasses, so they'd make pretty short work of a human.

CHAPTER SIX

But my life isn't all shite, you know. There are hundreds of wonderful things which have happened to me in the last few months that I could have told you about but decided not to.

There was the time when I stumbled upon a review of Tom Bland's book so abominably vicious that I had to ring him up to commiserate; the morning I got a letter from a literary agent saying that she really liked my column and had I ever thought about writing a novel?; the time Sam managed to procure some one hundred per cent pure Bolivian to accompany a blinding set at Brixton Academy by LTJ Bukem; the session on GLR's *Hit the Decks* when everything I said about the records we had to review was cool, witty and wise; the *Adam and Joe Show*'s puppet parody of *This Life*; clearing a record £2,500 for one week's articles; buying a big new Bosch Fridge Freezer; Sam's pregnancy test coming up negative . . .

In fact I'm sure that if I wanted to I could fill a whole book with tales of the wonderful things that have happened to me in the last few months. But I'm equally sure that if I were to write one about all the horrible things that have happened to me in the same period, it would be much, much longer. How much longer I'm not sure. And I've no intention of working it out. If any of us were to compare the number of hours we spend being unhappy with the number in which we experience transcendent bliss, I reckon the shortfall in happiness would be so depressingly vast that we'd all top ourselves.

Fortunately, every now and then there comes an experience so ineffably wonderful that all life's misery suddenly seems meaningless. Like, say, when you've managed to wangle a free diving holiday in the Red Sea. You've survived the charter flight to Sharm-El-Sheikh; you've enjoyed the matchless satisfaction which comes from discovering that your hotel is more attractive than any of the others you've seen your fellow travellers being dropped off at from the courtesy coach; you've unpacked your suitcase in a room whose size, cleanliness and sea-view balcony have exceeded your every expectation; you've celebrated with a sweaty fuck on the super-starched hotel cotton sheets; you've showered and changed into your jetsetters-by-night, we-do-this-all-the-time-you-know, sophisticated but casual holiday wear; you've ambled into the hotel's vast, exquisitely landscaped grounds just in time to catch the sun setting beyond the small, private beach; and as the big desert sky turns red and the cicadas sing and the scent of jasmine fills your nostrils and the warm breeze caresses your bare arms, it wells up inside you and builds and builds, this glorious sense of elation until you can contain yourself no longer and cry out, 'Fuck, this is brilliant!'

'And we've eight more days of hell like this to go,' says Sam.

'Seven, really,' I say. 'You can't count the day when we fly back from Eilat. That's going to be horrendous. Do you know we've got to get up at six and drive for five hours?'

'Thanks for reminding me,' says Sam.

'We might as well be prepared for it.'

'We were trying to enjoy the sunset, remember?'

'Oh right, yeah. Sorry. It's going to take me a while to wind down. That flight! If Mickey Mouse ran an airline it couldn't be more incompetent! And the food—'

'Joe!'

Our first proper holiday argument has to wait until after dinner. There are two restaurants: one indoors, one in the central garden area near the swimming pool. Ignoring my terror of mosquitoes, Sam decides it would be more romantic to eat al fresco. The little mushroom lamps dotted around the lawn near each table are perfectly placed, I notice, to attract ankle-biting insects. I douse and redouse myself in evil-smelling repellent until Sam tells me to stop being so silly. This will give me an excellent excuse to blame her should I get bitten.

There is no menu. We must choose, instead, from the impressive selection of fresh fish, poetically arranged inside an old boat draped with fishing nets. Sam makes orgasmic noises over this. I am not so sure. The boat looks suspiciously European. As indeed do the fish.

'Trout?' I say. 'You don't get trout in Egypt.'

'Maybe in the rivers,' says Sam.

'We're in the middle of a bloody great desert.'

'No one's forcing you to eat trout.'

'That's not the point. Why are they importing fish from Europe when they've got their own sea right on their doorstep?'

'Sole looks nice.'

'I'll bet that wasn't caught round here either.'

'Who cares?'

'Well, what if it's been airlifted over from the North Sea. It could be too expensive.'

'I thought the hotel was picking up the tab.'

'Maybe. I couldn't get much sense out of the receptionist.'

'Anyway, we're on holiday. We can afford to splash out.'

'I think we should ask at least.'

Though the fat, jolly chef has swarthy skin, twirly, Ottoman-style moustaches, a fez and an embroidered jellaba, he is no more authentically Egyptian than the seafood.

'Calamari,' he says. 'Pulpo . . .'

'No no. *Price!*' I say. 'How much? *Conto!*'

'Joe!' protests Sam.

'It means bill,' I explain. 'I think.'

The chef, less jolly now, scrawls a figure on his notepad. There are far too many 0s at the end.

'Not lire. Sterling. How much in sterling?'

The chef shrugs. After much gesticulating, I prevail upon him to give a figure in Egyptian pounds. This is no help either, partly because I have yet to get the hang of the local currency, partly because it's the price per kilo, which means about as much to me as leagues, fathoms and ells.

'Oh. Have your wretched sole,' I say to Sam. 'But this is the last time we're eating at this tourist trap, I can tell you.'

Dinner is, perhaps, less romantic than Sam might have liked. I'm sulking because my budget-order sardines, what little of them I can taste through the layer of mosquito repellent transferred on to them via my fingers, are redolent of liver, stale fish and salmonella. Sam is sulking because I'm a miserable skinflint bastard bent on spoiling everything.

I try steering the conversation to the pleasures ahead. A

hearty breakfast, collection by our dive master at eight, and then a whole day spent sunning ourselves on the boat and exploring the splendour of some of the world's finest coral reefs. Then perhaps an evening in Sharm-El-Sheikh sampling some authentic Egyptian food. Fresh, locally caught fish—

'Just run that first bit by me again,' says Sam.

'From what I can gather there are three prime dive sites . . .'

'No. The bit that came after the hearty breakfast.'

'Collection at 8 a.m.?'

'You were joking, weren't you?'

'Oh, come on. It's not as if we'll be going to bed that late.'

'You might not be.'

'This is Egypt, Sam. They don't have any nightlife.'

'I'm not expecting Cream, but – surely – there must be some sort of scene. Mustn't there?'

'Nope.'

'Well, you might have told me.'

'I thought you knew.'

'If I'd known I'd have said thanks but no thanks, we'll take your freebie to Ibiza instead.'

The evening is almost saved from further misery when the waiter presents us with a bill for the equivalent of six pounds. I'm just telling Sam how I take it all back and gosh, isn't it incredible what good value Third World countries can be, when the waiter returns and indicates that the banknote I have given him is inadequate. He requires ten times that amount to settle the bill.

A senior manager is summoned so that I can ascertain whether the meal will be included as part of my freebie package. It is not, he claims. But it must be, I splutter. There has been a terrible mistake. The manager returns with a fax which has been sent to him by the travel company PR. 'Bed and breakfast only' it says.

I slump forward on the table, cheeks resting on my fists, thinking dark thoughts.

'Coffee?' says Sam.

'What? At a tenner a throw.'

'I'll pay.'

'Cappuccino? Espresso?' asks the waiter.

'Qawah.' I reply.

'Nescafé?' asks the waiter.

'No. Arab coffee. You know. *Qawah*. Egyptian coffee.'

The waiter nods, which is Arab for no.

'Oh, for fuck's sake. This is ridiculous,' I tell Sam. I look up at the waiter. 'We are in Egypt. Why no Qawah? I want Qawah.'

'Leave him, Joe. It's not his fault.'

'If they're going to charge us these sort of prices, we might as well get what we want.'

The senior manager is summoned once more.

'Nescafé? Espresso? Cappuccino?'

'No. Qawah.'

'Qawah? No Qawah.'

'Why no Qawah? In Italy, cappuccino, espresso. In Egypt, Qawah.'

The senior manager nods.

'Are you going to be like this all holiday?' says Sam.

'Excuse me but I hardly think it's unreasonable to ask for proper Arab coffee in an Arab country. If I'd wanted cappuccino I'd have gone to frigging Rimini.'

'I wish you were in frigging Rimini!'

'Hey! Where are you going?'

'To get away from you.'

I am quite right, of course. What on earth is the point of flying all the way to Egypt if you're going to end up eating European food cooked by European chefs and paying European prices? I mean if that's really what all these Italians want, why don't they bloody well stay at home and leave the rest of the world free for those of us who can actually appreciate its cultural variety. And the same goes for all those English people who insist on frequenting pubs and fish and chip shops on the Costa del Sol. And the Americans who want their Big Macs to taste the same from Rio to Peking. Fuck off home, the lot of you. You don't deserve a passport!

All of which I would like to explain patiently to Sam. But I sense that now is not the time. We have been arguing far too frequently of late and though neither of us has ever stated it explicitly, I get the distinct impression that this holiday is, as far as our relationship is concerned, a make or break affair.

And I don't want our relationship to end. Not ever. Never mind the fact that Sam doesn't understand me, that she's a philistine, that she has crap friends and appalling taste in music, that she's a lush and a cokehead, that she stands in the way of my shagging whomsoever I please. Call it fear, call it conservatism, call me a romantic fool but I still love her madly and I'd do absolutely anything to stop us splitting up. Even . . .

Well, you're about to find out what that Even is. And believe me, Evens don't get much more drastic than this one. We're talking madness here. We're talking suicide. We're talking about something so stupid that you, who know me fairly well by now, will throw up your hands in despair and cry, 'Why? How could you be so foolish? You mad, mad, mad, *mad* bastard!'

Extending from the hotel's private beach into the sea is a wooden walkway on stilts, which broadens at the end to form a sunbathing deck-cum-swimming platform. It's here that I find Sam, sitting cross-legged, smoking a fag and staring out to sea.

'Hi,' I say.

'Hi,' she replies. The answer's a bit too short for me to tell how much humble pie I'm expected to eat.

I squat next to her and roll a cigarette. We sit in silence for a while, listening to the plash of the waves against the pontoon, gazing across the moonlit water towards a distant land mass. Possibly an island. Possibly Saudi Arabia.

At last I say the first thing that comes into my head after 'Sorry.' Only once I've said it does it occur that an apology might have been less painful. But I only mean it as a joke. Surely Sam will understand.

The thing I say is, 'Fancy a dip?'

'Do you?'

'Er, no.'

This is the understatement of the century. Repton and I once went to a lecture given by a professional shark photographer. Being as it was held at the Royal Geographic Institute, I'd feared that it was going to be a rather staid, solemn, rigorously scientific affair. I needn't have worried. Everyone in that well-heeled, middle-class audience had come for precisely the same reason. And the lecturer knew it.

He started by teasing us with the harmless plankton eaters – whale sharks and baskers; then he introduced us to some friendly reef sharks, some threshers and hammerheads.

Our excitement grew as we encountered the bulls and the tigers. 'And now,' he said – and we were hyperventilating like toddlers at their first pantomime – 'the great white!'

What is it about close-ups of great white sharks? Actually, I can tell you exactly what it is. It's that evil pointed snout, those huge pink gums, that gaping mouth and those rows of serrated triangular teeth. It is the physical manifestation of all our deepest, darkest fears.

Anyway, the point of my story is that, right at the end of the lecture, the photographer surveyed his audience and said, 'A lot of people, when they hear what I do for a living, tell me I must be mad. But I'm not, you know. The job I do isn't dangerous. Provided you know what you're doing, you keep your wits about you, and you know how to read a shark's body language, you're extremely unlikely to come to any harm. I've dived with sharks for fifteen years now and I've never felt in any serious danger.

'But, you know, there are still some things I'd never do under any circumstances. One of them is to dive with great whites without the protection of a cage. And the other is to go swimming off a beach in, say, Florida at night. Because that's the time when all the tiger sharks which spend the day three hundred feet below the surface, come right into the shallows to feed. Swimming in those conditions? Now that really is what I'd call madness.'

I'm sure I've told Sam this story before. And if I haven't, well, she must surely have a pretty good idea as to why I don't fancy a dip right now. But if she does, she's not letting on. She bum-shuffles towards the edge of the pontoon and dangles her toes into the water.

'Lovely and warm,' she says.

Just how the tiger sharks like it, I'm tempted to say.

'I'm going in,' she decides. 'Coming?'

This is not, I suspect, so casual an invitation as it sounds. If I refuse, it will confirm her view that I am a spineless obsessive whom she would do well to leave. But if I say 'yes' . . .

'Well?' says Sam, poised naked on the edge of the platform.

'Um. Are you sure it's, er—'

But already Sam has vanished beneath the water.

She does not resurface.

'Sam?'

I spot a dark shape in the water just a few feet from where she dived in.

'Sam? *Sam?*'

I tear off my clothes. This is what boyfriends are meant to do isn't it? Rescue their loved ones or die in the process.

'*SAM?*'

The sea is tingly and salty and terrifyingly dark. Looking down I can just make out the grey, moonlit pallor of my upper legs. As for the lower parts – for all I can see they might have been severed already by a—

'Ohmygodno!'

'Gotcha!' says Sam, resurfacing.

Before I can articulate my relief that Sam's alive and that she isn't a shark, before I can find words to express my disgust at the trick she has played, before I can plead with her to let us both flee this bottomless pit of watery death, she has disappeared once more. The next thing I glimpse is the spume kicked up by her feet as she powers towards the distant island.

All my instincts shriek that I should get back to the

safety of land this instant. At every splash of a wave, I whip my head round, eyes searching the foam for approaching fins. With each kick of my leg, I expect to feel the jagged rip of razor teeth through flesh. With each second that passes, the imaginary horrors multiply. Will it be death by the poisoned spike of a stonefish? Will I first be savaged by giant morays or barracuda? Will I be dragged out to sea by rip currents? What, in God's name, possessed me to dive in in the first place?

Bloody Sam, that's who. And much as she might deserve it, I cannot simply abandon her to die alone. Nor can I bear to stay where I am, alone, in the dark, strange waters, tormented by fear. The only other option is to do exactly what I'd do at home when attempting to flee my demons. I swim, as fast as I can, towards Sam. Lungs heaving, heart pounding, legs thrashing I surge through the water as if my life depended on it. And, who knows, perhaps it does. The sooner I reach her, the sooner I can talk some sense into the girl and get us both out.

'Hey!' says Sam. 'Isn't this fantastic?'

'Yeah,' I gasp, pulling myself close to her.

'You're scared, aren't you?'

'A bit.'

'Don't be.' She wraps her arms around me. And for just as long as we stay like that, a tiny island of warmth and love in an ocean of blackness, I feel safe. Happy. Elated even. I learn to see night swimming as Sam sees it: the silkiness of salt water against our naked bodies, the shimmering of phosphorescence, the vastness of the ocean, the majesty of the starry desert sky. But no sooner has she slackened her grip than the terror returns, more violent than before. I can feel it coming, closer and ever closer, its fat grey body questing through the water towards the vibrations of its trembling prey.

'Can we go back now?' I plead.

'Yes, darling. We can go back.'

And when we finally pull ourselves free of the water and reach the safety of the pontoon, I know that it's still out there. Cheated.

Diving in the Red Sea: not the ideal holiday, you might think, for one who professes to be terrified of sharks. But the way I look at it is this: if I were to spend the rest of my life cowering at home, never straying anywhere near shark-infested waters, then the enemy would have won. It's a point of principle.

Besides, I have done my homework. I know that the chances of being attacked while diving are risibly small; that, in fact, when you're underwater, the shark tends to be more wary of you than you are of him; that a shark sighting is a cause for jubilation rather than evasive action; that, indeed, there are few visions more magnificent than that of a lithe, streamlined body arcing through the blue, the perfect killing machine, unchanged since the dawn of time, etc. . . .

Some of this I have gathered from the Discovery Channel, the rest from our dive master Mohammed, a tall, wiry sex god whose resemblance to Imran Khan has not passed unnoticed by the female contingent on our dive boat. On the rare occasions I have managed to fight my way through his would-be harem – blonde Karin, blonder Anita, dark Maria and, yes, brown, treacherous Sam – I have questioned Mohammed closely as to the nature of the shark threat in these waters. 'Is it true that the sharks of the Red Sea are the fiercest in the world?' 'Are we likely to encounter any tigers?' 'How many recorded attacks have there been in recent memory?'

Besides being infuriatingly oversexed, Mohammed considers himself a bit of a wag. 'You have been reading too many of your *Tintin* books,' he replies to the first question. 'Only in India,' is his answer to the second. Mohammed has a degree in physical education from Loughborough University, you see, and is keen to show off his linguistic prowess and Anglo-Saxon wit. His harem giggles sycophantically. Mohammed barely seems to notice, as is the way with handsome instructors who have bedded so many tourists that they've shagged themselves bored.

Still, by remaining persistent and poker-faced, I eventually prise from this prize wanker the comforting information that the shark threat in these parts is only marginally greater than it is in 'your Piccadilly Circus'. Well, he would say that, wouldn't he? I've yet to meet the local who admits, 'No, my friend. Here are many, many dangerous sharks. It is not safe to swim off this beautiful beach.' But Mohammed has given me the answers I wanted to hear. And that's good enough for me.

In any case, there comes a point after four days' diving at innocuous sites with names like the Temple, White Knight and the Far Garden, when you grow rather bored of gawping at pretty little reef fish. Clowns, triggers, surgeons are all jolly cute and colourful, no doubt, but once you've seen one you've seen them all. You start hankering after something a bit bigger and more exotic. A turtle, say. Or a giant moray. Or better yet, a pelagic.

Pelagic, I have gathered, is the term hardcore, been-there-done-that divers use to describe really exciting fish like manta rays and barracudas and dolphins and whales and, of course, sharks. Until now, our pelagic-spotting opportunities have been rather limited because our dive sites have been too shallow and girlie. Today, however, our boat is heading for a proper grown-up dive site, where the coral wall plunges down to depths of up to a thousand feet, where the currents can be lethally strong, and where the big pelagics are wont to gather. Its name is Ras Mohammed.

'My favourite place,' announces Mohammed on his pre-dive briefing, the hilarious joke presumably being that it was named after him. The girls, whose swimwear has grown noticeably more scanty in the last few days, squat before him in an adoring semi-circle. They titter dutifully at his pleas-antry. Their forsaken boyfriends don't.

Mohammed runs through his by-now wearisome spiel about dive times, maximum permissible depths and safety procedures. He draws incomprehensible diagrams on a white-board, indicating the shape of the reef we will circumnavigate and the direction of the strong currents we can expect to encounter. Then he whets our appetite by telling us about all the pelagics he saw at the same site last week: a manta ray, a whale shark and three hammerheads, no less.

Needless to say, we don't see anything nearly so grand on the first dive of the day. Nor on the second. Though it's true we glimpse an impressive number of brightly coloured specimens at least six feet long from head to tail, they are not fish but shoals of Italian divers in flashy day-glo wetsuits, bent on trashing the fragile coral with their clumsy designer fins. The sharks are running scared.

Over the lunch break, the full extent of the problem becomes apparent. I count eight other dive boats moored within a five hundred yard radius of our own. At a conservative estimate of ten divers per boat, this means that, including our own contingent, there could be as many as ninety divers sharing the same small patch of reef at any one time in what's supposed to be a protected national park. 'Great,' I think. 'Conservation – Egyptian style.'

Not, you understand, that I'm trying to set myself up as some sort of crusading eco-warrior. It's the reason I stopped reading Carl Hiassen's thrillers, this habit he has of bludgeoning you with his man-is-evil, alligators-are-lovely, save-the-manatee diatribes. Sure I care about the depredation of the world's reefs; sure it pisses me off mightily that with one thoughtless kick, a diver can wipe out several hundred years' worth of coral growth. But the main reason I object to the presence of the other eighty-nine divers is that I'm a selfish bastard and I'd like to keep this reef all for myself. Oh, and maybe for Sam too, if she behaves herself.

The trip to Ras Mohammed has been a massive anticlimax. I'm so cross that I can scarcely digest the delicious fish stew prepared by Abdullah, the boat's chimp-like chef. As if in sympathy, the sun – which until today has shone relentlessly at temperatures of up to one hundred degrees – disappears behind a solitary cloud, the wind freshens and the boat starts to lurch from side to side. Which makes me even angrier, my stew more indigestible and drives me below decks where I flick, sulkily, through a few more pages of my Patrick O'Brian.

'Which one have you got there?' says a voice from a darkened corner. It belongs to the boyfriend of one of Mohammed's harem. John, I think his name is.

'*Treason's Harbour*,' I reply.

'Right. The Red Sea one.'

'Yeah. That's my excuse.'

'Why do you need an excuse?'

'Oh. Just, you know, I always think that when I'm on holiday I ought to be reading something more heavy duty. Learn something about the history and culture of the country I'm visiting, maybe. I've got a suitcase back at the hotel stuffed full of them: The Arabs, The Sinai, something thick and worthy by some Nobel-prizewinning Egyptian novelist I'm supposed to have heard of but haven't'.

'Naguib Mafouz?'

'That's the one.'

John laughs. 'Snap,' he says.

'God. You're not actually reading it?'

He flashes me the cover of his book. C. S. Forester's *The Young Hornblower* collection.

'Ah.' I smile.

'You know how it is,' says John. 'You start with the best of intentions. At last, a chance to taste the fruit of great world literature. Then you think, Naah. Sod it. Life's too short.'

'So who do you reckon's better: Forester or O'Brian?'

'Not much in it, I don't think,' he says. 'Hornblower's more consistent, more straightforward. O'Brian's stronger on technical detail.'

'The cunt splice?' I suggest

'The cunt splice. And you probably get more psychological insight than you do with Hornblower.'

'Mm, but it can get awfully wearing, can't it?' I say. 'Maturin's epic internal monologues. His metaphysical speculation. "Ah, just get on with it, you miserable sod," you want to say. "Go and spy on someone and get caught and have something interesting happen to you."'

'I don't mind a bit of digression,' he says. 'Gives you a chance to rest before the exciting bits.'

'Oh, digression's good, sure. As long as it's interesting digression. I mean I quite like that thing they do in contemporary novels where people just talk about the stuff that people talk about. Deconstructing *Star Wars*, children's TV—'

'Aubrey/Maturin versus Hornblower?'

'I'd buy that,' I say. 'As long as someone raised the most important point of all.'

'Which is?' he says.

'Their total neglect of the shark issue. Haven't you noticed? Hornblower and Jack Aubrey are forever leaping over the sides of their boats to rescue men overboard, yet not once – not even when they're in the Caribbean or the Indian Ocean – is the possibility of shark attack mentioned. And it flies in the face of all historical evidence. You know in the old days sailors were constantly being eaten by sharks. It's how the word first entered our language. After this disastrous expedition by Sir John Hawkins in the Caribbean, which is where shark comes from. It's Mayan. And no wonder the word stuck in their memory because do you know how many of them came back from that expedition? Fifteen. Most of the rest got eaten alive.'

'You've got a thing about sharks then?'

'Just a bit,' I say.

'Then you ought to know that there's actually a really good shark attack scene in one of the O'Brians. The one you're reading, I think. Pass it over and I'll see if I can find it . . . Yes. Here it is. Or do you want leave it till after this dive?'

'No. Fuck it. I'm not even sure I can be arsed to do another one anyway.'

I skim through the passage. It's a rather good one, involving a chirpy dragoman called Hairabedian who makes the big mistake of diving overboard Aubrey's ship, directly into the path of five prowling sharks. He gets ripped to shreds. In almost exactly the same waters where I'm about to dive.

'So now you're definitely not coming diving?' asks John.

'Probably not,' I say. 'But it's not what you think.'

''Course it isn't,' he says with friendly sarcasm.

But it isn't, it isn't, I promise. I just don't feel like another dive, that's all. I'm tired, the sores on my ankles – the result of ill-fitting fins – are giving me grief, and though we've been out of the water for a couple of hours now, I'm still shivering with cold.

At least I think it's because of the cold. The wind has certainly picked up, the sun's still obscured by cloud and the water's now so choppy that several of the other boats have already headed home. Even so, conditions are scarcely what you'd call arctic. According to the boat's thermometer, we're still in the high seventies. So why are my teeth chattering and the hairs on my arms stiff as bristles?

'Did that fish stew taste funny to you?' I ask Sam.

'No. Why?'

'Oh, I don't know. I think I might be sickening for something. Maybe I should sit this one out.'

'But you can't! We won't be coming here again. This is the best diving we're going to get all holiday.'

'Even so—'

'It's the name, isn't it?'

'What name?'

FIN

'Shark Reef.'

'I hadn't even noticed. Everything round here's called Shark Something.'

'Is there a problem?' says Mohammed.

'My dive buddy is getting cold feet,' explains Sam.

John's giving me a mocking look.

'Ah, yes,' jests Mohammed. 'The Indian tigers.'

'It has nothing to do with sharks. I'm feeling a bit ill, that's all.'

'Then perhaps it is better that you do not dive. The currents are very strong. This will be dangerous for a man who is . . . weak. You stay here, my friend. I will be your beautiful girlfriend's buddy.'

A buddy's jobs include checking the fasteners of his partner's Buoyancy Control Device (BCD – the life jacket which you inflate or deflate to give you the required buoyancy), helping them with their air tank, and sharing his air supply should his partner's run out.

I watch Mohammed perform the first of these tasks on Sam. He spends longer than is perhaps strictly necessary tightening the straps around her chest.

'Um, I think I've changed my mind,' I say.

'Then you must hurry,' says Mohammed.

Everyone glares at me as I fumble with my kit.

'Ready.'

One by one, we slip off the wooden platform at the stern of the boat into the sea. I'm very glad to be last in: if there are any sharks around, mine won't be the first pair of dangly legs to whet their appetite. The water is murkier and choppier and deeper than any we have dived in so far. It is the first time since that night swim with Sam that I have been seriously nervous. Already, the surface currents have begun

175

to pull our group apart. Mohammed indicates that we should submerge immediately. We give him the OK sign and obey.

Shark Reef comprises a huge pillar of coral which thrusts up from the ocean bed many hundreds of feet below. Our mission is to swim from one side to the other, sticking as close as we can to the edge, taking care not to sink below our maximum permissible depth of twenty-five metres.

It sounds easy enough. But diving in deep water is rather different from diving in shallow lagoons where you can always make out the sandy bottom below and the light from the sky above. In deep water, once you go below a certain level, you lose all your reference points. Up is blue, down is blue, forward is blue and sideways is blue. Sometimes it can become hard to tell which is which.

This is why it makes sense to check the depth gauge on your wrist every few seconds and to keep a close eye on the whereabouts of your fellow divers. Both of which codes I practise so religiously that there's barely time to investigate my surroundings. I'm dimly aware of the comforting pillar of coral to my right; I occasionally cast an anxious glance towards the expanse of blue murk to my left; but mostly, I keep my eyes fixed resolutely on my left wrist and on the divers strung out in a line ahead of me.

If this were Vietnam I would be very worried. As last in the patrol, I would be the person most likely to be crept up on by the Viet Cong and silently garrotted. But it isn't Vietnam and still I'm worried. With no one to guard my back, there's nothing to stop a shark sneaking up on me and biting my legs off. If only there were a way of swimming without letting your legs trail back in that 'Come on, sharky! Here's your hors d'oeuvres' manner.

I look over my shoulder to check that my legs are still

intact. Sometimes, apparently, you don't know you've been bitten until you see your own blood. No gore yet, it would seem, though I can't be absolutely sure because my rear view is obscured by my air tank. I had better turn round properly, just to be safe.

The good news is, my legs are still there. The bad news is that in the time it has taken me to execute this manoeuvre, I have very nearly lost my group. At the furthest extent of my visual range, I can just make out Sam, beckoning me furiously. Once I've caught up with her, she waggles her forefinger in front of my mask. I nod and slap my wrist on her behalf.

My jokey gesture implies a calmness, a flippancy even, that I do not remotely feel. Indeed, were I not horribly aware that sharks are attracted by human waste, I might well have shat myself by now. And what the hell am I doing down here anyway? I didn't need to come. I didn't want to come. Why didn't I want to come? Because I knew, I just knew, that something bad was going to happen. Perhaps that nearly-getting-lost experience was it. Perhaps – Oh God, let this be over soon – the worst is yet to come.

But the worst doesn't come. Not yet anyway. Instead, I witness something so beautiful, so jaw-droppingly awesome that my terror nearly evaporates. At first I mistake it for another vast pillar of coral that Mohammed neglected to mention. Except this one's not yellow but blue and flashing silver. And it moves.

As I swim closer, I realize that this shimmering tower is made up of circling fish. Fish far bigger than any I have seen before. Some clearly belong to the tuna family. Bluefins? Jacks? The silvery ones – and there must be at least five hundred of them – look very much like barracuda. In fact they're definitely barracuda because I'm now near enough to make out their tiger stripes and vicious, pin-sharp teeth. But the weird thing is, I don't find them remotely frightening. I feel – a disgusting word, I know, but it's true – I feel privileged to be here. I feel a tingling sense of joy and elation. I think this is bigger than the Empire State, cooler than Radiohead, trippier than the strongest acid. I want to live this moment, on freeze frame, for ever.

Just when I think that things can't possibly get better, they do. I'm right on the edge of the shimmering tower now, close enough to pick out the precise shape and colouring of each constituent specimen, when suddenly something vast and flat materializes from the blue beyond. The manta ray glides towards me, dark wings at least twenty feet across, mouth agape. It banks, exposing a pale belly mottled with black, then with one flap of its gargantuan wings it glides forward, and is gone as quickly as it came.

And the best thing of all is, I was the only one who saw it. Because the others, wherever they are – Yes. Where are they? Where the fuck are the others? And where's the reef wall? *Where am I?* Oh Jesus, this is the bad thing. This is the very terrible bad thing that I knew was going to happen and now it's happening. Now.

The water's so deep and dark and menacing. And I feel so helpless and alone. I want to be safe and warm and back in the boat now. I don't want to be down here with the things whose name I'm not going to mention because if I do I'll start panicking even more than I already am and – Jesus!

What was that?

What was *that*?

But of course, I know what it was. I know exactly what

it was even though I can't have glimpsed it for more than a second. It just flickered into vision. Then out again. All twenty, twenty-five feet of it. And it knows I'm here.

This isn't fear. This is something so terrible there isn't a word for it. This is rabbit-in-the-headlights, the guillotine's downward slide, the rumbling avalanche, the tidal wave's roar, the eye of the storm, the pit and the pendulum, the face of death . . .

Calm. Calm! Check your air supply. Fifty bars left. Check your depth gauge. Forty-one metres.

Forty-one metres!

Way, way, way too deep!

Forty-two now and going deeper.

Downward current. I'm caught in a downward current. Must act now.

Inflate BCD.

Still not enough. Pressure too great.

Inflate some more.

But not too much. Too much and you'll shoot to the surface and die of the bends. Too little and you'll sink down and ever down to the lightless domain of bug-eyed, luminous, implode-when-they're-dragged-to-the-surface-by-fishing-nets horror creatures which feast on your rotting corpse and—

It's happened already. I'm dead. Or very nearly dead because I'm no longer inside my stiff, shivering body. I'm outside, staring myself in the face. Livid flesh. Electric hair. Mask framing eyes bulging with terror.

Not my eyes. Mohammed's eyes. O blessed wonderful Mohammed with his powerful arms dragging me up towards the light. Towards the wall of coral comfort. Towards Sam.

There she is. Sam, Sam – O God, I'm so pleased to see you! There are the others. And there – O God be praised – is the mooring rope slanting upward towards the boat.

The stairway to heaven.

But halfway to heaven lies purgatory. Here, fifteen metres below the surface, I must wait in order to reduce the nitrogen levels accumulated at forty-two metres. I must wait here for – how long, Mohammed? Mohammed shows me ten fingers. For ten whole minutes. On my own. But not alone.

Do I need to describe the thoughts which pass through my head as the minutes on Mohammed's loaned diving watch tick by? I think not. You know me well enough by now. You know what I saw at forty-one metres below off Shark Reef at Ras Mohammed. You know why I keep looking round and round and round and round until I'm dizzy. You know that by the time I drag myself, shuddering, back on to the boat, I have solemnly vowed that I shall never go diving ever again.

It is not, I suspect, a resolution I shall find difficult to keep. Especially not after the discovery we make on returning to port. But first let me tell you briefly about the strange conversation I have with Mohammed on the voyage home. It happens just after Sam has walked off in a huff because I've told her about my vow. We've still three whole diving days to go and she's buggered if she's going to spend them hanging around the hotel because of my pathetic shark neurosis.

When Mohammed appears, I expect him to give me a ticking off. Instead, he claps me on the shoulder and says, 'Sometimes it is good that we listen to our heart.'

'Mm.' Is he talking about Sam, chicks in general, or what?

'Before, you did not wish to dive. I too did not wish to dive. Now we understand why we did not wish to dive.'

'You knew something bad was going to happen?'

Mohammed shrugs. 'You saw. Many of the other captains, they listened to their hearts. I did not. *He* did not.' He gestures towards the porthole. Through it we can see one of the rival dive boats, apparently trying to race us home.

We climb on deck for a better view. The rival captain clearly fancies himself a boy racer. He is pushing his boat as fast as it will go against the strong headwind, apparently oblivious of the huge waves that threaten to swamp his prow. We give his passengers a sympathetic wave. Rather them than us. They do not wave back, though one of them shouts something inaudible. Soon they are well past us.

Mohammed shakes his head and curses. A voice crackles on the radio. Mohammed answers back in Arabic. Presumably the two captains are exchanging insults. The rival captain sounds as if he's on the verge of hysteria. Mohammed too grows agitated.

'There has been an accident,' he explains.

'What kind of accident?'

'A diving accident,' he says, not meeting my eye.

We reach the port just in time to catch an ambulance and two motorcycle police outriders, sirens screeching, pushing their way outward through the crowd that has gathered round the rival dive boat. Standing to one side are the boat's uninjured passengers, shoulders hunched, far-off expressions in their eyes.

A thuggish South Londoner tells me what happened.

'We finish our dive same time as you and we're just going home when Debs there – that's my girl – sees this fin in the water. "Shark! Shark!" she starts screaming. "That's no shark," says Abdullah. He's our dive master. "That's a dolphin." Whole school of them as it happens. And Debs, well, it's always been her ambition to swim with dolphins. So we ask Abdullah if we can't jump in. Just with fins and snorkels, like. Soon as we've piled into the water – the whole lot of us, 'cause everyone wants to do it – the dolphins bugger off. And suddenly this geezer, nice bloke, Dave his name is – electrician from Swindon – he starts screaming. I didn't see much of what happened. Debs did though, didn't you, doll? You were that close—'

'Ooh, it was 'orrible. I felt it scrape past me. Here, you can see my arm's all grazed. And the water was all red and poor Dave was screaming—'

'It's all very quick. By the time we know what's happening, Abdullah's pulled the boat round and they've yanked the poor geezer out the water. Buckets of blood. Debs was sick when she saw what them teeth had done to his leg. They reckon he was lucky to survive. Tiger shark, they reckon it was. Twenty-footer, they reckon. You'd have thought a thing that size, someone would have seen it earlier.'

That night Sam and I have the best sex ever. It's as exciting and rude and adventurous as making love to a beautiful stranger. At the time, I put it down to our mutual relief at having escaped the jaws of death. On the final day of the holiday, however, I begin to wonder.

My insight comes while we're bouncing up and down on a potholed desert road, at speeds of up to ninety miles an hour, in a car with bald tyres and no suspension, driven by a madman. We didn't, of course, know that Kamal was mad when we chartered his taxi the previous evening. Indeed we chose him because he seemed the sanest, most responsible and least rapacious of the drivers touting for trade in the dusty parking area outside the hotel gates. But something appears to have turned his mind since our teatime stopover at the seaside, hippy resort of Dahab. The same something, I suspect, which is preying on the brains of his terrified passengers and transforming what should be just a routine 'journey from hell with crappy foreign taxi driver' into a parched-throated, head-spinning, nerve-shattering nightmare of apocalyptic horrendousness.

Sam was right. We should never have touched that Bedouin weed.

But then, Sam was always more of a pills and powder person. I, on the other hand, have made it one of my life missions to sample every variety of local marijuana, everywhere on earth. (Which, incidentally, is another powerful incentive for me not to give up travelling, despite the possibility that my plane will crash in shark-infested waters etc., etc.) And from what people say – and people are right – the Bedouin weed of Dahab is among the most brain-fuckingly noxious the horticulturalist's art has yet devised. To turn down the opportunity of trying it would be a crime.

Besides, we've earned it. We've had to rise at 6 a.m.; we've had to listen all day to Kamal's waily Arab pop music (I'm not averse to Rai, but we're talking the Egyptian equivalent of early Kylie here); we've been frazzled by the desert heat; we've overdosed on icons and early Christian culture at St Catherine's Monastery (just about worth it for grisly pile of bones in the *Killing Fields* style ossiary, I suppose); and we've survived seven whole days of annoying Italians, begging Egyptians and rapacious tiger sharks, without having enjoyed even the merest whiff of a spliff. So when the man from Dahab sidles up to me and says 'Smoke?', the man from Hackney, he say 'Yes!'

With hindsight, it might have made more sense to sample it in the safety of our hotel. Sam clearly thinks so. She doesn't say as much but her silence – angry, nauseous, accusatory – speaks volumes.

We rattle along the highway of death, locked in our private hell worlds, deafened by Kamal's 'music', roasted by the sun, choking on the fine desert dust, until eventually I can take no more.

'Strong, this stuff,' I say.

'Too strong,' says Sam.

'Interesting, though,' I suggest. It is for me anyway. We've just passed the wreckage of yet another roadside truck. I'm an Israeli Chieftain commander in the Yom Kippur War, powering through the desert in a trail of dust, pumping armour-piercing shells into the retreating Egyptian tanks, radioing the Phantom squadron for another airstrike . . .

'No,' says Sam.

'No what?'

'No it's not.'

'No what's not?'

'You said it was interesting,' says Sam, heavy with exasperation. 'And I'm saying no it's not interesting. It's horrible.'

'Oh.' At this rate we'll be in Cairo by teatime. Do Israeli tank commanders drink tea? Or coffee? Not with milk, either way. Unless perhaps, they haven't eaten meat for a while. God, my throat's dry. Why didn't we buy more water in Dahab? Cup of tea would be nice. With milk or without? Weird, these Jewish dietary laws. Do they ever drink milk with their tea? I could ask Sam, of course, but she might not understand. She's somewhere else. Bound to be. Shame really. Think how cool it would be if we were on the same trip all the time. No problem ever deciding what we'll do next. No rows—

'It's not working, Joe.'

'Oh, I don't know. I'm flying.'

'Us.'

'Us?'

'Our relationship. It's not working.'

Relationship? Does she mean relationship as in Relationship? Or some other sense of the word relationship that eludes me right at this moment?

'Uh. You mean, you and me? Us together? Going out?'

Sam is looking at me very, very directly. She nods.

FUCK!

'Shouldn't we maybe leave this stuff for when we're a bit less – gone?' (Though it must be said, I'm straightening up at a rate of knots.)

'Now. I want to talk about it now. While it's in my head.'

'Uh, yeah. I can see that. But maybe later it won't be in your head. And everything will be OK.'

'I've made up my mind.'

'What? When?'

'Oh come on, Joe. You must have seen this coming.'

'No. Not at all. Well, yes. I suppose you have been a bit quiet in the last couple of days. But I thought, you know, I thought it was because – oh, I don't know.'

'What?'

'The shark. I thought maybe it was shock. Guilt even.'

'Guilt!'

'Embarrassment then. You know how you've always said my shark fear is completely pathetic and then—'

'You amaze me sometimes, Joe. You really do. Is there a single issue in your life that doesn't revolve round sharks?'

'Oh, I'm *so* sorry. It really was totally my fault that I very nearly happened to be eaten by a fucking great tiger shark.'

Sam takes a deep breath. 'Joe, I've been seeing someone.'

It comes out so quickly, I nearly miss what she says. It doesn't register, anyway, because I say, 'We were talking about the shark.'

'I said I've been seeing someone. I've been sleeping with another man.'

'I heard.'

'Aren't you going to say something?'

'All right. Who?'

'You don't care, do you? It doesn't bother you one bit!'

'Who?'

'Marius Schenk.'

'You've been sleeping with Marius Schenk. Wow!'

'You weren't meant to be impressed.'

'Sorry. Can't help it. Big name, Marius Schenk.'

Sam looks at me, expecting more. I'm not going to give her that satisfaction.

'And that's all you're going to say?' she says at last.

'What do you want me to say?'

'Be angry. Be upset. I don't know.'

'I am angry and upset.'

Sam drags a finger across her eye and looks away. I rest my hand on her arm.

'Don't,' she says, shaking her head.

'Can't help it,' I say, leaving my hand where it is. 'I love you.'

FIN

I pull Sam close to me. She resists at first but I won't let her go. She relaxes after that, sobbing into my shoulder. In the rear-view mirror, Kamal gives me a conspiratorial smile. He thinks I've won. I'm not so sure.

THE MAKO

On the original 1977 poster for Jaws, the shark depicted is actually a mako, not a great white. Presumably this was because the artist decided that a mako's teeth look more scary. The artist was right. A great white's serrated, triangular teeth are horrible. A mako's – sharp and curved, as if he has a mouthful of claws – are truly horrendous.

Though there have been few recorded attacks on humans by the mako, this is not because he is a friendly fish. It's because he is shy and tends to hang out in mid-ocean. So the time to watch out for him is when your boat has sunk or your plane has crashed in really deep water.

Apart from his teeth, his dead black eyes (similar to those of a great white) and aggressive temperament, his nastiest distinctions are his maximum speed of 60mph (making him the fastest fish in the sea) and his ability to leap several times his own length above the water, enabling him to crash down and sink small boats.

CHAPTER SEVEN

Here are my three worst recurring nightmares:

1. It's the night before my first finals exam and, for reasons known only to the weaver of dread dreams, I have done no revision whatsoever. I scrabble through page after page of illegible notes, trying to commit to memory in one evening two years' worth of dates, names and key events. After a sleepless night, I realize why I've been finding it so difficult. I'm reading English, not History.

2. I'm a spy in Cold War Eastern Europe or a soldier in Vietnam. Either way I'm being pursued by malevolent baddies, whom I elude through a series of cunning ruses which take up many, many hours of dream time. In the spy version, there will be chases through Kafkaesque office blocks and multistorey car parks like the ones featured in every episode of *The Professionals*. In the Nam variant, I conceal myself in drainage ditches and up trees, using techniques I learned from one of those Tony Geraghty *Inside the SAS* books that everyone owns when they're fourteen. My favourite trick is the one where you strap yourself to a branch and fall asleep with one eye open. This I have found completely impossible to achieve in real life, though it seems to work well enough in dreams.

What never works in my dreams, unfortunately, is my

weaponry. I don't know why – again, only the weaver of dread dreams does – but my dream persona always seems to end up with really crap guns. Never once do I get to use something cool like an Uzi or a grenade launcher or a pump-action shotgun or an Ingram MAC 10 'spray and pray'. It's always something pathetic like a bolt-action rifle or a pistol. Which would be just about acceptable, I suppose, if the bloody things actually fired bullets. But they don't. When the crunch comes and I'm finally discovered, as always happens towards the end of the dream, I shoot at the enemy and my gun just melts. The barrel droops and the bullets plop uselessly on to the ground. Presumably this is the point where I die, though I've never stayed asleep long enough to find out. If you die in your dreams, you die in real life too. Apparently.

That melting gun barrel. I used to think that this was one of my own inventions. Apparently not, for rereading *Lolita* the other day, I noticed that Humbert Humbert once dreamt it too. So I suppose it must be a standard anxiety dream. Either that or I'm a closet paedophile.

3. Now this dream definitely is my invention. And if it isn't, I feel very sorry for the poor bastards who share it with me because it's an absolute nightmare of a nightmare. I did toy with the idea of telling it you straight, without the 'this is one of my dreams' preamble, and leaving it up to you to work out that it wasn't actually real. But then I thought, 'It's a hackneyed device. And anyway, it might tempt fate.' So here's the dream. No prizes for guessing what it involves.

I'm on a freebie at some unspecified, exotic foreign location: whitewashed hotel, palm trees, golden sands, crystal-clear blue water, etc. A bit like my Red Sea holiday with Sam, really, only better because unreality always is.

What's especially cruel about this dream is that I always start off being incredibly happy. 'Wow! This is so cool!' I think as I explore the multitude of bars and restaurants – all swarming with tanned ultrababes who would undoubtedly be willing to make love to me in any number of imaginative ways were this to be a wet dream and not a nightmare – before casting an approving eye over the palm trees, golden sands, crystal-clear blue water, etc.

But, as Kid Creole and the Coconuts once percipiently observed, there's something wrong in paradise. Et in arcadia ego, and all that. For it has been revealed to me in a vision – a bit like the one Fiver has at the beginning of *Watership Down* – that something truly terrible is going to happen. Needless to say, it involves sharks.

In this vision of mine, I learn that ten or twenty years ago these seemingly innocuous clear blue waters were visited by one of the biggest, most vicious great white sharks that ever chomped human flesh. Many swimmers perished. And I know that any moment now, this same shark – or perhaps its even bigger more vicious offspring – is going to come back for more.

When I try explaining this to my fellow guests, however, they won't believe me. Nor will the hotel staff, who insist that there is absolutely no danger of shark attack in this part of the world.

'But what about that incident ten years ago?' I ask.

'What incident?' they say.

And they're so persuasive that I almost believe them. I dip my toes into the water. Indeed it is warm and inviting. I go for a paddle. More pleasant still. I think about having a swim. Why not? Everyone else is doing it. The bay is full.

But something holds me back. It's at this point that I see

it. And, of course, being as it's a nightmare shark it's far, far bigger than the one in *Jaws*. Its fin is the size of a dinghy sail; its body fills half the bay. 'Shark!' I scream. 'Shark!' But still no one will listen. The carnage begins. Many die. How many I'm not sure because by that stage, I've woken up drenched in sweat.

'Can't you be a bit more original?' Sam usually groans once I've mumbled the details.

But not this morning.

'It's back!' I say. 'The shark's come back.' I'm still in that unpleasant, halfway state where you've yet to be fully convinced that it was all just a dream.

Still no response. If this goes on for much longer, I'll be wide awake enough not to need the solace of Sam's irritation.

I extend my arms to Sam's side of the bed. It's empty.

Empty as it has been for the month since we got back from the holiday, officially split up, and decided that Sam would move out and Black Cat would find temporary accommodation at Martha' garden maisonette while I stayed in the house until the rent contract expired – which it now has. Today's my last day here. Nobody loves me. I'm a failure. I'm all alone and I'm doomed to be eaten by a great white shark.

And it's not a dream.

And I've run out of oranges for my pre-swim juice boost. So I have a cigarette instead. And my car's being serviced and won't be ready till 10 a.m. So I walk to the swimming pool, wheezing. In the rain.

If God were on my side, He'd at least vouchsafe me a final glimpse Moroccan Babe's wank-friendly features. But Moroccan Babe isn't on cashier duty today. Nor is Mr Freebie. Nor is my old friend Kenneth, with the starched embroidered shirt and the penchant for classic English novels. Instead I am greeted by a sullen, acned teenager who doesn't know it's my last day ever at this swimming pool and wouldn't care if I told him.

At times like these, I wonder whether God is not a giant bumblebee. It's a thought that has haunted me ever since, aged eight, I massacred several of his innocent buzzy brethren by stunning them with a whippy stick and squashing them underfoot. 'Zzsso, my friend,' I can imagine him droning as I stand outside the pearly gates. 'You believed all that nonzzenzze about my being an old man with a beard, did you?' I'd fare no better, were God a giant ladybird. I used to burn them with magnifying glasses. Or if he were a fly (wings pulled off, natch), a wasp (drowning in jam jars), a mosquito (splat) or a goose (sorry, I just love foie gras).

Anyway, whatever he is – old man with beard, insect, goose, shark, etc. – he's definitely got it in for me. Why else would the pool be so unbearably crowded: three or four people to a lane, making it impossible to swim in a straight line?

I wouldn't mind so much if they were regulars. But I don't recognize anyone. It's as if I've wandered into a parallel universe where everything looks exactly the same except the people in it. Bob has turned into an Olympian black man and a pair of East End thugs; Not Bob has become three pensioners in floral swimming hats; Not Not Bob is now a pregnant woman, a child-molester and a city broker; and Fat Blubbery Bastard has exploded like a cluster bomb into six, twenty-something health Nazis who play squash and drink fake orange juice and work in marketing and earn more than me and surge up and down the lanes with such thuggish efficiency that I can't stand any more of this, I've got to get out now.

The showers are cold. And though I press the button in

for at least a minute they stay cold. I would complain – I love to complain; complaining makes my day – but what's the point? By the time they get it fixed, I'll be long gone. And I'm never coming back.

For the last time, I negotiate the corridors outside the cubicles, trying to avoid the myriad puddles. It's not the wetness I mind. It's the solids lurking at the bottom: flakes of athlete's foot, bits of child verucca, dirt carried in from the dog-poo-impregnated pavement, sodden fluff that clings to the bottom of your feet.

Charmingly, a nest of pubic hair has managed to lodge itself between my toes. As I pick it free I am reminded – madeleine-like – of Tom Bland's visit here with Repton, the morning of my thirtieth birthday party.

They've both stayed the night – too drunk to make it home – and we all have terrific hangovers. So I'm quite taken aback when they accept my invitation to join me for an 8 a.m. swim. Stupid of me not to twig immediately their ulterior motive. But I've always been of the old-fashioned opinion that swimming pools are for swimming in.

Behind the cashier's window Kenneth glances up from his copy of *Great Expectations*, looking vaguely troubled as usual.

'Morning,' I say. 'I've brought a couple of new customers for you.'

Kenneth smiles earnestly. 'I am very happy to make your acquaintance,' he says to Repton and Tom. 'Your friend always gives me great pleasure.'

'Really, Joe?' leers Repton, nudging my elbow. 'You dark horse, you.'

'Indeed,' says Kenneth, slightly bewildered. 'He has a manner of expressing himself which I find most beautiful.'

'Are you sure you've got the right person?' says Tom.

'There could be no mistaking your fine friend. He—'

'Kenneth, you're too sweet,' I interrupt, blushing. 'If you wouldn't mind putting these two reprobates on my card, I can get them under a cold shower. They're a little frisky this morning.'

Kenneth nods sadly.

As soon as we're out of his earshot, Repton and Tom burst into giggles. 'What was that all about?' says Tom.

'You're both very naughty,' I say. 'Keneth's my friend.'

'Your very special friend,' says Repton, exchanging a smirk with Tom.

And if this were the time or the place, maybe I'd try explaining that Kenneth was one of the first, real, actual black people I got to meet when I moved to Hackney; and how oddly flattered I'd felt when, after a period of shy non-communication I'd mistaken for chippy froideur, he'd finally chosen to give me – hateful, oppressive whitey – the time of day.

It seems stupid now, but before Sam and I arrived here, I'd convinced myself that the People's Republic of Hackney was choc-a-block with unwashed lesbians who'd eat you alive if you tried anything sexist like opening the door for them; with foetid crusties waiting for you to go on holiday so they could squat your home; with predatory gays, militant schoolteachers, aggressive beggars, anarchists, revolutionaries, and animal rights terrorists; and above all, with scary black people who, if they weren't high on crack or stealing your wallet, would be taking you to the Commission for Racial Equality for looking at them in a funny way.

And perhaps the People's Republic of Hackney is choc-a-block with such people. I'm sure it is. I just happen not to have bumped into any of them. The people I've met are the nice ones. People like Mark. My genuine, actual, black almost-friend Mark.

But this isn't the time or the place for going into any of this. So instead I just say to Repton and Tom:

'Oh fuck off, the pair of you. You wouldn't understand.'

Nor do they understand the niceties of swimming-pool etiquette. When you first start visiting a new pool, you must wait at least three months before any of the regulars deign to acknowledge your existence. Until then it is completely infra dig to attempt wishing anyone anything so impertinent as a 'good morning', let alone to join in any of the conversations you might hear being conducted in the showers or the neighbouring cubicles, no matter how fascinating you believe your contributions might be.

Repton and Tom, however, are having none of this. When I say my dutiful 'mornings' to my fellow regulars, they join in with 'mornings' of their own. And not just in embarrassed grunts, which might almost be permissible, but with excruciating jollity and enthusiasm. The consequences of this are truly terrible. Mr Fat Blubbery Bastard and his tittering sidekick Mr Grinny Beard mistake it for an invitation to further discourse.

'You're looking a bit peeky this morning,' chirrups Mr Grinny Beard, who has never, ever dared speak to me before.

'Mm,' I say, walking briskly on.

'It was his thirtieth birthday last night,' says Tom.

'And he took far, far, far too much cocaine,' adds Repton.

This, quite clearly, is the most exciting thing anyone has ever said to Messrs Fat Blubbery Bastard and Grinny Beard. For a moment — and this is definitely a first — they fall silent. They look at one another like toddlers who have just heard their kindergarten teacher say something incredibly naughty and funny like 'poo', their tiny brains overwhelmed by the flood of possible amusing rejoinders.

'Ha ha ha,' I say. 'He's only teasing.'

'You mean,' says Mr Grinny Beard, 'he was *crack*-ing a joke.'

'Crack-ing a joke!' chortles Mr Fat Blubbery Bastard.

'Do you get it? Crack as in crack cocaine?'

'And . . . and joke.' Mr Fat Blubbery Bastard is so pleased with this one, he can barely get it out. 'And joke as in *coke*.'

'Hee heee hee hee,' goes Mr Grinny Beard.

'Hahahahaha,' goes Mr Fat Blubbery Bastard.

'What's all this? What's all this?' calls out Not Bob from his cubicle.

'Private joke,' I call back grimly.

'Blimey,' he says on coming out to greet me. 'You're looking rough today, my friend.'

'Yeah, well,' I scowl. 'I've just lost my two best friends.'

The only consolation is that they both look ridiculous in the swimming trunks I've lent them. Tom's got the baggy grey ones which drag you underwater and cling around your crotch when they're wet so that everyone can see how shrivelled and small your willy is. Repton's got the designer silver ones which ride up your bottom crack and are so faded they're almost see-through. Annoyingly, neither of them seems remotely bothered. In fact, knowing Repton, he probably thinks it's a bonus.

More annoyingly still, Repton turns out to be a really good swimmer. Much better than me – and I do it every day, almost, while I'll bet he doesn't do it more than a couple of times a year. I suppose there must be some sort of gay gene which makes you instinctively athletic so that you don't make a prat of yourself while you're trying to pull down at the gym. Or in the swimming pool.

As Repton keeps telling me, swimming pools are one of the best gay pick-up joints going. 'Yeah, I know,' I say. 'I've read *The Swimming Pool Library.*' And blimey, did it make me sick! I mean, that scene where he's on the tube and he catches a bloke's eye and ends up following him off the train for a frenzied shag: how many times does that sort of shenanigan take place in the heterosexual world? Fucking never, that's how many times. Only in my dreams and 'reader's true experience' letters, anyway. Another reason that book pisses me off is that it's set in a swimming pool, which I've often considered during my tedious progress up and down the lanes would have made a really brilliant and original location for a novel. If Alan bastard Hollinghurst hadn't got there first.

Of course, had Hollinghurst done his research here rather than Porchester Baths, he would have been a bit stuck for pornographic inspiration. Everyone who uses my pool is probably frigid and definitely straight, apart from the ones who go to the special Thursday evening swimming club called Spartacus, the precise nature of whose nocturnal aquatic activities I prefer not to imagine. 'Do you think they actually have sex with one another? Actually in the pool?' I once ask Repton. 'Oh, bound to,' he replies. 'It's all gay men ever do.' The next Friday I go swimming, I spend the whole time peering through my goggles in search of pearly strands which might have escaped the pool's filtration system. It's an evil thing sperm. Especially the way it clings to your pubes and solidifies after you've been wanking in the bath.

Anyway, as I was saying, Repton's an annoyingly good swimmer. Almost as good as the Olympic professional in the cordoned-off lane. And about on a par with the second best swimmer, the smooth dark Latino with a triangular torso, who doesn't come here all that often but pisses me off when he does because he always manages to grab the only decent shower with the powerful nozzle seconds before I want to use it myself. They're sharing a lane and, as boys will, they're in hot competition, muscling through the water like a pair of killer whales at show time.

Tom, on the other hand, is a pleasingly crap swimmer. Lest he hasn't noticed, I swim three lengths – very close to him and smiling each time we pass – in the time it takes him to do one. I reach the shallow end just before he does, ready to greet him with some teasing remark. But Tom isn't playing. Instead, his attention is turned towards the steps in the far corner of the shallow end. Or rather, to the shapely woman in the black costume descending them.

I can understand why he's looking at her. I have often been distracted by her presence myself. She's thirtyish, slim-ish, pretty-ish – easily the most attractive woman in the pool. Quite how attractive, I've never dared ascertain. Not even on those delicious days when we happen to be sharing a lane together and she pauses at one end to do her stretching exercises. I just can't bring myself to do what a more lecherous bloke would do: stop bang next to her, pretend to be taking a breather or adjusting my goggles or something, and give her the full once-over. It would be too impertinent, too brazen. But I have to say that what little I have seen of her – especially when her fine, firm legs are opening and closing in front of me underwater as she does her breast stroke – is very, very tempting.

What makes her more tantalizing yet is that she's a single mother. And as Tom once told me, all single mothers are gagging for it because they can't afford to go out on the pull very often. Not that I know for sure she's a single mother. But she does have a baby which she brings along in a pushchair. The attendants coo and cluck over it while she does her lengths. Whenever the baby cries, she gets out of the pool to check it's all right, giving those who wish a few moments to drool over her dripping body before she slips back into the water.

I'm not one of the droolers myself. Partly it's good manners – the same good manners I apply when following a young woman down a lonely street at night: I'll always overtake her quickly or cross to the other side of the road, so she doesn't think I'm a rapist or something. Partly it's lechery: if I examine her too closely for too long I fear it might spoil the fantasy image I have of her in my head when I'm doing my lengths. And partly, it's a question of fear. Once, in another pool, I saw a man being accused of sexual harassment.

He was a pleasant-looking young man with long straggly hair. He didn't look like the sort of weirdo who hangs out in pools to molest women. He didn't lurk in the shallows, leering. He ploughed up and down the pool, just like me. Then out of the blue, a woman who'd just swum past him started screaming.

'You pig!' she yelled, jabbing her finger towards him. 'You bastard! You *know* what you were trying to do to me! You *know*! You *know*!'

Everyone else in the pool slowed down to glance surreptitiously at the scene. But only very briefly. It was too complicated. Too disturbing. It interrupted our routine. We wanted it to go away. And soon we'd all resumed our lengths, as if nothing was happening. Even though it still was.

The woman stood, hand on hips, in the shallow end and screamed at the female lifeguard, 'That man molested me! Aren't you going to do anything about it?'

The man gave the lifeguard a 'What can you do? The woman's clearly a nutter' shrug, and carried on swimming regardless.

'Well?' said the woman to the lifeguard.

The lifeguard gestured helplessly, as anyone would in his position. How could he possibly judge who was to blame?

I certainly couldn't. Not at first. But then it struck me how bizarrely unruffled the man had been by the accusation. Almost as if he'd been prepared for it. And I knew then that he was guilty as sin. And even if he wasn't, there was one thing of which I was absolutely sure: I never wanted to find myself in the same position as him.

That's why, when I do my lengths, I take care never to ogle too obviously any of the female pool-users. That way, should the false accusation ever come, I can rely on the pool staff to say, 'Him? No! He's not the sort. Takes his swimming very seriously does this one.'

Tom Bland, however, is clearly impervious to such concerns. Barely has the single mother entered the water than he has pounced, with a cheery greeting I don't catch because I'm too busy trying to put as much distance between myself and him as possible before the first shriek of 'Rape!' Because I know that Single Mum just isn't the type to welcome the attentions of lascivious strangers. Like me, she's a serious swimmer. She comes in, bosh, does her sixty lengths and gets out without a backward glance.

Once I've reached the deep end, I feel safe enough to risk a glance towards Tom and his prey. They are still talking. Which is very antisocial because they're blocking the end of one lane, forcing the people who've come here to swim rather than flirt to keep dodging round them when they want to do their racing turns.

Disgusted, I do a couple more lengths. And still, I see, they're talking.

Even more disgusted, I do two more. Now Tom's floating on his back, arms over his shoulders so that his hands can grasp the railing, in a gesture I suppose he thinks makes him look relaxed and cool. And far from trying to escape, Single Mum actually seems to be enjoying his company. She's sitting there by the steps, smiling and laughing, completely oblivious to the needs of her baby. Or, indeed, of the sensitivities of anyone who might find such public displays of affection quite outrageous at 8.30 on a weekday morning.

Not Bob, for example.

'I'm terribly sorry,' I say as he pulls in next to me.

'What you gone and done now?' he asks.

'Not me. My friend.' I nod towards the far end of the pool.

'Ah, it's a wonderful thing, young love,' says Not Bob.

'He's not that young and that's certainly not love,' I say.

Suddenly there's a loud female shriek, closely followed by a male bellow and a good deal of splashing. About bloody time, I think. Until I realize that it's not the violent rebuff I'd hoped. The lovebirds are simply having a race.

I look around for Repton. At least he'll be up for a good bitch about Tom's lechery. Or he would if I could find him. But he appears to have disappeared. The lane he was sharing with Latino Orca Boy is empty and I can't see him on the poolside. I suppose all that strenuous activity must have exhausted him. Quite strange of him, though, to get out without telling me.

Unless . . .

Oh my God.

And I'm so cross I want to leave right now. Except I daren't go anywhere near the men's changing rooms when Repton and Latino Orca Boy might well be doing heaven knows what in the cubicles, the loos or the showers. And I don't want to stay here either, watching Tom and Single Mum cooing and billing in flagrant and grotesque contravention of the pool's 'No-petting' rules. And I can't talk to Not Bob because he'll only annoy me even more by telling me I'm jealous or something. So I do the only bloody thing I can do. I keep my head down and swim, swim, swim, swim and bastard fucking swim.

'Good swim?' asks Tom, later in the changing rooms.

'Great, thanks. You?'

'You probably noticed. I didn't get much swimming done.'

'Yes, what on earth were you talking about?'

'Oh, you know. Babies, errant husbands, the miseries of single motherhood.'

'About which you know so much, of course.'

'You'd be amazed how easily it comes when the need arises.'

'Rather a lot of effort, though,' I say. 'Given that you're never going to see her again.'

'Oh, I shouldn't be so sure of that,' says Tom. 'I'm meeting her at her place. For "coffee". In ten minutes.'

'Pity,' I say. 'I was hoping we might all pop down to Pellicci's for breakfast.'

'Never mind, Joe,' calls out Repton. He emerges from the labyrinth of cubicles with Latino Orca Boy, both wearing nothing but a towel and a smug grin. 'You can make up a threesome with me and Paco instead.'

After that hateful morning, a whole month passes before I dare return to the pool. In the interim, I investigate a couple of rival establishments. But neither has nearly the same charm. The one in Dalston is smarter and cleaner but the water's piss-warm and the showers are mixed, which means you can't take off your trunks and give your bottom a proper clean. The one in Bethnal Green is bigger and more professional, but the atmosphere's too clinical, the clientele are oppressively sportif and there's nowhere to park.

So I'm glad when I return to my cosily shambolic old haunt with its dodgy showers, filthy floors, peeling ceilings and eccentric clientele. Even if it does mean avoiding eye contact with Single Mum, steering clear of the showers when Latino Orca Boy's in the vicinity, and pointedly ignoring Mr Fat Blubbery Bastard and Mr Grinny Beard when they try greeting me by rubbing their fingers conspiratorially against the side of their noses. At least Bob, Not Bob and Not Not Bob are pleased to see me. At least I can still lech over Moroccan Babe when she's on duty. At least Mr Freebie can flatter me into believing I'm something of a local celebrity. At least Kenneth can brighten my mornings by looking more solemn and careworn than me.

And now, here I am on my last day, and not one of my old chums is here to say goodbye. No one, save Mr Freebie, whom I catch striding briskly past as I'm towelling myself dry.

'Hello there!' I say.

'Awright? How's the book going?' he says.

'Don't ask. Hey, you know it's my last day?'

'Hollywood beckons?'

'Soho, actually. Where is everyone today?'

'Who was you looking for?'

'Uh, the pensioners. Bob and his mates.'

'Frightened off by the crowds, I should think.'

'And the girl at the cash desk. Darkish skin?'

'Cath? She went to Britannia Leisure.'

'And Kenneth?'

'Oh. Didn't you know?'

'Know what?'

'He died.'

'No!'

'Must have been two weeks ago, now. Car accident.'

'Nice Kenneth? Black guy? Starched white shirts? Always reading long novels?'

'That's him. Friend of yours, was he?'

'Yeah. Sort of. I mean ... Oh, I dunno. It's just a bit strange, you know, when people you know just vanish off the face of the earth like that. Without any warning.'

'Happens to us all in the end, I s'pose.'

'Well, quite. That's the problem.'

On the way home I compose a letter to Kenneth's widow, explaining that though I scarcely knew her husband, I valued our morning chats and will miss him hugely. I imagine her smiling through her tears at the kindly stranger's touching gesture. Which makes me come over all misty-eyed myself.

Not, it must be said, that I've needed much excuse to come over all misty-eyed in the period since Sam dumped me. But I'll spare you the mawkish details. Suffice to say that Friday nights, when Sam and I used to veg in front of the TV with a large spliff, have been hell; and Sunday mornings even worse; that our favourite hang-outs have been turned into emotional no-go areas; and that there have been bouts of weepiness. Most of these, of course, have been self-induced, by playing one of the records to which Sam and I would smooch when first we met. Scott Walker singing 'If You Go Away'; virtually anything else by Jacques Brel; the first Tindersticks album, especially 'Jism'; Nick Cave's 'Let Love In'; The Afghan Whigs' 'Gentlemen', and so on. You get the idea. You know how it feels to be chucked.

It's not that I'm a heartless bastard or anything. I really am cut up about Sam. It's just that there's only so much time left and I'd prefer to save it for the trivia, the absurdities, the quirks that people never really talk about. Because these are things that interest me. Take the death of Kenneth. Why would anyone bother to write about the random, meaningless death of a swimming-pool attendant they scarcely knew. What would be the point? Who'd give a shit?

I suppose one option would be to make the reader give a shit by building him up a bit more. Perhaps I could make him more colourful and eccentric, like one of Dickens's walk-on grotesques. He could be, say, an incredibly brilliant professor of sociology who's only pretending to be a swimming-pool attendant in order to study – I don't know – 'Sexism, Racism, Ageism and Class Warfare as Evinced by the Natational Behaviour of Swimmers in the North East London Region'.

Alternatively, I could keep him pretty much as he was in real life, but invest our relationship with greater significance. I could quote far more of our matutinal dialogue than that snippet about the 'Save Our Sharks' poster I gave you at the beginning. I could turn him into a touchstone of rough-hewn wisdom, like the news-sellers you often find in movies set in New York. I could make out that his touching remark about the quality of my spoken English was the only thing that kept me from committing suicide. And then – move over, Little Nell – I could turn his death and its aftermath into one of the novel's great setpieces, concluding with the heartrending scene where my character gets to meet Kenneth's widow and she thanks me for my kindness.

But it wouldn't be true. Especially not the last bit because – and I do feel bad about this – I never get round to writing that moving letter. I've too many other things to do: bags to pack, editors to phone so I can give them my temporary number at Repton's, coffee to make, fags to smoke, my date with Martha to look forward to.

Ah yes. My date with Martha. You didn't know about that. But let's not get too excited. It's bound to be a complete disaster. Whatever Repton might choose to believe.

Repton, you see, is absolutely convinced that Martha and I are made for one another. Always have been, he claims extravagantly. Why else would he have suggested that she offer a home to Black Cat. There was a time when I might have agreed with him. But that was when I was going out with Sam: you always want the thing you cannot have.

Now that I'm single I'm not so sure. Martha the potential new girlfriend is an altogether scarier proposition than Martha the unattainable fantasy figure.

'I mean what, besides sharks and a shared love of a certain magnificent black feline, do we have in common?' I ask Repton when he first raises the Martha issue. It's a few days after my return from the Red Sea disaster holiday and I've gone round to his place for a consolatory drink and smoke.

'Apart from the fact that she's a girl who looks like a boy and she's totally, totally made for you, you mean?'

'*Repton.* I've only just split up with Sam.'

'So?'

'So she was only the girl of my dreams and the most gorgeous babe I'll ever pull in a million years. And now I've lost her.'

'So find someone else. Someone with brains, a sense of humour, personality . . .'

'Yeah, right, because Sam doesn't have any of those.'

'I didn't say that.'

'You always hated her, didn't you?'

'I've always thought Sam charming, funny, attractive –'

'Liar.'

' – But completely the wrong person for you.'

I stare miserably at the floor.

'I see,' I murmur.

'No you don't,' says Repton.

'You're bloody right I don't. And you're going to regret that remark if Sam and I get back together.'

'Do you think that's a possibility?'

'Maybe.'

'Well, good luck to you.'

'God, you really do hate her.'

'I don't. I just think you could do better.'

'Better than Sam? Who do you know who's better looking than Sam?'

'Looks aren't everything.'

'Oh, that's right. Because I always see *you* going out with boys over twenty-one who are really ugly but have bags of personality.'

'I'm a lost cause. It's why I'm so keen that you shouldn't follow my example,' he says.

'Shagging a succession of brainless young models? Sounds a pretty good example to me,' I say.

'I'd give it all up tomorrow for the right person.'

'Why don't you go out with Martha, then. If she's really so bloody wonderful.'

'Fine. I won't mention her again,' he says.

'No, go on. What's so special about her?' I say.

'You've met her. You tell me.'

'I'm not doing your job for you.'

'Yes, but the problem is, I know her so well I've forgotten what it is I like about her. Maybe you can remind me. Here. Grab some inspiration.'

Repton passes me the joint and another bottle of Budvar.

'A Fish Out Of Water,' I say, after a few contemplative puffs. 'She knows about that. And she knows about seventies black and white children's TV series. Like *Belle and Sebastian*. Sam thinks that's just the name of a band. Too young to remember the original. But Martha ... how old is she anyway?'

'Older than you think.'

'How old?'

'What does it matter? The point is she remembers classic seventies children's TV.'

'Right. And she knows other cool stuff as well. Like that it was the Andaman Islands where all those Japanese soldiers got eaten by the estuarine crocodiles. And that sharks follow big boats into harbours. Important stuff. Stuff that chicks aren't usually interested in. In fact, come to think of it, she isn't really a girl at all, is she? She's a bloke in disguise.'

'Would that she were.'

'You have evidence to the contrary?'

'I've seen her kit-free, if that's what you're asking.'

'Shame on you, Repton. When?'

'I'm an honorary girl. There are no secrets between us.'

'And?'

'Nice body. Very nice body.'

'You're just saying that.'

'You seem very interested all of a sudden.'

'Well, it cannot be denied. A girl who looks like a boy, thinks like a boy, and has the lithe body of a gorgeous female is not the sort of girl you kick out of bed if she farts.'

'Oh, she does fart. And very smelly they can be.'

'I thought you were meant to be giving me the hard sell.'

'You're doing a good enough job yourself.'

'God, you're a devious bastard.'

'Moi?'

So that's how we leave it. Repton a good deal more excited about it than I am. But I've got to admit that as the appointed evening has drawn closer, I've started thinking about it more and more. This might not be unconnected with my failure to make contact with any other remotely eligible female, let alone score, in the last few weeks. But I can't help wondering whether perhaps Repton mightn't have a point. Perhaps Martha really is the girl for me. And if she isn't, well, there's always the possibility that we can have at least one experimental bout of meaningless sex before we decide that we're better off staying just good friends.

Until then, though, we've got a day of horrifying logistics to get through. So let's not dwell on gorgeous gamine Martha with her half-parted lips and her thighs moist with antici-pation and—

All right. No more. I promise. There is work to be done. There are phone calls to make. One of them is to the editor who commissioned my piece on diving in the Red Sea. She is running it this weekend.

'Any queries?' I ask.

'Don't think so,' she says.

I knew that already. If there had been any queries, she'd have rung and asked, wouldn't she? What I actually wanted to know was 'Was my piece brilliant? Or was it brilliant?'

'Oh,' I say. 'So it was all OK, then?'

'Fine,' she says.

Fine? *Fine?* God I hate it when editors tell me my pieces are fine!

'We've got another piece lined up for you, if you're interested,' she adds.

'Yeah, sure.' I try not to sound too enthusiastic, lest she think I'm desperate. Of all journalistic gigs, travel commissions are the most difficult to secure. Every hack in Christendom likes a nice, fat, juicy, all-exes-paid trip abroad, after all.

'Have you been to South Africa before?'

'No. But I think I can handle it.'

'I think you can too. It's right up your street. A week in Capetown. Another in Durban. But it's only the first bit we're interested in. You'll be travelling to Dyer Island, a couple of hours outside Capetown. What we'll need is a 1500-word colour piece on what it's like diving with great white sharks.'

'Uh. Sorry?'

'You'll be in a cage, of course.'

'Mm. Sure. But, um – are you sure I'm quite the right person for the job? You know, after what I said in my piece.'

'Remind me.'

'The bit where I said that I'm terrified of sharks, that I almost died of fright and that I never want to go diving ever again.'

'That wasn't journalistic licence?'

'No.'

'Ah. Don't suppose you can think of anyone who might be interested?'

'Great whites do have this unfortunate reputation.'

213

'Tell me about it. I wasn't going to mention this but did you see that documentary the other night where the great white actually broke into the diver's cage?'

'No. But hey. Come to think of it, I can think of someone stupid enough to do it. He's a novelist mainly. But he still does a bit of journalism . . .'

Now before you start accusing me of attempted murder, let me say this in my defence: anyone who professes to be as unafraid of sharks as Tom Bland deserves everything they get. In any case, Tom thinks I've done him a huge favour, as he tells me half an hour later.

'I didn't know you cared,' he says.

'I don't. I want you to die because I'm jealous of your vast sexual and literary success.'

Tom laughs uncertainly. Am I deploying that baffling thing called irony, he wonders.

'I shouldn't be,' he says.

He sounds down. My heart leaps.

'But you're doing so well,' I say, all innocence. 'The book. That lovely Scottish girl whatsername.'

'Nadine. And it's all over.'

'You got bored?'

'No. She did.'

'Makes a change.'

'I know.'

'Never mind. There's plenty more where she came from.'

'Are there?'

'God, you are in a bad way.'

'Mm. I am rather. I thought that she was the one, you see.'

'Bloody hell, Tom. What's got into you?'

'I don't know. Is it an age thing, perhaps? Or – I know the book hasn't exactly helped.'

'Oh come on. Everyone gets one bad review,' I say.

'There was rather more than one,' he says.

(Yes! *Yes!*)

'Well, hey. What do they know?' I say.

'You read it then?'

'I keep meaning to.'

'I shouldn't bother.'

'Tom, this is terrible' – No it's not. It's absolutely bloody brilliant. Now I remember why it is that I like you – 'Let's meet up soon and we can have a proper wallow. You heard about—?'

'Mm. Sorry,' he says. 'Meant to ask how you were.'

'Oh, you know,' I say. 'Pretty shit.'

'Fun evening we're going to have. How about tonight?'

'Can't. I'm seeing Repton.'

'I'm sure he won't mind,' he says.

ALERT! ALERT! NUCLEAR WARNING SIRENS! DATE IN JEOPARDY. DATE IN JEOPARDY!

'I don't know. There's some boring friend of his I've got to meet.'

'Male or female?'

'Oh, Tom, really! How're you fixed for the rest of the week?'

'Choc-a-block, I'm afraid.'

'Oh well. Give me a call when you're free, eh?'

'Sure. Oh. And thanks again for the shark mission.'

'The pleasure's all mine.'

Perhaps God isn't a giant bumblebee, after all, for when I arrive an hour early for my evening rendezvous, the streets

of Soho are sparkling gold and every pretty girl that passes
my chair outside the Bar Italia says, 'Christ, I fancy you. And
by the way I swallow.'

They don't say this literally, of course. They don't even
say it figuratively, if truth be told. But I can see it in their
body language: the way, instead of stiffening when they cross
my stare-line, they give me a half-look, sometimes even a
half-smile, of 'Don't think I've noticed you because I haven't.
I really haven't' acknowledgement.

I don't think I'm imagining it either. You know how
some days you feel good-looking and some days you don't,
even though no one else can ever tell the difference? Well,
today, I'm feeling good-looking.

Not too good-looking, though. I'm not one of those
Bland-style wankers who thinks that every girl that passes is
his, as of right. But nor, on the other hand, am I one of
those saddoes who believes that even the most houndsome
of hounds is out of his league. I'm somewhere in the middle
– the golden mean – the perfect place to be on a warm
spring evening when the sap is rising and all the beautiful
girls of London have started to shed their winter coats.

By the time I've finished my second cappuccino (decaf,
if I drink real coffee after 4 p.m. I can't sleep), I must have
counted a good thirty viable one-night stands, ten potential
long-term relationships and at least half a dozen loves-of-
my-life. So many and varied are the possibilities that I feel
almost grateful to Sam for having chucked me. I'm a free
man once more. The sensual world is my lobster.

And being single in your thirties is much more exciting
than it is in your teens or twenties. Your tastes have grown
so much broader. The younger you are, the fewer women

you consider worthy of your attention. Not only do you dismiss anything over thirty as old enough to be your grandmother, but you're that much more picky about the girls within your age group: a funny accent, a dodgy haircut, an uncool item of clothing, the smallest imperfection can set your alarm bells ringing.

By the time you've hit thirty, however, your spectrum has broadened quite considerably. You remain a connoisseur of nubile young flesh – everything from 16-year-old Bambis fresh from the womb to 22-year-old sweeties who think they're so mature and sophisticated because they've been to university. And it scarcely matters how good-looking they are. Their very youth is an aphrodisiac. But no more so than the fecund charms of the older woman, whose ripe allure, bruised beauty, knowledge and experience – you now appreciate – are every bit the match of the baby-faced, lithe-limbed, silky-skinned teenager or the pouting, twentysomething missy.

The irony is, of course, that by the time you're old enough to appreciate the ineffable shaggability of almost every woman in the world, you've invariably gone and narrowed your options by getting hitched to just one of them.

But not me. I'm one of the lucky ones. I'm free.

Almost. There is, of course, that small matter of my date with Martha. Or rather, my drink with Repton and Martha which could turn into a date if Repton decides that things are going well enough for him to leave us alone. If not, well, there's always alcohol and drugs, I suppose.

The important thing is not to look too desperate. Women find it very off-putting. But at the same time, I mustn't look as if I don't give a damn. Otherwise, she'll think I'm just a casual philanderer trying to notch off another easy kill on the side of my Spitfire.

So here's the plan. I will arrive fifteen minutes late, signalling that I am a busy man whose life is not dominated by his urge to get laid. But I will come bearing a carefully chosen gift, indicating that despite my hectic schedule, I can still find time to be sensitive and thoughtful.

What to bring?

Not scent obviously. Too forward.

Not flowers, either. Too obvious.

A book perhaps? Too easy to get wrong.

A CD then? Bingo. I'll get her that Bentley Rhythm Ace album she seemed to like at my dinner party.

Instead of paying full whack for the album at Tower Records in Piccadilly, I decide to look for a second-hand copy at Vinyl Frontier off Wardour Street. This is partly because I am constitutionally incapable of shelling out £15 for a product I normally get for free, and partly because spending that much money on a girl you scarcely know is tantamount to telling her, 'Right. You owe me a shag.'

Or maybe I'm just a tightfisted bastard. Anyway, the CDs in Vinyl Frontier are often in as good condition as the ones you buy new anywhere else. A lot of their stock comes from reviewers who've sold on their freebies after one listen. I don't sell any of my CDs there, though. The staff are too scary and rude.

True to form, the grim beardie behind the counter affects not to notice my entrance. He pretends to be sorting and cataloguing the huge pile of CDs in front of him and refuses to catch my eye, even when I clear my throat noisily.

'Um, Bentley Rhythm Ace?' I say at last.

'Who?' says beardie.

'Dance,' I explain.

Beardie gives me a disgusted look and gestures towards the basement stairwell.

Downstairs, behind another counter, a creature about my age with lank hair and bad skin, is listening to some unlistenable electronica.

'Bentley Rhythm Ace?' I say brightly.

'If it's here, it'll be there,' he says, pointing to a revolving CD rack.

It is there. In OK condition and priced at only £6.

'Excellent,' I say.

'No it's not,' says the creature.

Ten, fifteen years ago, I would have been quite intimidated by this remark. I might have said something like 'Oh. Isn't it? What would you recommend instead?' Or I might have gone ahead and bought it but never played it – not ever – because The Man In The Record Shop had decreed that it was no good. And I would have wanted to slit my wrists because I would have known for absolute certain that I was horribly uncool and that I had really crappy taste in music and that it had been an act of quite unspeakable impertinence for me even to have dreamt of dragging my wretched carcass into this prestigious emporium in the first place.

But this is one of the advantages of getting old. There comes a point when you realize 'I don't need to take this shit.'

Nor do I. Having paid for the CD, I look lank-hair directly in the eyes and say, 'Listen, tosser. I came here to buy a record, not to hear you tell me whether or not it's any good. That's my job. I'm a record critic. I earn at least four times as much as you. I get sacks and sacks of free CDs every week. I'm read by up to a million people every Friday. You, on the other hand, are just a shop assistant. You are nothing. No one cares a flying fuck what you think. And if they do, they're an even sadder wanker than you. If that's possible, which I very much doubt, you sad, sad, sad, pathetic, snivelling insignificant piece of stale toss.'

No I don't. But I feel much better for having thought it.

'Thanks,' I say to lank hair, smiling sweetly. 'Thanks. Bye,' I say to miserable git upstairs. I walk down Old Compton Street, past the gay pub to which Repton has sometimes taken me for that authentic straight-man-in-homosexual-haunt-clenched-buttock experience, towards Soho House and my rendezvous with Martha.

I've nothing against Soho House in particular. Just trendy London drinking clubs in general. They make me nervous.

When I ring the buzzer I feel about as welcome as a leper on a Paris catwalk. 'Who?'

I used to think that the reason I felt so insecure in these establishments was that I wasn't a member. Then I joined one. And still the icy, power-chick receptionists treated me as though I were an impostor. 'No, I am a member. Really I am,' I wanted to insist as I signed myself in. As I entered the bar, a dozen pairs of eyes would flicker towards me, suss that I didn't count, and look away. The barmen never recognized me. I would never belong. I resigned after a year.

Upstairs, a not-too-scary girl behind a counter directs me through the labyrinth. I take a wrong turning up a small staircase leading to the Gents. I retrace my steps and find myself in a half-empty bar. I try again. Third time lucky. Martha is sitting at a corner table, engrossed in conversation with someone whose back is turned to me. A table-hopping acquaintance, I hope. If it's Repton, I'll kill him. The whole bloody point of the evening was that he should arrive a good hour after me, so that Martha and I could have some time to ourselves.

I'm halfway across the room, tingling with anticipation and Martha still hasn't seen me. Perhaps it's just lust but she looks a lot prettier than I remembered. Maybe she's got one of those faces that appreciates with time. Maybe it's the spring air. Maybe, who knows, maybe she has been looking forward to this evening as much as I have. Maybe—

No!

The person she's talking to. It's Tom Bland. Tom fucking bastard fucking Bland!

And I would turn around and leave right now – that would show her! the tart! – except that she has chosen this very moment to notice me. She's smiling. And – though I really haven't a clue how my facial muscles have managed it – I'm smiling back. A thin Heinrich Himmler smile.

I'm trembling. All the blood has drained to my feet. Affecting not to notice Tom, I kiss Martha on both cheeks.

'Hey! Good to see you.'

'Yeah!' she says, with an emphasis I might have found deliriously promising had it not been for Tom's lurking presence.

'Here. Present for you.'

Martha studies the CD cover.

'Thanks. Thanks a lot. Do I like these people?'

'That was the idea. Yes. You heard them at dinner, remember?'

'Wow! I am popular tonight,' says Martha. She gives the CD one more look and then slips it the handbag at her feet.

Next to it is a bouquet of painfully expensive-looking flowers.

'Aren't you going to say hello?' says Tom.

'Eh?' I do a very unconvincing double take. 'Tom! This is a surprise. I thought—'

'Don't worry. I okayed it with Repton.'

'Oh. Well, that's all right then.' Not too much sarcasm. Just enough to let him get the message.

Which of course, Tom being Tom, he still doesn't.

'Just some boring friend of Repton's, you told me,' he says, nodding, with a slimy grin, towards Martha.

'I did? Oh. I must have got my dates muddled. I mean . . . not date as in date . . . but. Oh, fuck it. I think I need a drink. What're you having, Martha?'

'I'm all right for the moment, thanks.'

'Tom?'

'Another lager. Thanks.'

And maybe it is a little childish of me to gob discreetly into my palm and slip the spit into Tom's lager froth. But after what follows, I have no regrets.

'Cigarette?' I ask Martha.

'I've already offered,' says Tom. 'She's trying to give up.'

'Really?' I say.

'Really,' says Martha.

'Not even a rollie?'

'We-ell,' says Martha. She's blushing.

'If she wants to give up, let her give up. It's the first few days that are the worst. Isn't that right, Martha?'

'Uh, yes,' she says. She blinks at me. 'Sorry.'

Time for opening gambit number two.

'Oh, by the way. I've been dying to tell you. I've got my shark story.'

'Here we go,' sighs Tom.

'Excuse me but Martha likes shark stories.'

'Yes, but two in a row?'

'Tom's been telling me about his great white expedition,' Martha explains.

'Oh well,' I sneer at Tom. 'Nothing I say is ever going to match your heroic journey into the jaws of White Death.'

'Go on, Joe,' says Martha.

'No, it's all right. I'll tell you some other time.'

'Please. I'm interested. And I'm sure Tom is too.'

'I was the first time I heard it,' says Tom.

'Fuck off, Tom.'

'Boys, boys. You're like a pair of sharks yourselves. Fighting over a plump seal.'

'I wouldn't call you plump,' says Tom. Another split second and I'd have thought that one up myself.

'Is that what it is? You're fighting over me?'

'Not at all,' I protest because frankly, this is getting far too embarrassing.

'Liar,' says Tom because, frankly, he's an unscrupulous, self-serving shit.

'Seriously though,' says Martha, after a good gulp of her gin, 'how are we going to find you two lonely hearts the love of a good woman?'

'Ask me that at breakfast,' says Tom, giving Martha his most soulful gaze.

'I think I will have that cigarette after all,' says Martha. 'Would you mind?'

'My pleasure.'

I roll Martha the neatest, most uniformly cylindrical, smooth-drawing, life-enhancing Virginia cigarette since Walter Raleigh. A small victory but not, I fear, a decisive one.

223

Martha takes a long, orgasmic drag.

'You're right,' says Tom, 'smoking suits you.'

Martha looks at Tom, flushed, then turns to me. 'Is he always like this?' she asks.

'Unfortunately,' I say. In my agitation, I elbow my lighter off the table. As I bend down to pick it up, I notice that Tom's leg is pressed against Martha's. She pulls hers away, guiltily.

'So what's the plan for this evening?' asks Tom.

'Not sure,' says Martha. 'Repton was pretty vague. Any idea, Joe?'

'No.'

'Well, I'm starving,' says Martha.

'Me too,' says Tom.

I suppose I'm meant to say 'me too' but I don't and there's a long, gratifying silence.

After an eternity, several anxious glances in my direction and two more rounds of drinks, neither of which Tom pays for, Repton arrives flaunting the number of a 'peach of a boy' he's just met in Comptons. The gin I have been drinking to enhance my despondency has worked its magic. Or perhaps it's just the effect of having endured Tom playing for the sympathy vote by bemoaning the failure of his book and then having seen, on my next lighter-retrieval expedition, that he is now resting a hand on Martha's knee. Whatever, I have now grown monosyllabic and suicidal.

So when Repton proposes dinner, I murmur that, if it's all the same with everyone, I'll be heading home. I'm feeling a bit tired and I've got a headache and – Oh, you know.

'But we've only just started,' says Tom.

'Yes. You can't go yet,' says Martha, with less conviction than I might have liked.

'You sure?' says Repton, with a meaningful look. He understands.

'I'm sure.'

And the streets of Soho are swarming with Friday night revellers and couples all blissfully in love. Even the beggars are having fun. And I slink towards Repton's flat, bathed in a Ready Brek glow of suicidal misery, hating Tom, hating Martha, hating Repton, hating myself, hating the whole evil world. I slump on Repton's sofa and stare at the TV, not bothering to turn it on. Then I rifle through his drawers until I find his stash of dope, roll a terrifying spliff, smoke myself stupid and watch *Father Ted*, *Frasier*, *King of the Hill* and the *Adam and Joe Show* without finding any of them funny. Then I watch *TFI Friday* and I hate Chris Evans. Then Repton comes home, with booze on his breath, takes a drag from the spliff stub in the ashtray, sits next to me and drapes an arm around my shoulder.

'Sorry, mate,' he says.

'So?'

'What could I say? He rings me up sounding so sorry for himself. You know what Tom's like when he's feeling sorry for himself.'

'And?'

'Oh, you know. We had a few more drinks. Ate at the club. Got wrecked. And here I am.'

'And did they, er—?'

'Shared a cab home but I don't think that means anything. They were both heading the same way.'

'Repton, I'm not an imbecile. You saw them together. You know Tom.'

'I do.'

'They're probably doing it now.'

'You need another spliff.'

'I'll bet it's all stringy and warty. And dripping with gonorrhoea. And herpes and AIDs. And Ebola, probably.'

'Poor girl.'

'No more than the bitch deserves.'

'Do you think so?'

'Oh, Repton. I don't know. I really don't know. I just thought – ' if I'm not careful, I think I'm going to cry ' – she was more intelligent than that.'

'She's confused, that's all. Being single for so long and then having two men fighting over you like that.'

'But why *him*?'

'Sartorial elegance? Raffish style?'

'Yeah. Right. God, though, you should have heard some of the crap he was coming up with. "Smoking suits you." "You have eyes like a young gazelle—"'

'He never said that?'

'Almost. I mean is that what women really want?'

'You're asking the wrong man.'

''Cos if it is then I'm fucked. Seriously, I am. I just can't do that sort of bullshit. It's so tacky. So embarrassing. If that's really what Martha's after, then I'm well rid of her.'

'So you are.'

'Except—'

'Smoke?'

'Cheers. Except – ' I'm shaking my head and trying to inhale before the tears come. But it doesn't work. Not even Repton's grass, Repton's elephant-slaying, mind-destroying killer weed, is enough to hold them back. ' – Except I thought she really did like me!' I sob.

Repton hugs me tight and the tears flow.

BRONZE WHALER

As every schoolboy knows, the most famous shark victim of all time is Rodney Fox, the Australian spear fisherman savaged off Adelaide in 1963. This is largely thanks to the marvellously gory pictures of his injuries, reprinted in every shark book ever. One photograph shows his eighty-seven stitches, extending in a curved bite shape all the way from his left upper arm to his belly button. The other, taken before the stitches, shows his exposed, glistening guts. It looks like an open tin of Pedigree Chum dogfood.

It was done by a bronze whaler.

CHAPTER EIGHT

It has just gone 8 a.m. Obscenely early but I can't sleep and I won't let Repton either. I've lured him out of bed with a couple of Pat Val croissants, a Bar Italia cappuccino and a pale blue box of B&H Cairo from his deep-freeze. Now we're sitting on his roof terrace in the sun. Repton, dressed like the enormous queen he is in a Noël Coward style silk dressing gown, is doing his best to console me.

'And she's old,' he says.

'You said it didn't matter,' I say.

'Wait until you know how old she is,' he says.

'Thirty? Thirty-two?'

'Thirty-seven,' he says.

'She only looks thirty.'

'You're not being very helpful.'

'Sorry. She's a raddled old crone.'

'A raddled, gangrenous, leprous old crone. Who does very smelly farts.'

'God. I hope you don't talk this way about me behind my back,' I say.

'Do you want me to help or not?' he says.

'OK, she's old, ugly and leprous,' I say without conviction.

'And you know she spent five years living with a smack addict.'

'No.'

'There you are, you see. You know nothing about her. For all you know she could be heavily into country and western.'

'I like Johnny Cash.'

'Line dancing, even.'

'The coming thing, I'm told.'

'Pig fucking—'

'So she likes a bit of sexual adventure.'

'Face it, Joe. You're on the rebound. You're just in love with the idea of being in love. The Martha you think you know has nothing to do with the one that actually exists.'

'Then why, pray, Cunt Face, did you spend so much time trying to persuade me that she was my perfect match?'

'Because, Anal Cleft, I'm an arsing romantic, is why. Because I never quite realized what a heartless, evil bitch she is.'

'Do you reckon?'

'No. What she is is a nice girl who's got lousy taste in men.'

'What was the smack addict like?'

'Charmer. Absolute charmer. Especially when he was on smack.'

'So you can hardly blame her. All the cool girls go out with smack addicts.'

'I'm not blaming her. I'm just saying she's got seriously dodgy taste. As witness—'

'We still don't know that they did anything.'

'Come on. You know Tom.'

'That's not what you said last night.'

'Perhaps I was being unduly optimistic.'

'P'raps you weren't.'

'Let's give her a ring and find out, shall we?'

'No!' I shriek, diving for my tobacco.

Repton smiles triumphantly and sets about another croissant.

'So what I propose,' he says, after a few mouthfuls, 'is that we roll ourselves a small, post-breakfast sharpener; cruise on down to the market to procure ourselves some dinner; pause outside the Bar Italia to admire the local flora and fauna; grab a bite to eat at – where? – the Ivy perhaps? And then cast our minds towards the evening's clubbing which was so cruelly denied me yesterday thanks to my misguided attempts to engender a romantic liaison between the two friends I now recognize are hopelessly incompatible. How does that sound?'

'Jesus!'

'A little tame, perhaps?'

'God, no. I was just thinking. Is that what it's like being gay?'

'On a dull day.'

'Blimey. If I'd known what I'd been missing all these years . . .'

'Babe. You ain't seen nothin' yet,' he says, eyeing me sceptically. 'But if you are going to accompany me as I trawl my manor, might I suggest that you remove those awful eighties jeans and that terrible baggy T-shirt and slip into something a little less comfortable.'

Shat, showered, shaved, blunted and ready to begin my thrilling new existence as a single man in Soho, I'm suddenly gripped by a niggling stoner 'what if' which just won't go away.

'Er, Repton,' I say. 'Do you think maybe we shouldn't try giving her a ring? Just in case.'

'Absolutely,' he says. 'We most definitely shouldn't try giving her a ring.'

I scowl.

'Just make it quick. Her number's in the book by my bed.'

'Can't you do it for me?'

Repton sighs. 'And say what exactly? "Hi, Martha. It's only me. Just calling to ask whether or not you shagged Tom Bland last night"?'

'You needn't put it quite like that.'

'I'll do it on one condition. We don't hear another word about Martha for at least the next decade. Promise?'

'Promise.'

While Repton dials, I bury my head under his duvet.

'It's ringing,' Repton calls out. 'Still ringing . . . still ringing . . . nope. Just the answer machine.'

I pop my head out. 'Maybe she's asleep.'

'Do you want me to try Tom's?'

'No!'

'Do you want to know or don't you?'

'Go on then.'

This time I scuttle out into Repton's sitting room and shut the door behind me. 'Please! Please!' I whisper to myself, both fingers crossed, barely able to breathe. I wish I hadn't smoked that joint.

Decades later, Repton pokes his head round the door.

'Do you want the bad news or the bad news?' he says.

'Oh shit.'

'Answer machine.'

'Is that bad news?'

'Definitely. No one ever fails to pick up the phone at 9.30 in the morning unless they're shagging.'

'Or asleep.'

'Tom has his phone right by his bed.'

'So he's a heavy sleeper.'

'Joe. I kept my side of the bargain. Now you keep yours.'

We lock the door behind us. And I know that however magnificent the flora and fauna outside the Bar Italia, however delicious our lunch at the Ivy, however strong tonight's drugs, however banging the techno, I'm still not going to appreciate any of it one jot. My life is in ruins.

Halfway down the stairs, we hear a muffled ringing from the Repton's flat.

'I'm not in,' says Repton.

'But it might be—'

'You promised.'

'Please!'

Laboriously, Repton works his way through the multiple locks on his door.

He picks up the phone.

'Oh. Hi,' he says. It can't be who I hope it is because, though he's smiling, he's not looking at me and making thumbs-up signals. He's just staring at the floor.

'Ah,' he says. 'I like to be mysterious.'

It's his peach of a boy. Must be.

'1471. Yes. Hadn't thought of that.'

Unless. No. It's Tom. It's got to be Tom.

'So anyway, you got back OK last night?'

That's a question you ask girls. Not boys.

'No reason. Just . . . Did he now? Did he?'

Oh fuck.

'No? *No?* You've got to be joking. *Leopard-print poser pouch?* What a player!'

Oh no. Oh no, no, no, no, no!

'Five inches? And that's optimistic? Well, well, well. I know someone who'll be pleased.'

Repton beckons me over. 'No way!' I gesture.

'Oh. Just someone. But listen, I think Joe wants a word

with you . . . Not sure. Better ask him yourself . . . Joe? *Joe?* . . .
He seems to have run away . . . *Joe?* Ah. Here is . . . Ow! *Ow!*
He's hitting me, Martha. Don't trust him, Martha! He's a
rabid, frenzied beast!'

I'm staring into the Thames, wondering what my chances
would be of surviving if I dived in for a bet, when I feel a
light tap on my arm.

'Seen any fins?' asks Martha.

'Hundreds.'

'Bull sharks, I expect. You know they once found one
over a thousand miles up the Mississippi?'

'You, Martha, are a sad, sad case.'

She smiles wickedly. 'And you are a rabid, frenzied beast
who's not to be trusted.'

'But you won't find me in a leopard-print poser pouch.'

Martha's smile vanishes. 'Oh,' she says unhappily, 'you
heard.'

'Sorry. Wasn't I meant to?'

'I did promise Tom I wouldn't tell anyone. He was
terribly embarrassed. And I suppose it was all partly my
fault.'

I'd love to enquire further but I sense that I've done
enough damage. Bloody Tom Bland! Even when he's not
there, even when I invoke his name to act as a foil to my
own sweet-natured wondrousness, the bastard still manages
to mess things up for me!

'Anyway,' I say, 'you're here, that's the main thing.'

I haven't given her a greeting kiss yet, so maybe I should
now. But as I'm lurching forward, Martha looks away. I try
pulling out but the momentum carries me forward. A split

second before impact, Martha turns back – startled – and my lips smash into the bottom of her chin.

'Oh,' she says, proffering her other cheek.

But I'm so busy being squirmy and mortified that I don't notice until it's too late. Martha now has to pretend that she wasn't really expecting a second kiss. She was just turning away to look at something.

'Hadn't we better go in?' says Martha, slightly flushed.

'Oh yes. Right. What time did you say you had to meet that friend?'

'Lunchtime – ish.'

This isn't going to work, I can tell already. At least not according to the fevered 'let's skip the sharks and head straight to my place' fantasy gameplan I'd devised for us both on my cab journey down to Waterloo. Her lunchtime engagement is almost certainly a convenient fictional get-out, and even if it weren't, it's perfectly obvious that we're physically incompatible.

I suppose I should be disappointed. Instead, as we saunter side by side towards the aquarium entrance, I feel a surge of relief. Elation almost. No need to feel gawky or self-conscious any more. No need to worry about saying the right thing, nor to agonize about when to make the next move. No need to analyse her every word and gesture, like some Kremlinographer trying to decipher her coded hints as to whether or not she really fancies me. We're doomed to end up as good friends. Just good friends.

We've picked a bad time to visit the aquarium. It's crowded, close and very noisy. The aisles are blocked by pushchairs and the view to every tank is obscured by doting parents, pressing their young offspring against the glass and

cooing, 'Look at the fishy, darling. Isn't he pretty?' Not that
Martha and I are unduly bothered. We're only here to see
one thing, really. Two shark junkies craving their horror fix
of jaws and fins. I'm all for heading there straightaway.

'We can't,' insists Martha.

'Why not?'

'It would be like sex without the foreplay.' Which she
definitely wouldn't have said, I'm sure, if she'd meant our
outing to be anything other than platonic.

Then again ... There's a moment when we're standing
in front of a tank full of rocks and pipes, trying to decide
whether the electric eel that's supposed to be there really
exists, when Martha's bare arm brushes against mine. She
pulls it away quickly. But not before I've enjoyed a sensation
akin to – well – akin to being zapped by the creature in the
tank.

Just my imagination, I'm sure. But lest my libido tell me
otherwise, I hastily remind myself of the myriad reasons as
to why a relationship with Martha would never work. She's
old. She goes out with smack addicts and losers. She's not as
pretty as Sam. And she doesn't smoke dope. Yes. That's a
good one. She doesn't smoke dope!

Imagine! Going out with a girl who doesn't smoke dope!
It would be unbearable. How could you chill out? How could
you ever cope with the traumas of cold reality? And you'd
lie there, treating her to all the wondrous insights you'd just
gained into the meaning of life, the universe, Radiohead and
DJ Shadow and she'd look at you – dead straight – and go,
'You do talk an awful lot of rubbish.' Or worse, she'd try
and convert you. 'That stuff's doing you no good,' she'd say.
'You're edgy, you're paranoid, you can never get up in the
morning. Ever thought about laying off for a while?'

To which the honest answer would be 'Yes.' I think about giving up all the time. The problem is, I'm so screwed up by dope that I have to keep smoking the stuff in order to console myself for being so screwed up. So maybe a relationship with a straight person is exactly what I need. Maybe – Oh stop this at once, you pathetic, snivelling wretch! Dope is good. Dope is fun. And don't you dare let this prissy, straightlaced, boring old bag tell you otherwise.

There. Much better. She's wrong for you. You're wrong for her. And – ohmygod she's just gone and brushed my arm again and unless I'm very much mistaken which I'm not, I'm definitely not, she did it on purpose. Help!

'What are you thinking?' says Martha. Her teeth are blue, her skin green in the aquarium light. She's gorgeous.

'Oh, you know,' I say. 'Stuff.'

'Good stuff or bad stuff?'

'Uh, good. I think. How about you?'

'Good too.'

'Well, that's good, isn't it?'

'And it's going to get better.'

Wow!

'The rays,' she adds. 'And then the sharks.'

Oh. Them.

Actually, though, the rays and skates are brilliant. They're swishing around in a big, open pool and if you're really lucky they'll swim up to your fingers and let you stroke them.

'Just like little kittens,' I say.

'Ye-es,' Martha says. 'Apart from the fact that they're flat, they're scaly, they've got wings instead of legs, they live under the sea and—'

I pinch her. 'You know what I meant.'

'Here, kitty-kitty! Here, kitty-kitty!' Martha says to the rays.

A little girl looks at her curiously, giggles and whispers something to her mother.

'Here, kitty-kitty!' says Martha.

'Can't take you anywhere,' I say, dragging her by the wrist towards the next room. Which, being as it's the shark room, gives me the perfect excuse not to let go of her. Not that she seems to mind as I squeeze her hand tight for comfort.

'Urrgh!' I say with an involuntary shudder.

'Aaagh!' Martha agrees.

They're not maneaters exactly. Just harmless browns and sand tigers, no more than six or seven feet long. But they're still sharks, all right, with fins and teeth and stary eyes and sinister, sinuous torpedo-shaped bodies. And that's good enough for us.

The sand tigers look especially menacing. They swim with their mouths open, exposing their peculiarly evil-looking sharp, ragged teeth. I'm reminded of a revolting documentary called *Animal Cannibals* I saw once. It showed how young sand tigers start eating their siblings the moment they hatch in their mother's womb.

We gaze, entranced, for a while as the sharks make their leisurely, graceful circuit of the towering aquarium. I could stand like this for hours, half-mesmerized, half-horrified. But Martha, self-conscious suddenly, lets go of my hand. She presses her face and hands against the glass as a big shark glides by and then turns to me, pupils wide.

'You know what would be really cool?' she says.

'What?'

'Coming here when you're stoned.'

'But you don't smoke.'

'Don't I?'

'Well, I thought—'

'Right,' she says testily. 'You just assumed. Like you assumed that I'd be quite happy to drop everything at ten minutes' notice on a Saturday morning to come here with you.'

'Um—' Christ! What did I do to deserve this? 'Well, I'm glad you did anyway.'

After studying me fiercely for a second or two, Martha relaxes.

'Sorry,' she says, brushing a finger against the back of my hand. 'It's just that some people take too many things for granted.' And with that, she makes for the ramp which leads to the basement shark-viewing zone.

I choose not to follow immediately. She doesn't deserve it and anyway I need time to collect my thoughts. Is she blowing hot and cold in order to appear more alluring? Because she hasn't made up her mind? Because it's her time of the month? Because of something I said or didn't say? Because she's still upset by whatever it was that Tom Bland did? Because she's now realized that she wishes she'd let him do more of it? Because she has suddenly got the hots for that big, sexy sand tiger?

Incomprehensibility, thy name is woman.

What's so frustrating is that, for a while back there, I really thought I'd reached it: that ineffably wondrous point in a new relationship when you first know for certain that she likes you, you like her and that the only question that remains before you start banging each other's brains out is 'Your place or mine?'

Fat chance! For all I know, she might find me hideously

unattractive. I mean, what evidence do I have for thinking otherwise? Two occasions when she accidentally touched my arm and one brief moment of hand-holding when she got slightly scared of the sharks. Great! If only I'd listened to my own advice: steer well clear – she's old, she's boring, she's not as pretty as Sam, she doesn't smoke dope—

'Joe, come down here!' calls Martha from the ramp. 'You get a much better view.'

What sort of walk to adopt? Blithe unconcern or bolshie teenager?

I go for bolshie teenager. She notices.

'Disappointed?' she asks.

I study my footwear. 'A bit.'

'I know what you mean,' she says. 'It's always so much better in the imagination than it is in real life.'

'Mm.' Here it comes: the kiss-off. Chucked before it's even begun.

She takes my hand and slips something small and hard into my palm. A square of polythene-wrapped hash.

'Only if you want to,' she says.

'Do sharks have pointy teeth?' I reply.

Martha has devised a cunning plan. I skin up in the men's loos. We persuade a member of the aquarium staff that Martha badly needs some fresh air so would they mind bending the 'No re-entry' rule for the sake of a pregnant woman? Then we wander up and down the Thames-side walkway, steering clear of passers-by and close to the river, so as to disperse the tell-tale smoke in the breeze and to avoid undue attention. At last, our perceptions suitably enhanced and warped, we return, giggling, to the shark enclosure.

Yes, the snaggle-toothed denizens of the deep have

indeed grown spookier and more menacing. The water is bluer; the tank more strikingly deep and mysterious; the subterranean darkness more sensual and enveloping.

More importantly, though, I now have the perfect excuse for doing things that I might otherwise have found embarrassing. Like taking Martha's hand; and giving her hot palm a gentle stroke; and – no complaints yet – entwining my fingers in hers; and raising them gently to my lips—

'Oi.'

'Sorry!' I quickly release her hand. Suddenly twitchy, paranoid. We're being observed. The families, the scary straight people, they know we're stoned. They don't like us. We don't belong. Martha hates me. We've got to get out of here.

Martha's drawing her fingertips down my arm. She gives my hand a reassuring squeeze.

'No, you can,' she says. 'Just not here.'

'What happened?' Martha asks, mock-incredulous.

'Search me,' I reply. Though you'd scarcely need the deductive genius of Sherlock Holmes to work it out.

If you looked out of the bedroom window – bedroom, there's a big clue – towards the lawn, you'd see a rug and the remains of the picnic lunch we chose to eat in preference to dining in the West End.

'Much cheaper,' Martha said, though we both knew money wasn't the issue. 'And it would be a crime to eat indoors on a day like this,' I added, though for all I cared about the weather it could have been pissing down with rain. 'And we don't want to bump into Repton,' said Martha, as if there were the remotest possibility. 'And I'd love to see where you live,' I said. Though 'where you sleep' might have been nearer the truth. 'Not to mention Black Cat,' I add, as if right now I give the merest smidgeon of a toss.

So the 'picnic' we planned may have had big inverted commas round it but we went through the motions all the same: Ciabatta with olive oil, sun-dried tomatoes, smoked ham, three sorts of salami, and some deep, crumbly-based custard cakes picked up from the Café Lisboa on the way home. Almost all of it uneaten, of course.

We just weren't feeling very hungry, that was all. Anyway, it was far too hot to sit outside. Or was it too breezy? Whatever, it would definitely be more comfortable indoors and besides, hadn't Martha promised me a guided tour?

Kitchen. Yes, small, very kitchen-like, pots, pans, sink, oven, etc., etc. *Next*.

Sitting room. L-shaped. TV. Shelves. Books. Lots and lots of books. Probably worth a browse sometime but not now. Definitely not now. Armchair occupied by smug Black Cat completely uninterested in his old master. Crummy sofa which looks as if it would be pretty uncomfortable to sit on, let alone lie down on while she straddles you and—

Bathroom. Loo. Bath. Bit narrow and short for two people to share but who cares when you're sponging her back and soaping her breasts and—

Bedroom. Ulp! No, hang on. Desk in the corner. Word processor. Put-you-up. She doesn't sleep here. Which can only mean it's the other room. The place – aagh, help! help! – where we're going now.

Bedroom. Her actual bedroom. Wardrobe. Filled with *her* clothes. Clothes rail. Lined with *her* dresses. Drawers. Containing *her* underwear. Dresser. Mirror. Scent, lotions, powder, unguents. Mysterious feminine things. Bed.

Bed. A big double bed with a thick, rich, very white cotton cover. Pristine. Inviolate. Inviting.

Perch on the edge, maybe. She won't mind that. Pretend, you know, that you just want to feel how bouncy it is. Just like anyone would when visiting a stranger's bedroom. And maybe, just a quick lie-down. Stretch. Very comfortable.

'Very comfortable.'

'Do you think?'

And she's lying down next to you as if it's the first time she's ever considered the vexed question as to whether or not her bed's comfortable.

'Aaah!' she sighs.

'Aaah!' you agree, accidentally letting your arm drift towards hers. Leaving it there till you're absolutely sure she doesn't mind. Absent-mindedly slipping it towards the back of her head and caressing her hair gently. Lifting the strands and letting them fall. Stroking the nape of her neck until, enough.

You lunge.

You're pressing your mouth against hers. You're devouring her. She's devouring you. You want to lick every inch of her body and plunge your tongue into every orifice. You just can't get her clothes off quickly enough. You're fighting with her bra strap. She's wrestling with your shirt buttons, your belt, your fly and—

God this is brilliant. This is the best. You want it to go on forever and ever!

'*Examine if you will, Doctor Watson, the undergarments strewn across the floor with what appear to be an untoward abandon. Regard the flushed, naked bodies of both participants in this shameful act! And let me draw your attention to the patch, indubitably wet and sticky, at the centre of the bed. It is my firm conviction that this young man and woman have but recently enjoyed carnal knowledge of one another.'*

'I beg your pardon, Holmes?'

'To whit, Watson, they have been fucking each other senseless.'

'Cigarette,' I decide.

'Me too,' says Martha.

'You don't smoke,' I say.

'And I certainly don't sleep with people on the first date.'

'Don't you?'

'No!'

'I meant "don't you?" as in "I'm really flattered you made an exception."'

'So you should be.'

'Well, I am.'

We smoke our cigarettes. Delighted by how clever and rude and naughty we've been.

'I never thought you would, you know,' I say.

'I never thought *you* would.'

'What!'

'Well, you could have made more of an effort. Last night, for example.'

'Last night! You were all over Tom Bland!'

'I was not,' she says.

'You were too. Don't think I didn't notice all that business under the table.'

'What was I supposed to do?'

'Resist, I'd have thought,' I say.

'Maybe I would have done if you'd shown a bit more interest,' she says.

'You were trying to make me jealous?' I say.

'Maybe,' she says.

'If I'd known that . . .'

I plant a kiss on Martha's cheek.

She smiles prettily.

'So what did happen, anyway?' I ask.

'I can't tell you that.'

'Oh, go on.'

'It's embarrassing.'

'Why else would I be so eager to find out?'

'Then I'm definitely not telling.'

'All right. I'll guess. You're sharing a cab home. A bit tiddly. Completely gutted that the gorgeous, hunky man of your dreams has failed to pick up on any of the blatant signs you've given off that you fancy him rotten. Like, er, giving his arch-rival free rein to maul your upper thighs . . .'

'Pig!'

'So you're thinking, "If I can't have the best, then I suppose I'll have to make do with this Tom Bland bloke. He seems keen enough. Or is it just an accident that he's slipped his hand up my skirt."'

'He did not, you pig!' squeals Martha, quite amused.

'Bet at least you had a snog. Go on. Bet you anything you like.'

Martha reddens.

'You did! You actually exchanged saliva with Tom Bland! Do you have any idea where that tongue has – no. Best not to think of such things.'

'I was drunk.'

'And desperate.'

'Confused,' Martha corrects. 'I thought I was going to spend the evening – well, you know what I thought. And when you flounced off—'

'I did not flounce.'

'Mooch? Slink? Crawl?'

'So there you are. Tongues down each other's throats. When Tom prises himself away from your tonsils just long enough to gasp, "Fancy a coffee back at my place?"'

'Actually his exact words were, "I could invite you back for a coffee. But that's not what I want right now and I don't think it's what you want either."'

'And you said "yes" after that!'

'We all make mistakes. Look at what happened just now!'

We exchange self-congratulatory grins. God, if anyone were watching us now, I think they'd retch!

'And I knew it was a mistake too,' she says. 'As soon as I was out of the cab. I did actually try to get in again but Tom grabbed hold of my wrist and said, "It's OK. I won't do anything you don't want." And I was thinking, "Too right you won't," because by then I'd got the distinct impression that he was a right old perve.'

'And was he?'

'He started reasonably enough. Dimmed all the lights. Put on some music. Offered me a drink—'

'What was the music?'

'Spandau Ballet.'

'Oh classy. Very classy!'

'And I'm saying to him, "Look, I'm not sure what you meant back there. But to be honest, a coffee's exactly what I want and make it as strong as you like because I'm really pretty drunk and I'd like to get my head together before I go home which is what I'd like to do as soon as I've had that coffee, if that's OK by you." Except he doesn't hear the last bit because by then he's calling out from what I assume is

246

the kitchen, "That's OK, I've just what you want and I'll make it as strong as you like." Which sounds pretty ominous. Especially when he calls out a few minutes later, "Shut your eyes!" I don't of course and he says, "You're looking, I can tell. Please shut your eyes or it'll spoil the surprise." So God knows why but I do. And I can hear the creak of his footsteps getting nearer and nearer and I'm dying to look, I really am, but I'm thinking what if it's a *nice* surprise. You know, what if he's made me, um, an Irish coffee or something—'

'Oh sure. Sure.'

'Look, I was giving him the benefit of the doubt. And I had sort of led him on. So I kept my eyes closed out of politeness more than anything. And I can hear him breathing really heavily right in front of me. "Put out your hand," he says. And I can't. I just can't. "Put out your hand!" he says. And maybe there are some girls who like the dominant, commanding type. But not me. So I don't put out my hand. I open my eyes and there it is. All shuddery and pink. Poking its little head out of this tiny leopard-print poser pouch!'

'Aaagh!'

'Well, exactly. What's a girl to do in a situation like that?'

'What did you do?'

'Oh, it's awful. Really, really awful. I started giggling. And he's going in a husky voice, "Take me! Suck me! Do what*ever* you want to me!" But it's just so ridiculous that I can't stop giggling. And the poor man is starting to get really upset. I mean it's obvious because his little chap has started to shrink back. Like a baby snail retreating into its shell. And he's saying, "I'm sorry. I'm sorry." And I'm saying – or trying to say because I'm laughing so hard there's snot coming out of my nose – "No, I'm sorry. I'm sorry!" And he's saying, "Please don't tell anyone. Please." And I'm saying, "I won't, I promise!" And I'm out of the flat as fast as I can. Not because I'm scared but because I just can't bear to cause him any more pain. Poor guy!'

'Poor guy!'

'And now I've made it even worse by telling you and Repton. Promise me you won't mention it to him. Promise!'

'Martha, even I am not that big a bastard.'

'Promise me you won't then.'

'I promise.'

'Never?'

'Never.'

'So why are you looking at me like that?'

'Oh. Just thinking.'

'What?'

'I was thinking you're clearly not a girl who likes the brazen approach.'

'Definitely not.'

'That's a pity. Because I was going to say, I've got this little surprise that you might be interested in.'

'Really? Oh –' Martha rolls her eyes ' – *that* sort of surprise. Well, I suppose in your case, I can always make an exception.'

OCEANIC WHITE TIPS

One of the more horrible shark-related disasters of all time was the torpedoing of the American battleship USS Indianapolis near Guam in the South Pacific on 30 July 1945. Two thirds of the ship's 1200 crew survived the sinking, but when the victims were finally discovered by a spotter plane three days later, only 316 were still alive. Many of the rest had been eaten by sharks.

Besides being recounted by Quint in the waiting-for-the-shark-to-arrive scene in Jaws, the incident was turned into a not-half-bad film called Mission of the Shark starring Stacey Keach as Captain McVay, whose life raft (both in the movie and in real life) was harried by an enormous shark with a distinctive fin 'almost as white as a sheet of paper'. McVay and his men attempted to club the shark with their oars but to no avail. The shark would simply swim off only to return a few minutes later.

But at least McVay had a raft to hide on. Many of his fellow survivors didn't and were left floating in their life jackets, in groups of between 50 and 200, while dozens of sharks circled around them. When the sharks closed in for the kill, the men would kick and scream to drive them away. Sometimes this worked. Sometimes, however, according to survivors' reports, a shark 'would have singled out his victim and no amount of shouts or pounding of the water would turn him away. There would be a piercing scream and the water would be churned red and the shark cut his victim to ribbons.' No wonder that many of the men silently committed suicide by slipping out of their life jackets in the night.

Anyway, the reason I mention this story is that many of the sharks involved were almost certainly oceanic white tips. They never come close to shore, preferring to hang out in deep water, waiting to eat you when your plane crashes or your boat sinks. Unlike other maneaters, they have enlarged, rounded dorsal fins with white tips and long, paddle-shaped pectoral fins. So if you ever find yourself close enough to recognize those distinctive features, I'd advise you to start praying – sharpish.

CHAPTER NINE

At 1.15 a.m. I'm woken by a sharp twang on my guy rope and a muttered 'You sure it was this far up?' At 1.16 a.m. someone shouts, 'Guys! *Guys!* Over here.' At 1.32 a.m. the music starts. Not the comforting ambient rumble of a thousand distant sound systems, but something altogether more immediate and threatening. The dread noise of 'Definitely Maybe', played at full volume on a ghetto blaster.

At 1.35 a.m. there's a muffled cry of 'Turn that bloody music down.' The music is turned down a fraction. At 1.37 a.m. the music is turned up again, louder than before. At 2.15 the music stops, which is almost worse because now you can hear five or six teenagers, talking the sort of adolescent bollocks teenagers do when they're drunk, stoned and away from Mummy and Daddy for the first time in their pathetic know-nothing lives.

At 2.19 a.m. the music starts again. No, this is worse. This is definitely worse. It's 'What's The Story? (Morning Glory)'. At 2.32 a.m. I think, 'I knew I hated Oasis. But I would never have believed I could hate them this much.' At 2.41 a.m. someone shouts, 'Anyone got any skins?'

At 3.05 a hush descends.

At 3.06 someone says, 'Whizz, anyone?' At 3.08 the music starts again. 'Be Here Now'. Wish I wasn't. At 3.15 I try to think of Things In The World That I Hate More Than Oasis. At 3.17 I give up. At 4 a.m. the album ends. 'Skin up, Fish!' says someone.

At 4.05 the music starts. 'Wish You Were Here'. Good. I like the Floyd. At 4.15 I think, 'Well, I used to anyway.' At 4.16 I think, 'I hate Pink Floyd even more than Oasis.' At 4.17 I think, 'My God, my God, why hast thou forsaken me?'

At 5.15 I am awoken by birdsong. At 5.16 I decide I hate birds even more than Oasis and Pink Floyd put together.

At 6 a.m. I am reawoken by the green glow of the tent in the morning sun.

At 7 a.m. I am reawoken by the patter of rain on canvas.

At 10 a.m. I am reawoken by the very bright green glow of the tent, the even heavier patter of rain on canvas, the boom of distant sound systems, the squawk of feedback and a voice in a microphone going *Two! Two!*, the zipping and unzipping of tents, the brushing of teeth, the splat of spit on wet grass, the crunch of boots, the twang of guy ropes, the dankness of my sleeping bag, the ache in my back and Repton going, 'Joe. You awake?'

'No.'

'Me neither. Bastards!'

I unzip my tent and crawl forwards, taking care to avoid the patch of grass beneath the outer sheet on which I pissed during the night because I couldn't be arsed to put on my boots and do it outside. I undo the outer zip. Repton's face is pale, his Drizabone dripping heavily.

'Is it as horrible out there as it looks?' I ask him.

'Worse.'

'Better skin up then.'

'You've got the stuff.'

'I haven't.'

'I gave it to you last night.'

'When?'

'Last night.'

'Oh, come on. You know how untogether I am. You'd never have given me the stuff.'

'I did.'

'This is stupid. Search your pockets.'

'You search yours.'

'We'll both search. But I promise you. I definitely haven't got it.'

I scrummage through every one of my myriad pockets. Those in my jeans, in my spare jeans, in my shorts, in my rucksack, in my waterproofs. I look inside my sleeping bag and under my carry mat. I scour every inch of my tent. Then, increasingly desperate, I scrummage through all my pockets again until I hear Repton say, 'Got it!'

'Thank God,' I say.

'I said, "Have you got it?"' he says.

'No!' I say.

'Bugger!'

'This is disastrous. What are we going to do?' I say.

'Try to stay calm,' he says.

'How are we supposed to stay calm when we've just gone and lost half a frigging ounce of red-bearded skunk?' I say.

'We'll have a spliff.'

'Oh ha ha. Very funny.'

'Chill, Joe. Chill. I found a blim. Just enough for one J.'

We smoke the joint. It's hash. Not nearly as strong as I might have liked, but enough to blunt the unspeakable ghastliness of our predicament and to enable us to devise a cunning plan. We will have breakfast. We will attempt to retrace last night's steps and find – fat chance – the missing bag. En route, we will try to score.

Repton extinguishes the stub. 'Real Meat Sausage Company?'

'What about Martha?'

'What *about* Martha?'

'Well, I was rather hoping to lose my Real Meat Sausage virginity with her.'

'When did you say we had to meet her?'

'Two p.m., back right of the *NME* stage mixing desk.'

'It's called the Other Stage.'

'Fuck.'

'You know it's called the Other Stage. It was last year.'

'Fuck!'

'Is that all you can say? Fuck!'

'I can't fucking help it. This is a major, major fucking disaster. It's the worst fucking Glastonbury ever!'

The only good news so far is that the encampment belonging to Fish and his noisy chums is in pleasing disarray. One tent has collapsed during the night, forcing its occupants to shelter under a strip of blue, industrial plastic sheeting. The others have been so badly pitched that they are sagging in the middle with rainwater which is no doubt dripping on the unhealthy specimens inside. This is where the teenagers will remain for the rest of the festival, victims of Glasto first-night burn-out syndrome. As Repton and I stride over their guy ropes, I make sure to give them a good yank.

We head down hill on a pathway made of ridged metal sheets bolted together. Annoyingly, they have been bolted the wrong way so that the ridges run lengthwise instead of crosswise. This makes them almost as slippery underfoot as the mud on either side. Files of shell-shocked kids tramp wearily back and forth. The cleaner ones going uphill, carrying tents and sleeping bags, wear an expression which says, 'Jesus! Did I really spend eighty pounds for this?' The expression on the battle-hardened regulars going downhill says, 'You ain't seen nothing yet.'

In years past, the route would have been flanked at intervals by shabby black men and even shabbier crusties going ''Ash. Blackash. 'Ash for cash' and 'Thai. Thai. No stalks. No seeds. Just 'eads.' This year, there are none. Nor are there any in the triangular copse where the travellers used to park their trucks and serve good, strong coffee on cushions beneath camouflage nets. We used to call this place the Enchanted Wood. Today, it has lost its magic. The travellers are gone; the drug-dealers are gone, supplanted – in a heinous act of philistinism – by a rank of urinals.

Not even the Real Meat Sausage tastes quite as good as it used to. It's meant to be chilli flavour but it isn't nearly spicy enough and the fried egg is hard even though I distinctly asked for it to be cooked runny. 'We need drugs!' I tell Repton. 'Badly.'

'So you keep saying.'

'Tell me I'm not right.'

'You're right. We definitely need some drugs.'

So we retrace last night's steps.

The Tiny Tea Tent, where we skinned up and drank tea out of real mugs. Which is pretty much what everyone is doing there now, apart from us. We're just doing the boring tea part.

The Caravan at the far end of the Green Field, where we skinned up and drank Turkish coffee. But the nice woman in charge says she hasn't seen our dope.

The Tent with the Garden in the Healing Field, where we skinned up and drank herbal tea. But the bloke behind the counter just laughs when we tell him why we've come. 'Anyone found a big bag of skunk?' he calls to one of his colleagues. And everyone in the tent laughs at our predicament. Which strikes me as a not very Glastonbury thing to do.

But then Glastonbury itself isn't being very Glastonbury this year. Indeed, by the time we have reached the stone circle, I have begun seriously to question whether it ever was.

Martha is going to be horribly disappointed. Disappointed and not a little smug. She knew it was going to be wet and miserable and muddy, she said. Glastonbury always was. 'Oh and you'd know I suppose. Having been there so many times.' And we ended up having the first official argument of our relationship.

'So let me get this right,' said Martha. 'You spend three nights in a tent – '

'Four. You have to get there on Thursday to get a decent spot.'

' – swimming in mud – '

'It's never muddy. Hardly. Last year was an aberration.'

' – you watch two dozen bands you've never heard of – '

'Doesn't matter. The line-up's irrelevant. In fact Glasto's famous for having crap line-ups.'

'So the bands are all crap – '

'No, they're not. You think they're going to be crap and then they turn out to be really amazing.'

'And you live on veggie burgers.'

'Or Thai. Or Indian. Or Chinese. Or sausages. You

haven't lived until you've tried a Real Meat Sausage Company sausage for breakfast with runny fried egg and – '

'I'll take your word for it.'

'You're determined to have a bad time, aren't you?'

'I'm not going to have a bad time because I'm not going.'

'Are you mad? Are you totally insane?'

'Give me one good reason why I should.'

'But – but it's impossible to explain. You only know how good it is once you've been.'

'Try.'

'The vibe.'

'Oh, right.' Martha makes an inverted commas sign. '*The Vibe.*'

And now the vibe has gone and Martha's going to blame me for dragging her all this way and we're going to have another row. If we ever meet up, that is, because thanks to the bastard *NME* Stage changing its name to the pathetic Other Stage we're going to end up—

'Repton. What time is it?'

'Ten to two.'

'Shit!'

We reach the back right-hand corner of the Other Stage's mixing desk twenty minutes later. Martha is not there. At least I don't think she is. It's hard to tell because all the people who might be her are turned towards the stage, their heads concealed beneath hooded waterproofs. Like the horrible stabby creature from *Don't Look Now*.

I push my way forward through the crowd, then back again, examining the faces one by one. Under normal circumstances people might be freaked out by this sort of behaviour. But not at Glastonbury, where staring weirdos are the norm.

Still no sign of Martha. Which either means that she arrived on time, gave up after ten minutes and went looking for me; or that she's out there searching for an *NME* stage that no longer exists; or that she's found the right stage but not the right place because she doesn't know what a mixing desk is; or that she has been caught up in the traffic on the A361, or that she's lost her ticket or that her car's broken down or that she's had an accident or that—

This is horrible. This is truly, truly, maddeningly, terrifyingly horrible. Right now Martha could be absolutely anywhere. She'll be worried, she'll be frightened, she'll be cross, she'll be hating Glastonbury even more than I do right now, if that's at all possible. She'll be—

'Hey,' says Martha, giving me an enormous kiss. 'Isn't this just totally brilliant?'

'Er—' I'm blinking. Recovering from the shock. 'Is it?'

'Come on, let's dump my stuff and get moving. Red Snapper's on any minute and I've heard he's really good. He's on the jazz stage. Know where the Jazz Stage is? 'Course you do. So how's it been, boys? Who've you seen so far?'

'No one.'

'What have you been doing?'

'It's a long and painful story.'

'And it ends very unhappily with your boyfriend losing half an ounce of skunk.'

'Joe!'

'I bloody well did not. It was Repton who had it last.'

'I gave it to you, I remember because – hey, Martha. You didn't by any chance bring any—?'

'I was relying on you. Anyway, who needs drugs at a place like this? It's weird enough already.'

Repton and I exchange horrified glances.

'Martha,' I say, 'you don't understand. Glastonbury without drugs is like . . . like. . . .'

'Wimbledon without strawberries,' suggests Repton.

'Or drum 'n' bass without the drum,' I say.

'Or the bass,' agrees Repton.

'Or sex without foreplay.'

'And post-play,' says Repton.

'And during-play,' I say.

'So what you're saying is we can't see any bands or have any fun until we've scored some drugs?'

Repton and I nod seriously.

'OK,' says Martha. 'So let's score.'

'We've tried. The place is completely dry.'

Martha glances heavenwards. 'Oh yeah?'

'I'll tell you, if you'd been here in – what was it Repton? – '92 or '93?'

' '93. Vintage year.'

'Or what. Every second person was dealing. We'd just pitched our tent when this crustie comes up to us. The Wizard, I think his name was. Or Gandalf. Something like that. Anyway, he's turned up with this Bedford truck absolutely chock full of druggy comestibles. Skunk. Sensi. Thai sticks. Black. Whizz . . .'

'Right,' says Martha, 'but since we don't have a time machine, why don't we just ask the man I saw selling drugs by the gate?'

'Bet he's gone by the time we get there,' I say.

'There's only one way of finding out,' says Martha.

The man selling drugs by the gate is still there. But there's one small problem, as I whisper to Martha.

'He's black.'

'That is soo racist!' says Martha.

259

'Shh! He'll hear.'

'Serves you right if he hears. You—'

'Look, it's got nothing to do with the colour of the skin. It's what he represents. He's not here because of the Glasto vibe. He's just here to make money.'

'So? He's a dealer.'

'Exactly. So he'll charge us dealer's rates and give us a dealer's deal. What we need is someone who's mainly here for fun but happens to be selling drugs on the side. Someone like The Wizard.'

'Someone white, you mean,' says Martha.

'Well. Probably. Yeah.'

'We're on,' interrupts Repton, returning from the latrines. 'Dealers. Whole gang of them. By the fence.'

'Not a group of frightful negroes, I do hope,' says Martha.

Repton hands me £30. 'I'll go halves with you.'

'Oh, I'm scoring, am I?'

'You lost the dope.'

'I did not lose the fucking dope. You did.'

'I'll do it then,' says Martha.

'I'll do it,' I say. 'You might get ripped.'

Which probably makes Martha come over all knee-jerk feminist and 'Just because you're a bloke doesn't mean, etc., etc.' But I don't hang around long enough to find out. Anyway, I'm right, because the dealers Repton has spotted are pretty unsavoury – Scouse accents, shell suits, very unGlasto – and would undoubtedly have grabbed her £60 and scarpered. Me, I'm much more careful. I make sure I have a good sniff of the merchandise before showing my money. I beat them down from £60 to £50, and they don't get a note until the drugs are in my hand.

Repton has the papers and baccy all ready.

'What did you say this stuff was?' he says, inspecting the weed. Unusually it's wrapped in newspaper.

'Purple Haze, they said.'

Repton sniffs it, crumbles it between his fingers and sniffs again.

'Bloody isn't,' he says. 'It's Ore-cunting-gano.'

'Orecuntingano. Is that good?' asks Martha.

'No, it is not fucking good. It is a fucking, fucking nightmare. Your boyfriend, your moronic fucking boyfriend has just blown sixty quid . . .'

'Fifty actually.'

'Oh, well done. You really struck a hard fucking bargain. Only fifty quid for fifty wretched ps worth of Schwartz bloody Italian herbs. Let's celebrate. Let's have a pizza!'

Martha sniggers.

'It was you who spotted them,' I protest.

'Oh good. That's just what I wanted to hear. It's my fault you lost the skunk and now it's my fault you got burned.'

'All right, it's not your fault. It's those evil fucking Scousers. And you and I are going to go back there right this minute—'

'And they're going to give us our fifty quid back just like that? Dream on, matey.'

'Well, if they don't we'll shop 'em.'

'Right. Right. Excuse me, officer. I would like to report a serious breach of the trades' descriptions act.'

'But we can't just let them get away with it.'

'They have just got away with it.'

'Joint, anyone?' interrupts Martha.

'Please, hon, this is serious,' I say.

'Quite,' she says, unwrapping a chunk of black hash

evidently purchased from the cruelly maligned black dealer. 'So we'd better make it a very, very large one.'

And as if by magic the shopkeeper appears with his cheery red fez and his passport to a better, happier, more colourful, carefree world where mud is fun and rain is fun and getting ripped off by evil bastard drug dealers is sort of fun in an anecdote-to-tell-your-friends-later kind of way. And stumbling along for miles and miles on slippery paths is fun and queuing for the latrines is fun and entering a cubicle which reeks of plastic, urine and ordure, wiping the piss off the seat, wrestling to pull your trousers down far enough over your filthy boots for you to be able to squat down above the Everest of festering turds while struggling to ensure that your arse-cheeks don't stray so far below that they actually touch the peak of that evil brown mountain and then rising once more, your Augean challenge accomplished is, well, not fun, exactly, but interesting. Definitely interesting.

Which is almost as good as fun. In fact it's definitely as good as fun. Interesting is as good as fun. Which means that even crapping in a Glastonbury latrine is fun. And if even crapping in a Glastonbury latrine is fun, then how much more fun does that make all the other things you do at Glastonbury? Like:

Watching the incredible man in the Circus Field who cycles thirty feet above the ground along a tight rope, without a safety net. And then, as you're going 'Noooo. Don't do it! Don't do it!', watching him do the same trick on a bicycle so small you could almost fit it in your pocket. Backwards. Wearing a blindfold.

Skinning up.

Passing a large papier-mâché dragon with, in front, three buckets full of paint and a sign saying 'Splash The Dragon'.

And thinking 'Naah. Can't do that. That's embarrassing. That's stupid.' And then watching someone else dip a wad of paper in a paint bucket and hurl it so that it hits the dragon with a satisfying colour-splodge. And thinking, 'Hang on. This is a bloody brilliant idea! This is sheer genius! I must splash the dragon! I must splash the dragon!'

Skinning up.

Agonizing over the vexed question of whether to have an 'award-winning' Cornish pasty, a Masala Dosa or falafels with pitta bread, salad and chilli sauce. Then realizing it doesn't matter because with two and a half days still to go you can actually have all three, as many times as you want. And another Real Meat Sausage roll. And a crêpe with maple syrup and banana. And a carrot cake, a flapjack and a greasy, sugary bag of doughnuts.

Skinning up.

Sitting in the Tiny Tea Tent and watching the weirdies go by: babes, goths, crusties, scallies, hippies, Japanese trendies, indie kids, ravers, anoraks, mutants, and straight people with children in pushchairs. Studying their faces to work out which ones aren't stoned. Realizing that the answer is 'none', except for maybe the straight people with children in pushchairs. Who are the weirdest people of all.

Skinning up to celebrate the fact that everyone's stoned and to make absolutely sure that no one's more stoned than you.

Prising the accumulated mud from your boots and discovering how much easier it is to walk now that you're no longer carrying an acre of Somerset on each foot.

Seeing Red Snapper, Dawn of the Replicants, Laika, Kristen Hersh and Rolf Harris. With Portishead, The Chemical Brothers, Lo-Fidelity Allstars, Spiritualised, Nick Cave and Julian Cope still to come. And, should you be feeling suitably ironic, Robbie Williams and Tony Bennett too.

Discovering that you're totally drenched and completely knackered after all that wandering through mud with nowhere dry to sit down and getting more and more paranoid because you're still out in the pissing rain and it's raining harder and harder and you've nowhere to shelter and the last joint's wearing off, either that or it's just not working any more, and you're beginning to think, well maybe this isn't such a good time I've been having, I'm cold and I'm wet and I need somewhere dry to sit down and I need a joint and what are we going to do? What are we going to do? When suddenly you spy a big white marquee, which is even whiter inside, with film of polar bears being projected on the walls and a DJ playing trippy ambient music and gym mats and cushions and low skinning-up tables on the floor. And you buy a cup of tea, settle down on the dry, springy mats, not bothered any more about the mud from your boots fouling your trousers because you're past that stage now, and you skin up and you realize that everyone in the room is as monged and as glad to be here as you are and you think, 'This place is very heaven.' And Martha's thinking the same thing because she looks at you and then at Repton with a beatific smile on her face, takes a huge drag on the reefer, exhales and says, 'Now I get it.'

'Thought you might.'

'Poor Joe,' says Repton, 'he was terrified you wouldn't, you know. Thought he might have to chuck you if you didn't pass the Glasto test.'

Martha looks at me reproachfully. 'And have I passed the Glasto test?'

'Definitely,' I say.

'Oh good,' she says. 'Does that mean we can go now?'

For some reason I find this very, very funny. Repton thinks so too.

Martha, however, remains straight-faced. And when we've stopped rolling around she says, 'Well. Can we?'

'Crikey!' I say to Repton. 'I think she means it.' And we both start laughing again.

'Actually though,' Repton says at last, 'that's not such a bad idea.'

'Yeah, right,' I say, giggling, 'if you were having a Really Crap Idea competition.'

'Is it a crap idea?' asks Martha.

'Driving back to London? In this state?'

'We-ell,' says Martha. 'There's this couple I know. They don't live too far from here. And I did mention we might be dropping by.'

'Oh, you did, did you?' Even I'm taken aback by the nastiness of my tone. But, damn it, I feel betrayed. She's been planning this early escape all along.

'It was just an idea,' says Martha, all pathetic. Which is enough to bring Repton on-side.

'It's a very good idea,' he says. 'What were you planning to do in this mud-bath, anyway?'

'What we usually do,' I reply, fixing him with a baleful stare. 'Score some Es—'

'Cat-worming pills more like. To judge by your scoring prowess.'

'It's a point of principle. I've never quit a Glastonbury yet and I'm not about to start now.'

'Suit yourself,' says Repton, reaching for his mobile phone. He turns to Martha. 'Here. Want to let them know we're coming?'

Martha makes a long, enthusiastic phone call to her incredibly boring friends. 'Now I know what my great-grandpa went through at Passchendaele . . . Yes. Yes . . . Oh ha! Ha ha! . . .' etc. Huffing furiously, I roll and smoke another joint.

'They're putting the electric blankets on and they're going to make us a lamb tagine,' says Martha.

'How very cosy.'

'Oh, come on, Joe. They're really looking forward to meeting you. And the kids—'

'Kids? I'm definitely not coming.'

'You're going to stay here all on your own?' says Martha.

'If you insist on leaving me, what choice do I have?'

'Come with us, obviously,' says Repton.

'And play Snap with screaming children and make boring small talk with boring grown-ups I've never met and "Oh really, Mrs Humdrum. That was quite the most delicious lamb tagine I've eaten. And why don't we all turn in for a nice early night because I'm dying to try out your electric blankets and, let's face it, it's so much more fun than boshing loads of Es and dancing your tits off in the Dance Tent to the Chemical Brothers." I don't think!'

'Melanie and Xan aren't like that,' protests Martha.

'Leave him, Martha,' says Repton. 'If he wants to play the lonely martyr that's his problem.'

'OK. OK. Even supposing "Melanie" and "Xan" are the nicest, coolest, funniest people in the world, I'm still not coming because it's a point of principle. The day I quit Glastonbury early is the day I hit middle age, and the day I might just as well give up and die. So there.'

On the long mournful trudge back to the tents Martha slips her hand into mine and gives me a pitiful look. I pull my fingers free and accelerate ahead of her and Repton where I stay, watching my boots go squelch squelch squelch through the mire, thinking dark, hateful thoughts. And secretly wishing that Martha would catch up with me and try holding my hand again because if she did I'd let her. But she doesn't.

Where the path joins the disused rail track, a man in a hooded rainproof chants, 'Doves. Doves.'

I walk past.

'There's someone back there selling Es,' says Repton, catching up with me.

'It's no fun on your own,' I say.

'You can still change you mind,' he says.

And I'm about to reply – I might even have said, 'You're right. I think I will' – when I'm distracted by a pair of day-glo orange combat trousers on a tall, absurdly good-looking man coming towards us. He's entwined in the arms of an equally absurdly good-looking girl. They're radiantly happy and completely oblivious of their surroundings. Which is fortunate because the girl is Sam, the man – presumably – DJ Marius Schenk, and they walk past without noticing me.

That settles it.

'I'm staying,' I tell Repton and I feel fantastic. Fantastic-ally bad, that is. So fantastically bad, indeed, that it's almost as thrilling as feeling fantastically good. No matter how happy my ex-girlfriend may be, I congratulate myself, the extremity of her joy can't even come close to matching the severity of my misery.

I've blown it. I've managed to turn a petty point of principle into a full-blown rift with Martha. I've insulted her friends, I've implied that anyone who quits Glastonbury is too boring and middle-aged to go out with me, I've rejected her attempts to make it up. I've ruined the most promising relationship of my life.

And there's more disastrousness still to come. When we get to our encampment – and we know it's definitely ours because Fish and his crew are still there and clearly haven't budged all day – our tents have vanished. Not just our tents but our sleeping bags, our rucksacks, our spare clothes, my concealed wodge of spare cash. Everything.

'Bastards!' cries Repton.

'Bastards,' I agree. And, of course, I'm not going to let on that actually those thieving bastards have done me a huge, huge favour.

So I do get to spend the night in a bed warmed by an electric blanket. And I do get to try that delicious lamb tagine.

I also get to try some of Melanie and Xan's hydroponic homegrown, which is a good deal stronger than anything I could have scored at Glastonbury.

And I get to rifle through Mel and Xan's CD collection, as you do, and discover to my surprise that the sticks aren't solely inhabited by culture-free troglodytes.

'Found, um, anything you like?' Xan asks.

'Well may you sound nervous,' says Repton. 'You realize that Joe writes . . .'

'We have been warned,' says Mel.

Everyone stares at me. Like I'm some totally evil music fascist.

'Well?' says Martha.

'Just looking,' I say all innocence.

'You're incapable of just looking,' says Repton. 'You judge.'

'So,' asks Mel. 'Guilty or not guilty?'

'Vinyl Justice,' says Xan.

'Hey. *Adam and Joe*,' I say.

'Good one, Xan,' says Repton. 'You have met with the Führer's approval.'

'Actually Vinyl Justice is my least favourite bit.'

'Be afraid, Xan,' says Repton. 'Be very afraid.'

'Hey, stop ganging up on me. I'm allowed to have opinions, aren't I?'

''Course you are,' says Xan, 'and I agree. Vinyl Justice sucks.'

'See, Repton, see? I don't just have opinions. I have right opinions.'

'Very Right.'

'OK, I'm a Nazi. Satisfied? I'm a Nazi and I'm hateful and I'm wrong and somebody else can choose a record because obviously I haven't a clue about music and—'

'He's so pretty when he's being petulant. Don't you think, Mel?' says Martha.

'I like the way his blink rate goes up. Such sweet eyelashes,' agrees Repton.

'Oh piss off,' I say.

'Yes, leave him alone. Both of you,' says Mel. 'Now come on, Joe. We want to know. Do we have good taste or bad taste?'

'Good.'

'You're just saying that.'

'Oh, I don't think so,' says Martha. 'Joe always speaks his mind.'

'Really?' says Xan.

'Oh good,' says Mel. 'And do we have good taste? Or very good taste?'

'Very good taste.'

'Joe, sweetheart. You're welcome here any time.'

'And you can definitely pick the next record,' says Xan. 'What's it going to be?'

'You'll see,' I say, easing the disc from its cardboard sleeve.

'Oh God,' groans Martha, 'it's one of those boysy tests.'

'Well, I'm never going to get it, am I, hon,' says Mel to Xan. 'I never remember any of these groups' names.'

'Bet I get it in under five seconds,' says Xan.

'Bet I can get it in under one,' says Repton. 'Radiohead. Bound to be.'

'Nope,' I say. 'It's even better than Radiohead.'

'Better than Radiohead. Not possible.'

'As good as, anyway.'

'Oh no, it gets worse,' says Martha. 'It's one of those if Martha doesn't like it then she's chucked scenarios.'

'You'll like it.' I hit the play button.

'And if I don't?'

'Shh!'

'Got it,' says Mel, less than five seconds in. 'It's that one that starts with the funny jazzy stuff and the speaky bits.'

'They're called samples,' says Xan. 'And it's DJ Shadow. *Entroducing DJ Shadow*. Good call!'

I give him a big smile and a double thumbs-up.

'Phew!' says Martha. 'Now can we play games and skin up?'

Which is what we precede to do, much to my relief since (a) *Entroducing DJ Shadow* just isn't the same unless you're really stoned and (b) I want Martha to be distracted.

You see, I've already gone and broken the cardinal rule of introducing someone to a really brilliant record: don't pre-sell it. Because all that happens then is that you raise their expectations so high that they're bound to be disappointed. What you really want to do is put it on surreptitiously, let it seep in slowly, naturally and wait for them to go, 'This is all right. What is it?'

But Martha hasn't responded yet and I'm starting to worry. No. Not starting. I've been worried from the very beginning. It's a difficult record, *Entroducing*, and it would be crazy to expect anyone to get into it after – let alone during – one listen. But that's what I'm hoping Martha does nonetheless. Not, of course, that I dare prod her for an opinion. I daren't even look at her, in case she's frowning or looking bored or shoving her fingers in her ears. That really would be the end. I don't think I could ever truly love a woman who failed to understand the God-like genius of DJ Shadow.

Everyone else is immersed in a round of Switch. I can't concentrate and keep forgetting my go. I can't even enjoy the music. I'm trying to imagine I'm hearing it for the first time, wincing on behalf of Martha whenever it gets remotely discordant, steeling myself for the really hairy bit that I know is coming soon. The passage in the middle where it gets almost unbearably cacophonous and messy and nerve-jangling and your average fairweather listener turns to you and yells above the din, 'Got anything a bit easier on the ear?'

The moment passes.

'Joe?' says Martha.

'Mm.'

'Your go.'

'I've just had my go.'

'And I put down a Joker. So back to you.'

'Oh.'

But I'm not the only one who's losing the plot. Repton forgets that an eight means you skip the next player. Xan gormlessly discards a Queen of Hearts on a Jack of Diamonds. Melanie gets called into the playroom because the small brat keeps pressing the stop button on the bigger one's *Thomas the Tank Engine* video.

When she returns the DJ Shadow appreciation society is in full swing. We've got to the tinklingly mesmerizing keyboard bit which sounds vaguely like the *Exorcist* theme tune only prettier and more shimmery. From this point it gets better and better.

'Perdition catch my soul but I do love this track,' says Repton.

'Top,' agrees Xan.

'It's the build, that's the secret,' I say. 'It's how you can always tell a really great record. When they start off straight and then just get trippier and trippier.'

'Yes, like the *Goldberg Variations*,' says Martha.

'Eh?' says Xan.

'I think she's taking the piss,' I say. 'Evil Martha!'

She smiles.

'So you don't reckon this is the greatest album ever?' I ask.

'Oh, for sure,' she says. 'Right up there with *Brothers in Arms*.'

'Know any nice chicks?' I say to Xan. 'Only I've just recently split up with my girlfriend – musical differences – and I – urrrgh.'

Martha has grabbed me round the neck in a mock stranglehold.

'He would too, you know,' she tells the others.

'Perfectly reasonable grounds for divorce if you ask me,' says Xan.

'Xan!' chides Melanie.

'Yo brother,' I say. 'Tell yo' ho' like it is.'

'So it's just the three of us who'll be enjoying my delicious tagine,' says Melanie to Martha and Repton. 'Come on, girls. You can keep me company in the kitchen. We're leaving the brothers to bath the kids.'

'And we're taking this with us,' says Martha, removing the CD from the player. 'DJ Shadow is far, far too good to be wasted on philistines like you.'

Blimey, I think. No one has ever taken my *Entroducing DJ Shadow* from me in mid-play and lived to tell the tale, let alone been rewarded with a beneficent smile. Maybe this is love.

And I'm beginning to realize that my sudden plunge into terminal middle-agedom – if that's what this is – might not be so great a disaster as I'd feared. Because it has to be said that playing games and dining well and chilling out with an enormous spliff in front of a log fire and watching the Glastonbury highlights on TV with people as simpatico as Melanie and Xan is a sight more entertaining than doing it for real in the Somme-like conditions fifteen miles down the road.

Oh, and the kids aren't too evil either. The small one smiles at me and makes gurgling noises. The bigger one forces me to play Jenga and Pick Up Sticks, both of which are pretty cool when you're stoned. In fact the brats almost make me feel a bit broody. Not that I'm going to mention any such thing to Martha. Not just yet.

What I will go so far as to concede as we lie side by side,

blissfully monged, in a real bed with real sheets, underneath a solid roof that doesn't leak and a bathroom outside with a flushing loo and stone walls so thick that even if there were a bunch of adolescents with names like Fish snorting speed and playing Oasis and Pink Floyd next door till dawn breaks you wouldn't hear them . . . What I will concede is this: 'Martha. You know when I said earlier about your idea being a strong contender for a Really Crap Ideas competition?'

'Ye-es.'

'Well, I was wrong. It would definitely have lost.'

Martha seems to think this constitutes a crushing admission of defeat. She laughs. And I laugh too. But then in our state, we'd probably laugh at anything. It's good stuff, as I said, this hydroponic weed. Giggly, heady but – and this is a problem when you're trying to get to sleep – a bit trippy.

'Do you think we should try to get some sleep?' says Martha.

'We could try.'

'Night night.'

'Night night.'

'Sleep tight.'

'Sleep tight.'

'Love you.'

'Love you.'

But it's not going to work I can tell. My thoughts are racing. And as racing thoughts do – mine anyway – they inevitably turn to sharks.

'Martha,' I say, 'have you ever had that horrible thought where you imagine that the last thing you say at night is also going to be the last thing you'll say before you die?'

'No.'

'Well, it's horrible.'

'I'll bet.'

'Say, for example, you said, "Night night." Well, that would be fairly safe because you might say it before you ceased upon the midnight with no pain. But you'd never say "night night" to somebody if you were floating in shark-infested seas waiting to be eaten.'

'No.'

'But you might say "I love you." I mean, suppose we'd both survived a shipwreck together and this huge shark was circling around us and we knew we were going to die. Well, obviously we'd talk about lots of things. Try to keep each other calm. Say how much we meant to each other. But I reckon as the shark closed in for the kill, the last thing we'd say is "I love you." Don't you reckon?'

'I suppose so. But it's not going to happen, is it?'

'I wouldn't let it happen. I'd swim off. Try and attract the shark away from you so you'd survive. I've never said this to anyone before, Martha. Not to anyone. But I'd do anything for you, you know. Anything. I'd swim through shark-infested seas for you.'

'I wouldn't let you. I wouldn't want to live without you.'

'That's nice.'

'It's true. I wouldn't. So don't do it, all right? Don't ever, ever, ever swim through shark-infested seas for me. Ever. All right?'

'All right.'

'Do you promise?'

'I promise.'

'I love you.'

'I love you. Wait. I can't let that be the last thing I say to you because—'

'OK. We'll try something different. How about "Make love to me. Now!"'

'That's a good one. You'd never say that just before you were eaten by a shark.'

'No. I mean it. Make love to me. Now.'

THE BULL

Though his reputation is not so fearsome as those of the great white and the tiger, the bull may yet be responsible for more human deaths than any other shark. Besides being bulky, aggressive and virtually omniverous, he has the unusual ability to survive in both fresh and salt water. This means that when swimming in tropical rivers, you are every bit as likely to be gobbled up by a bull shark as you are by alligators, crocodiles or piranhas. Bull sharks have been found as far as 1750 miles up the Mississippi and 2500 miles up the Amazon.

The dreaded Matawan Creek incident of 1916, in which the New Jersey coastline was terrorized for twelve days by sharks, leaving four people dead and one injured, may well have been the work of bulls. Since the incident was the main inspiration for Jaws, it almost makes you feel sorry for the much-maligned great white. Almost.

CHAPTER TEN

Repton has discovered a fascinating rumour about Christine Villeneuve on the Internet. Apparently, she has been undergoing treatment in a Swiss clinic for rampant nymphomania.

'Was that before or after she shot JFK?' I ask, grateful for the excuse to put my game of *Final Fantasy VII* on pause. It's quite disgusting and immoral indulging at this hour of a working day, but Martha got it for my birthday last weekend and I feel I owe it to her to play with it as often as possible.

'Don't believe me then,' he says.

'She doesn't look like a nympho,' I say.

'What are nymphos supposed to look like?'

'I dunno. Not like Christine Villeneuve. She's pure. She's aloof.'

'And she goes like a train.'

'So what am I supposed to do about it?'

'Nothing. I should hope. You're married.'

'Exactly. So it's bloody irresponsible of you to put evil ideas into my head.'

'Forewarned is forearmed. Suppose she suddenly leaps on you and says, "Joe. Joe. Mon chéri. Je veux faire l'amour avec toi"?'

'Things like that just don't happen in interviews. Especially not with big shot movie actresses. They've always got some hatchet-faced PR on hand to stop you asking personal questions. They don't flirt with you. They don't even tell you anything interesting. They just plug their latest film. Besides, actresses never look fanciable in real life.'

'Is that what you told Martha?'

'Yes.'

Repton laughs.

What's annoying, of course, is that the bastard's absolutely right. I have indeed been considering the horrifying possibility that Christine Villeneuve might interrupt this afternoon's interview to make passionate love to me on the floor of her Dorchester suite. Or perhaps up against the wall. Or in the shower. Or tied to the bed. With whips. Baby oil. And a huge vibrator.

None of which, of course, holds any appeal to me at all. Not even the tiniest, inciest, winciest bit.

Well, all right. Maybe just the tiniest, inciest, winciest bit. She is Christine Villeneuve, after all.

So: would I or wouldn't I?

It's for tricky moral dilemmas like this that distracting games like *Final Fantasy VII* were invented.

I unpause it and soon my characters – I have wittily changed their official names from Cloud, Barrett and Tifa into the more entertaining Wanka, Rimcheese and Orgasma – are embroiled in a fierce battle with a boss that fires poison bubbles at you.

'God, that music's annoying,' says Repton.

'Mm.'

'Really, really, really annoying.'

'Mm.'

'Enjoy your freedom while it lasts, I should. Come Saturday, you'll be washing dishes and changing plugs and queuing at Sainsbury's and IKEA. You'll have no time left for Wanka and Rimcheese.'

With a sigh I abandon the game. One of the annoying things about *Final Fantasy VII* is that in the early bits, you can't save when you want to. You have to go looking for a special question-mark-shaped save point and clearly, with Repton yabbering at me, I'm not going to have time.

I reach for the pouch of Golden Virginia on the breakfast table.

'I have lived with chicks before, you know,' I say.

'A fine job they did of domesticating you. I tell you, if Martha has to spend as much time cleaning up after you as I have—'

'Oh, Repton, sweetie. You're really going to miss me, I can tell.'

I try planting a kiss on his cheek.

Repton recoils.

'Yes, please don't go, Joe,' he says. 'Please carry on ruining my love life and fouling my spare bedroom and leaving your discarded wank tissues on the bathroom floor.'

'I'll have you know I haven't had a single wank for over a month. That girl, Repton, I'm telling you. She's insatiable.'

'Wait till domesticity strikes. It'll be once a fortnight if you're lucky.'

'You think it's a bad idea, moving in?'

'No. These things have to be done. I just do wonder sometimes – you breeders – I mean, on the one hand, I really envy you all that togetherness, knowing exactly what you'll be doing for Sunday lunch, sex on tap and so on. But on the other, well, that whole monogamy business. It just seems so unnatural. For a man anyway.'

'You're right. It's a pisser. All that stuff women say about

"Our sex drive is exactly the same as yours." It's total bollocks. I mean look at your lot. Shagging anything with a pulse.'

'Thanks.'

'Yes, but you know what I mean. Left to his own devices, a man's going to do what a man's meant to do. Spread his seed as widely and frequently as possible. It's in our nature.'

'Oh, it is,' agrees Repton, with a lascivious smile.

'Whereas with women it's quite the opposite. All they want to do is get themselves fertilized by a single alpha male and then keep him trapped so he can get on with the hunter-gathering. Which would be fine if they admitted as much. But they won't. They keep spouting all this feminist propaganda that it's as normal for a man to be faithful as it is for woman. And it so obviously isn't.'

'Well, quite. That's why I was asking. Suppose you get the chance to sleep with someone like Christine Villeneuve, what do you do?'

'You just say no. You have to. Don't you?'

Repton shrugs.

'Oh, come on,' I say. 'You know how happy Martha and I are together. It would be madness to blow it all just for the sake of a shag.'

'Even if she never found out?'

'Yeah, but you can never guarantee that, can you? And even if she didn't find out, do I really want to spend the rest of my life with this dark, horrible, guilty secret? I couldn't, Repton, I couldn't.'

'I'm sure she'd be pleased to hear you say that.'

'What? Did she put you up to this?'

'Oh per-lease. I was just interested, that's all. And I'm

really impressed. Shows just how good Martha is for you. You've grown up.'

'Don't say that. Please don't say that.'

'Well, you have. Wish I could be half so mature.'

'Mature! That's even worse.'

'God, is that the time? I'd better be going. You're sorted for this evening, aren't you? Remember I've got you-know-who coming round and I don't want you cramping my style.'

'Yeah. Yeah. You're safe. I'm meeting up with Sam.'

'God, you're not. Why?'

'Oh, you know. Show we're still friends. Rub her nose in the fact that I'm so radiantly, radiantly happy with Martha. Take loads of class A drugs—'

'And back to her place for a lively threesome with Marius?'

'Oh, I'll be all used up by then. My afternoon making love to Christine Villeneuve, remember?'

Not, it must be said, that there's slightest chance of that. Her body language, as I enter the interview suite, tells me all I need to know. She sits enthroned on a repro antique chair, legs crossed, arms folded, cigarette in slender hand, bored gaze directed a couple of inches above my head as she dismisses my questions with a weary 'Bof. Je sais pas.' I'm slumped subserviently beneath her at one end of a sofa, wired on coffee, dry-mouthed after too many cigarettes, wondering how the hell I'm going to turn her platitudes and non-sequiturs into a witty 1200-word appreciation of the life and career of Christine Villeneuve.

It's always a mistake to interview people you really admire. You want them to be your new best friend but they can't even be bothered to remember your name. You want them to tell you things they've never told anyone before. But they've already had a thousand other journalists ask them precisely the same questions to which they've responded with precisely the same pat answers. Why should you be any different?

Of course, I should have learned this by now. But you always hope that the next time is going to be different. Next time you're really going to bond; you're going to get the definitive interview; you're going to be invited to the superstar's home in LA/Miami/Cap d'Antibes and hang out by the pool with Bobby and Quentin and Uma and Gwyneth; you're going to be told 'Hey. You're pretty cool. Do you mind if I pay you $100,000 to doctor this screenplay/help me with the lyrics for my new album/play the love interest in my new movie?' Not this time, unfortunately. Definitely not this time.

For, as I predicted to Repton, Christine Villeneuve is indeed slightly dowdier in the flesh than she looks on celluloid. Not that she's ugly, by any stretch. But she's definitely more girl-next-door than utterly-entrancing-fantasy-sex-goddess. Which is just as well, I suppose, since otherwise I might never have been able to string a vaguely cogent series of questions together. Nor I suspect – and I still wish I hadn't – would I have dared mention at the beginning of our meeting that she is at the very pinnacle of my all-time top shag list.

Though naturally, I don't express this quite so bluntly. What I actually say is that my girlfriend will be very jealous that I am meeting her because, um, well, er, even more than Uma Thurman, Gwyneth Paltrow and Natalie Imbruglia—

'Qui?'

'C'est une pop star Australienne.'

'Ah bon.'

I consider her to be, um, très, très jolie.

For just a second she meets my eye. Her look says, 'Jesus. That is the most stunningly banal and obvious thing anyone has ever said to me. Now get on with the interview, ask me about my latest film and then piss off out of here, will you?'

Something like that. So I do exactly what her look seems to have told me. I ask her about her latest film. Christine Villeneuve gives me a boring answer. I ask her another question about her latest film. Christine Villeneuve gives me an evasive answer. I slip in a question about her personal life. Christine Villeneuve tells me she doesn't answer questions about her personal life. So I ask her another question about her latest film.

At last there's a rap on the door, her PR pokes his head into the room, to say that my hour's up. Christine Villeneuve waves him away. And with considerable relief, I scoop up my notes and tape-recorder, and make to leave.

'You are disappointed?' says Christine, after I've thanked her for her time.

'Not at all,' I say.

'The English. They lie so beautifully,' she says.

'Why thank you,' I say.

'Quand même,' she says. 'You are not lying when you say you think I am beautiful.'

'Certainly not.'

'And you will like to make love to me, n'est-ce pas?'

'Oh yes. Ha ha ha ha ha.'

'Tu le veux?'

'Pardon?'

'Tu veux coucher avec moi?'

'Um, well, um, you see the thing is I have this girlfriend and um, we're sort of, er – are you serious?'

'Bien sûr.'

'Well, er. Yeah. Sure. I suppose.'

'So then you must take a shower.'

'You want me to have a shower?' Oh, I get it. This is some warped technique she's devised to humiliate journalists she doesn't like.

'Yes. First you take a shower. Then we make love.'

Still, worth a try, isn't it? I mean it's not every day that Christine Villeneuve asks you to make love to her.

So I retire to the bathroom, lock the door primly behind me, strip off and take a shower. There's something very 'Have that boy bathed and brought to my bedchamber' about this scenario. Something very, very unreal. In fact, if this were a wank fantasy, I'm sure I'd interject at this point with a stern: 'More realism, please.' Because divine beings like Christine Villeneuve simply don't do this sort of thing with scuzzy mortals like me. Do they?

Do they?

Of course they don't. Any second now I'm going to leave the bathroom to find a camera crew waiting to capture my horrified expression. Then Jeremy fucking Beadle is going to creep from under the bed and go, 'Surprise! Surprise!' No. That's Cilla. What is it that Jeremy Beadle says? Something equally annoying no doubt. And I'm going to have to pretend that I find this hilarious practical joke as chuckle-some as he does. I'm going to have to let it be known, somehow, that I knew it was a practical joke all along because otherwise when Martha gets to see me on TV—

No. Best not to think about Martha. I'll only feel worse than I do already. Which is bad. Very, very bad.

There's only one way I'm going to wriggle out of this one. I'm going to get out of the shower now. Give that semi hard-on – sorry, mate – a knock on the head. Get dressed. Leave quickly and pretend nothing ever happened.

Which is exactly what I do. The getting out of the shower and the getting dressed bit, anyway. But when I've got my hand round the bathroom door handle, it suddenly strikes me. What if it isn't a practical joke? What if it's for real? What if I were to become the first man in the world ever to turn down the opportunity of making love to Christine Villeneuve? I'd never forgive myself. I'd be like John Betjeman, filmed in the twilight of his life on the white cliffs of Dover, musing that he only ever had one regret in life. He wished he'd had more sex. And I don't want to be John Betjeman. I want to be me. Joe Davenport. The man who once in his life – just once – got to live out his wildest fantasy and make love to Christine Villeneuve.

So I take the compromise option. I undress again, slip on a thick white towelling bathrobe and, assuming an expression which says 'I've just had a quick shower. To get myself clean. As any normal journalist would when he's just interviewed a movie actress,' I walk into the bedroom.

The camera crew isn't there. Nor is Jeremy Beadle. There's just Christine Villeneuve. Stark naked. On the bed. Waiting to make love to me, Joe Davenport.

'God, you're beautiful,' I gasp.

She is too. She's, well you must have seen that nude scene she did in the remake of *Le Grand Meaulnes*, and that's exactly how she looks. Only more three-dimensional. And more available.

I join her on the bed and make to kiss her. She shakes her head and draws mine down past her smooth, pale belly towards her pubic mound. Towards Christine Villeneuve's actual pubic mound, as seen in the movies. As previously explored, so it's rumoured, by Gerard Depardieu, Serge Gainsbourg, Yves Montand and, perhaps less fortunately, Roman Polanski. As previously fantasized about by every sentient male on the planet.

I feel the wiry hair against my nose and mouth. I inhale her earthy perfume. I part her soft pink lips with my fingers and probe deep inside with my tongue.

'Doucement,' she gasps.

I flicker my tongue more gently. I lick and I suck and I lick and lick until my tongue is stiff and my jaw aches. But it doesn't matter. I'm going down on Christine Villeneuve, that's all I can think of. I'm actually going down on Christine Villeneuve.

And suddenly she's reaching down and slipping a condom on me and then I'm actually fucking Christine Villeneuve. I'm actually fucking Christine Villeneuve. I'm actually—

Fuck!

I roll from on top of the girl who suddenly bears very little resemblance to Christine Villeneuve.

'You seemed very distant,' she remarks.

My desperation to speak to Repton the next morning is only exceeded by my terror of catching him in flagrante with his catamite du jour.

I wait outside his bedroom for two hours, chain-smoking, chain-drinking coffee, channel-hopping between *GMTV*, *The Big Breakfast*, *Kilroy* and Children's BBC, sweating, grinding my teeth, clawing at my hair, loathing myself more deeply with each passing second.

At last he emerges.

'Are you alone?' I hiss.

'Only the very privileged few get bed *and* breakfast in this little bordello. Good night?'

'What does it look like?'

'Oh dear. If you'll just let me grab a coffee—'

'Here.' I hand him a cup.

Repton takes a sip. 'Bit cold.'

'*Repton,*' I plead.

Repton sighs and searches for a cigarette. I hand him one of those too.

'So you had a row with Sam?' he says.

'Worse,' I say.

'You got on so well with Sam that you had second thoughts about Martha?'

'Worse.'

'No! You didn't? You can't have—?'

'I did.'

'You actually slept with Christine Villeneuve?'

'Oh, just shut up and listen, will you?'

So I tell him about my very nearly perfect evening with Sam. Martinis at the Met Bar, an absinthe at the Groucho, dinner at this amazing place in Smithfield which serves cool things like foie gras and cassoulet in tiny portions so you can eat lots and lots and which is absolutely impossible to get into unless you're amazingly well connected. Which, of course, Sam is. God, how she is. She can get us into any club we want to go to, any members-only bar, any restaurant. Whether it's because she's in PR or because she's young and beautiful or because she's Marius Schenk's girlfriend I don't know and I really don't care. The point is that this girl holds the key to everything that is cool and groovy and wonderful in the whole fucking metropolis. And tonight, Matthew, she's going to open all those doors for me. Just for me.

And for the first time in, blimey, probably the first time in five years, I remember just what it was I saw in Sam. It's not that she's stunningly beautiful (though boy does it feel great getting so many jealous looks from every bloke in every place we visit); it's not that she's carrying grams and grams of top quality coke (you think we could have survived all that Martini and absinthe and champagne unassisted?); it's not that she's footing the bill for an evening which might otherwise have cost me a week's earnings (cheers, Marius!); and it's not that she introduces me to more supermodels, DJs, rock stars and movie actors in one night than I've met in a whole career of celebrity-infested journalism (though it all contributes to my generally beneficent state of mind, obviously). But no. These groovy accoutrements are merely the icing on the cake. The thing that most impresses me is, well, Sam herself. Her astonishing social ease; her infectious laugh; her fluent repartee; her terminal joie de vivre. There's just no one else in the world like her. She's so – *UP*!

Too up, almost. Because after all that fizz and foie gras at Club Gascon, frankly, I'd be quite happy to call it a night. Unlike Sam who absolutely insists we've got to pop into Turnmills, it's so near, and since we're in the area we might just as well move on to the Blue Note. And I really don't know how I manage it – well, obviously, I do, I do, my streaming nostrils and motor-mouth give me a pretty good idea – but at 2 a.m. I'm still juddering like a bastard to some hardcore drum 'n' bass and thinking 'I'm young, I'm young, I'm still young, I should do more of this', till Sam yells, 'It's winding down. Time to move on,' and I suddenly realize, no, this really is it, I've had enough.

So we compromise and end up at Marius's obscenely huge warehouse apartment, dancing to one of his trancier mix tapes, me catatonic and stiff, Sam daisy-fresh and lithe, snaking and shimmying like one of those tanned ultrababes you see on those special poseur platforms at Ibizan clubs.

Marius isn't there, of course. DJ-ing in Iceland or somewhere. Which is unfortunate, since if he were here, I obviously wouldn't be in a position to do the terrible, terrible thing I end up doing.

All I can say in my defence is that my mind is not in full working order. It's pure feral instinct which leads me to place a hand either side of Sam's bare midriff, so that I feel her warm flesh pulsing against my palms. Sam fixes me with a look which may be significant, may be the drugs or may be my imagination. Whatever, she keeps on dancing and my hands stay where they are.

'This is nice,' I think. 'We can still be intimate without any of that sex nonsense rearing its ugly head.'

Just to make sure, I slip my hands higher up her waist, beneath her skimpy T-shirt. Sam still doesn't respond. Apart, maybe, from thrusting her hips just that little bit more energetically.

After a while I move my hands still higher, almost but not quite touching her breasts which – amazing that I didn't notice this before – appear to be bare. Even nicer, that. That I can still very nearly touch her bare breasts without Sam minding, without me deluding myself that the gesture is anything more than a sign of platonic affection.

So surely it won't do any harm if I give my old friends a nostalgic squeeze. Will it?

'That's not allowed,' says Sam, when I try.

'Isn't it?' Her nipples are hard.

'No,' she says, allowing me to tweak her nipples until they're harder still.

'I'd better stop then,' I say, raising her shirt and burying a breast in my mouth.

'Yes,' she gasps as I press a hand tight against her crotch, almost lifting her from the ground. She rubs herself rhythmically against my fingers.

'This is a very bad idea,' I say.

'Very bad,' she says, pulling my hand from beneath her. She leads me towards the far end of the apartment. Towards the enormous, top-international-DJ-style bed.

We make love. At first it's really good. Better than I can ever remember with Sam. A proper, full-on, frenzied rapprochement fuck. Then, as they do with drugs, the niggling doubts begin to set in. I think, 'I'm fucking my ex-girlfriend on her new boyfriend's bed.' I think, 'I'm fucking my ex-girlfriend three days before I move in with my new one.' I think, 'I'm only doing this because I'm out of my tree on drink and drugs.' I think, 'I'll regret this in the morning.' I think, 'If I go on thinking like this, I'll lose my hard-on.' I think, 'I am losing my hard-on.' I think, 'Quick. Quick. Think some erotic thoughts. Think – sex with Martha? No. No. That'll make things even harder. Even, limper rather. Think – sex with Christine Villeneuve. She's there in your brain. Still fresh. It could have worked out. It could have. Instead of saying goodbye at the end, she could have called you back. She could have said, yes, yes, she could have said, "Tu veux coucher avec moi?" And you would have thought it was a fantasy, that. But it isn't a fantasy, you can tell it's not a fantasy, because you're doing it now. You're fucking Christine Villeneuve. It's real, it's real and it's happening now.'

'And that's it,' I say to Repton. 'That's what happened. And God, I wish it hadn't and I wish I hadn't told you but I had to tell someone and – Jesus, Repton – what the fuck am I going to do?'

'There's only one thing you can do,' he replies. 'Forget about it.'

'Forget about it! It's the only detail in my whole miserable bastard life I can remember.'

'Well, obviously. It only happened a few hours ago.'

'She'll know, won't she?'

'Not necessarily.'

'Not necessarily. That means yes. They know these things, women. They always know.'

'So come clean. Tell her everything. You never know. She might respect you for it.'

'Oh yeah, right. I can just imagine: 'Thanks, Joe, for telling me you've fucked your ex-girlfriend three days before moving in with me. Now I know you're the man for me.'

'Mm. Now you put it like that—'

'So?'

'So you keep quiet and hope she never finds out. How can she find out? Sam's not going to say anything, is she?'

'God no. She's even more embarrassed than I am.'

'There you are then. Anyway, Sam's an ex. Fucking exes doesn't count as infidelity.'

'It doesn't?'

'Hardly. You slept with her often enough before you went out with Martha. Who's counting one extra fuck?'

'Martha?'

'Don't tell and she won't know.'

'Me, then.'

'Oh per-lease.'

'It's all right for you. Living in a moral vacuum. But some of us have principles.'

'Except when you're round your lubricious ex-girlfriend's place, up to your tits in champagne and charlie, and you suddenly think it would be a nice idea if you put those principles on hold for half an hour and—'

'God, you can be a cunt sometimes.'

'If I'm a cunt, what on earth does that make you? Get real for a moment, Joe. You messed up. You've no one to blame but yourself. You ask me for advice and I'll give it. As cuntishly as I see fit.'

'But you're telling me to lie to her. How can I lie to someone who trusts me?'

'Best sort of person to lie to, I'd have thought. Anyway, who said you had to lie?'

'Well, suppose she asks me how my evening with Sam went. Which she's bound to do.'

'Tell her the truth. Tell her it was a total disaster.'

'And when she asks for details?'

'Do what you did last night. Use your imagination.'

'Repton, this isn't funny.'

'Joe, do you think you're the first person in the world to have been unfaithful to his partner? Thousands of us do it, every day.'

'You don't have a partner.'

'I can promise you that if I did and I found myself in your position, I'd lie my arse off rather than ruin a good relationship.'

'I thought good relationships were ones where you don't have to lie.'

'Funny that. Only this time yesterday I was talking to

someone rather like you. And that's just the sort of glib idealism he would have dismissed as feminist bollocks.'

'Maybe the feminists were right.'

'Maybe you have lost the plot completely.'

'Maybe I have and I don't care. I'm going to ring her now and tell her everything. If she can't find a way to forgive me, well, maybe it was never meant to be.'

'OK,' says Repton. 'Just so long as I don't have to hear any of it. Use the phone in my bedroom, I should.' He sounds grumpy.

'You think this is a mistake, don't you?'

'Yes,' he says.

'I'm doing it for her, Repton.'

'You're doing it for yourself. Because you haven't got the courage to live with your guilty conscience.'

'Then I'm sorry.'

I shut the bedroom door behind me and pick up the phone.

'Oh, please don't pick it up,' I think. 'Please don't pick it up.'

She doesn't. Her answer message clicks on.

'Hi, I'm not in right now, so if you want to leave a message – just speak after the beep.'

So perky. I remember when she recorded it, just after we'd decided that I was going to move in. She'd wanted to re-record it. Thought it sounded too giggly, too happy – especially the girlie inflection at the end. And I'd said no, keep it. Why be shy of sounding how you feel?

'Because then They'll know how I feel. And maybe They'll try to stop me,' she said.

And she was right. *They* have.

295

I dial her number at work. Then I put down the phone. Work's not the right place to break the news. Nor's home, for that matter. Nor's anywhere. There's no right place or right time to tell Martha I've fucked up, I'm not worthy of her and she might as well forget about me.

And I realize Repton's right. I am only doing this to salve my guilty conscience; to feel better by making Martha feel as bad as I do. The only person who deserves to suffer is me. Boy, do I deserve to suffer. The more horribly the better. Only then can I purge myself of all my sins. Only then can I prove to Martha how sorry I am, how badly I want to win her back.

There's a way of doing it, too. The very worst, most horrible way imaginable.

I pick up the phone and make two calls. The first is to the hotel where I will temporarily stay, beyond anyone's contact, until my flight departs. The second is to Tom Bland, appealing to his better nature to let me undertake the shark mission which had originally been offered to me. Tom's better nature is not in evidence. When I bring up the small matter of leopard-print poser pouches, however, Tom agrees that on balance, perhaps I am a more deserving candidate to enter the jaws of death than he.

After Repton has gone to work, I write him a long letter. I write another even longer one to Martha. I don't tell either of them where I'm going. I just say at the end that I've gone away for a while to think things over.

I post them both just before I leave to take my flight from Heathrow.

TIGER

This is the one that gets you when you're surfing in Hawaii, diving in the Maldives, swimming in Durban, escaping from Cuba to Florida on your pitifully inadequate home-made raft or in fact virtually anywhere in the world where the water's warm. If you're unlucky, you'll recognize him by the stripey, tiger-like bars on his side. If you're even more unlucky, you won't because once he's grown really big, his warning stripes fade.

He is undoubtedly the world's most evil shark after the great white, partly because of his size (up to twenty-four feet) and ferocity, partly because he tends to hang out in exactly the sort of water in which you're most likely to swim, but mainly because of his voracious and undiscriminating appetite. The tiger shark will eat absolutely anything from raincoats and tennis shoes to any pigs, horses, cows and, of course, humans, unfortunate enough to find themselves in his domain. Hence his nickname: 'the dustbin of the seas'.

The tiger shark story I really hate is the one about the Australian shrimp boat which capsized off the coast of Queensland in 1983. Of the three people on board, only the skipper survived after scrambling on to a coral reef. You can guess what happened to the other two.

What's so awful about the story is that the shark was

circling them for hours before it struck. First the deckhand got his leg bitten off and nobly swam away from his mates to distract the shark. Then, just when the skipper had persuaded the other survivor – a girl in her early twenties – that everything was going to be OK, the shark returned.

'I was still holding her by the hand as he shook her about three or four times,' the skipper recalled. 'She only let out one little squeal as soon as it hit and I knew almost instantly that she was dead.'

That little squeal. Can't you just hear it now?

CHAPTER ELEVEN

Suppose you were going to write a book about a man who believed it was his destiny to be eaten by a shark. And suppose that, for some incredibly stupid reason, this man was going to get on an aeroplane, fly to South Africa and then lower himself into a cage in seas infested with great white sharks. How do you think you might describe his journey?

I know how I'd describe it. I'd have the poor bastard dose himself with a very large gin as soon as he'd checked in; then he'd down at least a couple more once he'd cleared customs; and then he'd stagger on to the aircraft, collapse into his seat, swallow a handful of valium pills and slip into a hellish netherworld where waking visions and sleeping dreams merged in a terrible miasma of apocalyptic hallucinations where stewardesses with razor teeth served vomitous airline soup swirling with fins while a shark-headed pilot set the controls for the heart of a pitilessly dark ocean whose surging waters ripped screaming passengers from their seats while the jagged fuselage tore chunks from their flesh as deep red arterial blood pumped from their gaping wounds, attracting white sharks and tiger sharks and bull sharks and hammerheads and makoes and oceanic white tips . . .

But that's fiction for you. Reality, in my experience, is

invariably far less interesting. And so it proves when I come to make that journey myself. I don't drink any alcohol at the airport because I know it'll make me dehydrated on the plane; I don't take any valium because I haven't got any; and though the stewardesses certainly look pretty scary with their pancake make-up, perma-tans and perma-grins, none of them appears to have triangular, razor teeth. Nor, I feel fairly confident, is the pilot a shark bent on crashing the plane so that his passengers can get eaten by his finny brethren.

Instead, my flight passes much like any other: short bursts of terror when the plane hits turbulence and the wings start flapping and you think they're going to fall off giving you maybe a minute or two to pray or scream or grab the nearest vaguely attractive female passenger and enjoy one last fuck before you die, though enjoy's scarcely the right word under the circumstances and anyway it wouldn't be physically possible in zero gravity when you're strapped in your seat and the plane's spinning out of control and briefcases and bags of duty free are careering out of the overhead lockers and dashing people's brains out, and even if it were physically possible the girl you picked would be bound to say no because hey she scarcely knows you and besides it would be awfully embarrassing if you were both in flagrante when it suddenly emerged that the wings hadn't actually fallen off and you were all going to survive after all; and long, long periods of reading, boredom, eating, boredom, sleeping, boredom, boredom, boredom and more boredom.

Personally, I prefer the short bursts of terror. At least, then, I can feel as if I'm being properly punished for my infidelity, whereas in the long boring bits I simply feel full of self-hatred and guilt. And boredom, of course.

To compensate, I try reminding myself of the horrific ordeal which lies ahead; I try picturing myself beneath the waves in the cage of death as the hungry maneaters close in; I try to imagine the first bite. But my mind won't co-operate. It has decided, apparently, that what I am about to do is so impossibly silly that it refuses to believe that I am actually going to go ahead with it.

Either that or it's just being wilfully perverse. Perhaps it wants to thwart my attempts to alleviate my guilt about Martha. Perhaps it's trying to deny me the tension-building 'thoughts of a condemned man as he journeys towards the jaws of death' intro I'd been hoping to use in my article. In the event of my surviving, that is.

After dinner, I strike up conversation with my neighbour, a grizzled New Yorker who is travelling with his wife to visit their son and daughter-in-law in Cape Town. He seems quite taken aback when I tell him why I'm going to South Africa. It turns out that he is even more squeamish about sharks than I am.

'But you're American,' I say. 'Americans aren't supposed to be scared of sharks.'

'Don't you believe it,' he replies. 'Which country do you think it was that made *Jaws*?'

I ask him whether he's ever seen a shark.

'Not a shark, no,' he says. 'But I've seen what they can do.'

I wait for him to go on, which he does after ascertaining that his wife is asleep.

'I was serving with the US Navy in the Yellow Sea,' he says. 'One of our fliers was down. It was my job to pick him up. What was left of him.' He stares ahead of him, moustache twitching. Then he turns to me and says funereally, 'And you've chosen to dive in a cage with great white sharks!'

'I know it sounds stupid to someone of your generation,' I begin – play this one right and I could be in line for a juicy war anecdote – 'but for those of us who've never been called up to serve our country, well, we have to find other ways of proving ourselves. You've no doubt heard of Dr Johnson. "Every man thinks meanly of himself for not having been a soldier"—'

'You'd like to have seen combat. That it?'

'Well, yes and no. I mean—'

'Let me tell you a story. It might have some bearing on what you've been telling me. It might not. It concerns my own service during the Korean war—'

Bingo!

'Now I spent part of my tour of duty on the front line, as a forward observer for the US Navy. It was my good fortune to serve there towards the end of the war, when most of the fighting was done. The Chinese and Koreans had their hills. We had ours. And that was the way we all expected things to stay until the peace treaty was signed.

'But until that treaty was signed, we had to carry on showing that we meant business. Both sides did. So every night, our infantry would send out reconnaissance patrols. And so would theirs. The principal aim of both sides being to avoid encountering the enemy. No one wanted to get himself killed so close to the end of the war.

'And – pretty much – no one did. Until one day we had a platoon of volunteers come up from the rear – clerks, cooks, ordinance – guys who'd never seen combat before but kind of wanted to while they still could. If you served in the combat zone, see, you got yourself a special medal. You also got your discharge from the military that much quicker. So that, I guess, was why they volunteered. Maybe earlier in the war, guys like that would never have been allowed out on patrol. But I guess people figured, nothing bad was going to happen to them at this stage.

'But – you know – it did. I remember the day well. It was real cold. Snow was on the ground. Dawn came and still those guys hadn't returned. Maybe they'd got themselves lost in the dark, I don't know, but I had a feeling there was going to be trouble because they'd now have to cross open ground in daylight. First we saw of them was a starburst. And we soon knew exactly where they were because of the mortar fire exploding around them. We called in covering fire and smoke soon as we could, but by then the damage had been done. Fifteen of them went out. Only seven came back alive and most of them were wounded. And do you know what one of them said to me, as he took cover in my dug-out? He said, "This wasn't meant to happen." And I had to agree with him that it wasn't. Because those guys should never have put themselves in that position. Nobody ordered them to. Nobody even asked them to. They did it because they wanted to test themselves. And that test was exactly what they got.'

I know I should probably feel chastened after this moving moral tale and I do my best to make the appropriate noises so as not to disappoint the old Korea vet, but my heart's really not in it. In fact I find his presumption rather galling. I am not a clerk or a cook about to get myself shot on patrol in Korea. I am me, Joe Davenport, about to go down in a cage with great white sharks. And I'm going to come up smiling, all limbs intact and very much alive.

Steeled by this bizarre and inexplicable conviction, I

manage to have my first ever good night's sleep on an aeroplane. I disembark at Cape Town refreshed, happy and almost exultant. I'm going to live! I'm going to live!

And the annoying thing is – annoying at least for the purposes of my 'Jesus I was so scared' article and for my urge to purge myself of Martha-related guilt – that this conviction refuses to go away. It enables me to say, quite confidently, to the car rental people at the airport, 'Back in a week.' And to the man in the dive equipment hire shop, 'See you in three days.' And it lingers still on the two-hour drive through Cape Town's eastern suburbs, over Sir Lowry's Pass and down the winding mountain roads which lead to a rugged coastline fringed with blue-tinged mountains.

It's here, just after I've passed a place called Hermanus (celebrated for its whale watching, the sign outside says), that reality redescends with a nauseating thud. It happens during my umpteenth attempt to tune the radio to a halfway decent music station. If they exist in the Cape Town region, the stereo in my car is incapable of picking them up. All it has found so far is a Moslem phone-in show and an evangelical Christian programme full of uplifting songs about how wonderful life is once you let Jesus into your heart. I've been listening to the latter for a good half hour, partly for kitsch value, partly out of the same impulse that in the past has driven me to do stupid things like standing on the very, very edge of the Grand Canyon or putting my hand as close as I can to the red-hot ring on an electric cooker without actually touching it.

Anyway, as I'm tweaking my way through the fuzz, I suddenly hear a word that stops me in my tracks. The word, almost inevitably, is 'shark'. It's preceded by great white. And it's followed by a news report describing how a scuba diver has been killed by the aforementioned beast just a few miles along the coast from the bay in which I'm planning to dive.

Now I suppose the rational response to this is 'Shit happens. I'm going to be in a ginormous steel cage. He wasn't.' But where sharks are concerned rational responses are not my forte. I pull over to the side of the road, hyperventilating and trembling. Clearly, it was no accident that I should have tuned in to the news report at the very moment it was describing this poor man's death. It was a warning; a sign from above that this expedition of mine was never meant to be.

So what do I do? Turn back for home, face the wrath of my travel editor, ruin my journalistic credibility, end up paying for my flights, my accommodation and all my other expenses, attract the scorn of Tom Bland, prove to Martha that I don't love her enough to risk my life for her, and spend the rest of my days knowing that I am a slimy, despicable coward who chickened out of an assignment he might very easily have survived? Or keep going and get eaten?

Tricky. Very, very tricky. The only way of resolving dilemmas like this, I find, is to have a cigarette. So I do and, sure enough, no sooner have I taken the first drag than a brilliant solution occurs. I will follow the advice of the Christian radio station and let God decide. If He lets four – no, let's make it five – cars pass in the time it takes me to finish the cigarette, then it means I mustn't go down in the cage. Otherwise I will.

Four cars pass. Well, one of them's a truck and I'm not sure whether or not that counts. Then a fifth one appears on the horizon. It's coming towards me fast and though I'm still smoking the cigarette, I'm close enough to the end to justify throwing it on the ground and calling it finished if I want to. Which makes me realize how stupid this game is. The decision's really up to me, not God. I'm still holding the cigarette, I notice, which probably means that deep down I don't want to be eaten. But there's still time to change my mind. Though not much. Less and less by the second. The car's getting nearer and nearer and nearer and—

It has pulled over. Just behind mine.

'Need any help?' the driver asks.

'Oh, that's awfully kind of you but I'm fine, thanks. I just stopped for a cigarette,' I reply, tossing the butt on to the ground. The car passes mine.

Oh dear. So death it's going to be.

Gaansbai is the sort of town you'd normally drive through without stopping. Unless maybe you needed some petrol from the garage, a packet of crisps from the 7–11 grocery, a crappy shell souvenir from the crappy shell souvenir shop, or a shark poster, shark postcard, shark T-shirt or shark hat from the shark shop. Fishing apart, sharks are the one thing that Gaansbai is really good at. Which makes it very much not my kind of town.

I suppose. Though to be fair, the couple who run my bed and breakfast are incredibly friendly, as is the man who directs me to the bar where I head to pick up some local colour, as are the deceptively fearsome-looking occupants of the bar, most of whom are seven feet tall with tree-trunk legs and heads the size and colour of pumpkins and whose forebears were almost certainly responsible for wiping out my ancestral compatriots at battles like Spion Kop and Majuba Hill. In fact, everyone's so nice that I start to get rather worried. Do they know something I don't? Is there some sort of *Stepford Wives* scenario occurring here?

To which the answer is probably yes as I've already had an inkling during my wander to the bar. While lost in one of the residential roads, I have chanced upon a house with what looks like a giant lobster pot in its yard. It's about seven feet tall, drum-shaped and made of criss-cross steel mesh. Presumably, the lobsters climb in through the hole about a foot from the top, fall in and get stuck at the bottom. Not that I really care about such technicalities. It's just good to know that the lobster on tonight's menu is going to be very cheap.

I'm about to move on when I see a local staring at me. 'I hope they're in season!' I say brightly, pointing at the cage. 'The lobsters,' I add, since he appears not to understand. Perhaps he only speaks Afrikaans. To enlighten him, I make snapping pincer gestures with my hands. He says, 'Thet isn't for lobsters, man. Thet's a shock cage.' Oh, yes, I think. The fabled Boer sense of humour. I laugh heartily for his benefit and ask him for directions to Ernie's Bar.

Ernie's Bar only serves beer in cans which is annoying since it means the stuff's too fizzy and tastes of metal but it does serve very good mussels, two plates of which I consume at £1.60 a throw while trying to converse with the blonde proprietress. 'Oh ja,' she says. 'You mustn't worry. The shock diving here is really safe. We have niver hed iny exidents.' Has she been down herself I wonder. 'Not yit, no,' she says. 'But I would like to very much.' She must be in her forties. She has lived here all her life. She's mad keen to go down in a shark cage. And yet she hasn't got round to doing it. A likely story. The reason she hasn't done it is because she knows how bloody dangerous it is.

My suspicions are confirmed following the arrival of two young Americans, in windcheaters, waterproof trousers and deck shoes. They look like refugees from the Pepsi Max commercial. They smell of fish.

'Jeez,' says one. 'Do I need a beer? Or do I need a beer?'

'You need a beer,' says his friend.

They both down their cans in one go.

'That,' exclaims one, wiping his mouth with the back of his hand, 'Was Beyond Awesome!'

'Um. You haven't been cage diving by any chance?' I enquire.

'Sure,' he replies. 'You too?'

'Tomorrow,' I say.

'Man, you are in for quite a trip,' he says.

'So it's as scary as they say?'

'Scary Is Not The Word!'

'Put it this way,' says his friend. 'You done bungee jumping? Altitude sky-diving? Whitewater rafting?'

'No.'

'Only say you had, you'd still have no idea – no idea at all – just how scary cage diving can be.'

We introduce ourselves. The one with the frizzy beard is called Wilton; the one who speaks in capital letters, Marty. I offer to buy them a drink. They insist that the honour should be theirs. 'It's the least we can do for a guy who's going down in a cage with *Charcharodon carcharias*!' says Wilton.

'But it's not actually dangerous. Is it?' I ask.

Marty laughs.

'You seen the cages they use?' asks Wilton.

'No.'

'Put it this way. They Ain't Fort Knox!' says Marty.

'You expect them to be big and square with thick steel bars. Like in the movies. But they ain't. They're made of chicken wire.'

'Shit! I think I have seen one. Are they round with a sort of gap near the top?'

'That's the viewing window. And you know what? It's big enough for a baby shark to get inside the cage!'

'No!'

'Straight up. Happens all the time. It's one of the things they don't tell you before you've paid your hundred and fifty bucks.'

'Tell him about The Rope,' says Marty.

'He doesn't want to hear about the rope,' says Wilton.

'What about the rope?'

'Oh, it's just a rope which ties the cage to the back of the boat.'

'Only trouble is,' says Marty, 'the shark sometimes gets Tangled In The Rope. And That Ain't Good. Round here, see, they care about sharks more than they care about tourists. They have to cut the rope, so the shark can get himself free. Which is cool so long as the shark does get himself free. But if he doesn't—' Marty shakes his head.

'If he doesn't— What?'

'Some of the sharks round here, they're real big. Real strong,' says Wilton. 'Now I guess you know that the shark cage floats on the surface. But a big shark, he can pull down that cage to the sea bottom. Easy.'

'Which kinda leaves you with a problem. See your air line runs to your air tank inside the boat. But your air line just ain't long enough to reach to the sea bottom. So you're underwater and you can't breathe. Which means you either got to hold your breath and hope that the shark comes back up before you suffocate—'

' – Or you gotta climb out of the window and swim back to the boat.'

'Very, very quickly.'

'I think I need another drink,' I say.

At the bar one of the pumpkin-heads nudges my arm.

'They're trying to scare you, boy,' he mutters.

'They're succeeding,' I reply.

'The shocks in this bay are frindly shocks. They have never given us any trouble.'

'I'm sure you're right but there was a report on the radio today—'

'That was different. He was spear-fishing. He was tying the fish around his body. The shark smells the blood. He wants to eat the fish. He eats the spear-fisherman too.'

'Even so. It's not exactly what you'd call friendly.'

'That shock was not a friendly shock.'

'Hey, mister,' calls Marty. 'Pardon me for butting in. But do you think maybe that shark was The Submarine?'

'Ja. It was the Submarine. No question.'

'I take it that the Submarine is a very big shark?' I say.

'You know Jaws?' says Marty. 'Jaws *Is* The Submarine.'

'Hang on. That book came out twenty-five years ago. It can't be the same shark, surely?'

'Sure it's the same shark,' says Marty. 'Only, since then, it's grown some. What is it they reckon now? Thirty, thirty-two feet?'

'Plus, minus ten metres,' agrees pumpkin-head.

'And boy is he mean! He hates humans. It all started with that fisherman – what's the guy's name?'

'His name is Bryan. Bryan Mendoza,' says pumpkin-head.

'That's the guy. You've seen Quint in *Jaws*? You know the story. He's out fishing one day when he feels something big, real big, on his line. So he starts hauling it in. It takes him hours. All day in fact. Because this fish is fighting real hard. And his arms are aching and his hands are raw but he knows it's worth it because this is the mother of all sharks. It might even make the world record. Anyhow, it's started getting dark, his strength is giving out, but he's seen the shark break the surface and man is it big. It is huge. "Just a little longer," he's saying to himself. "Just a little longer." And he can see the shark thrashing and fighting and thrashing and fighting. And he's almost landed this mother when something Totally Incredible happens! It is just Totally Fucking Unbelievable! This shark – Even Bigger than the one on the end of his line, comes shooting up from underneath the boat, grabs the other shark in his jaws and just carries it away like it was a tiny piece of bait. Can You Imagine?'

'Unfortunately.'

'Yeah, well, that's just the start of it. From then on, this guy Bryan, it becomes His Mission to catch that shark. Nothing else matters any more. The other sharks – they're just pilchards. He Wants The Submarine. And a shark that size, there just ain't a hook big enough to catch it. So he makes one himself. Out of steel. The biggest fish hook ever. And he goes out. It takes him weeks. But eventually he finds that shark and he starts hauling it in, just like the one before. Only this shark really knows how to fight. This shark makes the other one look easy. This shark is going to cost him every ounce of strength in his body. Maybe more, even, than he can give. But what the hell, he's going to try anyway. By that night, he's doing pretty well, he thinks. The Submarine's still a long way off but he's seen it break water a couple of times and he's feeling pretty hopeful. Until, suddenly, the line goes slack and he knows he's got that shark beat. Least he thinks he has until he pulls the line right in and finds this huge steel hook he made. The hook has been Bent Straight. And the guy is thinking, "Just how strong do you have to be to bend a hook straight?" And he's thinking, "This shark was Not Even Trying. He was just playing with me. He was doing this for fun!"

'But hey, this guy's a sports fisherman. There's nothing he likes more than a challenge. So he makes himself a bigger hook. And the same thing happens. Bent straight. So he makes himself an even bigger hook. Same thing again. So he goes and finds himself the toughest steel and makes a hook so big – we're talking ship's anchors here – that nothing on earth can bend it. And he goes out. And this time he knows it's gonna be make or break. Either he's gonna get that shark. Or he's gonna die trying.

'And he damn near does too. He fights for that shark a whole day and a night. Dawn comes. The guy's close to exhaustion but he knows the shark must be too. Not even The Submarine can keep going as long as that. And when he feels the line slacken, the guy thinks, "This time, I've got this shark beat." And he starts reeling in as fast as he can, in case the shark changes his mind, but he can't reel in fast enough, the line's still slack, and suddenly he understands why. The shark *is* beat, almost. Problem is, The Submarine knows he's almost beat. Which is why he's decided to change his strategy. He ain't gonna waste any more energy on trying to escape. He's gonna use it to sink the boat. And that's just what he does. He comes swimming, fast, toward the boat. He leaps out of the water. Comes crashing down into the stern. Now, Theo, he's got himself a pretty big boat. But you know how much a full-grown white shark weighs? Three tons, that's how much. And that's just an ordinary full-grown white shark. The Submarine's closer on four. Four Tons! That Is A Lot Of White Shark. We Are Talking Serious Damage. And sure enough, that boat is starting to sink. And Bryan is already on his radio calling Mayday, Mayday. And The Submarine is coming round for another pass. Up into the air and *bang*! Hard down on the boat. And Bryan knows that unless someone answers his call real soon, He Is Going To Die.

'This scares him. 'Course it scares him. But the strange thing is, fear is not the only thing he is feeling. He's also feeling respect for that shark. That shark is a worthy opponent. And if The Submarine is gonna kill him, he's thinking that maybe it's earned the right. But if he is gonna survive – and he makes this vow right then – he's never going to hunt the shark ever again. Not The Submarine nor any shark. Because he knows that these creatures ain't nearly as dumb as he thought they were. Maybe it's the guys who fish for them who are the dumb ones. And maybe he should spend his life protecting these sharks, not killing them. And that's exactly what he's been doing since. Another boat came and rescued him just before his sank. Cute story, huh?'

'What about the Submarine?'

'That's not so cute. Seeing he wasn't going to get the guy, he pulled away so hard that the hook tore through his mouth. You can still see the scar, apparently, if you're unlucky enough to get that close. Guess he's never forgotten what happened. And never forgiven, neither. Just go ask that spear-fisherman. What there is left of him.'

*

'Am I going to die?' I ask.

And almost everyone laughs: the middle-aged, middle-class English dad; the young French-speaking couple; the elderly American with the binoculars; and Piet, the boat's taciturn skipper.

Only Miles, English dad's bolshie teenaged son, and Adam, the wiry South African in charge of our expedition, remain po-faced.

'Ja, for sure you're going to die,' says Adam. 'Cigarettes are bad for your health. Especially when you smoke them inside my nice clean boat. I have already told you, smoking on deck only!'

But I'm not smoking inside his nice clean boat. Not really. I'm standing just inside the doorway which leads to the shelter of the wheelhouse, taking care to keep my cigarette hand outside so that the smoke gets blown away by the bitter wind which is sweeping the boat's unprotected stern. The combination of wind, spray and waves makes it very dangerous to obey Adam's instructions to the letter. As is demonstrated when I do step outside to take my last few drags and the boat crashes headlong into an unusually large wave, drenching me in spray and nearly hurling me overboard.

I waddle, sodden, back inside.

Adam gives me a told-you-so look.

Miles looks up from his book and sniggers. English dad goes, 'Oh. Poor you.' The French couple, Simone and Thierry, make room for me on their side of the bench. Simone offers me a towel.

'Le grand chef des requins. Il parle français?' I ask her.

'Non. Pas du tout.'

'Bon. Parce que je voulais dire, c'est un vrai branleur, n'est-ce pas?'

Simone and Thierry laugh. They are terribly impressed that I know the French word for 'wanker'. Apparently, they reached this conclusion themselves two days ago.

'So what are you doing here?' I ask. (Our conversation takes place in French by the way, but I'm translating it all into English, in case you think I'm trying to show off.)

'We have no choice,' Thierry replies. 'We paid our money in advance for a week's diving.'

'And I tried asking for it back. But the wanker said no,' says Simone, who incidentally is stunningly gorgeous and would probably strike me as enormously shaggable were it not for her worrying and guilt-inducing resemblance to Sam.

'But the sharks. You have seen them already?'

'Unfortunately, no,' says Thierry.

'No?' I ask. 'You've been here two days and you still haven't seen a shark?'

'Oh yes. We've seen a shark. The fin. The mouth which goes – ' Simone pulls up her upper lip to expose her gums, opens her mouth wide and chomps like a great white in feeding mode.

'And?'

'It was nice,' says Simone.

'Very nice,' says Thierry.

'But after a time, it becomes boring,' says Simone. 'We want to see the sharks from inside the cage but so far it has not been possible.'

'Why not?'

Thierry shrugs. 'You must ask the big shark chief wanker.'

The big shark chief wanker is talking, in Afrikaans, to Piet. I decide that it's not worth interrupting. He'll only come up with another smartarse answer designed to make me look stupid. I read my book, *Alamein to Zem Zem*, instead.

It's an eyewitness account of the Western desert campaign, written by a young tank commander called Keith Douglas, and it's one of the best military memoirs I've ever read. What's interesting about it is that he describes the experience of war from the viewpoint of a total novice: going to the front line for the first time; how it feels on the eve of battle; what it's like seeing your first dead body; the fear, the boredom, the exhilaration, the confusion, the sheer randomness of it all.

It's this sheer-randomness element that bothers me most. My old art master Mr Jennings – the one who fought with the Long Range Desert Group – once told me that you never thought it would be you who was going to cop a bullet. It was always going to be someone else. But presumably the people who did end up copping a bullet thought exactly the same thing until they got killed. So really, a conviction that you're not going to die just yet is a pretty useless defence against mortality.

Douglas doesn't think he's going to die either. Nor does he during the desert campaign, which is why it's very tempting to identify with him as he charges those deadly 88 mm guns in his thinly armoured Crusader and emerges, unlike the majority of his comrades, unscathed. But you don't want to identify with him too much because, as you learn from the poignant foreword, he ends up being killed a couple of years later during the D-Day invasion.

So I leave Douglas to his fate and head outside for

another consolatory fag. The sea's much calmer now because we're entering a sheltered channel between two narrow rocky islands. Dyer, the bigger of the two, is speckled white with sea birds. 'Jackass penguins!' exclaims the American with the binoculars. The other island, Geyser, is blubbering with seals. The majority sprawl oafishly on the rocks. The braver ones are gathered in rafts on the water's edge or playing and diving amid the crashing surf. Which just goes to show how stupid seals are because, as their parents, grandparents and great-grandparents must surely have told them by now, the sea round here is absolutely teeming with creatures hell-bent on eating them.

That's why the channel is called Shark Alley. It contains probably the highest concentration of great whites anywhere in the world. And the insanely stupid thing is, I'm actually about to jump into it, protected only by a cage with bars so thin that they could scarcely hold out a fierce kitten, let alone a three-ton monster. The thought is not a happy one.

Piet anchors the boat in mid-channel. It's quiet. Too quiet. Actually that's not true. The seals are making a terrible din, some of them baaing like sheep, some of them groaning like humans in pain, and some of them even sounding a bit like seals. So it isn't quiet, exactly. What I mean is that it *feels* quiet. Ominously tranquil.

This, I imagine, is what it's like when you drift into the Bermuda Triangle or the Sargasso Sea. You half expect Captain Nemo to emerge from the depths, playing Bach's *Toccata and Fugue* on his great organ. Or a giant squid to wrap its tentacles round the boat. Use your imagination – and mine's working overtime right now – and you could easily confuse the snake-headed strands of slimy brown kelp poking above the water for sea monsters. And that weird whipped-cream froth floating on the surface a few hundred yards downstream – caused by the action of the waves on the kelp carbohydrates, Mr Binoculars is telling anyone who's interested – looks to me like a group of distant icebergs. So we have *Jaws*, *Ten Thousand Leagues Under the Sea*, the *Titanic* and the Bermuda Triangle all rolled into one deceptively placid hellhole. Great.

I peer queasily over the side of the boat. The water's much clearer than I expected. In fact, I think I can just make out the sea bottom – encouraging really, since somehow the idea of being killed in shallow water seems marginally less horrible than dying in the bottomless blue.

Adam hands me a thick wooden pole about the size of a baseball bat. Belatedly I remember that a great white could quite easily leap out of the sea, snatch me in mid-air and drag me back into the water. 'Thanks.'

I practise a few swipes. The place to go for is the snout, apparently. Or the eyes.

'If you want to play the bloody fool, find another boat,' Adam snaps. He indicates a large steel drum in which he has slopped a mixture of pilchards and fish oil. My punishment, it would appear.

The chum smells vile. And the harder I pummel the oily fishy mess, the viler it gets. I try mashing with my arms outstretched but my muscles soon tire; then I try with my head pulled back but that just gives me a stiff neck. The only efficient method, unfortunately, is for me to stand right next to the drum with my nose directly over the noisome slop, mouth closed so as to avoid tasting the stray bits of red mush which keep spurting on to my face.

I've just begun to get the hang of it when the wind changes direction. Now, the fishy smell is blown away from my nose. But it's replaced by something even more horrible – the pungent, throat-curdling blend of stale urine and rancid dung, wafted on the wind from a million and one incontinent seals. I make it to the side of the boat just in time. The vomit drifts in an oily trail past the stern and small fish emerge to peck at the chunkier morsels. Adam claps me on the back. 'If that doesn't bring in the shocks, nothing will!' he says.

As it turns out, nothing does. Not my sick. Not the ladles of chum which Adam pours over the side. Not the chunks of whale blubber and butchered seal trailing by a rope from the stern. Not anything. For after five hours, the tally of sharks attracted to our boat remains at precisely zero.

Perhaps this wouldn't matter so much if it weren't for the three other boats now moored in the channel, each with its own cage and party of shark watchers. They arrived after us and yet, infuriatingly, every one of them has managed to attract its own personal shark. The nearest shark is no more than thirty feet away, circling a red Dory-type, open-topped speed boat with White Death Safaris emblazoned on the side.

This is my first ever great white sighting and to be honest it's a bit of an anticlimax. Clearly the shark in question has not seen *Jaws*. If he had, he would know that it was his job to scud menacingly along the surface, fin in full sail, while the dur-dum dur-dum dum-dum-dum-dum-dum-dum-dum-dum theme plays in the background. He would then swallow the seal bait whole and, very possibly, drag the White Death Safari boat to the bottom of the sea and pick off its occupants one by one.

But this shark is a pathetic shark. He spends most of the time skulking underwater, only surfacing to inspect his prey at the very last minute, giving just a brief flash of his dorsal and tail fin before diving down again for another pass. And he won't even bite the seal bait. He just sniffs it, circles and sniffs again, like a picky cat who has been denied his Whiskas and been offered a tin of supermarket own-brand instead.

I suppose this should come as a relief. But my main feeling is one of intense frustration. If the sharks won't come to our boat, there'll be no point in going down in the cage. And if I can't go down in the cage, it means I'll have to come back tomorrow. Or the day after. Or the day after that. And what if the sharks never come? What if I have to fly home without ever having undergone my ordeal in the cage of death? What will my cousin and Repton and Tom Bland think? How will I ever be able to face Martha?

Lunch is a predictably dismal affair. We congregate on deck, chewing stale bread rolls (cheap marge, a sliver of unripe tomato, budget salami), and watch enviously as the occupants of the White Death Safari boat take turns to enter their shark cage. When they emerge, they gibber excitedly, making thumbs-up signs and 'it was this big' gestures. Our seal and whale bait remains untouched.

'Maybe we're using the wrong sort of bait,' I suggest. Adam says nothing.

'Well, we're obviously doing something wrong,' I persist. 'I mean why else would the sharks have stayed away from this boat for three days running?'

'If you don't like it, you can swim out to White Death Safaris. It's only twenty metres,' he says.

'If we carry on like this, I might!' I reply.

I almost mean it too. My fear of sharks has been almost totally overwhelmed by my fury at Adam's incompetence; my intense jealousy of the White Death divers; and the urgency of my desire to get this whole wretched cage ordeal over and done with so that I can fly home and get on with my life.

And still the sharks refuse to come. The wind picks up. Mr Binoculars gets seasick and cowers below deck. It starts to drizzle. The French couple have a row. The rival boats up-anchor and head home. Middle-class dad politely enquires whether he'll get any money back if the expedition's unsuccessful. Adam bites his head off. Bolshie teenager sniggers. Then middle-class dad bites *his* head off. Bolshie teenager goes to sulk on the flying bridge. Piet says something to Adam. Adam nods and Piet heads for'ard to wrestle with the anchor. We all exchange mournful glances. It's over.

Well, almost. The thing that happens next is so boring I can scarcely be arsed to tell you. But the gist of it is, just before we leave, one of those pathetic sharks finally does decide to make a few desultory passes at our bait. We lower the cage and take turns to get inside. When my turn comes, I'm totally – and I mean totally – unscared. The shark turns up, hovers around my cage for about five minutes – the bastard's only about six feet long and he refuses to open his savage jaws or rattle my cage or do anything authentically evil and shark-like – before buggering off into the blue. And that's it.

While the others go for a celebratory round at Ernie's, I sulk in my hotel room. Though I managed to say all the right things on the boat journey home – 'Yeah. Totally amazing. The ultimate!' etc., etc. – I know that after a few beers I'll only end up saying what I really think. And what I really think is so depressing that I scarcely dare admit it to myself, let alone to a party of bomb-happy revellers.

I have survived my ordeal. And nothing has changed. I

don't feel any braver, I don't feel any happier, I don't feel any more fulfilled. I don't feel anything except a terrible, aching emptiness.

Tomorrow morning, I will drive back to Cape Town. I will spend two or three days doing all the things tourists are supposed to do: a lobster lunch at Panama Jacks, dinner at Blues, a cable-car ride up Table Mountain, a tour of the wine region, a trip down to the Cape of Good Hope. Then I'll fly home to the same old life and the same old job and the same old anxieties. And then I'll die.

Of course, if I wanted to be big and grown-up and sensible about it all I'd ask myself, 'Well, what did you expect?' I mean, there are ways and means of changing one's life – winning the pools, say, or finding God, or coming out of the closet, or going to live in a pretty mas in Provence – but jumping into a cage, seeing a great white shark, and then getting out again is not generally thought to be one of them.

But I don't want to be big and grown-up and sensible. Not about anything. Ever. What I want to happen is all the things I subconsciously hoped would happen once my ordeal was over.

Like: rediscovering my zest for life; becoming incredibly famous; finding that I own a large Queen Anne town house in Central London with huge rooms, high ceilings, original period features, and a two hundred foot garden; and another house in the country with about fifty acres of land and a tennis court and swimming pool and servants; suddenly remembering that I have written my novel – the best of the century – and that I've already been given a huge advance and that it's being published next week and that I'm going to be even more incredibly famous than I was ten seconds ago; growing a new set of lungs which are immune to smoking; discovering that I am, in fact, immortal and that I'm going to remain exactly as I am for ever only with better eyesight, no back trouble and the fitness of an athlete, the suppleness of a gymnast and an IQ of 160; and that I have the ability to confer this miraculous state on anyone I like; being forgiven by Martha, marrying her and living happily ever after in a relationship where I'm allowed to sleep with anyone else I want, not that I do because I'm so blissfully happy that I have eyes only for her . . .

All right. So maybe it was just a little unrealistic for my subconscious to have expected these things. But that's what subconsciouses do, isn't it? They come up with the desire. While the mind deals with the grim reality.

Reality, for example, like the sudden ringing of a bedroom phone which you really can't be arsed to answer because you're feeling so depressed.

Ring-ring. Ring-ring. Ring-ring.

Oh fuck off, will you?

Ring-ring. Ring-ring. Ring—

'Yeah?'

'Joe?'

'Martha!'

'You're alive.'

'Yes, I'm alive. How did you—?'

'From your travel people. After about an hour's pleading. I think they thought I was a nutter. Suppose I might have sounded a bit hysterical.'

'I'm sorry.'

'You might have left me a number.'

'I'm really, really sorry.'

'I know.'

'You do?'

'"I'll swim through shark-infested seas for you." Ring a bell?'

'Oh. That. Yeah.'

'Did you think that's what I really wanted?'

'Um. No?'

'No. It was the very last thing I wanted. Do you think what I saw in Hong Kong wasn't enough for one lifetime.'

'It was you? Why didn't you say?'

'I thought you would have guessed.'

'I'm sorry.'

'So you keep saying. Wouldn't it have been easier to have said it to my face?'

'I felt too bad.'

'You felt bad! How do you think I felt when I got your note? Mm? You think I went "Oh yippee. My boyfriend's slept with his ex. But it's all OK because to show he loves me, he's flown to South Africa to get eaten by a great white shark!"'

'But I do love you.'

'I know.'

'Can you forgive me?'

'I don't know.'

'I wouldn't blame you if you didn't.'

'Please. No more burning flesh or I think I'll scream. Just tell me how you are.'

'Fine.'

'And the sharks?'

'They were fine too.'

'There's something you're not telling me.'

'Is there?'

'Never mind. You can tell me tomorrow.'

'Why tomorrow?'

'It's when my flight gets into Cape Town.'

Sure, sure, I know what you're thinking, 'You jammy bastard. You got off that one pretty lightly.' Personally I'm not so sure. I mean, of course, it's totally fantastic that Martha still cares, that she's coming out to see me, that we're almost certain to make things up. But there's one thing that bothers me. That remark she made about the something I hadn't told her. She was right. Absolutely right.

I have lost my fear of sharks.

There. I've said it.

I have lost my fear of sharks.

Which should be the best thing that has ever happened to me. But it's not. It's a total fucking disaster.

I have lost my fear of sharks.

Let's consider for a moment what that means.

It means, for one thing, that I will now have to find something else to be scared of. Lung cancer, bowel cancer, throat cancer, pancreatic cancer, testicular cancer, say. Or brain tumours, leukaemia, emphysema, AIDs, Creutzfeldt–Jacob's disease and necrotizing fasciitis. Or that fungal disease you get from the ancient spores in mummies' tombs; or that fish that swims up your urine stream while you're pissing into the Amazon, lodges itself inside your bladder and starts to breed, giving you a slow agonizing death which can only be averted by chopping your penis off.

Not to mention being killed by crocodiles, alligators, polar bears, grizzly bears, lions, tigers, Cape buffalo, hippos. Or cows. They're dangerous too, you know. Especially during calving. They gang up on you and crush you to death. As do pigs. Then there's wolves and rabid dogs; soldier ants, scorpions, snakes and spiders; and stonefish and killer whales. And bees, of course. They're responsible for more human deaths than any other animal on the planet.

And there are plane crashes, car crashes, motorbike crashes and train crashes; there's drowning and being burned alive—

And you know what? Dying by any one of the above hideous methods is in fact far, far more likely than being eaten by a shark. Because, let's face it, there are only an average fifty shark attacks a year, very few of which are fatal. Which, of course, I knew all along. But until now I was never particularly bothered by the statistical improbability because I believed I'd be the exception to the rule. And in a funny way that belief protected me from worrying too much about the other vile deaths I've just mentioned. In fact, with hindsight, I can now see that shark fear was my friend, my paranoia protector, my guardian angel.

Now that I've lost that friend, my whole existence seems a sham. All those 'Why I'm scared of being eaten by a shark' conversations I used to enjoy: they were a total waste of time. All the laughs I got as a result of my eccentricity, all the jokes at my expense, all the attention: they're history.

I've turned into the po-faced, eco-minded party-pooper I used to hate. The chap who butts into your conversation and says, 'You know, actually, sharks really aren't as danger-ous as they're cracked up to be. In fact they need protecting from us far more than we do from them. Consider their beauty, their grace, their fluidity, their evolutionary suprem-acy. The perfect killing machine unchanged since the dawn of . . .' Oh, piss off, will you? We were trying to have fun.

Just imagine if I'd been like that at Marc and Jennifer Stone's party. Perhaps, who knows, I might still have chatted to Martha. But we would never have bonded so soon. In fact I'm sure I would have forgotten about her the moment we parted. And we would never have taken that trip to the London Aquarium. And we would never have fallen in love. And we would never have known that we were perfect for one another. Because, well, we wouldn't have been.

Sure, Martha and I have plenty in common besides sharks. But our shared fear was the glue which bound us. And now that I've lost my fear, while hers has grown stronger as a result of my stupid mission, I feel as if I've betrayed her far more cruelly than ever I did over that meaningless shag with Sam.

There is no doubt about it. Our relationship is doomed. She's going to find out. I know she will. And there's absolutely nothing I can do to stop it.

THE GREAT WHITE

I have only two things to say about great white sharks. They must die. They must die.

Actually, that's not true. I have hundreds and hundreds of things to say about great white sharks, starting with the dread international eco-conspiracy which has caused them to be declared a protected species by virtually every civilized nation on earth.

I use the word civilized advisedly. Because frankly, if that's civilisation then let's bring back the Dark Ages. At least in the Dark Ages man knew where he stood. It was kill or be killed. And kill, as I say, is exactly what we should do to the world's (with luck) ever-dwindling supply of great white sharks.

Sure I'm familiar with all the tedious arguments in the great white's defence. The sea is his domain, not ours. He is a vital part of the food chain. He is, in his foul, ravening-jawed, brutish, evil, murderous way, a rather magnificent creature who has changed little since the dawn of time. The perfect killing machine etc., etc.

But so fucking what? If we're so keen to eradicate the tsetse fly and the malarial mosquito, why can't we have the courage of our convictions and go for the big one – charcharodon carcharias – as well?

Maybe it will mess up the food chain a bit if we wipe out

all the world's known maneaters. But that's just something we'll have to live with. After all, which would you rather have: too many seals or the ever-present threat of being gobbled up by a great white? If you ask me, it's a no-brainer. Good news for the fur trade, too.

'Oh, but it's just not fair,' I hear a handful of bearded eco-freaks whining. 'I mean, gee, it's not like the great white means us any harm. Human beings are not part of his diet. He only bites us by mistake. It's just our bad luck that he hasn't got very good eyesight. That from underwater, a surfer or a canoe or a scuba diver looks a bit like a seal.'

Huh. Try telling that to the dozens of surfers, canoers, scuba divers and swimmers who've been bitten in half by the half-blind motherfucker over the last few decades. I'm sure they'd feel so much happier to learn that they only died as a result of mistaken identity.

These are the facts: the great white shark is the deadliest fish in the ocean; he can grow more than twenty-six feet long and weigh over three tons; he has huge jaws, horrid pink gums, and nasty serrated teeth; he feeds using the 'bite and spit' method, thrusting his powerful, retractable jaws forward so as to inflict a massive bite on his victim before leaving it to bleed to death; he is hateful, ugly, merciless and evil and if he had his way he would kill us all.

Oh, and you don't just find him off the coasts of California, Mexico, South Africa and Australia. He is also responsible for several human fatalities in the Mediterranean, most recently that of Italian diver Luciano Costanza in 1989. Something to think about next time you're splashing around off Porto Ercole.

CHAPTER TWELVE

'Shark! *Shark!*' someone cries.

'Yeah, yeah,' I think, glancing up from my book. 'Been there, done that.'

But everyone else hurries sternwards to gawp at our visitor and I suppose it would be rude not to join them.

'By God, it's a whopper!' enthuses an Englishman about my age. 'Perhaps it's the one you saw earlier,' he adds.

'Probably,' I say.

Except the one I saw earlier doesn't exist. It couldn't do. No shark in the ocean – not even the Submarine – could ever grow as big as that.

I see it – or rather don't see it – before lunch, when I'm having a pee over the side of the boat. So I can't give it my fullest attention: not with one hand clinging for dear life on to the handrail, the other simultaneously trying to keep my flies open and to direct my urine flow into the sea rather than down my leg or the side of the boat or into the wind like some pillock did earlier, spraying everyone on deck.

Whatever it is is quite a long way distant, just beyond the point where Shark Alley meets the open sea. And I only glimpse it very briefly out of the corner of my eye, so I can't describe it in massive detail.

But this thing I see – or rather, think I see – reminds

me quite a bit of the poster for *Jaws*: the one which shows a shark's head surging upwards through the water to eat the swimmer. It doesn't have its jagged teeth bared or anything obvious like that. But it does definitely look like a shark's head – which, allowing for the perspective and distance, must make it a very, very, very big shark's head – sticking out of the sea. Except I know real sharks don't stick their heads out of the water like that. They only do that in movies.

By the time I've zipped up and gone to the prow for a better look the thing has disappeared. Very likely, I decide, it was a whale, or the conning tower of a submarine, or a protruding strand of kelp, somehow distorted by a trick of the light, or maybe just a mirage, the result of wishful thinking. The whole reason I've come back for a second day's cage diving, after all, is because of this pathetic fantasy of mine that I might end up seeing a shark so totally evil, huge and scary that I'll somehow regain my fear.

Fat chance of that, whatever Adam might say.

'Yesterday's sharks not good enough for your story, eh?' he asks me when I join the party of newcomers at the dock. Everyone's looking anxiously out to sea. Today it's so rough that it's touch and go whether we'll be able to launch the boat.

'They were OK,' I reply. 'But if you want it to make the lead feature, you're going to have to find me something a bit more – interesting.'

'I think I can guarantee you that,' says Adam.

'Really?'

'Sure. For your interesting shark these conditions are ideal. We call it strong water. When the sea is rough, the seals don't like to hunt in open water. They swim in Shark

Alley instead, where it's calm. The sharks know this. Especially the interesting sharks.'

'I see. And how will we be able to tell these interesting sharks from an ordinary shark?'

'Maybe you won't,' he says with a nasty grin. 'Maybe when you do, it will be too late, eh?'

Yeah, well, he would say that. Being a wanker and all.

Still I have to say that the shark currently hanging around our boat goes some way towards filling my requirements. It's at least twice the size of the six-foot tiddler we saw yesterday. And a lot more aggressive. Already, it has dispatched the chunk of whale blubber we put out as bait. Now it's circling angrily, while Piet frantically prepares the next lure: a dead seal pup whose entrails are spilling out on to the deck, leaking blood through the hole at the back of the boat and into the water. The shark wants more.

Barely has Piet tossed the seal astern than the shark has seized it. Grey snout retracted, jaws thrust forth, a raw, bloody cavern of razor-teeth and shredded gore. Bait clamped between its teeth, it thrashes and smashes from side to side, sending up great walls of spume on to the deck. Some of the more timid members our party flee to the safety and dryness of the cabin. I stay on deck, appraising the beast with my newfound professional detachment.

Piet stops wrestling with the line and inspects his rope-burned palms. He shakes his head and says something in Afrikaans to Adam. They both look at me and laugh.

'What's this?' I say, trying to look good-humoured.

'He says this shark has your name on it,' Adam replies.

It reminds me of a birthday card my cousin once made for me. On the front was a picture of a black fin with the word 'Joe' scrawled across it in bloody lettering.

'Come on, what are you waiting for?' Adam snaps. 'Suit up! I want you in first.'

I'd like to ascribe the sudden twinge I feel in my stomach to burgeoning fear. But I'm afraid it owes rather more to the swell of the sea and another meagre stale roll and marge lunch. Certainly, I manage to slip into my wetsuit with the accomplished ease of a hardened veteran. No fumbling, no where-does-this-bit go?, no shakes.

I don't look up but I can feel the others watching me. Bet they're really impressed, the way I can be so cool and confident just moments before slipping into that tiny hole at the top of the cage, right next to a bloody great shark in feeding mode.

They're bound to have heard all the horror stories. How, if the boat lurches at the wrong moment, you end up in the open sea rather than the cage. But I know that's just a myth put about by hardcore divers like me to scare rookies. Cage diving's safe. Nothing ever really goes wrong. Just watch me.

But no one does. My thunder has been stolen by an apparition on the port side of the boat. Another shark. Ho hum.

'What's it doing?' someone asks.

Adam goes to inspect. 'Spy-hopping,' he says.

Spy-hopping? I go to investigate.

Spy-hopping, it turns out, is when a shark pokes his head out of the water and looks around. Like that huge thing I saw in the distance this morning. The one I'd told myself couldn't possibly be a shark because sharks only do that sort of thing in movies.

'Come on. Come on. What're you waiting for?' Adam barks.

'Um.'

'You're not turning chicken on us, are you?'

Heads turn from the spy-hopping shark towards me. What's this? The party's resident Jacques Cousteau getting cold feet?

Piet slaps me on the back. 'He's OK,' he says. 'Aren't you, boy?'

'Yeah, yeah. I'm OK.'

I'm OK. I'm OK, I keep telling myself, as Piet takes my hand and helps me over the back of the boat. One step forward. And I'm in.

I'm OK. I'm OK. I'm OK.

Down to the cage bottom. Find the air line. Clear the mask. It won't clear. It's full of water. My eyes are stinging. I can't see. Calm. Calm! You're panicking. You can't panic. Now clear the mask. Clear the mask!

Good.

You've cleared the mask. You can see now. You can see.

I can see – Oh my God – I can see the shark coming towards me. Coming directly towards me.

Get back. Get back.

But what if there's one behind me?

Get back!

It's opening its mouth. It's going to bite. It is biting! It's got its fucking horrible fucking white fucking teeth round my fucking cage—

And it's gone.

And you survived.

An actual great white swam up to your cage. Bit it. And you survived.

And you're going to survive the next time it does it too.

It's going to do it again?

Of course it's going to do it again. It's what sharks do. But that's OK. You're going to survive.

How do you know?

Because – you just will.

But how do you *know*?

Stop thinking like that. If you start thinking like that—

I've started.

No!

Too late. I'm thinking it now and I can't stop thinking it. I've thought it while I'm at my desk and I've thought it in the swimming pool and I've thought it at parties and I've thought it on the beach and I've thought it in bed and I've thought it at breakfast and I've thought it almost everywhere on earth I've been. But I've never thought it before at a time and a place like this because if I had the fear would grow so strong I think it would drive me insane.

And the thought I'm thinking is the thing I mentioned at the very beginning. The thing so scary that I didn't dare tell you about it because I feared it might increase its chances of coming true. But now it is coming true, I suppose I might as well come clean and share with you my deepest, darkest secret. It's so secret that not even Martha knows about it yet. She'll find out soon enough, though, when she opens the letter I've left for her at my bed and breakfast. It's marked 'Only to be opened in the event of my death'. And it goes something like this.

Dear Martha,

I do hope you've disobeyed the instructions on the front of this letter. Because if you haven't, it'll mean I'm dead.

FIN

Sorry if I sound a bit flippant but the problem is that at the time of writing I am very much alive and still can't take the possibility of being dead as seriously as I should. You might find that strange, being as I'm about to go diving in utterly filthy conditions with great white sharks. Then again, you might not. When we spoke last night, you guessed that there was something wrong. And you were right, as ever. For some bizarre reason I had convinced myself that I wasn't scared of sharks any more. As we now know, this was a somewhat foolish notion.

Damn. There I go again with my wry understatement. I guess I'm never going to get the tone quite right. And I'm certainly never going to be able to cram in all the things that I'd like to say to you if, as I'm afraid I still can't bring myself to believe, this really is the last you're ever going to hear from me.

But first and foremost I love you very, very much. You're the best thing that ever happened to me and I only wish we could have lived happily ever after, as I'm sure we deserved if there'd been any justice. But you probably don't want to hear that at a time like this. It'll only make things worse than they already are. What's important now is that you go out and live your life as happily as you can. Forget about me. Well, don't forget about me, obviously. I just mean, you know, try not to let me ruin your life. OK? Otherwise I may have to come back and haunt you.

Anyway, I don't know whether this is going to help at all but I wanted to tell you something about me and sharks. I never told you before because I thought it would scare you. But now the worst-case scenario has actually happened, I think it may offer you a strange source of comfort.

You see, I've always known deep down that it was my destiny to be eaten by a shark. I don't know how I knew. I just knew. Naturally, I've always done my best to deny that I knew: to kid myself that it was just paranoia, hypochondria, whatever. But – and this is going to sound really weird – I think I've actually known it since before I was born.

Now hang on. It gets weirder still. It's my belief that before I was born, I wasn't merely cursed with the ability to foresee my death. I was also blessed with the power to make it less painful, less terrifying, less horrible.

Yeah sure, I know what you're thinking. It's those bloody drugs again. And you're probably right. I think I did come to this conclusion at a time when I was doing rather too much acid. But hey, who says the insights you get on LSD aren't the truth: the doors of perception and all that?

Anyway, I believe in this theory and I hope you do to, because if I'm right it'll mean I won't have suffered at all when I died. Nor in the moments before.

So let me explain how the system works. Suppose you're going to die in a really horrible way. Let's just pluck an example from the air and choose shark attack, shall we? Right. Now suppose that rather than experience that death at the very end, you can instead choose to spread out those final moments throughout your life. Death by instalments, as it were.

You're a clever girl, Martha. You must have seen what I'm getting at by now. You must see what sense it makes. All those moments throughout my life when I've been agonizing about death by shark, with thoughts so vivid it almost seemed it was happening for real . . . well, in a strange way, it was happening for real. I was taking chunks out of my evil future and exorcizing them in the present. I was taking away death's sting.

At least I hope I was. No. Scrub that. I'm absolutely, positively, one hundred per cent sure I was.

Trust me, Martha, I didn't feel a thing. No pain. No fear. Nothing but sweet oblivion.

I love you, Martha, and always will.

Your treacherous, idiotic, infuriating (but actually not too bad once you get to know him, really) Joe.

xxxxxxx

So that, more or less, is what I'm thinking about right now. Except, of course, I'm still clinging on to the hope that I may yet have got it completely wrong and that any second now, I'm going to feel a tug on my air line, I'm going to climb back in the boat and that everything's going to be fine and dandy.

You might be wondering why I don't just climb back into the boat straightaway. Personally, I think the answer's blindingly obvious but I'll tell you anyway. First, the cage is still floating ten feet away from the boat and I can't get out until Adam pulls it in. Second, it would be utter madness to attempt to surface when, at any moment, one of the sharks in the neighbourhood could decide to launch another attack on the cage. Third, even if I wanted to I couldn't because I'm paralysed with fear.

It's all coming back, now. I haven't felt this way since the moment I sensed the tiger stalking me in the Red Sea. Except that this time the sensation is more intense.

Ahead of me, I can see nothing but dull, grey water; the odd small fish; shreds of mashed pilchard and strands of kelp. Nothing to worry about there. Nothing I can see anyway. So why do I feel as if I'm in the presence of some ineffable evil? Why is it that I'm staring, wide-eyed, ahead of me when I know that if I wanted to feel really secure, I'd sneak a quick glance behind me as well?

Why do you think?

Because I know that that's where it is.

Behind me.

And I also know that this isn't like those nights in childhood when you can't sleep because as soon as you do the man in the cupboard will come out and get you. It isn't a problem that can be resolved simply by hopping out of bed, opening the cupboard door, peering inside and discovering to your joy that the man in the cupboard isn't there.

Because it is there. That thing behind me. It's definitely there.

And not looking won't make any difference. It will still be there.

I turn round. Slowly.

I see an eye. A huge, huge eye.

Black.

Cold.

Dead.

And around that eye are white scars. Around those scars is a mass of rough, dark skin. And beneath that rough, dark skin is a mouth. A mouth bigger than me. Bigger than the cage. And in that mouth I can see—

No. Not the teeth. I won't look at the teeth. I won't!

I turn away. I don't know how long it is before I look back again. But when I do, the Submarine has gone.

And I think, maybe it was never there. Maybe I just imagined it. Because surely if I hadn't imagined it, Adam would be tugging on my air line and pulling that cage towards the boat as fast as he could.

Unless. My God, he wouldn't have seen it. He would have been looking out from the stern of the boat. But the Submarine must have come from the front and swum directly beneath the boat.

I'd better warn him. I'd better surface right now and—

There's a tug on my air line so hard that my regulator is nearly ripped from my mouth. It's followed, a split second later, by a massive impact which hurls me to the far side of the cage. Looking up, I catch a flash of white belly. Now I'm choking on sea water. The air line has been severed. The cage is being tossed from side to side. There's something thrashing against it. A shark has been caught in the rope. I'm being hurled from side to side. And I'm drowning.

Got to breathe. Got to get to the surface.

I do. Just. A quick gulp of air and then I'm under again. Going deeper. The shark is still caught in the rope and it's dragging the cage down. Teeth and heaving grey flesh just inches from my body. I'm being battered. I'm being crushed. I'm drowning.

I need air. Got to get some air.

We've hit the sea bottom. Got to get out.

Avoid the snapping teeth. The writhing grey body. Through the cage roof. I'm out. I'm out of the cage. Going up. Air's coming. Going up.

I can breathe.

Oh, the relief. Oxygen! I can breathe! I can breathe!

Where am I?

Where's the boat?

Oh my God, the boat's miles away. I've been carried

downstream. The current's so strong. Further and further all the time.

On the boat they're waving and screaming.

'We're coming.'

When are you coming? Get me out of here now. Oh please, God, please get me out of this cold, cold water now. I don't want to die. I don't want to die.

Sharks.

There are sharks in this water.

Big sharks.

The biggest.

The Submarine.

Why won't the boat come?

What was that?

What is that?

My God what is that between me and the boat?

That thing coming towards me.

That huge, huge triangular thing.

Oh my God, this is it! Oh my God, this is it!

There's a roaring in my head. Like the sound of a boat's engine.

I'm imagining it. Must be. It's not coming from the direction of the boat. It's coming from behind me.

The fin's coming too. Closer and closer.

I'm going to die. I'm going to die. I'm going to—

They say that when a shark bites you you don't feel a thing. At least not real pain. Just a sort of a numb squeezing sensation.

Now I know that this is true because when I regain my senses – I must have blacked out for a second or two – I feel a strong pressure on my upper arms. Then, as if in slow

motion, I feel myself rising up and up until my whole body
is out of the water.

And I know what's happening. I've seen it with seals on
documentaries. The shark flings them high into the air and
then snaps them in two as they land in its jaws. Except this
isn't a documentary. This is what's happening to me now.

And now I've begun my descent. I'm going down. And
down. And down.

And there's no fear. There's no pain. Just a strange sense
of detachment. Relief almost. For my whole life I have been
dreading this moment. And now it's happening. It has
happened. It's over.

I'm dying. Perhaps I'm dead already. Perhaps this is what
the afterlife is like. Voices. Looming faces. My forebears have
come to welcome me into paradise. They're smiling. I'm
smiling.

'Joe,' says a voice I know so well. 'Joe?'

If I didn't know better I would think that it belonged to
Martha.

And that man standing next to her. Looking down at
me. He's a dead ringer for that pumpkin-headed Afrikaaner
who once told me in a bar that the sharks round here were
'frindly shocks'.

'Joe?'

Oh, give me a break, will you? I've just been eaten by a
great white shark. I haven't got used to this being dead
business yet.

'*Joe?*'

'Martha?'

'I got your letter.'

'Fuck! So I really am dead?'

'No, Joe. You're alive. You're in a boat. You're alive and we're going home.'

'Give me a cigarette. Quick. I need to be sure I'm not hallucinating.'

The Afrikaaner hands me a cigarette.

I look at Martha.

'I'd rather have a rollie.'

'Really?'

'Really.'